dissonance

dissonance

ERICA O'ROURKE

SIMON & SCHUSTER BFYR

NEW YORK • LONDON • TORONTO • SYDNEY • NEW DELHI

SIMON & SCHUSTER BFYR

An imprint of Simon & Schuster Children's Publishing Division

1230 Avenue of the Americas, New York, New York 10020

For information about special discounts for bulk purchases, please contact Simon & Schuster Special Sales at 1-866-506-1949 or business@simonandschuster.com.

The Simon & Schuster Speakers Bureau can bring authors to your live event. For more information or to book an event, contact the Simon & Schuster Speakers Bureau at 1-866-248-3049 or visit our website at www.simonspeakers.com.

Jacket design by Lizzy Bromley

Interior design by Hilary Zarycky

The text for this book is set in Granjon LT Std.

Manufactured in the United States of America

2 4 6 8 10 9 7 5 3 1

Library of Congress Cataloging-in-Publication Data

O'Rourke, Erica.

Dissonance / Erica O'Rourke. — First edition.

pages cm

Summary: "Every time someone makes a choice, a new, parallel world is spun off the existing one and Del's job is to keep the dimensions in harmony"—Provided by publisher.

ISBN 978-1-4424-6024-9 (hardback) — ISBN 978-1-4424-6026-3 (eBook)

[1. Choice—Fiction. 2. Love—Fiction. 3. Science fiction.] I. Title.

PZ7.O649Di 2014

[Fic]—dc23

2013033578

To Danny, who I would cross worlds for.
And to my girls, who make my world shine.

ACKNOWLEDGMENTS

During the first conversation we ever had, Joanna Volpe said: Write this book. So I did, because she is fierce and brilliant and tireless and never wrong. (All excellent qualities in an agent, not to mention a human being.) I am continually grateful for the opportunity to work with her. I'm also thankful for the amazing team at New Leaf Literary: Kathleen Ortiz, for her foreign rights wizardry; Danielle Barthel, for cheering me on at every turn; and Suzie Townsend, Jaida Temperly, and Pouya Shahbazian, for all-around awesomeness.

Zareen Jaffery's intelligence, clear-sightedness, creativity, and heart brought this book to life, and shaped it into the story I had only dreamed it could be. Working with her—and learning from her—has been an absolute gift. The people at Simon & Schuster BFYR have given *Dissonance* the best home a girl could ask for, especially Justin Chanda, Julia Maguire, Jenica Nasworthy, Brian Luster, Paul Crichton, Katy Hershberger, Siena Koncsol, Alexandra Cooper, and Amy Rosenbaum. Lizzy Bromely's beautiful, breathtaking cover captures Del's story perfectly.

The women of Chicago-North RWA have been a source of inspiration, learning, and support. I'm particularly grateful for Clara Kensie, Lynne Hartzer, Ryann Murphy, and Melonie Johnson—supremely talented, wickedly funny women. I'm equally indebted to Paula Forman, Lisa McKernan, Genevieve O'Keefe, Lexie Craig, and Judy Bergman for their willingness to drag me out of my office when I need it most. Jenn Rush, Susan Dennard, Leigh Bardugo, Sarah J. Maas, and Monica Vavra gave me knowing nods and supportive e-mails at every turn.

I begged Holly McDowell, Thomas Purnell, and Joelle Charbonneau for assistance on all things musical, which they graciously provided. My genius cousin, Dr. Katie Woodhams, explained genetics using small words and pictures, which was exactly the right speed for me. Lisa Tonkery has provided encouragement, snarky texts, and basketball pointers as only a Hoosier can. KC Solano provided key plot-bouncing services yet again. Kim McCarron, Vanessa Barneveld, Sara Kendall, and Hanna Martine read countless drafts and gave invaluable feedback and encouragement. Loretta Nyhan is wise and kind, a true storyteller and an incredible friend.

Without my beloved Eliza Evans, this book wouldn't exist. I'd also be a much crankier person, with a much shakier grip on pop culture. She is astonishing in the best sense of the word, and I am so thankful for her insight, her humor, and her generous soul.

Thank you to my parents—not only for their love and support, but for teaching me that books were as essential as food or air. In doing so, they gave me the world, a million times. Thanks also to my amazing sister, Kris, who inspires me with her strength and bravery. My entire extended family has cheered me on, but none more so than my aunt, Patricia Layton, who loved romance novels and Christmas and family, and who is dearly, dearly missed.

Every single day, my daughters delight me with their intelligence, their wit, their independence and their boundless hearts. Thank you, my loves, for being excited about my writing, entertaining yourselves during deadlines, and being exquisitely, unequivocally you.

Above all, the biggest thanks go to Danny, for making me laugh and swoon in equal measure, for giving me solid ground and space to dream, for building this life with me. You are my heart and my home, for infinity.

In the beginning was the dark, and the Lord spoke and chose the light, and the world cleaved, and the song of the new world was pleasing to His ears. Worlds begat worlds like the branches of a tree, and each favored branch was touched with His song. He anointed the ears and hands of His most favored children, and granted them freedom to Walk among the branches so they might preserve and magnify His song.

—The Walker Bible, Genesis, Chapter 1, Verses 1–3

The duty of each Walker is to preserve the course and integrity of the Key World, the One True World from which the Multiverse sprang, and to protect it from the blight of Echoes. To be a Walker requires obedience, diligence, and sacrifice. The calling to Walk between worlds is both a gift and a burden, and this textbook will guide you accordingly.

—Authors' Note,
Principles and Practices of Cleaving, Year Five

BEGIN
FIRST
MOVEMENT

CHAPTER ONE

IT SEEMED LIKE A LOUSY WAY TO REMEMBER someone: two aging strips of wood nailed together in the shape of a cross, stuck into a weed-choked ditch on the side of the road. A name, careful cursive in fading black marker, looped across the middle, and a tattered supermarket bouquet—carnations, daisies, baby's breath—slumped against the base.

It wasn't much, but it would be enough.

More than enough, if you asked me. Which no one did.

The two-lane road on the edge of town wasn't busy, but the curve was surprisingly sharp if you didn't know to look for it, or didn't care because you were young and thought you'd live forever. Backpack over my shoulder, I started into the ditch, tromping over prickler weeds and knee-high grasses. The ground squelched under my feet, but I ignored it, listening for the hum that meant I was close.

My phone rang, and I shoved it deeper in my pocket. I'd gotten the most important message just after lunch.

"Del, it's Dad. I'm sorry to cancel our Walk again, but I've got an emergency meeting with the Consort this afternoon. Your mother says your assignment's due tomorrow, so why don't you . . ."

I hadn't bothered listening to the rest. I'd heard it—or a variation of it—enough times. Emergencies were the status quo at my house. There was always a problem my parents needed to fix, a fresh crisis demanding their attention. A situation so important everything else was pushed to the side.

More often than not, I was the "everything else." But the upside of being ignored is that people forget to tell you no.

Burrs clung to my sweater as I picked my way across the muddy terrain. Clouds blanketed the sky, and the air carried a heavy, earthy scent that signaled more rain to come. With any luck I'd be back before the storm hit.

My assignment was easy enough: Walk to a nearby Echo, locate the trouble spots, Walk home. I'd done it countless times, knew the steps well enough that I didn't need a chaperone. My parents might disagree, but if they were *really* worried, they would have made the time to come with, like they were supposed to.

I could handle this on my own.

The problem was, the only person who believed me was my grandfather. When other kids were playing park district soccer or climbing trees, Monty had taken me wandering among a different set of branches—the multiverse, the infinity of worlds spreading out from ours like the limbs of a tree. It was Monty who'd first shown me how a single choice could create two distinct realities—the world we lived in and the road not traveled. He'd shown me how to move between those realities, listening for the unique frequency each was set to, using the sound as a pathway across. I'd grown up with his voice in my ear, whispering the secrets of the multiverse, while the sounds of the Echo worlds rang through me like a bell. He'd taught me more about Walking than I'd ever learned from my parents, my older sister, Addison, or Shaw, my teacher at the Consort.

As far as they were concerned, I needed training. Someone to hold my hand while I took baby steps, when all I wanted was to run.

Today I was free to go as fast and as far as I liked.

I held my hand out, palm down, next to the wooden cross. Instantly I felt a thrumming over my skin, like a harp string roughly plucked. It was the pivot, a gate between realities, a sound so faint only one in a hundred thousand people—literally—could hear it.

There are more than six billion people in the world, but only sixty thousand licensed Walkers. Nine hundred in the greater Chicagoland area. Four of them were in my family, and by summer, I'd be the fifth.

Usually pivots are easier to hear than see, but the air around the memorial trembled like leaves in a high wind. It made sense; the strongest pivots form at places where a choice causes a sudden, significant change, and nothing's more sudden or significant than an unexpected death.

I eased inside the vibrating pocket of air, the rift expanding around me. The dissonance slid over my skin like a dusting of snow. With each step the noise in my head increased, countless frequencies competing for my attention. A pivot directly connects two worlds, but once you're inside, you can use it to travel to any other Echo in the multiverse. The trick is knowing what to listen for.

Over breakfast, my mom had played a sample of my target frequency, the one I'd need for today's Walk. But my assignment could wait for a while.

One foot in the Key World, one inside the pivot, I reached into the fabric of the multiverse, choosing a random thread from the dense, rippling weave. The vibration turned my limbs effervescent, while the air grew heavy as water. I hummed, matching the pitch of the string in my hands. The path cleared, resistance fading along with my vision. Another step, and the pivot went wispy and gray.

Another, and I left behind the rules and disappointments and weight of the old world . . .

. . . and walked directly into oncoming traffic.

CHAPTER TWO

Exercise caution when crossing a pivot, as conditions may prove unexpectedly hazardous.

—Chapter Two, "Navigation,"
Principles and Practices of Cleaving, Year Five

RUSH HOUR SWALLOWED ME WHOLE.

Cars whipped by, sending my hair into a blinding tangle. Trucks belched exhaust fumes, and a Harley roared so loudly I fell backward, gravel biting into my palms. The pivot's buzz was lost in the chaos. I scrambled out of the path of a beat-up Chrysler, nearly losing my backpack beneath the wheels.

Not a single car honked or swerved.

Technically I wasn't invisible—Echoes could see Walkers once we touched them. Otherwise we hovered on the edges of their peripheral vision, present but not worth noticing. Usually this was a good thing, allowing us to move freely in Echo worlds. Right now it increased my odds of being flattened.

A semi barreled toward me. I fumbled for the pivot with both hands, searching for a string—any string—to use. One sang out and I latched on to it.

The truck blew by, a burst of diesel-scented air slamming into my back as I dashed through the rift.

Nobody ever said Walking was safe. Nobody ever said it was boring, either.

The pavement under my feet was pitted and crumbling, with weeds sprouting up through the cracks. On the opposite side of the parking lot stood a rundown apartment complex, the balconies sagging, stick-on numbers missing from half the units. A low, monotone pitch filled my ears, and I gasped in relief.

Adrenaline pumped through my veins, replacing fear with triumph. Sometimes Walking felt like a drug. The aching anticipation, the quicksilver rush, the craving for more—but it was completely legal. Even better, it was *expected*. I might not be the Walker my parents wanted; that was Addie's job. But it was my calling, and my life, and the only thing I ever wanted to do.

Best of all, it was infinite.

You could find an endless number of worlds in a single location. If one Echo didn't suit you, a few steps and a flick of your fingers would bring you to another. The rush never had to end.

Again and again I crossed the pivot, choosing new frequencies each time. I visited hospitals and strip malls, farmhouses and factories, reveling in the sensation of slipping between worlds. I never stayed long, and it never got old, watching the differences that sprang up, each Echo a unique combination of choices and circumstances.

In every world I left a tiny origami star, no bigger than a

quarter. Breadcrumbs, my grandfather called them. A piece of the Key World, left behind to mark the way home. As a child, I'd done it to humor him. Now it was part habit and part superstition, my own private ritual.

My world hopping caught up with me in a forest preserve. A dull ache spread through my skull, and my ears rang with the key change. Time to get to work and head home. I could terrify Eliot with my near miss, find out what new disaster my parents had fixed.

Humming the frequency my mom had given me, I stepped into the rift. The string responded, gaining strength, and I followed it through. The massive oak trees disappeared, and when my vision cleared, the dirt path underfoot had shifted to asphalt. Leaf-strewn grass spread out on either side of me. The clouds parted, late-afternoon sunlight warm on my face. I turned in a slow circle, taking in the changes. A big jump in frequencies, for this world to look so different from ours.

On the other side of the pivot, the roadside memorial flickered like the afterimage when you stare at a bright light for too long.

Then it vanished, only a slight ripple marking where someone had died and the world had split in two.

CHAPTER THREE

Vibrato fractums (commonly called "breaks") are areas of instability within an Echo and an indicator of significant problems. Direct contact with vibrato fractums should be kept to a minimum.

—Chapter One, "Structure and Formation,"
Principles and Practices of Cleaving, Year Five

ACCORDING TO FAMILY LEGEND, I TOOK MY first Walk when I was eight months old—long before my first steps and years before most other kids. Wearing nothing but Pampers and a dimple, I'd crawled through a pivot outside our living room, leaving behind my stuffed panda and my outraged older sister.

Even at four, Addie was a fan of rules, and rule number one in our house was no Walking without an adult. So she fetched our grandfather, Monty, and he came after me.

Addie might have caught me, but Monty brought me back.

My grandfather liked to say it was the first sign I was something special, even among Walkers. Addie said it was the first sign I was going to be a pain in the ass. Everyone agreed it was a sign of things to come. I'd been named the problem child; Addie was the good girl. Sixteen years later, and the labels stuck fast.

I gritted my teeth at the frequency surrounding me. My mom had predicted this world would be mildly off-key, but the wavering pitch was stronger—and more unstable—than expected. At most I could last a couple of hours.

I followed the jogging trail around the perimeter of the park, past the duck pond and the picnic shelter, heading for the playground. It would have been pretty, if the whole Echo didn't sound so awful. Two guys played Frisbee at the water's edge, the ebb and flow of their laughter obscured by a screeching that made me wince.

Break by the duck pond. Noted.

For an Echo to sound this unstable, there had to be multiple breaks nearby overtaking the primary frequency. I listened for them, ears straining as I put some distance between me and the Frisbee game.

The wind shifted in the trees, bringing the rich smell of autumn with it. Joggers and cyclists passed by, oblivious to the noise surrounding them, their eyes sliding over me.

The playground teemed with shrieking kids leaping off the monkey bars, going down the slide headfirst, playing freeze tag. Two moms pushed their toddlers on the swings, gossiping about playgroups and marital woes. Distracted and jittery from the discord, I slid a pale purple square of paper from my backpack, creasing and folding until a four-pointed star took shape. As I worked, another noise fought for my attention. More ragged, less musical. Annoying. I looked around.

A little girl, four or five, huddled at the base of a tree, sobbing in the unashamed, exceedingly wet way kids do—snot and tears and misery plastered down her front, her wails nearly as loud as the world's pitch.

Except for breaks, everything in an Echo, living or dead, should resonate at the same frequency. I moved closer, brushing a hand along the girl's dimpled elbow, wondering if I'd missed something.

I hadn't. Her signal matched, which meant she was off-limits. Interacting with her would only make things worse, could actually *create* a break. Smarter to move along and leave her to her sobfest.

The problem was, touching an Echo—even a stable one—caused them to notice you. The kid snuffled and clutched my sleeve, tipping back her tearstained face to look directly at me.

Once one Echo sees you in their world, they all can. But nobody on the playground was paying attention to either of us. Not a single turned head or furrowed brow. It was easier for people to ignore her than listen to her, and I knew what that was like.

I pried her fingers off my arm. "What's wrong?"

She scrubbed at her eyes. "I was playing and I saw the ducks and I wanted to show them my balloon. And I went on the grass to show the ducks my balloon and I fell and the string went up and now it's gone and it was *red*. And red is my favorite color, but my red balloon is *gone*." She spoke in one unbroken rush.

"Your balloon is gone."

"And it was *red*," she wailed, a fresh flow of gunk cascading down her face. She pointed skyward. "See?"

I did see—caught in the tree branches overhead was a bedraggled red balloon. "Can your mom buy you a new one?"

"Mommy went to work. I came with Shelby."

"Shelby?" The little girl pointed to a bored-looking brunette Addie's age, sucking down a smoothie and texting nonstop. "Nanny?"

She nodded, chin quivering.

A tiny tweak wouldn't matter, considering how unstable this world was. It was like a symphony—a single wrong note in a perfect performance could ruin the whole thing. But if the song was already riddled with mistakes, one more wouldn't make a difference.

"No problem."

Had I known I'd be climbing park benches in an attempt to rescue wayward balloons, I would have dressed differently that morning. Still, I dropped the backpack and climbed up, hoping a sudden breeze off the pond wouldn't cause my skirt to pull a Marilyn Monroe.

"Almost there," I said, wishing I were taller. Even atop a park bench in my motorcycle boots, I could not reach the ribbon. The kid eyed me dubiously. "Back of the bench should do it."

I put one foot on the back of the bench, wobbling in my heavy boots, the string dangling inches away.

So much for a quick fix.

"Need a hand?" came a new voice.

Startled, I lost my balance. Someone grabbed me, one hand on my leg, the other at my waist. I looked at the fingers curving

around my thigh—a guy's hand, wide and strong, slightly calloused, with a leather cuff around the wrist—as dissonance
roared through me, twice as loud as before. My knees buckled.

I knew him. A version of him anyway. I'd spent a lot of time
studying those hands when I should have been focused on math
or history or Bach. They belonged to Simon Lane. And Simon
Lane, even back home, belonged to an entirely different world
than I did.

He guided me down until I was standing on the seat, balance
restored, dignity shaky. He let go, but the noise remained. *He*
was the break by the duck pond. I focused on his sweatshirt, the
faded blue logo of Washington's basketball team, and willed the
discord away.

He glanced at the kid. "Balloon got stuck?"

Her lower lip trembled. "This girl isn't big enough."

It was tempting to point out, standing atop the bench, that
I was currently taller than Simon. But he was standing closer
than he ever had at school, and his dark brown hair was a good
two inches longer and shaggier than I was used to, and I got distracted. He knew it too, judging from the flash of amusement in
his eyes.

"I can do it myself," I said.

"She's stubborn," he told the girl, as if he was confiding in
her. "If she'd lean on me, we'd have your balloon down by now."

"You lean," she ordered.

"Charming," I said.

He nodded. "So I'm told."

Some things—eye color, gravity, mountain ranges—were constant no matter how far you Walked. And Simon's reputation as the guy all the girls wanted, even though they knew better, was apparently one of them.

I shook my head to clear the ringing.

"Fine. But don't drop me." I braced one hand on his shoulder and climbed up, both feet perched on the narrow back of the bench, feeling myself sway. His hands closed over my waist and I stretched, catching the string of the balloon, tugging until it came free of the branches. "Got it."

"Jump," he said, and I did. His thumbs brushed against my rib cage, lingering when they didn't need to. This close, his eyes were a darker blue than I'd realized, more thickly lashed, and there was a tiny scar at the corner of his mouth I'd never seen before. *Simon Lane*, I thought dizzily, and pulled away.

I tied the balloon around the girl's wrist, and she ran off without another word.

"You're welcome," I called after her.

"No good deed goes unpunished," he said, grinning at me. "I'm Simon, by the way. You look familiar."

"Del," I said. "I go to Washington. With you."

He squinted, trying to place me. It wasn't his fault. Walkers didn't have Echoes, the way regular people did. But we left an impression through the worlds, like a daydream. When I was in class with his Original, this Echo would see my impression hovering in his peripheral vision. If he tried to look at me directly, the image would fade away, and he'd forget about me.

Which was not so different from the Key World, now that I thought about it.

"Aren't you supposed to be in class?" I asked.

He ducked his head for a moment, then looked up with a mischievous smile. *Trouble,* I thought. Way more than his Original, which was saying something. "Aren't *you?*"

A voice from behind me, bossy and superior, said, "You have *got* to be kidding me."

Addie.

Simon didn't hear her, of course. Unlike me, Addie would have been careful to avoid touching any Echoes. Casually I looked over my shoulder. My sister stood ten feet away, hands on hips, foot tapping, eyebrows drawn together in disapproval.

"You cut class again?" she said.

"It's only school," I replied, keeping my eyes on Simon, answering both questions at once. "Most useless part of my day."

I didn't mention that I found my classmates equally so. They'd probably say the same about me.

Suddenly a soaking wet chocolate Lab raced past us, Frisbee clamped in his teeth, a red bandana around his neck. He circled Addie twice and dropped the orange plastic disc at my feet. He let out a thunderous bark and panted up at me as if looking for approval.

"Iggy," Simon said warningly at the same time I said, "Good puppy."

Which was all the encouragement Iggy needed to shake himself off, spraying pond water all over me.

"No!" groaned Simon. "Bad dog!"

I brushed at my clothes as Iggy romped around. "Serves you right," Addie said, snickering. "You know Mom and Dad don't like you Walking alone."

Iggy woofed in her direction and put his paw out for me to shake. Gingerly I took it. Monty said animals liked Walkers because they could hear the difference in our frequencies, and we sounded good. Whatever the reason, the dog was all lolling tongue and blissful unrepentance, even when Simon grabbed his collar.

"Leave her alone, Ig." The dog ignored him. "Sorry. I think he likes you."

"Animals do," I said, pulling at my drenched sweater.

"He's got good taste."

Addie tapped her watch, her face drawn. The noise was already getting to her. Iggy must have heard it too, pressing damply against my leg and whining.

"Chill, boy," Simon said, scratching the dog's ears. "Let me make this up to you? There's a kick-ass band playing at Grundy's tonight, and we just got new IDs. You should come with."

"Absolutely not. Tell him no," Addie said.

The real Simon would never go to a bar during basketball season. He had too much to lose. I must have frowned, because his eyebrows lifted, dark lines over dark blue eyes. "Okay, not Grundy's. What about the Depot?"

In the Key World the Depot was a coffee shop on the south side of town, in the old train station. After a huge crash decades ago, the city built a new station on the north side, and the Depot became a landmark and a place for locals to get lattes.

Walkers believed every accident came from a choice. Nearly forty people had died that morning; another hundred were injured, simply because the engineer picked the wrong time to throw the brake. Countless worlds had sprung up in the aftermath, a lesson in the way a single decision could transform the fabric of the multiverse.

I wondered what choices had shaped this version of Simon, who cut class and used a fake ID. Despite his dissonance, I was tempted to find out. He was definitely the break, and it was just my luck that the one time he noticed me, there was something fundamentally wrong with him.

Iggy bumped my legs, and I fell heavily into Simon again. His arms came around me, and for an instant I let mine circle him. Then I took a quick, unsteady step back. "I'll think about it."

Now it was his turn to frown. Most girls would have been falling all over him for that kind of invitation, but I wasn't most girls.

"Playtime's over," Addie said, her expression like a storm front. "Wrap this up."

I gave Iggy one last pat. "See you around."

"Count on it," he said, scooping up the Frisbee and tossing it toward the pond. Iggy raced away, Simon followed, and I turned, awaiting the wrath of Addie.

"We're not here to troll for guys, Del."

"You're not, anyway. I'm sure we could find you someone." I

pointed to a girl biking on the other side of the pond. "She's cute."

Playing matchmaker for Addie wasn't a bad idea. Not that the outdoorsy type was right for her. She needed someone as effortlessly polished as herself. But if she had a girlfriend, maybe she'd be too busy to notice my mistakes.

Her green eyes took on a warning gleam. "Leave it alone, Del. Him too."

I shrugged. "He's a break. I was getting a reading for my homework."

"Some reading," she replied.

"How long have you been spying on me?" I asked, trying to draw her attention away from Simon.

"Long enough to see you get the balloon down. There was nothing wrong with that kid. You should have left her alone." She crossed her arms, her face taking on the pinched, fussy look that made her look older, and not in a good way. "We have rules for a reason, Del."

I studied my nail polish, plum colored and starting to chip.

"She was miserable."

"So? She's an Echo. It doesn't matter."

It matters to me, I wanted to say. But Addie was right. Echoes weren't real people, only copies of Originals, no matter how alive they seemed. Still, her response, practical and dismissive, nettled me.

"Whatever." I glanced over at Simon, roughhousing with Iggy. The discord surrounding them scraped along my nerves, growing louder the longer I watched. "Why are you here?"

"Dad asked me to help you with your homework. I left you three different messages."

"Didn't get them," I said airily, pulling Simon's wallet out of my pocket. I held up the out-of-state license that claimed he was twenty-four. "This is a terrible ID. They'd totally bust him."

"You picked his pocket? Did Monty teach you?"

"Who else?" She frowned as I continued. "Simon's Original is the star basketball player at my school. He'd never try to sneak into a bar. What's the harm in keeping this one out of jail too?"

"It's pointless," she said, swiping at a wisp of strawberry blond hair that dared escape the neat twist at the nape of her neck. I never understood how she was able to get her hair to behave. Mine was a perpetual mess—reddish brown, unruly as tree bark, black at the ends like they'd been dipped in a pot of india ink. "He's not even real."

Simon's palm on my bare leg had felt pretty damn real, but I kept that tidbit to myself.

I couldn't say why, exactly, I'd nicked his wallet. Because it was fun. Because I wanted to test myself. Because while this Simon flirted, the one back home barely noticed me. Because even if he was only an Echo, I'd hate for him to end up in juvie. Because Addie couldn't. A million reasons, but mostly . . . because I could.

I shook my head and slipped the wallet back into my pocket. "I hope he didn't pay a lot for this. It's awful."

"Leave it here." Her tone and temper were both growing short, but so were mine. "You know it's dangerous to bring it back."

"It's not radioactive. It won't hurt anything." According to the Consort, bringing Echo objects to the Key World was like introducing bubonic plague, but they'd never explained why. It made sense for big things, like pets. Clear violation of the rules to bring Iggy back, since the *real* Iggy was already frolicking about somewhere. But an object as small as Simon's wallet wouldn't affect my world, the same way a single grain of sand wouldn't hold back the tide.

Even so, it was easier to let Addie think she'd won, especially with a migraine brewing. I tossed the ID in the trash and the wallet on a nearby table, where he'd spot it on his way out. "Happy now?"

"Not really," she said. "Let's get started on your homework. The first step is to locate the vibrato fractums."

"Already did. Simon's one. Jogger's two." I jerked a thumb toward the trail where a stout, balding man was running. "Minivan's three, but it pulled out while I was talking to Simon. Swing set makes four. Did I miss anything?"

I hadn't, but it was fun to make her admit it.

She scowled. "Since you've got it figured out, go get your readings."

"I already checked Simon," I said, and flashed my phone. I hadn't just picked his pocket—I'd recorded his frequency so I could determine exactly how bad the break was. "I can skip the others."

"Three breaks, three readings," she said firmly.

The thing about Walking is you're always playing catch-up.

It's not time travel. You can't go back and prevent a problem. Once a decision is made, a branch—the choice you didn't take, an alternate pathway, an alternate world—is created. Most of the time, it's no big deal. The alternate world, populated by Echoes, goes its own way. It creates Echoes of its own and never interferes with the Key World again.

Every once in a while, for reasons unknown, something goes wrong. There's a snag in the fabric of reality, a frequency that's grown too strong or too unstable. Left alone, it will spread, destabilizing the Key World and weakening the other branches of the multiverse. And that's where Walkers come in—crossing through pivots, cutting off one reality to preserve the rest. Cleaving.

Breaks are the first sign of a problem, but they aren't necessarily fatal. Like infections, some are more serious than others, so we have to determine which ones can be left under observation and which require cleaving. I didn't doubt this world would end up cleaved—it was sounding worse by the minute—but Addie would never let me bail early.

I'd heard the jogger's pitch warbling across the park, but the assignment required I get a direct reading to be sure. I started toward him as he came around the curve, checking his pulse, his face red and his shirt sweat-soaked. I shuddered.

I picked up the pace as he approached, his signature growing louder. *Get away clean,* Monty always said, and I hustled the last few steps, phone clutched in my hand.

Our paths intersected, my shoulder brushing against his

arm. He stumbled onto the grass, yelped, and swore.

"Oops," I said, and kept going. He threw up his hands and continued running. The touch had been brief, but long enough to turn my screen cherry red. I headed back to Addie. "That was gross."

She fixed me with an expectant look. "Well?"

"Yes, obviously." I showed her my phone. "I didn't need a direct read to know he's a bad break."

"*Augmented* break," she corrected, tugging at the hem of her tweed blazer. "He's not good or bad; it's a question of how far his individual frequency has degraded."

"Whatever. Can we go now? This place sounds awful, and I have plans." A sharp ping, like a violin string breaking, split the air. The wobble in the frequency sped up.

"A date with Eliot is not a sufficient reason to blow off training." She rubbed her temples as she spoke. "Check the swing set."

"It's not a date," I ground out. "It's *Eliot*."

Everything is possible, for a Walker. The multiverse is infinite, like an ancient tree with branches in every direction, each branch sending out countless shoots, each shoot sprouting an endless number of worlds. Walk far enough, carefully enough, and you could find whatever world you wanted. But you would never find a world where Eliot Mitchell and I were a couple. It was hard to feel romantic about someone you'd gone through potty training with.

I stomped across the playground to the swings and gripped the chain with one hand.

Discord knifed through me, and I let go as if scalded.

Immediately the noise receded. I bent over, hands on knees, waiting for the nausea to pass before rejoining Addie.

"Done. Bet you they cleave this place by lunch tomorrow," I said.

"The Consort's not going to cleave a world because a fifth-year Walker said so," she scoffed. "On the other hand, if *I* said so . . . I bet they'd let me help."

Naturally they'd listen to her over me. "*I* found it."

"You stole a wallet and let an Echo get grabby. You will not be helping." She set off toward the pivot we'd come through. If I squinted, I could see the roadside marker flickering in and out of view, a sign this world was rapidly destabilizing.

I chased after her. "That's not fair. I should at least get to try it."

A thrill ran through me as I spoke, dark and compelling. My fingers twitched, sliding through the atmosphere, through time and space and perception until they touched the fabric of this world, the threads raucous and trembling. Like a key in a lock I hadn't known was there, the sensation called up something more instinctive than memory, a sudden yearning to fix the snarled, too-tight lines straining against my skin. I hummed a half-forgotten song, only to be cut off by Addie.

"You. Aren't. *Licensed.*" She took my arm, looking frazzled. "We go home. We tell Dad. We let the Consort handle it."

"Why not save them the trouble?"

"Like you'd even know how."

Over her shoulder I saw Simon lift a hand to wave at me. I

smiled back, then caught myself. Not real. The Original Simon wouldn't wave at me. He wouldn't notice me. He definitely wouldn't invite me out to hear a band or grab coffee or anything else. He wouldn't have made me feel this uncomfortable regret. Not real—but very dangerous.

"It's not hard," I said, the heart of the world vibrating under my fingers, as reckless and chaotic as my own. "All you have to do is start."

CHAPTER FOUR

When interacting with Echoes, do not let emotions cloud your judgment or divert you from your duty.
—Chapter Three, "Echo Properties and Protocols,"
Principles and Practices of Cleaving, Year Five

IT SHOULDN'T BE SO EASY TO END A WORLD.

When you think about it, unraveling the fabric of reality should require more effort than clipping your nails. As it turns out, all you need to do is find the right thread and yank.

Or hold on to the thread while your sister yanks you.

The strings slid away with such force I thought they'd slice my fingertips, the remaining fabric slack and gauzy. The ground at our feet warped like a Salvador Dalí painting, nearby trees going liquid and limp, the sky a smear of blue and white.

"What did you do?" Addie looked around wildly.

"It wasn't my fault! You grabbed me!" A line of silver shot from the playground to the pond, which turned gray and began to fade.

"You shouldn't have been messing around," she snapped, pulling me toward solid ground.

"They were going to cleave it anyway," I said. According

to the Consort, cleavings were complicated procedures that required tools, and training, and time.

I'd done it completely by accident.

My stomach churned as I watched the ducks bobbing along the increasingly dim surface. They flickered, turning grainy black-and-white like an old movie, and then a blob of static, and they were gone.

White noise, like listening to a seashell, filled the air.

Simon threw the Frisbee and Iggy leaped, the color leaching out of the bandana around his neck. My chest squeezed painfully at the sight. I'd expected something . . . cleaner. A quick winking out of existence, like stars at sunrise. "I didn't mean to."

"Like that matters? We have to go." She started toward the portal but stopped when she saw I wasn't moving.

One by one, the cars in the parking lot guttered like candle flames. Even the ones with people inside them. "I did this," I said hollowly. "I should watch."

Addie's voice was unexpectedly sympathetic, despite the note of panic creeping in. "Del, they're not alive. They were never alive, just Echoes."

"They don't know that."

"No, but we do. It's cleaving too fast," she said. "It's supposed to start at the breaks and spread out from there. This is . . . random."

She was right. The whole point of our training was to manage cleaving in an orderly way. Cleavers cut away the damaged branch, then rewove the strings, ensuring the healthy world stayed strong. The Echo was left to unravel at its own pace, triggering a domino effect. The worlds that sprang from the cleaved Echo would unravel as the effects spread. It was like pruning a shrub: Cut the base of a branch, and all the twigs and leaves attached would fall away too. The effects would take time, but cleavings were irreversible.

The chaos before us shouldn't have happened for days, but already the wooded area beyond the paths had turned to a misty gray wall, the unraveling flowing across the field. The roaring in my ears increased with every Echo that disappeared. I turned, looking for the rift we'd come through.

"Addie?"

The grass around our pivot was silvery with hoarfrost.

"Come on!" She sprinted, graceful even when she was running for her life. I followed as best I could in my clunky boots and overloaded backpack. The asphalt was starting to soften and the curve ahead was fading. I could see where the edges of the world didn't quite align, and hear the Key World's frequency drifting through like a beacon.

Inches away from the pivot, the signpost for the park dissolved into a lumpy puddle. There was no way we'd reach it in time.

"Wait!" I caught the hem of her jacket. She ignored me, and I yanked harder. "We'll never make it through—we'll be caught in the cleaving."

She whirled, eyes bright with fear. "We're caught unless we get out of here, you moron!"

"Look," I said. The signpost disappeared. An instant later, the pivot was gone too, replaced with the same formless gray overtaking the park.

Addie made a sound like a drowning kitten and went limp. "We're stuck."

The silver-coated ground crept toward us like fog. I tugged at her. "Back this way. The park." For once, she didn't argue. "There has to be an emergency plan."

"Yeah. Don't cleave a world while you're standing in the middle of it!"

We reached the playground, where the disintegration was already setting in. The benches bowed toward the ground, the moms and nannies oblivious. The kids climbed on the jungle gym, unconcerned by the bars warping beneath their hands.

"No pivot points," Addie said. "That's the only way in or out."

She was right. The ooze had overtaken the far end of the playground and the parking lot, where the strongest concentration of pivots was. It was impossible to cross. Iggy and Simon had been replaced by a sea of grayish light; so had the swingset and the spot where I'd bumped into the jogger. The Echoes never noticed. They'd fade before they realized what was happening, reabsorbed into the fabric of the universe.

We wouldn't be reabsorbed. We'd be dead.

Addie dropped onto the bench and started to cry. I tried not to throw up. A few feet away the little girl with the balloon twirled, the balloon's color bleeding away.

The balloon.

The balloon should have been tangled in the tree overhead.

I'd fixed it, and the kid had gone back to playing, instead of crying at the base of the tree.

And she was still here. Only . . . not for much longer.

"Move!" I hauled Addie up.

"It's too small, Del. We'll never get through."

"You have a better option? Move your ass, or we're dead!" I skidded to a halt inches from the girl. I listened as hard as I could for a frequency—any frequency—not obscured by the white noise of the cleaving.

"Hurry," Addie said.

"Shut up!"

The balloon flickered as I heard one—E minor, haunting and sweet. Light filtered through the pivot, pale as dust and barely visible. I lunged for it, clutching my sister's hand.

The last thing I saw was the little girl disappearing in a burst of static.

CHAPTER FIVE

The term "accident" is a misnomer. Every consequence, no matter how unexpected, is rooted in a choice.

—Chapter Ten, "Ethics and Governance,"
Principles and Practices of Cleaving, Year Five

LANDED HARD. MY PALMS AND KNEES STUNG from the impact, and my ears rang in the sudden silence. Less than a foot away, the edges of the portal fluttered like the wings of a monarch and sealed themselves. Slowly, I sat up and brushed wood chips from my hair.

Addie lay nearby, flat on her back, panting and staring at the sky. The blue, blue sky. Azure. Lapis. Cornflower. Glorious, rich, head-spinning color. After the relentless gray of the world we'd escaped, I was practically drunk on it. I hauled myself up, using the jungle gym to keep my balance.

The scene before me was identical to the cleaved world. Joggers and kids and nannies. Ducks bobbing on the pond. Simon and his friend playing Frisbee with Iggy. My throat tightened and my breath eased simultaneously. Everything was exactly as it had been.

Almost. The little girl sat next to her nanny, head bent,

shoulders shaking. I looked up and saw the balloon, caught in the highest branches of the tree. Soon the wind would carry it away.

I thrust my hands in my pockets and found my star, crumpled and half-finished. Smoothing it out, I folded the rest from memory, the movements familiar and reassuring.

Addie stood, her face white and set.

"Not bad, right?" I tried to smile, but it felt as wobbly as my legs.

"No, Del. That was bad. Very, very bad." She swiped a finger underneath each eye, erasing the tracks of mascara. "We have to keep moving."

"We're safe."

She shook her head and studied the playground. "When that world finishes cleaving, this one will start. It's a domino effect, and you knocked over the first one."

My stomach twisted, and I nearly dropped to my knees again. The Key World was safe, but every Echo originating in Park World would unravel and fade. Because of me. "What about the people?"

"Del. Focus. We have to find a pivot we can use to get home. Where's our best shot?"

She must have been seriously rattled to ask me for advice, instead of ordering me around. It was almost funny. Almost, the way that this world was almost the same as the one we'd fled. "Almost," as it turned out, meant "not at all."

A sour taste flooded my mouth. "Parking lot," I said. "There's a ton of decisions in a parking lot."

"Then let's go. And don't touch anything." I glanced over my shoulder at the little girl, still crying.

"Thanks, kid," I murmured, and followed Addie toward the rows of cars and pivots. The instant before I crossed over, I tossed the paper star toward the signpost. Pointless, considering this world would soon vanish, but it was habit.

A breadcrumb, just like Monty had taught me.

For someone who spent so much time talking up how she was the mature one in the family, Addie wasted no time reverting to childhood when we arrived home.

"I'm telling Mom," she said, slamming the car door extra hard and marching up the driveway.

I chased after her. "You're tattling on me? Seriously? Are we five now?"

"Five-year-olds have better impulse control," she hissed. "We could have been killed. Do you think the Consort won't notice? *You cleaved a world.*"

"You grabbed me," I said, fighting back the fear that enveloped me. "I didn't mean to do it."

"It doesn't matter what you meant. It's what you did. And don't try to blame me—you shouldn't have been touching the strings in the first place. This is completely on you, Del." She stalked inside.

I stood in the driveway, shivering as a chill worked its way under my sweater. Our kitchen windows glowed warm and yellow, the peeling paint less visible in the dusk. It looked homey.

Safe. Cheerful. But I knew exactly what kind of welcome awaited me when I crossed the threshold, and it was none of those things.

The barberry bushes bordering the yard rustled, and a moment later Monty popped out, his cardigan catching on the thorns. He swatted at them, not noticing when his hands came away scratched.

"You're back?" he asked, his voice thin and reedy like an oboe. Monty had been a big man once, but he'd diminished over the years. Most Walkers developed frequency poisoning as they aged, but his was especially severe. Too much time spent in bad frequencies had left his shoulders bent and his gait slower. He lost time, forgetting my grandmother was gone. Worst of all, his hearing was ruined. Without hearing, a Walker had to rely on touch to navigate through the multiverse. Difficult and dangerous, but it didn't stop him.

"Hey, Grandpa." I took him by the elbow. "How long have you been out here?"

"I was going out. Where was I going?" He patted his pockets, pulled out a cheap little spiral notebook and a pencil stub. "I wrote it down. I drew a map."

Walker maps didn't look anything like the jumble of lines and musical notes he was peering at. He'd end up lost. Real maps showed only the major, stable branches of an Echo, their important pivots color coded to show strength and stability. Computers had made them easier to maintain—the old bound versions, drawn on onionskin paper, were inches thick and instantly outdated. Even with technology and experience on our side, tracing a path through the multiverse was no more accurate than chart-ing wind currents.

"You're not supposed to Walk by yourself," I said, taking the notebook. Then again, neither was I.

A cagey light entered his eyes. "We can go together."

"I—" The screen door flew open and my mother appeared, anger visible in the rigid lines of her posture. Addie stood behind her like a self-righteous shadow. "Mom—"

"Not a word, Delancey. Not. A. Word." She pointed to the kitchen table, and I slunk past her to my usual chair. Monty fol-lowed me inside.

"Foster!" she called into the twilight. From his office in the garage, my dad shouted back something unintelligible, and then hustled inside. Nobody messed around when my mom used that tone.

Monty patted my arm. "She's in a temper, isn't she? Been snappish all day."

"Do not move from that spot," Mom said, her glare nailing me to my seat. Addie smirked as they filed into Mom's office and shut the door.

"You've been out a long time." Monty drew two glass bottles out of the fridge. "Root beer?"

"Not thirsty," I mumbled as he pried off their tops.

He brought both bottles over and drained half of his. I rolled mine between my hands, listening to the faint hiss and snap of the carbonation.

"I screwed up," I said. "Big."

He belched gently, and I wrinkled my nose. "Nothing's done that can't be un-, Delancey."

It's what he'd always said, when I was a kid and we'd gone Walking together. A song he'd invented, special for me.

Nothing's done that can't be un-,
Nothing's lost that can't be found,
Make a choice and make a world,
Find another way around.

It had cheered me whenever our Walks had gone awry, and with Monty, they usually did. But I'd figured out by now that plenty of things—and people—stayed lost forever.

People like my grandmother. She had been a medic—the Walker equivalent of a doctor—charged with keeping Cleavers like my grandfather and my father healthy during their trips through the multiverse. A few months before I was born, she'd gone out on a Walk and never returned.

My parents and Addie had been living in New York at the time; Monty and Rose were here, in this house. According to my mom, the Consort's teams had searched for weeks, but she'd vanished completely. Their official verdict was that Rose had been caught on the wrong side of a cleaving, like we'd been today.

Monty wouldn't accept it. They were meant to be together, he insisted—Montrose and Rosemont, two halves of a whole. He'd wandered the multiverse alone, looking for her, until the Consort had stepped in and issued a second verdict: Either my parents come back to take care of Monty, or they'd send him to a home. So, a month after I was born, we returned permanently.

It was Walker tradition to name a kid after big pivots in their parents' hometown, and few pivots were bigger than train stops, where decisions accrued on a regular basis, day after day. Everyone else in my family was named for Chicago, but I'd been named for New York, a reminder of what could have been. My grandmother's disappearance had given me my name and an entirely different life.

When someone vanishes, it leaves behind a scar. Some heal better than others. My grandmother had unwittingly left her mark on our whole family. My mom saw the world as a collection of messes to be contained. Addie was so desperate to please her, she'd taken that need for order and translated it as a need for perfection. My dad tried to keep everyone happy, ever the peacemaker. The only path left to me was the one marked trouble.

Even now Monty didn't believe my grandmother was really gone. He slipped away whenever he could to continue the search. But instead of finding Rose, he'd lost his mind.

His song had failed us both, but I didn't tell him so.

"Now," he said, leaning back in his chair and lacing his hands over his stomach. "What's this about?"

"I cleaved an Echo," I said. The words felt leaden as I spoke them, and Monty's head snapped back as if he'd taken a punch. I hurried to explain.

"Not on purpose. I touched the strings for a second and it sort of . . . happened. Everything fell apart crazy fast. I've never

37

been inside a cleaving. I didn't know . . ." My throat clogged up. "There was a guy from school—an *Echo* of a guy from school. Simon Lane. One minute I was talking to him and the next he was gone." Monty's eyebrows lifted, his watery blue gaze turning sharp. "I know they're not real, but . . . that's not how it felt. It felt awful."

He nodded. "As it should."

"We barely got out in time, Grandpa. I thought unravelings took days."

He looked like I'd given him a prize instead of a problem. "How'd you manage to escape?"

When I explained about the balloon, he chuckled. "Clever girl."

I didn't feel clever. I felt sick. "I didn't mean to. It was an accident."

"There are no accidents," said my mother from the doorway. My father's hand rested on her shoulders, a unified front.

I turned to plead my case. "I only wanted to know what the threads felt like. I'd never been anywhere so out of tune. Then Addie yanked me away, and they split. That's it."

"That's it?" Mom's voice was like a lash. My father stepped between us.

"You two must be starving. We'll talk after dinner."

I barely touched my food. Monty smacked his lips, slathering butter and jam on a biscuit. How could he be so cheerful after what I'd told him? My parents were ominously quiet, while Addie spooned up delicate bites of lentil soup with a satisfied air.

Whatever punishment they'd decided on, she was happy. It must be bad.

Finally my dad pushed his bowl away. "Your actions today were reckless. And dangerous. Do you know what could have happened to you and your sister?"

I stared at the brown ooze congealing in front of me.

"You could have been killed. And we'd never have known. This is exactly why we don't like you going out by yourself. Did you even think about us? What it would have done to your mother, living through that again?" Dad asked.

"This isn't about me," said my mom. She folded her napkin precisely and set it on the table. "This is about you, and your behavior, and your constant need to flout every rule that has been laid out for your own protection and the protection of the Key World."

"I'm sorry." I slid lower in my chair. "I didn't mean for it to happen."

"You never do," my mom said. "You rush in and trust that your gifts will be enough to get you out of any mess you create."

I poked at my bowl. I'd screwed up, but I'd also saved us. That should count for something, shouldn't it?

"It was a neat trick," Monty said. "Getting out of there. You should give her some credit."

Gratitude rushed through me. Monty understood.

"She wouldn't have needed a trick if she'd followed the rules," Mom replied. "Addie made it through five years of training and we never once saw this kind of behavior."

No, of course not. I'd figured out a long time ago that I couldn't beat Addie at her own game, so I stopped trying.

My father added, "Cleaving can't be handled by one person. The protocol mandates three Cleavers to manage it safely."

"Hogwash," said Monty. "They send three Cleavers so no one knows who cut the last string. Keeps 'em from feeling too guilty."

"Why would someone feel guilty?" asked Addie. "They're only Echoes."

Monty shook his head in disgust.

"A faulty cleaving causes more harm than good," my father said. "It leaves the Key World weak."

There was no greater crime than damaging the Key World. My voice sounded very small when I said, "We can fix it, right? We don't have to report it?"

I thought about the stories I'd heard, Walkers stripped of their licenses, forced to live like ordinary people, never again venturing outside the Key World. Walkers who vanished altogether, sent to an oubliette.

Oubliettes were prisons, hidden behind rumor and speculation. The story was, to contain the worst of our criminals, the Consort had played with the fabric of the multiverse. They'd created worlds no bigger than a jail cell, severing them from the Key World and Echoes except for a single thread. A world with all possibilities eliminated, impossible to escape. No one had ever come back from an oubliette, so no one knew the truth.

But I'd been reckless, not malicious. I wasn't even seventeen— surely the Consort wouldn't want to sentence a teenage girl to life

in a prison world. Even so, I wasn't eager to test the theory. "Dad, please. We can't tell the Consort."

Regret tempered the firmness in his voice. "We already have."

"You're supposed to be on my side!" I'd expected that kind of betrayal from Addie. But not my parents. Not my dad.

"We are. A cleaving that big can't be covered up, and it's better to admit what you've done. Take responsibility for your actions," he said.

"It was an accident!"

"The Consort has rules, Del. If you want to be a Walker, you have to prove you can follow them." My mom's frown made it clear she wasn't willing to bend the rules for me. Addie's penchant for the straight and narrow was as genetic as our ability to Walk.

I wanted to remind her it wasn't rules that had saved our lives today, but the breaking of them. And that I wasn't going to be an Echo of my sister, no matter where we Walked. I didn't say any of those things, though, because my mom would never truly hear them.

Monty had dozed off, crumbs scattered across his cardigan. Addie toyed with her necklace, pretending not to listen. My dad's hand laced with my mom's in a silent gesture of support.

I was on my own.

CHAPTER SIX

Counterpoint is the combination of two independent melodic lines into a single harmonious relationship.

—Chapter Five, "Composition,"
An Introduction to Music Theory

GO BACK TO THE PART ABOUT THE BALLOON," Eliot said the next morning.

"Really? I cleave a world, barely make it out alive, my parents narc on me to the Consort, and the freaking *balloon* is the part that interests you?" I threw my physics book into my locker and slammed the door. "My parents couldn't even tell me what happens next. We have to wait for the Consort to decide. What if they put me in an oubliette?"

"They won't," he said. "There has to be an explanation for why the world cleaved so easily. And the only weird thing was the balloon, right? The rest of the Walk was by the book. So we're missing something." Behind his glasses, his brown eyes took on a familiar, faraway look. Deep in the supercomputer that was Eliot's brain, he was sifting through everything I'd told him, searching for a clue, a pattern, a reason. "We're definitely missing something."

"Nothing important," I said, thinking of Simon's fingers curving around my thigh.

"Everything's important, Del."

I shifted my books from one arm to the other. Walkers kept their abilities secret from the rest of the world. I kept all sorts of things secret from my family. But Eliot and I had *never* kept secrets from each other. I'd explained Echo Simon and Iggy and the fake ID easily enough. But when it came to our encounter at the bench, I wasn't ready to share.

Despite the crowded hallways, we reached the music classroom with time to spare. Eliot pulled at my sleeve to prevent me from going in. "If we can prove there was something wrong with the world, and that's why it cleaved, they'll have to go easier on you."

"It's the Consort. They can do whatever they want."

"They can't rewrite your DNA."

He had a point. The Consort couldn't take away my *ability* to Walk, but they could make it illegal. I'd be monitored for the rest of my life, unable to Walk without an accompanist. "What if they never grant me a license? I'd be stuck here."

I'd be like an Original, only worse, because I'd know what I was missing.

"I'll take you anywhere you want. All you have to do is ask," Eliot said.

His eyes were oddly serious, despite the smile, and I had the distinct feeling that now I was the one missing something. Before I could ask, our teacher, Ms. Powell, appeared in the doorway.

"Am I interrupting, you two?" Smiling, she motioned us inside.

"Nope," I mumbled.

If school was a wasteland, orchestra and music theory were my oasis—a break from the monotony of my day, a place where people spoke my native tongue. Ms. Powell was the only teacher who didn't treat me like a delinquent.

Eliot and I slid into our seats at the back of the room. Simon sat at the desk in front of me, his dark hair starting to curl along the nape of his neck. As usual, it looked slightly unkempt, like he'd just rolled out of bed. Rumor had it that he'd rolled out of a *lot* of beds.

Park World Simon's hair had been shaggier, falling past his collar, nearly hiding his eyes. The memory sent a stab of guilt through me. Simon must have felt me staring, because he twisted in his chair, flashed me a smile.

My own smile rose in answer—and disappeared as the girl sitting next to him noticed me too. Bree Carlson, star of the drama department, lead of nearly every musical and school play since the sixth grade. Pretty but not so gorgeous that the other girls hated her, popular but not so cutthroat that she had to watch her back, Bree was a chameleon; she acted whatever part would put her in the spotlight.

She and Simon had been together at the start of the year, but they'd split up about a month ago. The relationship had followed his typical pattern—a slow, easygoing shift from flirtation to coupledom to friends. Being dumped by Simon Lane was practically a badge of honor. I was surprised his exes didn't have an official club, with a page in the yearbook.

Judging from the way she trailed her fingers over his shoulder, I could see she'd decided to reprise her role as Simon's girlfriend. But in all the time I'd been watching him, he'd never gone out with the same girl twice. She had a better chance of nabbing a Broadway lead.

Which didn't ease the sting when he turned back to her as if I wasn't there.

"Since when do you smile at that guy?" Eliot grumbled.

I elbowed him. "Jealous much?"

Ms. Powell hit the lights and launched into her lecture on counterpoint, complete with slides. I tuned out Eliot's sputtering and tried to focus. Even so, my thoughts kept drifting to Park World Simon versus real Simon. Bedhead wasn't the only difference between the two. The leather cuff on his wrist was gone, replaced by a sporty, complicated-looking digital watch. This Simon had shadows under his eyes, the kind that took longer than a single late night to acquire. I wondered what—or who—had put them there. Eliot had always been better than me at pinpointing the changes between realities, but asking for his take on it would have meant admitting how close I'd gotten to Simon during the Great Balloon Rescue.

Forty minutes later the lights came back up, and Ms. Powell slapped her hands together with undisguised glee. She looked like a cross between a mad scientist and a 1950s housewife, wiry blond hair piled on her head and secured with pencils, a shirtdress printed with bluebirds, and a pair of orange patent-leather heels.

"So, your next project, to be done with a partner, is to develop and perform your own example of counterpoint, sixteen measures long. Fun, right?"

"This was supposed to be my blow-off class," Bree hissed to Simon, who shrugged. Despite being my parents age, Ms. Powell was new this year and naive enough to believe everyone was here because they loved music as much as she did. It was kind of endearing.

Ms. Powell continued. "This time around I decided it would be good to shake things up."

Nothing good had ever come from a teacher's desire to shake things up, and I braced myself.

"Rather than pick your own partners for this composition, I'm going to assign them." She chuckled at the groans that rose up. "You know what they say—familiarity breeds contempt."

There was plenty of contempt in the room, but it was all aimed at her. I might have felt sorry for her, if I hadn't felt like she was pitching her little speech directly to me. Walker training or school projects, Eliot and I were a team, and she was about to split us up. I slouched down as she yanked on the screen. It rolled up, displaying neat columns of names.

Eliot made a choking noise, but I couldn't tell if it was because he was partnered with Bree—who didn't look any more thrilled than he did—or because I was paired up with Simon.

"We can switch partners, can't we?" Bree asked, tossing her hair back. "If both groups agree?"

"If I wanted you to pick your own partners, I would have said so from the beginning," Ms. Powell replied, unfazed by Bree's venomous look.

Bree huffed and flounced without leaving her seat, then bent over to whisper something to Simon.

"You okay?" Eliot murmured. "You look weird."

"Thanks," I said through gritted teeth. "I'm fine."

He spun a mechanical pencil between his fingers, an over-under pattern I knew he'd spent hours practicing. "Watch him, okay? He's . . ."

"I know what he is." Trouble. My area of expertise. "Better than being stuck with Bree."

"She's not terrible," Eliot said, and pushed his glasses back up his nose. "Not terrible to look at, anyway."

It wasn't jealousy, exactly, that zinged through me. More like annoyance that he'd fallen under her spell so quickly, like he was any other guy. Worry, too. I knew how much experience he had with girls, and none of it was enough for him to deal with Bree. She'd have him for a midmorning snack and forget about him by lunch.

"Longest sixteen measures of your life," I said, and froze as Simon twisted around to face me again.

"Hey," he said, friendly despite the tension swirling around the four of us.

"Hey," I said, feeling stupid and obvious. I stared at the scar at the corner of his mouth, the one I'd seen in another world.

Ms. Powell spoke. "Now that you have your partners, take a

few minutes to get acquainted, and we'll—" The bell rang, off-key enough that Eliot and I both winced. "Never mind. We'll pick this up tomorrow."

"See you tomorrow, partner," Simon said, and turned to gather up his books.

"Today," I said, and he swiveled back, looking confused. "We have history together? Last period?"

He nodded slowly, but it was clear he'd never noticed. Heat rose in my cheeks.

"Can you *believe* Powell?" Bree said, tugging him toward the door. "This class is such a waste." He didn't give me a second glance. As usual.

I shoved everything into my backpack and followed Eliot into the hallway. "She actually split us up."

Eliot looked up from his phone and blinked. "Huh? Yeah, it sucks. Why'd your mom send you and Addie to that Echo?"

"She didn't. The assignment was to pick the Echo ourselves, remember? And it wasn't supposed to be Addie. My dad bailed at the last minute."

"But why did she approve it? I've been looking at the data you brought back, and those breaks were way outside acceptable stability parameters. She should have noticed when she ran the map."

"The map was fine when she ran it." My training Walks had to be analyzed by a licensed Walker before I could go out. Years ago that meant a navigator had to check each Echo in person. These days they ran the proposed route through a computer, and an algorithm would determine if it was safe to visit. My mom was one of the best navigators around; if she said a world was stable enough for a homework assignment, it was. "Echoes go bad all the time."

"A branch that big should take weeks to degrade. Yours changed in hours." He shook his head. "Maybe your mom screwed up. If the world was damaged before you arrived, you're not to blame. She is."

The Consort would be a lot tougher on a full-fledged Walker. She could lose her position—or worse. "My mom doesn't make those kinds of mistakes."

"Neither do I," he said. "This wasn't your fault, Del."

I remembered the sensation of the strings, knotted and straining against my fingertips, and wondered if, for once, Eliot was wrong.

The day did not improve. "Delaney," Bree called out with forced cheer on my way to ninth hour. I kept walking.

"Delaney." She tapped my shoulder sharply. "I was calling you."

"Delancey," I said. "Not Delaney."

Bree waved a hand. "Whatever. Can you believe Powell?"

I should have known she wasn't going to let the assignment go. We weren't friends. I didn't *have* any Original friends, and if I did, she wouldn't be one of them. I folded my arms and waited.

"We should be allowed to switch partners," she said, oozing chumminess. "Don't you think? It's not fair that we have to depend on someone we don't even know for a grade. What if we don't get along? What if they're a complete idiot?"

I bristled, but kept my tone syrupy. "Eliot won't hold that against you. He's very patient."

Her mask slipped as my words registered. "You don't have to be a bitch about it. Won't you be happier sticking with you own kind?"

"My own kind?" I didn't think she meant Walkers.

She simpered. "You know. Socially speaking. I'm only trying to help."

"Sweet of you to worry. But Powell won't let us switch."

"She will if *you* ask. For some reason, she likes you." She looked me over, the brightness in her voice ringing like steel. "Convince her to let us trade."

Annoyance shifted to anger. "Why? So you can climb all over Simon? He was tired of you back in September, Bree. He won't be interested in a rerun." I turned on my heel and left her fuming in the hallway.

Bree and her friends viewed everyone as either a stepping stone or a target. I was the weird girl who was constantly skipping class and blowing off homework, so far on the fringes of the social scene I didn't qualify as either. I wasn't dazzled by her talent or taken in by her performances, but I'd never tried to outshine her. At most, I'd been an afterthought.

Now I was a threat.

"Del," said Mrs. Gregory as I slid into my seat. "Good of you to join us. We missed you yesterday. As we so often do."

"Not all of us," said Bree, coming in behind me. Snickers crackled through the room.

"Family emergency," I said.

"And yet the office has no record of either one of your parents calling to inform us of this . . . emergency. Which means, as you're certainly aware by now, your absence is unexcused."

I sighed. The Walks I took during school weren't part of any assignment. They were my own secret ramblings, illegal but irresistible. I couldn't stand being cooped up in a classroom, not when the multiverse beckoned to me from every pivot I passed, new frequencies calling to me like a siren song. The War of 1812 or quadratic equations couldn't compete. Hence, my familiarity with the inside of the dean's office.

Gathering up my books, I waved halfheartedly. "See you tomorrow."

"Don't leave yet." She gave me a stack of papers and a thin smile. "Pass these out, if you will. You can see the dean *after* our pop quiz."

Like one quiz would make a difference to my abysmal grade. Wordlessly I started circling the room. When I reached Bree's desk, she took a paper and casually, deliberately, knocked the rest out of my hands.

"Sorry," she said.

I bent to scoop up the papers, and she added, "At least he knows I exist."

"Excuse me?" I reached for another quiz, and she planted her leopard-print ballet flat on top of it.

"Simon. Did you honestly think one stupid project would give you a shot with him? You could disappear tomorrow and he'd never notice. He doesn't even know your name."

I stood, papers crumpling in my fist. Mrs. Gregory called, "Del, the quizzes? We don't have all day."

Sotto voce, Bree murmured, "Watch yourself, freak."

I forced my fingers to uncurl. She settled back, triumphant, her ponytail swishing as she surveyed the room. I looked at the sheaf of papers in my hand, the questions so foreign I might as well not bother.

So I didn't.

"Del! What are you doing?" Mrs. Gregory called.

"Saving time," I said, swinging my backpack over my shoulder. "I'll tell the dean you said hello."

CHAPTER SEVEN

Every Walker leaves an audible trail when moving through Echoes, as does any object brought from the Key World. Over time, the signal will weaken until it becomes untraceable, though inanimate objects hold signatures longer than people.

—Chapter Two, "Navigation,"
Principles and Practices of Cleaving, Year Five

WHEN I GOT HOME FROM SCHOOL, DISCIplinary paperwork stuffed into the bottom of my backpack, my mom was sitting at the kitchen table. A glass jar of buttons stood at her elbow and one of Monty's sweaters lay in her lap. "The school called."

"I know." I'd been sitting in the dean's office when he dialed. "I'll be more careful next time."

"There'd better not be a next time," she replied, and snipped a loose thread. "Have a seat."

I dropped into my chair. "You heard from the Consort?"

"They want to see you tonight." She tugged at the button and made a small, satisfied noise. "Daddy and I will take you in."

The last thing I wanted was an hour-long lecture in the car. I glanced at the teapot, squat and fire-engine red, the same color as the little girl's balloon. My throat tightened, but I said, "I'm going with Eliot."

"He can ride with us. We need to be there."

"You *don't* need to. You've already turned me in, Mom. Isn't that enough?"

"That's not—" She broke off as Monty wandered in, clutching the sports section of the newspaper.

"I'm cold," he complained.

"Perfect timing," Mom replied with forced cheer, and helped him into the sweater. He must have given her a rough time today—the more difficult he was, the more upbeat she got, as if she could reverse his decline solely through willpower. "Honestly, Dad, I don't know how you manage to lose so many buttons."

Monty winked at me and put his finger to his lips. I stifled a laugh, despite my mood.

"Good as new, and here's my best girl in the bargain." He gave me a whiskery kiss on the cheek. "Have you been out Walking? Did you see Rose?"

"I was at school, Grandpa."

"It's late. She should be home by now," he said, and swiped a handful of buttons from the jar. "We should look for her."

"How about a snack?" Mom said. She packed up the sewing kit with exaggerated care, like the precise arrangement of threads and needles would somehow make everything else fall into place.

He paused, his hand on the doorknob. "A snack?"

"I'll fix you something," I said quickly. When Monty lost

time, distraction was the only way to stop him from taking off. "How about granola? With honey on top?"

He scratched his chin, considering, and then sat as if he was doing us a favor. My mom exhaled. "I'm going to finish up some work. Del, we're leaving in an hour."

I didn't answer.

"Have you been out Walking?" Monty asked again when she left. "Did you see Rose?"

"Nope. School, remember?" He did this a lot, asking the same questions over and over, as if the answer would change.

"You're in trouble," he said. "I heard them talking."

"Yep." I kept my tone even and my face hidden behind the pantry door. "I . . . made a mistake. When I was Walking with Addie."

He made a harrumphing noise. "Nothing's done . . ."

I was not in the mood for rhymes. Not with so much at stake. "I cleaved a world, Grandpa. It doesn't get any more done." I spoke more softly. "It was an accident. I know they don't believe me, but it was."

Monty didn't say anything, and I dug through the shelves for the giant mason jar of granola. "You know what I don't understand? If Echoes are such a threat, why am I in trouble for cleaving one?"

The air around me quivered. As quietly as I could, so as not to disturb the chord, I backed out of the pantry and turned my head toward the table.

"Damn it, Grandpa!"

Monty was gone, the pivot point he'd used trembling faintly. If I hurried, I might be able to catch him before my mom realized he'd wandered off. In a way, I admired how neatly he'd played us, but I doubted my parents would see it that way.

If they found out.

I'd need to be fast, not only to keep my mom from discovering I'd let Monty escape, but because his signature would only last a little while. I had to find him before the trail went cold.

Grabbing my backpack—even on a quick trip, I wanted my tools nearby—I followed him through the rift.

Monty had been tracing my grandmother's path for so long, he was Walking between worlds at random, searching for a hint of the frequency that meant she'd been there. He'd never found one.

I was luckier. I let the cacophony of the pivot swallow me up, searching for the smooth, crystalline pitch of the Key World. Only a few minutes had passed, and Monty hadn't gone far—his signal was loud and clear, nestled in an Echo with a frequency close to ours.

This Echo was old. Someone else had moved into this version of our house and rehabbed it, the empty kitchen gleaming and catalog worthy, with artful flower arrangements and perfectly staged clutter instead of the *actual* clutter that filled every surface of our house, despite my mom's efforts. A neat line of monogrammed backpacks hung from hooks by the open back door.

I dashed outside and heard the next pivot point, whirring

like crickets at dusk. When I crossed through, a giant spruce had replaced the crimson-leafed maple in my backyard. Nestled against the trunk was a bright yellow button, resonating at the Key World's frequency.

Monty's breadcrumb.

I got lost once, when I was five. My parents had been busy working, Addie was practicing piano, and I'd slipped outside on my own. I'd found an unfamiliar Echo of our backyard, with a full swing set—a slide and glider and monkey bars instead of the single rope swing my dad had made for Addie and me to share. I'd loved it, until I lost track of time. The pitch that had started out as intriguing transformed into overwhelming. I couldn't find the pivot I'd come through, and I couldn't hear any others.

That's when Monty appeared, button in hand. He'd scooped me up in his arms and called me his best, most clever girl. A glow spread through me at his words. Even back then, I'd grown tired of hearing how smart my sister was. He'd given me the button, ringing with the sound of the Key World frequency, and promised that as long as I left a trail of breadcrumbs, he would always find me, and together we would find the way home.

These days I usually didn't want to be found. But I left a trail of paper stars when I Walked anyway, both habit and reminder of the fun we'd had.

When I stepped through the next portal, he was waiting for me, leaning against a mailbox shaped like a giant fish.

"You scared me!"

"Nothing to be scared of," he said, pulling a shiny silver

button from his pocket. "I wanted to stretch my legs."

"Mom's going to kill me," I said. "We have to go back."

"It's a beautiful afternoon, Delancey. Walk with me."

He flipped the button to the ground and set off, singing under his breath. I could see the village water tower in the distance, the same view I'd grown up with, but we were standing in a development of Tudor-style townhomes, with steeply pitched roofs and wooden cutouts decorating the balconies, exactly where our once-stately Queen Anne should have been.

You learn pretty quickly not to mourn the changes in a world. It wasn't a Walker's place to decide which Echoes were better, only to decide which ones were threats to the Key World. Sadly, chintzy housing was not considered dangerous.

I chased after Monty, linking my arm with his.

"Grandpa, the Consort wants to see me. Tonight."

"Bah. There's time enough." He stopped short. "Feel that?"

His mind might have been going, and his hearing was shot, but he retained the touch. I stretched out my hand, quieted my mind, and felt the quiver of a pivot point I would have missed on my own.

Again and again, the ground changed under our feet—from sidewalk to dirt road to cement to blacktop to grass—a sign we were making big jumps between worlds. In every one, he dropped another button and smiled slyly, like a kid who'd gotten away with something. We were far from the Key World now, wandering among Echoes of Echoes.

I loved how vast the multiverse felt on these Walks, hungered for the possibilities. Someday I'd travel not only in the Echoes of the world I knew, but all over the globe. If I could find this much variety when we'd covered only a few miles, what would it be like to explore Echoes of Rome, or India, or Antarctica?

My steps slowed. How many Echoes had I destroyed with my cleaving? How many possibilities had I unraveled?

"You've cleaved worlds before, haven't you?" I asked Monty. "Back when you were a First Chair?"

"When I was young and foolish." His tone softened. "It bothers you, what happened."

"I keep thinking about them." About those people, rippling away, as if they'd never existed in the first place. "Did it bother you?"

He studied the cracked sidewalk and finally said, "Still does. As it should."

"They're just Echoes," I said. "That's what everyone says."

"Not everyone." He brightened, our conversation forgotten. "You choose the next one."

"I choose we go home." I checked my watch—Eliot would be at my place soon. If I intercepted him, we could head out before my mom realized we'd left. We could cross directly from here to the Key World, but we'd still need to get from downtown to our house.

"We used to have such fun," he wheedled. His chin had taken on a stubborn set. "One more."

"One, and then we go home." I surveyed the grungy Echo we'd stopped in. Every third storefront was boarded up; graffiti scrawled across the plywood; the gutter was littered with food wrappers and cigarette butts and pulpy shreds of newspaper. At home we would have been standing directly outside a juice bar.

He grinned crookedly. "Are you hungry?"

We watched as a woman in Snoopy-print scrubs hesitated at the intersection, then decided to wait for the WALK sign. A pivot sprang up.

An instant later a Ford sedan blew through the light.

I shuddered. On the other side of the pivot, had her newly formed Echo made it across?

Either way, her choice had given us an opening. Monty hummed a target pitch and motioned to the rift. "Go on. Nimble fingers."

Another childhood song from our Walks, as ingrained in my mind as the ABCs.

Nimble fingers, open mind,
Hum a tune both deft and kind;
Nimble fingers, open mind,
Help to seek what you would find.

I reached inside, the right frequency snagging my attention like a radio signal breaking through static. Keeping a firm hold on Monty's sleeve, I eased into the next Echo. When we were safely on the other side, I took a deep breath, tasting sugar in the air. Across the street was a bakery with a pink-striped awning and a window full of sweets.

"Doughnuts!" He rubbed his hands together. "Don't tell your mother. She'll say I spoiled my dinner."

"Trust me, I won't say a word. How did you find this place?"

"I ramble," he said distantly, tugging on my sleeve. "Don't suppose you'd like to buy an old man a treat?"

I knew he'd had a reason for bringing me here. The frequency was off-key, but not grating. We could stop for a few minutes. I handed him a crumpled five, hoping it matched this world's currency. "One doughnut. And be fast, okay? I need to get home."

He patted my arm. "We're right on schedule."

I trailed after him as he crossed the street. This version of downtown was miles better than the one we'd left. The sidewalks were clean, the storefronts filled, even if they weren't quite as upscale as home—a hardware store instead of an art gallery, a pawn shop instead of an antique store, a pharmacy instead of a yoga studio. The street was lined with cars, and plenty of people chatted on the sidewalk. Monty made sure to brush against one as he entered the store, so he was now fully visible. Outside the bakery, a dog was tied to the armrest of a bench. A chocolate Lab. With a red bandana.

"Iggy?" I whispered. Echoes often overlapped, but seeing Iggy so soon after watching him unravel was as jarring as any frequency I'd encountered.

His answering barks shook the windows, and he leaped up, straining at the leash.

I blinked. Some animals' hearing was so sensitive, they could recognize Walkers before we made contact. Iggy was obviously one of them.

"Good boy," I crooned, inching forward with my hand extended. "What are you doing here?"

As if in answer, the bakery door opened and Simon strolled out, white paper bag in hand. A different Simon, I reminded myself, taking in the layers of flannel and denim and leather, the messy hair, the battered work boots. Not a basketball in sight.

"Settle down," he said, untying the leash. The dog bolted, seventy-odd pounds of enthusiastic fur crashing into me. I rubbed his silky ears, staring at my third Simon in two days, trying to recall Park World's frequency. This one was less grating—and much more stable. My stomach unclenched at the knowledge this Simon was safe. I didn't think I could handle seeing him unravel again.

He grabbed Iggy's collar, his hand brushing mine. The strength of his signal sent me reeling, and he met my eyes, interest sparking in his own. "You're making me look bad, Ig."

Not much made Simon look bad. Even his legion of exes sighed and talked about his eyes or his hands or his laugh. He wasn't the type to stick, they said, but it was fun while it lasted.

I was not interested in fun.

"Iggy won't bite, I promise," Simon said, misinterpreting my frozen silence. I looked at his hand, wrapped around the leash. Instead of the leather cuff or digital watch, he wore what looked like a silver railroad spike hammered into a circle around his wrist. But his hands looked the same, strong and capable and slightly calloused. "Don't I know you?"

My nerves kicked up, a swarm of butterflies spreading from my stomach through my body, a hundred thousand wings beating in unison.

"Del," I said, my voice scratchy. "School, maybe?"

"Maybe," he said. "Or maybe I need to get my eyes checked."

"Oh?" I asked, checking the bakery. Through the window, I could see Monty peering at the pastry cases.

Simon's voice dropped, warm and inviting. "Something must be wrong if I haven't noticed you."

I turned back. "Really? That's the best you can do?"

At home I would have stuttered and stumbled. It was easier to deal with him here, when it wasn't real and didn't matter. His smile turned rueful and somehow even more charming. "Too obvious?"

"You're not going to win any points for originality. What are you doing here?"

"It's Thursday," he said, holding up the white paper bag. "My night to make dinner. I always pick up cookies for my mom, to make up for the inevitable kitchen disaster."

"You could learn to cook," I pointed out.

"I don't mind," he said with a shrug. "Besides, if I hadn't stopped by, I wouldn't have run into you."

There was an Echo where he hadn't, and I was unreasonably, alarmingly happy to be in this world instead.

"There's a band playing at Grundy's tonight," he said. "They're supposed to be pretty good. Want to meet up?"

This invitation was as surprising as the first one. It wasn't unusual for Echoes to mimic each other, if their branches were close enough. And just like in Park World, I had a million reasons to say no. But sometimes the best decisions are the ones made on instinct and impulse. Sometimes a choice isn't a simple yes or no, but the truth made visible, strong enough to hold up a world.

I wasn't sure I was ready for that kind of truth.

The bell over the bakery door jingled and Monty appeared, long john in one hand, coffee in the other, a cruller clamped between his teeth. "I have to go."

Probably not the reaction Simon usually got when he asked a girl out. His forehead wrinkled. "Is that a yes?"

I bit my lip. "It's a maybe. Bye, Iggy. Stay out of trouble."

Grabbing Monty's arm, I steered him back toward the pivot.

"Making friends?" Monty asked around his cruller. His gaze, sharper than usual, followed Simon and Iggy as they crossed the street and climbed into a battered black Jeep.

"Simon Lane. He's a guy from school." I checked my watch. Eliot would be arriving at my house soon.

"Simon," Monty said. "Wasn't he the boy—"

"From the cleaving," I finished. "Yeah."

He nodded, obviously pleased with himself for remembering. The walk back to the Key World was fast and easy. We turned onto our block as Eliot pulled up in his mom's Subaru, parking in Addie's usual spot. She was typically back from her apprenticeship by now—she would arrive home a few minutes before Eliot and I left for training, offer advice we hadn't asked for, and then go inside to finish up her day's paperwork.

"Where's Addie?" I asked.

Monty licked a bit of frosting from his thumb. "Your mother said she was meeting with the Consort."

"By herself?" That didn't make sense. Mom had been adamant I not see the Consort alone. Why would Addie be any different?

"Seems so."

If Addie could deal with the Consort by herself, I could too. "Can you get in by yourself? You won't wander off?"

"Don't worry about me," he said, patting my hand. "Now go on, before your mother catches you."

I kissed his cheek and ran for Eliot's car as Monty ambled around the side of the house.

"Go!" I said, throwing my bag onto the seat and sliding inside.

"Hello to you, too. Is there a problem?" Eliot asked.

"Not unless my mom catches us. Drive, will you? I want to make the early train."

"Seat belt," he replied, shifting into reverse. "I feel like I'm driving a getaway car."

"Then act like it." As we pulled away, my mom stepped onto the front porch, hands on hips.

"Delancey!" The shout was faint, but I was sure she'd make up for it later.

CHAPTER EIGHT

While Walkers share the Key World with Originals, we occupy very different spheres. Casual acquaintances and business interactions are acceptable, but strong attachments are discouraged.

Most importantly, revealing the existence and abilities of Walkers is *strictly* forbidden. Originals cannot understand the scope of our responsibilities and would seek to take advantage of both us and the multiverse, resulting in disaster.
— Chapter Ten, "Ethics and Governance,"
Principles and Practices of Cleaving, Year Five

ELIOT AND I HAD BEEN COMING TO THE Consort Building for years—as little kids on family outings, and later as eleven-year-olds beginning our training, dropped off by his mom or mine. Eventually we'd graduated to taking the train on our own, once they trusted us not to wander through the pivots riddling Union Station. Class met four times a week, and I learned more in a single session of Walker training than in an entire month of regular high school.

To Originals, the Consort's headquarters looked like any other office building in Chicago's Loop. Even the name on the front door blended in: Consort Change Management. Nobody could tell you exactly what they did, but they'd been a quiet, unassuming presence in the city for as long as anyone could remember. My parents drew a paycheck from CCM; they filed their taxes every year, they had health insurance and pension plans. CCM had offices around the globe, entire communities of Walkers hiding in plain sight. The operation was funded by investments, using information gleaned in Echoes. They took insider trading to a whole new level.

We followed our usual path from Union Station, taking Adams across the river, forcing myself not to look at the gray-green water below, waiting impatiently for the light across Wacker.

"Everyone's going to know," I said, squeezing the straps of my backpack. "They're probably talking about me right now."

The light changed and Eliot hustled me across the intersection, dodging the commuters streaming past us. "Quit dragging your feet. You love it when people talk about you."

"Sure, when they're saying how kick-ass I am. This is not one of those times."

"They probably won't even know."

I snorted. "They'll be thrilled. And it's going to napalm my class rank."

Unlike Washington High, where my GPA consistently landed in the toilet, Walker training didn't give grades. Instead they relied on rankings, and mine was disappointingly average.

Ranking was based partly on fieldwork, which I dominated, and partly on classroom assignments, which I did not. Walking was easy for me. Navigating branches, moving through pivots, tracking signals . . . I moved as swift and sure as an arrow.

Classwork was another story. Nobody gave points for intuition or improvisation, only the meticulous repetition of Consort protocol. Eliot tried to help, but his patient explanations only underscored how differently my mind worked. In the Consort's eyes, "different" was the opposite of "better."

My ranking, combined with our final exam, determined where I'd be assigned during my apprenticeship. We could request a position, but the final say, as always, belonged to the Consort. Never before had I realized how much of my future lay in the hands of other people, and the knowledge made me want to kick something. Hard.

We stopped outside the glass doors of CCM. Inside was a nondescript lobby—marble floors, security desk, a bank of elevators, and a few low couches and tables. Our classmates were gathered in the corner, everyone leaning in, still wearing their coats and backpacks.

"Listen," Eliot said, eyeing the twin guards at the security desk. "When you see the Consort . . . act contrite. Like you regret what you did."

"I *do,*" I said, remembering the twist in my gut as the Echo unraveled. "It's not an act."

"Good," Eliot said. "Don't blame Addie, either. They think she's great, so it's logical they'd take her side."

"That's nothing new," I said.

He took my hand. "We don't want to be late."

I nodded, and he held open the door.

My skin tingled every time I crossed the threshold of this place. There's power in secrets, in knowledge hidden away. The deeper they're hidden, the greater the tension shimmering through the air. This building held secrets Originals couldn't dream of, and no matter how many Monet reproductions they hung on the walls or how tasteful the jazz they piped in, the hum of power couldn't be entirely muted.

This time when I walked in, dread curled through me, bitterly cold.

"Del!" Callie Moreno called from the corner. The group turned to gape at me. Muttering something under her breath, Callie shot them a dirty look, pushed off the couch, and strode across the lobby. In the too-quiet room, the heels of her boots rang out on the floor. She gave me a half smile, warm but worried. "Is it true? Logan said you—"

"Delancey Sullivan?" one of the security guards asked, stepping out from behind the desk. Callie's smile fell away, and Eliot shifted, putting himself between us. "You'll need to come with me."

I opened and closed my mouth soundlessly, like a fish thrown onto shore.

"Where?" Eliot asked. "Says who?"

Out of the corner of my eye, I spotted my classmates edging closer, as if they couldn't catch every word in the echoing lobby.

"To the sixteenth floor," the guard said, chest puffed out. "At the request of the Consort."

"Class starts in five minutes," I said, my voice rasping.

He smirked. "Not for you."

Eliot turned his back on the guard to look at me, his dark skin shiny with nerves. "I'll go with you."

The guard beckoned, and a woman in an identical uniform—badly cut black pants, white shirt with black trim, Taser and other paraphernalia hanging from a thick leather belt—joined him.

As a precaution against creating strong pivots in the building, Consort guards didn't carry lethal weapons. Before today I'd assumed the stun gun and pepper spray were to protect the Walkers from discovery by Originals. Now, as the second guard stared down my best friend, I reconsidered.

In a nasal, overloud voice, she said, "The summons is for Delancey alone. We will escort you to the chamber. The rest of you will proceed to training as usual."

Eliot met my eyes, ready to argue.

"I've got this," I told him, trying to keep the wobble from my voice. "See you in a few."

Maybe they would let me off with a warning. If they did, I'd be a model student for the rest of training. I'd help out at home. I'd be nicer to Addie. Anything, as long as they didn't take Walking from me.

Our path to the elevators was blocked by my classmates. Behind us, the younger kids were coming inside for their training, some of them accompanied by their parents. As the lobby filled and the murmurs grew, my face went fiery. I'd wanted to be known for my skill, not my screwups.

I kept my eyes fixed on the elevators, tuned out the whispers and snickers, and moved across the room on autopilot. Shame burned through me, hotter with every step. But it wasn't until I was inside, steel doors sliding shut, that I nearly lost it. The glimpse of Eliot, stricken and sympathetic, was infinitely worse than the onlookers' scorn.

Given a choice, it seems like pity would be easier to bear than mockery, but that's not true. Mockery hardens defenses; pity slips through, finds the softest places you have, and slices to the bone.

Pity will break you, every time.

One guard slid a card through a reader and pressed the button for the sixteenth floor. I thought about asking what would happen, but they looked straight ahead, feet braced wide and hands clasped behind their backs. They didn't seem like they'd welcome a conversation.

I wondered if they knew the full story, or if they'd simply done the Consort's bidding without asking for details. Probably the latter. Nobody questioned the Consort. Their rulings were absolute, their directives inviolate. Even my parents didn't challenge the orders they received.

The display counted steadily upward, and I knotted my fingers together as the elevator slowed. The doors opened and my lungs closed.

My parents stood in the cream-and-ebony foyer, their heads bent together. Monty perched on an upholstered black bench, looking around owlishly. He must have been here plenty of times, but he was acting as if he had never seen this place before.

One of the guards prodded me in the back, and I stumbled

into the hall. My mother's head snapped up, her mouth tightening in annoyance. "Del! Why did you run off? I told you we would come in together."

"And I told you I'd ride with Eliot," I said, palms sweating. "I can do this without you."

"You're a minor," she said. "The Consort can't sentence you unless we're present."

"Sentence me?" I repeated. "I'm on trial?"

"No, sweetheart." My father pulled me to his side, like he could protect me from the impact of his words. "The trial's over. They've called witnesses, reviewed the reports . . ."

I jerked away. "I didn't get to defend myself!"

"Your actions are your defense, Del. Intentions don't count. Explanations don't count. The only thing that matters is the end result," he said.

"Deaf and dumb," Monty grumbled. "Every one of them."

Mom shushed him. "Dad!"

He waved her off. "Rose used to say I should have been given a Consort seat. Thought I could do some good. Don't let them scare you, Del. You're worth ten of them."

My mom pinched the bridge of her nose. "Dad, you're not helping matters. Can you please keep it to yourself until we get home?"

Monty's disdain for the Consort was nothing new—their failure to find my grandmother was a grudge he'd nursed my whole life. But his words could be twisted if the wrong person overheard.

72

"I keep all kinds of things," he said, tapping his forehead with a gnarled finger. It would have been better for him to stay home, and I realized we were short one person.

"Where's Addie?" I asked.

My dad tugged at the knot of his tie. Cleavers rarely dressed up, and now I understood why. Hard to run in business casual. "She's inside."

Sympathy stirred within me, but it was comforting to know I wasn't the only one on trial. They must have already sentenced her, since she wasn't considered a minor.

The female guard touched her earpiece and gestured to the twin doors of the Consort's chamber. "Go in."

Monty levered himself up with a grunt. My mom helped me with my backpack and coat, handing them over to my dad. She started to say something, but stopped. Instead she tucked my hair behind my ears and sighed, as if it was the best she could do. My dad reached for the door handle, not meeting my eyes.

I started to shake, and the worst-case scenarios I'd been trying not to imagine crowded into my head. Prison. An oubliette. Another cleaving, one I couldn't escape.

A blue-veined hand closed over mine, cool and reassuring. Monty angled his head toward the door. "Together?"

At least Monty was looking out for me. "Together."

I looked up at the marble plaque above the chamber doors. The Key World frequency was carved into the polished white stone, a line of peaks and valleys in perfect symmetry. The motto beneath captured everything I'd ever been taught.

To the true song, all honor;

From the true song, all gifts.

For the first time in my life, the lines rang false. Walking was my birthright, my gift, but the people inside that room had the power to snatch it away. My whole future—the only one I'd ever wanted—had narrowed down to a single moment. A single decision.

And it wasn't mine to make.

CHAPTER NINE

The Minor Consorts number forty-eight, each responsible for a specific time zone on one side of the equator. They govern the branches and Walkers within their territories and are accountable only to the Major Consort.

—Chapter Ten, "Ethics and Governance,"
Principles and Practices of Cleaving, Year Five

THE CHAMBER OF THE MINOR CONSORT sounded impressive, but the room itself was spare and anonymous. Institutional gray carpet, white walls, and no chairs except for those behind the table at the front of the room. The three Consort members were already seated, tracking my movements closely. Addie was standing to the side, arms crossed over her stomach.

These Consort members had served for as long as I could remember. They'd probably worked with Monty. Before my grandmother disappeared, he'd risen pretty high in the ranks, leading a team of Cleavers to the most critical Echoes. But he gave no sign of recognizing them.

My mom guided him toward the wall, her voice so soft I couldn't make out the words. Addie joined them, taking her place next to my dad. She looked wan but resolute. They must have come down hard on her.

"Come forward, Delancey," said the woman in the center. "I'm Councilwoman Crane."

I knew who she was. I knew all of them, though we'd never met. The Consort was comprised of three members, one from each section: ethics, science, and cleaving The ethicists were the ones who made the rules and policies; the scientists studied the physics of the multiverse and the Key World; the cleavers dealt with the day-to-day effects and protocols of cleaving. All three were represented on the Consort to ensure their decisions were balanced—all their decisions were unanimous, to symbolically avoid pivots. Whatever my sentence, they'd agreed upon it.

Crane spoke in a faintly scratchy alto. Her white hair was cut short and severe, but her features were soft behind her frameless glasses. She didn't look kind, exactly, but she did look fair. As the ethicist, she'd be in charge of my sentencing.

I edged to the center of the room and tried to look contrite.

To her left sat another woman, Councilwoman Bolton, the head of the scientists. Her dark hair was as long as mine, arranged in countless tiny braids, heavily shot through with silver and caught in a low ponytail. Her eyes—a harder, sharper brown than Eliot's warm gaze—seemed to catalog every one of my faults. I curled my toes inside my shoes, and tried to read my future in their faces.

The man on the right was easier to read but no more reassuring. He had a narrow face, steely hair swept back from a high forehead, and a strong nose. On some people it would have been aristocratic. But he caught sight of Monty, and for an instant his lips peeled back. Aristocratic turned arrogant. Councilman Lattimer, who ran the Cleavers.

Before today these people had been only names—last names, no less, unlike the rest of the Walkers. They'd been printed across the bottom of the letters I received every June, congratulating me on another successful year and welcoming me to the next round of my training. They'd been mentioned over dinner, when my parents were discussing a policy change, or in class, during our unit on governance. I'd never envisioned them as real people.

Now they seemed even less human.

I looked back at Monty, hoping for reassurance. He'd deliberately turned away from the Consort, tugging fretfully at the buttons on his coat, inspecting the door as if he could escape.

"Let us begin," said Councilwoman Crane.

I locked my knees to keep them from giving out.

"Yesterday we received a report stating that, on an accompanied Walk, you unraveled a world resonating at the specific frequency of . . ." She read from a paper in front of her, rattling off a number at least twenty digits long, complete with decimals and exponents.

"It was an accident," I protested, my voice as high and plaintive as a child's.

"Within every accident lies a choice," Bolton said, her expression stern.

Before I could say anything else, Lattimer held up a hand. "We are not concerned with your excuses or opinions. Only the outcomes and evidence matter here."

Councilwoman Crane continued, setting the paper aside. "We've spoken with your instructor. The parameters of your assignment neither required nor permitted direct contact with the strings. Our investigators confirmed the frequency in question has ceased transmitting. According to the witness statement, you are the one responsible."

"The witness statement?" I whirled, but Addie wouldn't meet my eyes. "You sold me out?"

"As the only other Walker present, her testimony was required," Bolton said. "Based on the findings of our investigators, we believe her statement to be accurate and reliable."

Addie nibbled on her thumbnail, head bowed. I took a step toward her, and the guards at the door both shifted—hands on weapons, faces impassive, intent clear.

I dug my fingernails into my palms, trying to see through the haze of anger. It wasn't enough for Addie to be perfect, to be the one everybody fawned over. She had to screw me over, too.

Councilwoman Bolton read from her own paper. "Your interaction with the Echo child was unnecessary and increased the existing damage. You ignored the direction of your accompanist, and your actions endangered her life. Your cleaving was improperly conducted, resulting in a weakening at the cut site of the pivot."

"Any one of these is a serious infraction," Lattimer said. "To commit so many on a single Walk indicates a tendency toward recklessness that does not bode well for your future."

A hint of a smile snaked over his face and his gaze flickered to

Monty, then back to me. "You are suspended from your Walker training for the remainder of the year. You may not attend classes with your cohorts. You may not Walk alone, or with anyone but licensed family members.

"At the conclusion of your suspension, you will be expected to take the final licensing exam with your classmates. If you pass, you may continue on to your apprenticeship. If you fail or violate our terms, you will repeat your fifth year while your peers move on."

The room wavered along the edges. "The entire year? How am I supposed to pass the exam if I can't go to training?"

"That responsibility will fall to your family. We'll expect a weekly report of your lessons, to ensure you're receiving proper instruction. Naturally, this would be in addition to your parents' usual duties."

My parents couldn't find time to help with a homework assignment, much less an entire year of training. The fifth-year exam was notoriously hard—cumulative over all our years of training, covering every aspect of our work. The last three months of class were essentially a giant cram session, and Shaw made sure we were prepared. Without his help, I'd fail.

By June my classmates would have their licenses. Eliot would be off to his apprenticeship. Everyone would know I'd been left behind.

Walking was the only thing I was good at, and they were taking it away. Something inside me twisted sharply at the loss.

Councilwoman Crane cleared her throat, waiting for a response. Shock had stolen my words, and I eyed her mutely.

Her expression thawed. "Do you agree to comply with the terms of this sentence? The alternative is to permanently forfeit your right to Walk."

People weren't kidding when they said the Consort went out of their way to minimize choices. I'd do anything to be a Walker, and they knew it. I looked back at my parents, who appeared solemn but unsurprised. Maybe even relieved. Next to them, Addie stood frozen, fingers pressed to her lips.

"I object!" shouted Monty. My mom took his arm, but he shook her off, stomping past me toward the table. Crane and Bolton exchanged knowing looks, while a mottled red crept up Lattimer's neck.

"Overruled," Crane said calmly. "This is not a courtroom, Montrose. Surely you haven't forgotten that much."

"She's got more talent in her little finger than any of you. I trained her myself."

"Did you?" said Lattimer. He studied me with fresh curiosity, like a frog in biology class, right before dissection. "Quite the student she's turned out to be."

"We gave this matter considerable thought. We took into account her age and her abilities, your family's service, and your . . ." Crane trailed off, searching for the right word. ". . . sacrifice. It is our hope she will use this time to grow into her talents. But we have made our decision, and now she must make hers."

She shifted her gaze back to me. "Delancey?"

Sometimes, in the instant an Original makes a choice, you can feel the pivot forming. The air snaps and shifts, as if the world is breaking open to make room for the other reality taking shape. It doesn't happen for Walkers. Our pivots are too weak to last, and once our choice is made, we can only imagine what might have been.

So I said yes, and listened to the silence.

CHAPTER TEN

"WELL, THAT COULD HAVE GONE WORSE," MY father said after we filed out, trying to sound upbeat and missing by miles. He put his arm around my shoulder, but I yanked away.

"They kicked me out," I snapped. "I'm going to fail the exam. How could that have gone worse?"

Monty patted my hand.

"They could have sent you to an oubliette," my mother said sharply. Addie stood next to her, shoulders curling inward. "You should be—" Behind them, the chamber door swung open again.

"Winfield, Foster," said Councilwoman Crane, leaning on an ivory-handled stick. "We have another matter to discuss."

My parents exchanged glances. "Wait here," Mom said. "And behave yourselves. That includes you, Dad."

"Foolishness," Monty mumbled when they'd left, crushing his hat in his hands. "Hidebound foolishness."

"What do you think they're talking about?" Addie asked, ignoring him.

"Probably what a bitch you are," I said. "You got off scot-free, didn't you? That's why you were so eager to turn me in. You wanted to cut a deal?"

"There was no deal," she said, flushing pink. "They asked me what happened. I told the truth."

"*Your* truth." Not the same thing. *Truth is as fluid as water, as faceted as diamonds, as flawed as memory*, Monty used to say. People saw what they needed to believe in the moment. Not untrue, he'd remind me. Just not the entirety. And Addie needed to believe I was the villain. "I'm suspended, thanks to you."

"Thanks is right, you little brat," she shot back. "Lattimer was convinced you did it on purpose. Unsanctioned cleavings can be tried as treason, Del. Same with lying to the Consort. So, yeah. I told them what an idiot you were, and they went easy on you."

"Treason?" I said, ice filling my veins.

"You're welcome," she said grimly as Lattimer stepped into the corridor, immaculate and unsettling.

"I'm surprised to see you here, Montrose. Goodness, it's almost like old times." He said the words with relish. "All we're missing is Rose."

Monty jerked, and he leaned in like he was telling me a secret. His voice, however, carried through the empty hallway. "Rose never liked him."

A vein in Lattimer's temple pulsed, but he took in Monty's threadbare cardigan and disheveled hair, the unsteady hands and stooped shoulders, and smirked. "Her judgment wasn't exactly sound, was it? Otherwise she'd still be with us."

To my surprise, Monty didn't protest that my grandmother

was coming back. He sagged visibly, murmuring, "Like old times."

"Is he often like this?" Lattimer asked Addie.

"Some days are better than others," she hedged. "He's tired."

"Of course," he replied. "He was quite talented, you know. It's a shame, what his searching has done to him."

"What *you've* done," Monty growled.

There was an awkward pause before Addie stepped in. "I'm so sorry, Councilman. He gets confused."

"I see," Lattimer said, sounding sympathetic. He patted Monty's shoulder, ignoring the way he twitched. "I merely wanted to check up on you, old friend. I'd best return to my colleagues. Duty calls, you know."

He reached for the doorknob and my jaw unclenched.

Lattimer paused and turned back. "We appreciated your forthrightness this afternoon, Addison. One year left in your apprenticeship, I believe?"

She bobbed her head. "Yes, sir."

"Excellent. If you continue to impress us as you have, you'll have quite a bright career ahead of you."

"Thank you, sir," she mumbled.

"As for you, Delancey," he said, keeping his eyes on Monty. "You'd do well to pick your role models more carefully, if you hope to have a career of any sort."

The door shut behind him with a soft click.

"I really get the sense he's rooting for me," I said.

"He's bearing a grudge," Monty said, back to his old self. "And you've been caught up in it."

"What kind of grudge?" Addie asked.

"An old one," Monty said. "Ancient history."

I didn't believe that any more than the helpless, muddled routine he'd put on for Lattimer's benefit. Both ignited my curiosity.

He jammed the battered hat on his head. "Let's go. The sooner we're away, the better."

"Mom said to wait," Addie protested.

"Stay if you like," he told her, then directed his words to me. "There's nothing here for either of us now. Are you coming, Del?"

Monty had never steered me wrong before, so I went.

CHAPTER ELEVEN

When visiting an Echo world, interaction with its inhabitants should be limited to frequency analysis. Do not engage with Echoes in a frivolous manner or for personal gain.

—Chapter Three, "Echo Properties and Protocols,"
Principles and Practices of Cleaving, Year Five

DINNER," MOM SAID WHEN WE ARRIVED home. "Del, set the table."

I threw my coat on the couch. "I'm not hungry."

"Dinner," she repeated.

My mother had a thing about the whole family eating dinner together. Even when we were little and my dad was out cleaving, he made a point to be home for the evening meal. Sometimes we ate at four in the afternoon, sometimes nine at night, but it was always the five of us, clustered around the big pine table. A constant.

No one except Monty ate much. Finally I asked, "Which one of you is going to tutor me?"

I was hoping for my dad. A First Chair, he led teams of Cleavers into the most dissonant worlds, managing their unraveling. There was nothing he liked better than a lost cause, everyone joked.

Suddenly it didn't seem so funny.

Still, it was better than working with my mom. A navigator, she analyzed pivots branching off our part of the Key World, determining which Echoes needed cleaving. If she was in charge, I'd be stuck in her office for the next six months, charting frequencies and crunching numbers.

She rearranged her silverware, took a sip of water. Stalling. I knew the move, because I was an expert at it. "Your father and I are working on a project that will require a lot of our attention."

Addie straightened, like a hunting dog who'd scented a rabbit. "Is that why the Consort wanted to talk to you?"

My dad nodded. "The Major Consort is sending in teams from around the country, and they've asked us to coordinate."

"The Major Consort? That's huge," Addie said. "What kind of project?"

"A classified one," Mom said. "We're hoping it's a short-term assignment, but for now, it's our top priority."

Which meant I was not.

"There's no reason your training has to suffer," my dad put in, seeing my expression. "While we're handling this, Addie can work with you."

I slammed my water down. "Are you kidding? She's as much to blame as I am!"

"I am not!" Addie shouted. "You were supposed to listen to me, and you ignored every word I said."

"If I'd done what you told me to, we never would have gotten out. You're mad because you choked, and I had to save your ass."

"I'm not the one who's suspended, am I? I don't want to train her! What about my apprenticeship? I'm supposed to be focusing on my work, not holding her hand!"

"*Girls!*" My mom pinched the bridge of her nose. "Enough. We know it's not an ideal situation, but it's not up for debate."

"The Consort said you were supposed to teach me," I said, desperation creeping into my voice. "Not Addie."

"Technically, they said 'your family.' Addie qualifies."

"Unfortunately," I sniped.

Addie made a face. "The feeling's mutual."

"The Consort agrees this is the best solution for now. In fact, it was Councilman Lattimer who suggested you two work together. It should only be for a few weeks," my father said.

Monty blew a raspberry, and Mom rolled her eyes. "Dad, it's a good thing. The councilman must think highly of Addie to give her this kind of responsibility. It's an honor, really."

Addie didn't look honored. "Why am I being punished for Del's mistake?"

"You were responsible for her during that Walk," my dad said mildly. "It seems fair you should shoulder a portion of the consequences."

"Dad, why can't I tag along with you?" I turned to him in appeal. "I'd learn a ton. Way more than I will with Addie."

"No can do, kiddo."

"But . . ."

"I can watch over the pair of them," Monty said abruptly. "Be good to keep my hand in. And I'll bet I know some tricks that aren't in your books, Addie-girl."

"That's not really the point of the exercise." My mom set down her fork and frowned at him, but he was already drifting.

"I should exercise more often. Good for the heart. My heart," he said, his face softening. He stood up, his napkin dropping to the floor. "I'll be off, then."

"Dad, no." Mom scrambled after him. "Sit down."

"Rose needs me," he said. "She's out there, Winnie. Your mother. I promised I'd find her."

My mother was many things in our family—the glue, the backbone, the compass—but mostly she was the rock. She made the hard choices and the tough calls. We went to my dad when we scraped a knee, to be fixed with a Band-Aid and a kiss and an oatmeal cookie. We went to Mom when we broke a bone, to make sure we got to the emergency room safely. She moved through the world with such determination, such forcefulness, it was easy to forget that when my grandfather had lost his wife, she'd lost her mother. Her hand went slack on Monty's arm.

He took advantage of the moment and pulled away, hitching up his khaki pants, hand outstretched to find a nearby pivot. My dad tensed, ready to grab him, but I knew better. Confront Monty, and he'd bolt. Distraction was key.

"Brownies," I said cheerfully. "There are brownies for dessert. I saw them earlier. And ice cream. You don't want to miss brownies à la mode, do you?"

He paused. "À la mode."

"It means with ice cream," Addie said.

"I know what it means." He smoothed the wisps of white

hair sticking out at odd angles and considered the offer.

"You can have the corner piece," I wheedled.

Stiffly, like he was doing us a favor, he came back to the table. My mom blew out a breath, and my dad took her hand in his.

Without a word Addie rose and started dishing out dessert. Midway through his brownie, Monty spoke again. "It's settled, then. I'll supervise the girls."

"I don't need supervision," said Addie. "I'm the supervisor."

My parents had one of their wordless conversations—raised eyebrows, pursed lips, the tiniest of head tilts—a duet in a key only they understood. Reluctantly my dad said, "You'd need to keep a close eye on them, Montrose. Especially Del."

I scowled, but my mom gave a warning shake of her head—and this time the message was perfectly clear. *Don't argue.*

The idea of Monty in charge was ludicrous. Most days he couldn't remember what year it was or where we kept the milk. But he'd definitely be more fun than Addie, whose expression teetered between wounded pride and outrage at the thought of being replaced.

"Fine by me," I said. "I like spending time with Grandpa."

Mom looked at Addie. "Well?"

She smiled through clenched teeth. "Sure."

"Excellent. I'll let the Consort know." Mom dusted off her hands, like everything was in perfect order once again.

Monty wandered away from the table, my father close on his heels. Addie flounced upstairs to sulk, and I headed to the attic.

Addie and I had shared a room until I was ten, when my

parents had offered up the third-floor attic. I'd moved the same afternoon. It was boiling in summer and freezing in winter, but it was also private. The stairway, narrow and steep, tended to discourage visitors.

The room was an unfinished mishmash, with oddly shaped windows and slanted ceilings. I'd filled it with castoffs and pieces "liberated" from the rest of the house—a bottle-green chaise, a tattered leather chair, an enormous trunk with brass fittings. I'd propped an old door on sawhorses to make a desk, but you could barely see it under the piles of sheet music and maps.

Along the rafters and over the windows, I'd strung origami stars, my own twisting, multicolored galaxy. They jumped as I slammed the door and snatched up my violin.

Nothing took me away from myself like Bach. The music, a dense, exacting flurry of notes, demanded my full attention. The violin had been my grandmother's, and her grandmother's before that. The sound poured out, rich and sweet and heartbreaking. It was easy to lose myself in the finger work, to sweep the bow over the strings with the anger I hadn't been able to show the Consort.

Midway through the second movement, my mom let herself in.

"Very nice," she said. "But isn't that section marked largo?"

Of course she'd want me to slow down. I sped up for the last few measures, ending with a flourish. "I'm allowed to improvise, aren't I? Or is the Consort monitoring my orchestra grade?"

She sighed. "You might not believe this, but we're looking out for you."

I concentrated on loosening the bow and tucking it away.

"No one doubts that you're very talented, but you don't apply yourself. Walking isn't fun and games, Del. It requires discipline and practice. It's the same as your music—you have to know the rules before you can break them."

I could play the Bach Double backward—and had, on a dare from Eliot. My mom wouldn't have seen the humor in it. "Monty breaks tons of rules."

"Look where it's gotten him. If you need a lesson in why our rules are important, he's an excellent one." She lowered her voice, as if he might hear us. "He's getting worse."

I plucked at the violin strings, letting the sound travel through me. Underneath, strong as ever, was the frequency of the Key World. Monty had been my first teacher, and I didn't want to think about his decline. "He's not that hard to manage, if you've got something he wants."

"The only thing he wants is your grandmother. I know you and Addie don't need a chaperone, but he does."

Understanding dawned. "You want us to watch him," I said. "Not the other way around."

"Addie can supervise you both, and ultimately, she's in charge. But he listens to you better than any of us. He always has."

True enough. After Addie had started school, Monty and I were often left alone together. "Walk with me, Del," he'd say, holding out his hand, and we'd go exploring. Echoes had a music of their own, he swore, and he'd taught it to me alongside our piano lessons. I'd listened to him back then, and now he was returning the favor.

"We're going to have to do something about him, but . . ." She trailed off, touched the pendant hanging around her neck. A miniature tuning fork, identical to Addie's. Every Walker had one. Every *licensed* Walker. "I'm not ready to send him away."

To a facility. A "home" where he'd be supervised and medicated, tethered to the Key World. Nothing would kill him faster.

"Don't look at me like that. We're hoping that working with you will keep him out of trouble." She reached out, tucked a lock of hair behind my ear. "You look like her. My mother."

I'd seen the picture in the hallway, but not the resemblance. It was my grandparents' wedding portrait, my grandmother lifting her chin to face the camera straight on. Everything about her seemed strong and forthright, from her dark, intelligent eyes to her generous smile. She was the kind of beautiful that people called striking. The best I could hope for was "cute," but people were usually talking about my height, not my looks. I heard "lovely" a lot too, as in, "Del could be lovely if she'd do something about those clothes/that hair/her attitude."

"Is that why I'm his favorite?"

She straightened the sheet music propped on my stand, tracing the intricately carved mahogany. Like the violin, it had belonged to my grandmother. Monty had insisted I use them; they were my only connection to her. "You look like my mother, but you and Monty are peas in a pod. You'll watch out for him, won't you?"

I snapped the case shut. If it would keep him out of a home, how could I say no?

Later, while my family slept, I stared at the stars spinning from the rafters and tried to imagine what my life would be like if I failed. If I never Walked again. Every choice irrevocable, every decision fixed. Never seeing the beauty and possibility of Echoes again. How did people live like that? The thought made my skin feel two sizes too small, and my legs prickled like pins and needles.

Sometimes I worried about liking the Echoes too much. There's a danger in being drawn to something that's not real, in giving yourself to something you can never be a part of, instead of making your life where you are. But those infinite worlds, with their infinite potential, beckoned irresistibly.

I slipped out of bed, back into my bulky cardigan and a pair of old jeans. They were more holes than denim, but the fabric was worn to blankety softness. I twisted my hair back into a knot, tucked a pack of notepaper into my pocket, and crept outside.

Maybe it was stupid to go out by myself, especially after the Consort had told me not to. But the thought of being under Addie's thumb for the next six months was suffocating. I wanted one last night where my choices were my own.

I took small steps, shifting through incrementally different worlds, drawing out the feeling of power and freedom. I listened with my whole body—skin and muscle and blood and bones— my entire being attuned to the music of the universe. Most Walkers said the other worlds were full of noise, but they were wrong. There was beauty in it, if you listened.

The doughnut shop was closed for the night. The streetlights turned the plate-glass window reflective, and I looked pale and wild-eyed. But I looked happy, too, in a way I often didn't in the mirror over my dresser.

A few blocks away I could hear the twang of guitar and the throb of bass. The show at Grundy's. Simon's invitation. He might have changed his mind. He might not remember he'd asked me . . . but I wanted him to.

A light rain started to fall, and I headed toward the music, looking for Simon.

Simon and trouble.

CHAPTER TWELVE

Direct contact with an Echo will intensify your perception of a world's frequency and heighten their awareness of you. Therefore, it is essential to limit physical contact with individuals in Echo worlds.

—Chapter Five, "Physics,"
Principles and Practices of Cleaving, Year Five

DIM LIGHTING. ALT-COUNTRY BAND ON THE cramped stage. The smell of sweat and cheap beer and fresh pizza. The booths were filled with chattering women, biker couples, and Echoes of my classmates, wedged five to a side in booths meant to fit three. I veered to the opposite end of the room, tapped the bartender on the arm, and ordered a rum and Coke. When he asked, I passed over my fake ID—much higher quality than Park World Simon's—and feigned boredom while he scrutinized it.

Drink in hand, I eased closer to the stage and leaned against a wooden post. The band was good—exactly the right amount of ache in the singer's alto, raw but not emo, with the bright, unexpected notes of a mandolin weaving through. I didn't get to simply appreciate a song that often; some part of my brain kicked in and started analyzing it, as if a frequency might be hidden within the notes.

I sipped my drink, letting the sugar bolster me and the alcohol relax me, and scanned the crowd. No Simon. Maybe he'd decided not to come. If so, there was an Echo nearby where he'd done the opposite. I could find it if I was willing to put in the effort. Then again, tracking him down across a bunch of random realities was a lot of work for a guy I barely knew—in this universe or any other.

The glass was sweating. I wiped my hand on my jeans and tried not to feel hurt that he wasn't here. It was late. It was a school night. The practical thing to do was go home and crash.

"Drummer's not bad," Simon said from behind me, so close his breath ruffled my hair.

Practicality is overrated.

Pushing back the smile threatening to break loose, I turned. "Most people focus on the guitarist. Or the singer." I had a vague memory of Original Simon playing drums when we were in junior high. "You play?"

"Sometimes." He braced one arm against the post, silver spike glinting at his wrist. "I was starting to think you stood me up."

"I didn't realize this was a date." I hadn't even been certain he'd remember me. Then again, it had been less than twelve hours since we'd spoken. Not long enough for him to forget, but plenty of time for my life to be turned inside out. "You never asked me."

"I didn't?" The light was too low to read his expression—if he was teasing, or disappointed, or genuinely curious. All I had to go on was the sound of his voice—a little rough, a little warm. "Serious mistake on my part. I could ask you now."

"We're already here. The timing's off." Curious how a different Simon made me different too.

"What if we went somewhere else? Somewhere quieter?"

I choked on my drink. "That's kind of fast," I said. "Even for you."

"For coffee, Del." He laughed, his eyes full of mischief. "What did you think I meant?"

"Nothing." I felt the blush spread along my cheeks and hoped he wouldn't notice. He offered me his arm, and I took it, the muscles like iron under my hand. He sounded the same as he had in front of the bakery—dissonant but stable, a steady rhythm that matched my pulse. Already his frequency was etched in my mind. "Coffee?"

The corner of his mouth curved up. "For starters."

I punched him lightly, but didn't let go. "Was there a basketball game tonight?"

"No idea." I thought I saw a momentary sadness in his expression—but then it was gone, a trick of the light. "Not my thing these days."

He shrugged into his coat, the black leather well-worn and supple, his shoulders broad and straight. When his hand found mine, I didn't pull away.

The rain fell steadily, silver against the streetlights. The cold air felt good after the overwarm room, and I breathed deeply as we walked. Simon said, "You took off pretty fast today."

"I needed to get home." I stopped under an awning. "You know, I don't want coffee."

"No?" He joined me, the water beading like mercury on his coat and hair.

I shook my head, feeling dizzy—the frequency rippling along my skin, the air damp and clean, Simon stepping close to me, smelling of leather and rain.

"Why did you come back?" he asked.

"You invited me."

He tugged at the clip holding up my hair, and it tumbled around my shoulders in a rush. "You liked the music, but you left before their set was over. You ordered a drink, but barely touched it. You've said yourself it's not a date, and you don't want coffee. Did you come out here just to walk around in the rain?"

"You got all of that from ten minutes in a badly lit pizza place?"

Lately, no one noticed me, except to point out what I was doing wrong.

"So," he pressed. "Why are you here?"

This world wasn't mine. I could spill out my secrets and leave, and no one would ever know. He might remember me now, but in a few days I'd drift from his mind like smoke. But for the time I was here, I could forget myself.

"I'm grounded, kind of. Starting tomorrow, I'm pretty much under twenty-four-hour surveillance."

"You figured you'd break out? One last night of freedom?"

"Something like that."

He touched my chin. "Better make the most of it," he said, and when I looked up, he was only inches away, the heat of his body chasing away the cold. He pushed my heavy, rain-soaked hair back, his palm brushing my cheekbone. His gaze fixed on my mouth.

I couldn't look away from his smile, the way it tipped to the side, challenging me. Not a perfect smile—there was the familiar scar at the corner, and his front teeth were the slightest bit crooked. The imperfections kept him from being too pretty, the same way the faint air of recklessness around him kept him from being too nice.

Nice had never been my thing.

It wasn't like I'd never been kissed. But I'd never had a guy look at me with such single-mindedness, the entirety of his attention on the scant space between us.

He touched his lips to mine, a silent question. His dissonance drifted around me like dust motes, heightening my senses, and I leaned in and answered with another kiss, my fingers clutching his coat. The air seemed warmer, but it wasn't the air; it was Simon, pulling me closer, and my blood thrilled the way it did when I Walked into a world for the first time, so much mystery and possibility.

Not real, I tried to tell myself, but he felt real—entirely solid and strong and alive as his arms wrapped around me, anchoring me against him as the world started to spin. He tasted like mint and secrets, and I opened my mouth to his, craving more as his fingers traced languid circles down my back. I shivered at the sensation, tried to close the space between us completely. He broke the kiss, and tucked my head under his chin, his breathing ragged. "You're cold."

"I'm fine."

"My car's over there," he said, jerking a thumb toward the Jeep. "We could get out of the rain. Go someplace private."

I rubbed a hand over my mouth, where his lips had been a moment ago, the taste of him still fresh, my pulse unsteady.

"Or not," he said, dark eyebrows lifting. "Your choice."

Around us, I could hear the fissures forming, a hundred pivot points created by a single kiss, the universe cracking wide because of this one instant, this one boy.

Time is not static. You can never get a choice—or a moment—back. The best you can do is witness the effects.

I wanted the moment. Every nerve I had was screaming at me to take Simon's hand, get into the car, and drive.

Not truly Simon, though. This Simon was an Echo, and tomorrow I'd have to sit behind his Original in class and pretend like I didn't know the feel of his hands or the fit of his mouth. I'd have to watch his eyes pass over me without a hitch, because this never would have happened.

I couldn't stay.

Already the frequency was ringing in my ears, competing with the thudding of my heart. In two hours I'd have a headache. In three, a migraine. By sunrise I wouldn't be able to find my way home. I'd Walked too much today.

I drew a piece of paper, dark blue on one side, silver on the other, out of my pocket. It was damp from the rain, the creases soft edged. Simon watched as the star took shape in my hand.

"I'll take that as a no?"

I finished the last fold and set it on the windowsill. I didn't need a breadcrumb to find this world again. It was proof of this moment, something that wouldn't disappear when I did.

"Another time," I said, only half-believing it, and went up on tiptoe to kiss him again. His hands tightened on my hips, holding me fast as his lips traveled along my jaw.

"You don't want to leave."

"Never said I did." I pushed away, legs and resolve both shaky. "See you around."

"I'll drive you," he said, catching my hand.

I disentangled my fingers from his. "Thanks, but I'll walk."

As I rounded the corner, I looked back through the pouring rain. I wanted to see his face one more time, while he remembered I existed.

He'd picked up the star. He stood under the awning, spinning it between his thumb and forefinger, his eyes never leaving me.

CHAPTER THIRTEEN

While a Walker's decisions create pivots, our inability to form Echoes means the pivot is unable to sustain itself; almost immediately, the newly formed world is reabsorbed by the parent branch. This phenomenon is called "transposition." Transposition may also occur when Originals or Echoes make a choice that does manifest in a significant frequency change.

—Chapter One, "Structure and Formation,"
Principles and Practices of Cleaving, Year Five

"WHERE WERE YOU LAST NIGHT?" ELIOT ASKED as we trudged toward the cafeteria. "Didn't you get my texts?"

"Sorry. I crashed early." Guilt nibbled at me. First a secret, now a lie. I hadn't seen Eliot's messages until I'd returned from Doughnut World, too late to reply. And he would not be thrilled to hear I'd already violated my probation to make out with Simon's Echo.

I changed the subject. "What happened after I left last night?"

"Left" wasn't quite accurate, but it sounded better than "After the Consort guards escorted me to my doom."

Eliot looked away, and I wondered how much he was holding back to spare my feelings. "Just regular class. Boring without you."

"What are you working on next? More break analysis?" The answer would only make me feel worse, but I couldn't help asking.

"For another week or so. Shaw said we'll start inversions soon."

I ground my teeth. "It's so unfair. I'm stuck with Addie for the next six months while you'll be off having adventures and kicking ass."

"I'm only the navigator," he said. "Asskickery is your department."

I jammed my hands in the pockets of my sweater. "Do you think I can pass the test? I'm going to miss out on all the fieldwork."

"Addie's good at fieldwork," he said. "She was ranked first in her class, wasn't she?"

"Naturally. You know how she is. It'll be all textbooks and essays. I'm screwed."

He didn't contradict me. "We need to figure out why the Echo deteriorated so quickly."

"The Consort doesn't care. They thought I did it on purpose." My impulse in that moment hadn't been to cleave, but something else both foreign and familiar, a new verse to a song you knew by heart. "The only reason I'm not expelled is because Addie told them I was too dumb to know what I was doing."

"They listened to her?"

"Who wouldn't?" I said bitterly. "Now she's in charge of my training. She has to submit progress reports each week. Isn't that a conflict of interest? She turns me in *and* gets to grade me?"

"Hold up." He shoved his glasses farther up his nose and sat down at one of the couches clustered around the student commons. "I need to think."

While I waited for his latest flash of brilliance, I studied the trophy case on the far wall, crowded with evidence of Simon's basketball prowess. State championships and tournament wins, nets draped over the tops of their first-place trophies. Hanging behind them were team pictures, groups of tall, broad-shouldered boys wearing royal blue and matching scowls. It might be a game, but basketball was serious business around here. Even Simon looked solemn and determined . . . until you saw the faint curve at the corner of his mouth.

I thought back to the way Echo Simon had smiled at me last night. That had been a game too, in a way.

Eliot coughed, and I jumped like he'd caught me doing something wrong. "We need to prove you're not at fault. If we can do that, they'll have to review your sentencing. They'd reinstate you."

A loosening in my chest, the faintest stirrings of hope. But hope was a dangerous, fragile thing, easily shattered. I couldn't afford it.

"Nice plan, but the entire Echo's gone. If there was any proof, I destroyed it." I shuddered, remembering the melting sky and flickering children.

"Records," he said, with the same patient tone he used when explaining my trig homework. "Your mom's map. Frequency samples from previous Walks. Even similar branches might have relevant information. The Consort adds terabytes of data to the Archives every day. I'll bet you anything the answer's in there."

I didn't know how much a terabyte was, but it sounded big. And time-consuming. And like a very, very long shot. Hope fluttered again and I tamped down on it. "Addie's not going to let me spend my suspension going through records. She's got half the lessons planned already."

"I'll take care of the research," he said, holding open the cafeteria doors.

"What am I going to do while you're off scouring the Archives?" The noise and bustle of the cafeteria was overwhelming, the smell of steamed hamburgers and canned green beans turning my stomach.

"Funny you should ask," he said. "I have a theory I want you to test."

The tension left my shoulders. Eliot had theories about everything, and he was forever asking me to test them. Sometimes this turned out well, like when we figured out how to give people earworms by amplifying the Key World frequency in Top 40 hits. Sometimes it resulted in a sprained ankle and dislocated shoulder, like when we were eight, and I conclusively disproved his idea that you could fall *through* a pivot if you jumped from a high enough distance. Taking a seat at our usual table, I said, "I'm listening."

"Watch." He pulled out a sheet of paper and sketched the floor plan of the cafeteria. "Three pivots since we walked in." He circled three separate places—one just outside the doors, another at a table full of sophomore girls, and a third near the cash register—and hummed their frequencies.

I closed my eyes, letting the chatter of the room recede. "More than that. I've got at least a dozen."

"Half of those are diminished," he said confidently. "They'll blend back in any minute. The other three are off-key but stable. Forget them."

"How can you tell?" I stared at him. Most Walkers had to be standing in an Echo to judge its stability. Even I couldn't do it from this distance.

"Because I have a map." With a flourish he produced his phone, a prototype with a screen bigger than my hand. "And I need to test it."

"Gimme."

He handed it over. Tiny lights dotted the screen, like the stars on a clear night. "How does it work?"

"It's like a GPS. Instead of reading satellite information, it uses the microphone to plot nearby frequencies. Stronger frequencies are displayed as bigger circles, unstable ones flash, and pitch correlates to brightness."

"Big, bright, flashing circles are bad? Small, dim, steady ones are good?"

He ducked his head. "I know it's not subtle. . . ."

"Since when have I cared about subtle? You're a genius!" I threw my arms around his neck. "A map that updates in real time? You're going to be famous."

He hugged me back for a second, then pulled away, almost

bashful. "I don't need to be famous. I haven't even shown it to Shaw yet."

"Why not? Once he sees it, you'll own the class rankings."

"There are a few bugs in the software I'm trying to work out. If I install it on your phone, do you promise you'll use it?"

His tone was urgent, and I frowned. "Sure, if it helps you test it out. What are you so worried about?"

He shrugged. "That Echo deteriorated way too fast. It could happen again."

"Park World was a fluke."

"A fluke that almost killed you. I've been checking Echoes in the same frequency range, and they seem fine. But this will tell you if a world is too dangerous before you cross." He stared at his sketch of the cafeteria and tapped the biggest of the pivots. "Use the map, Del. Promise."

A burst of laughter from across the room distracted me—Simon, holding court at one of the big round tables near the windows, his chair tipped back on two legs, completely unaware of my presence.

Why would he notice me? He hadn't been the one to kiss me breathless in the rain. Last night was a secret known only to me and a boy who wasn't real.

Bree snuck up behind him, covering his eyes with her hands, and the chair dropped down with a thud. She let go, giggling as he reached back and caught her hand. It was the kind of casual gesture I was terrible at reading: Were they flirting? A couple? An *actual* couple?

Simon always had a girl on his arm. Frequently blond, typically adorable, and almost never serious. Probably Bree was no different. Until I saw the way her free hand toyed with the collar of his shirt—playful on the surface and possessive at the core.

"No time like the present," I said to Eliot, pushing away from our table. "Let's take your new toy for a test run."

"It's not a toy," he grumbled. "It's a serious piece of scientific equipment."

"It's so shiny!" I trilled, bumping my hip into his. Turning away from Simon, I headed toward a group of drama kids abuzz about tryouts for the winter play. A dozen pinpricks of light sprang up on the screen.

"There," he said, pointing to one of the circles. "Something's different."

"Somebody changed their mind about auditioning?" I murmured.

"Probably. Tryouts spawn a lot of pivots—so many possible choices." He gestured to the twinkling display.

"It's like a cheat sheet." Only I wasn't breaking any rules, for once in my life.

He zoomed out on the map and pointed. "Over there, see? This circle's getting bigger." I followed him out the doors to the water fountain. The rent in the air was easy to see, if you squinted. Without thinking, I brushed my fingers over the edge. The vibration felt as though it was calling to me.

"What triggered it?"

He peered at the map, then around the hall, nudging his glasses up again. "Not sure."

"Let's go look."

Eliot groaned. "No way. What if we get caught?"

"Who would catch us?" The hallway was practically deserted, and it was such a strange sight—a person disappearing into thin air—most Originals assumed they hadn't been looking close enough.

"We have class in five minutes."

"Five minutes," I said. "Add three more for passing period, that's eight. Bet I could find the source in eight minutes."

"Del . . ." He stopped fiddling with the phone.

"See you in eight," I said, and slipped through the gap.

The Echo looked identical, and the frequency warbled, gradually shifting away from the Key World like a violin part played by a cello. As events here diverged from the Key World, the threads of this reality would settle into place, taking on their final resonance.

I scanned the room, looking for clues to explain why this world had branched off ours.

Finally I spotted it: Beneath the water fountain was a stack of note cards, right where Eliot had been standing. They must have fallen out when their owner stopped for a drink. I picked them up, and the key change traveled up my arm.

Notes for a test, I figured, looking at the neat lines of chemical equations in a round, cheerful hand. If there'd been words instead of symbols on the cards, little hearts would have dotted the *I*s.

I'd never tracked the source of a pivot before. Would it sound different from the rest of the Echo? Louder? Would it be unstable, like a break? Easy enough to find out, and I set off for the science wing, taking the stairs two at a time.

"Del!" Eliot called behind me.

"Glad you could make it."

"It's dangerous to Walk by yourself," he said when he'd caught up. "What if something goes wrong?"

"You worry too much." Eliot's preference for navigation over Walking wasn't only because his brain was wired like a super-computer. His mom ran one of the Consort homes for elderly Walkers, the kind my mom wanted to send Monty to. Eliot had grown up witnessing the toll our abilities took. I looped my arm through his. "Besides, you're looking out for me. Safest Walk in the world."

"Why do I let you talk me into this?" he asked as we set off. He twisted to avoid the streams of people filling the hallway.

"Because I am irresistible. Who's giving a chem test today?"

"Doc Reese," he said. "I heard someone talking about it in lit this morning."

"Time to see Doc Reese." The bell rang, and we flinched.

"We'll be late for music. Again. I hate being late."

"Then we'd better hurry." We dashed through the halls, until he pulled on my elbow so hard I staggered.

"Here. This is longer than eight minutes."

People filed past us, and I wove around them, trying to avoid the contact that would draw their attention. Inside the classroom kids were settling into place, pulling out pencils, calculators, and . . . yep. Note cards.

Doc Reese stood behind the table at the head of the room, sporting his usual lab coat and bow tie. His bony hands clutched a thick sheaf of papers. "The sooner you're seated, the sooner we'll start," he said, his voice doleful.

The cards vibrated in my hand, gaining strength as the frequency crescendoed. I peered through the narrow window, studying the back of every girl in the room. They were perched on their lab stools like brightly colored birds, arranging pencils and reviewing notes—except for one girl, crouched on the floor, frantically emptying her backpack. "Bingo. Third row, left side."

Eliot checked the map again. "Great. Time's up."

I shook off his arm. "What if I gave her back the cards? What would happen?"

"We'd be even more tardy."

"Five minutes," I said. "Think of it as an experiment."

He scowled, but didn't stop me.

The room smelled of sulfur and nerves. I eased past the kids lined up at the pencil sharpener, dropping the cards a foot away from the girl's backpack. Her pitch grew sharper as I waited for her to notice.

Panic must have blinded her. She dug through her bag with staccato movements. Her sniffles were audible behind her curtain of light brown hair. The second bell sounded, and Eliot waved wildly from the doorway, pointing to his watch.

So much for limited interference. I touched her shoulder. "You dropped something."

She lifted her head, red-rimmed eyes startled. I pointed to the note cards, and she fell on them with a squeal. "Oh my God! Thank you!"

"No problem," I said, but she was too focused on the cards to respond.

Doc Reese, on the other hand, spotted me. "Can I help you?"

"Just leaving," I said, backing out the door.

"The pitch is changing," Eliot said. Onscreen, the dot of light was folding in on itself like a collapsing star.

"Because of the note cards?"

"Must be. It started right after you handed them over. I didn't think it was possible to alter an Echo's frequency."

"Me neither. It's kind of cool," I said as we headed down the corridor, my short legs struggling to keep up with his lanky ones. A strange quiver ran through the air.

"Did you hear that?" I asked, my steps slowing.

Eliot tapped the screen. "It's reverting to the Key World frequency."

I stopped. "Do not tell me we created a second Key World."

"You're good, Del. But not that good." He scanned the hallway we'd come from. The lockers blurred and snapped back into focus, like adjusting a camera. The lines on Eliot's forehead deepened, and fear sent a wave of dizziness crashing over me.

"Did I cleave it?"

"No," he muttered. "It think it's a transposition."

Choices create worlds, but not every world is sustainable. When you decide between strawberry and blueberry yogurt for breakfast, odds are good your morning will play out exactly the same way. When that happens, the multiverse autocorrects, absorbing the new branch into the older, more established one. The same thing happened when Walkers made a choice—without an Echo to sustain the pivot, the branch reabsorbed into the Key World almost immediately. The effect was called transposition.

The thing is, consequences are like people: hard to predict and harder to change. If the blueberry yogurt is expired, you could end up with food poisoning and spend three days in the hospital instead of at school—a big difference rooted in a small choice. We never knew which worlds would transpose and which would form significant Echoes, but since transpositions were both common and harmless, we barely touched on them in class.

Now that I was inside one, they didn't feel harmless. Across the hallway, the bio lab doubled and merged, the Key World room overtaking the Echo one.

"This is not good," Eliot said, eyes shifting between the map and the wavering corridor. "Since when can we cause transpositions?"

"Hell if I know," I said, and pulled him toward the stairs. "What happens if we don't get back before the Echo is absorbed?"

"The frequency will carry us back into the Key World wherever we're standing at the time. Like we're surfing into shore. Could be a rough landing, though."

It couldn't be any worse than escaping from a cleaving. "Won't people notice if we appear out of thin air?"

"Nope. It's a continuous transfer. Their Echoes see our impressions before the transposition and the Originals see us after. Once they've combined, they think we've been there the whole time."

It made sense. People ignored what they couldn't explain. It was more comfortable that way, and Walkers exploited that weakness all the time.

"Then why are we running?" I asked, and stopped short.

"We're late for music. Eight minutes, you said. This is more like fifteen."

"Maybe not," I said. "If we can sneak into class before the transposition's done, Powell will never notice we were late."

Eliot gestured toward the rapidly stabilizing staircase. "The transposition's nearly finished. She'll catch us."

"Pessimist," I said, and took off again, headed for the music wing.

The curving wall of cement block pulsed as the frequencies melded, the tile beneath my feet shifting. I lost my footing, and the transposition caught up with us, sending Eliot careening into me. My shoulder slammed into the wall, and I swore loudly.

When I looked up, Ms. Powell was standing outside the classroom, her expression puzzled. Confusion was replaced by exasperation as the Key World's signal overtook the Echo's, the sound locking into place.

She'd seen us. The transposition was complete, and we were too late.

"Sorry," Eliot wheezed as we struggled past her. "Really sorry."

Simon glanced back for an instant, but didn't say anything before returning his attention to Bree. I studied the nape of his neck, the breadth of his shoulders under the thin gray T-shirt—and took a few deep breaths, trying to recover from my sprint. The crisp scent of cotton and citrus rose off his skin, so different from his Echo.

"Eliot, Del," said Powell, as we flopped into our seats, "glad you two made it."

CHAPTER FOURTEEN

The ability to Walk is hereditary. Recent advancements in genetics and neurology have revealed a mutation on chromosome 8q24.21, corresponding to hyperdevelopment of the primary auditory cortex. This mutation enables Walkers to detect and manipulate matter on a quantum level. Other characteristics frequently tied to this chromosome include perfect pitch and a predisposition for early-onset dementia.

—Chapter Four, "Physiology,"
Principles and Practices of Cleaving, Year Five

Ms. POWELL LEANED AGAINST THE PODIUM like a lounge singer on a piano. "Since everyone's finally here, get together with your partner and start planning. This is your last big project before the semester exam, so you've got a solid month to write and rehearse your composition. I'll give you the whole period today, but the bulk of the work should be done on your own time."

My head snapped up. Time with Simon. The real Simon, the one I couldn't form proper sentences around. Anticipation and anxiety weren't so different, not under the skin, where my heart stuttered and my blood skipped.

While my classmates rearranged their desks to meet with their partners, I sat catching my breath, unsure how to approach Simon.

As it turned out, there was no need to figure out an approach.

He spun around in his chair, his legs knocking into mine and staying there. It was the kind of casual, flirtatious move I'd seen him use a million times with a million other girls. Now that I was on the receiving end, it felt anything but casual.

"So. Delancey."

He'd never said my name before. Not ever, in this world, and not my full name in any world, and the way he said it—slow and thoughtful, like he was considering the way each syllable felt in his mouth—stole my breath anew.

"Simon," I said, trying to mimic his tone, trying to shake off the weirdness, trying not to gape. "And it's Del."

"Del. You're good at this stuff, aren't you?" He held up the packet Ms. Powell had given us, full of rubrics and instructions and blank staff paper. "It's your thing."

"My thing?"

"Aren't you some kind of music prodigy? You always know the answer to Powell's trivia. Plus, she's made you play the violin for us a bunch of times. Piano, too."

I stared at my hands, my fingertips roughened from hours practicing. This is what he'd noticed about me? My freakish musical ability? "My family's big into music."

Not only my family. All Walkers had perfect pitch. While our love of music wasn't genetic, I'd never met one who didn't play at least three instruments.

"What about you?" I asked, wanting to shift his attention. His Echo had watched the band with the focus of a musician. How did his Original compare? "Didn't you used to play the drums?"

"In sixth grade, sure. A bunch of us thought we'd start a band in Matt Lancaster's garage." He shook his head. "I can't believe you remember that."

I remembered more than his ridiculous band. Sixth grade was the year his mom found out she had cancer, and the whole community pulled together—throwing car washes and bake sales, raffles and walkathons. Even my mom had helped out, dropping off casseroles and containers of soup. Mrs. Lane had recovered eventually, and every mother in town had wanted to adopt Simon. Five years later, they still did.

"My mom tried me on a bunch of instruments, but it was a total disaster. She says I couldn't carry a tune in a paper bag." His smile quirked and his voice dropped. "Be gentle with me."

"Composition isn't that hard, I promise." I cringed at the eagerness in my voice. I'd been brave enough to flirt back when I'd met him in Doughnut World; why couldn't I do the same here?

Because bravery comes easily when there's no cost to it. Anything was possible in Echoes; if I didn't like one world, another, better one was a few short steps away. I could kiss Doughnut Simon without fear of consequences. He wasn't real, no matter how hard he'd kissed me. It was heat and spark, with no chance of being burned.

I liked who I'd been last night, and I tried to recall her now, saying, "Do girls usually fall for the whole 'charming your way out of work' routine?"

A few feet away, Bree watched us through narrowed eyes, ignoring Eliot's attempts to catch her attention.

"Depends on the girl," he said. "Not you, I'm guessing."

"Not even close."

He studied me, tapping his pen on the desk. "We've had classes together before, haven't we?"

Freshman biology. Geometry and civics sophomore year. This year it was American history and music theory. But if he couldn't remember, I wasn't going to point it out. "Probably."

"That explains it."

"Why I'm immune to your charm?"

"Why you look familiar." He pretended to look insulted. "And who says you're immune? You're smiling."

"I'm not. . . ."

"Oh, yeah. Right . . . here." His thumb touched the corner of my mouth, the slightest pressure, his fingers curling under my chin, the Key World's frequency rising around us.

I didn't throw myself onto his lap, or anything quite so obvious. But I *felt* obvious. Clumsy and naive, definitely not the version of myself I wanted to be around him. The charge running through me at his touch must have been written across my face.

He was supposed to look smug. Everything I knew about Simon Lane prepared me for his eyes to light up with triumph, like the scoreboard after a three-pointer. Instead, he looked confused.

"Making progress?" inquired Ms. Powell, wandering past.

Simon let go of me, shook his head as if to clear it. "Excellent progress, ma'am."

For once, I kept my mouth shut.

CHAPTER FIFTEEN

Identifying the choice that triggered an Echo is exceedingly difficult. Historical analysis can be used with some degree of success, but unless the pivot formation is witnessed in real time, theories about why an Echo formed cannot be proven.
—Chapter One, "Structure and Formation,"
Principles and Practices of Cleaving, Year Five

ARE YOU SURE YOU CAN HANDLE HIM?" ELIOT asked once class was over.

A few feet ahead of us, Bree and Simon were walking together, his dark head bent over her fair one. It was as if our strange, electric moment was even more of an aberration than the time I'd stolen with his Echo.

"Absolutely," I said, forcing a lightness I didn't feel. "It can't be any worse than working with Bree. That looked super fun, by the way."

Eliot grimaced. "I never thought I'd say this, but I agree with her. Powell should let us switch."

He doesn't even know your name, Bree had said. "It's good for Bree to experience disappointment. Builds character."

Eliot transferred his frown to me. "Don't tell me you *want* to work with him."

Simon and Bree stopped outside the history room. After a short conversation—one where Bree stroked his arm and tossed her hair and batted her eyelashes, as subtle as a two-by-four upside the head—he ducked inside.

The moment he was out of sight, her friends swooped in with an audible squeal. "Did you ask him?" one asked in a mock-whisper.

Bree's smile slid away. "Maybe tomorrow." She caught my eye before they disappeared down the hall, the glare so unmistakable even Eliot recoiled.

"You might want to reconsider going to Mrs. Gregory's class today."

"I can handle Bree." Open hostility was easy to deal with. Simon's unpredictable, unexpected tension was more dangerous. "Give me your phone."

"Why?"

"To order a pizza," I said. "Why do you think? We have a sub in history again. I need something to do while she shows the movie."

"You could try watching the movie for once."

"Why bother?" I slipped a hand into his jacket pocket and tugged the phone out. "You're a sweetheart."

"I'm a pushover. Promise you won't get caught."

I blew him a kiss. "I never do."

The movie was as mind-numbing as I'd predicted. Five minutes after the opening credits, the sub was playing computer solitaire and the class was evenly divided between napping and texting.

Simon, legs sprawled in front of him and chin propped on fist, was in the first group.

I was playing with Eliot's new toy.

I was not thinking about Simon, and the feel of his thumb against my mouth. Or Simon in the rain. Or in the park. I was not thinking about any of those things when I zoomed in on the music room, examining the pivots that had sprung up during class.

Beginnings meant branches. Nobody in history was making decisions except the sub, and the display showed a dim, nearly lifeless room. But in music, each group had made a bunch of choices as we planned our projects—when to meet, how to divide the work, what instruments to use. The screen *should* have looked like a Christmas tree.

Instead, there was a single, overwhelming glow, growing steadily brighter as the edges of the circle spread out, one all-encompassing pivot.

And then the map crashed.

I tapped the screen and clicked the buttons, but nothing worked. I didn't know much about Eliot's gadgets, but whenever they glitched, he'd ask me a million techie questions. "What were you doing when the error occurred? What did the screen say? What settings were you using?"

He'd ask a million more now that I'd broken his baby. I'd be doing him a favor if I checked out the music room in person.

I approached the sub. "Bathroom pass?"

She waved at the door, too intent on her cards to worry about me. A few minutes later I was back in the music wing, phone rebooted and working again. Everything looked normal. Everything *sounded* normal—freshman band squawking away in one room while swing choir rehearsed in another—the Key World strong and sure. The map shone brightly as I peered into Powell's empty classroom, and when I opened the door, I caught the buzz of a solitary pivot.

A good-size one, I saw, big enough that the fluorescent lights seemed to catch on the edges of the rift, leaving shadows in mid-air. It was centered directly over Simon's seat. I thought back over our conversation. He'd noticed me, but that wasn't enough. A frequency as jarring as this one came from a deliberate, significant choice. What was it?

He'd touched me.

I'd thought it was his usual routine—heavy on the flirting, light on substance—but the quavering air above his desk suggested otherwise. If he'd touched me in the Key World, what had he done differently in the Echo?

According to Eliot's map, the pivot was stable enough to visit. I slipped the phone into the pocket of my sweater, found the star I'd been folding in class, and stepped through, holding my breath like I was diving into deep water.

The room I surfaced in stood empty. Whatever choice Simon made wasn't visible, but the pitch was unexpectedly loud. If I was going to figure out what had changed, I'd need to do it fast.

My best shot at pinpointing the change was to find his Echo. I dropped the star on the piano and headed to history.

No one in Echo history noticed my entrance. The movie

played on as I slid into the seat next to his, deliberately jostling him awake. His dissonance sent a shock through me, but he smiled, sheepish and sleepy lidded. "Del. What's up?"

His whisper found its way under my skin. I squashed the urge to lean in closer, to recreate our connection. Hooking up with Simon was a bad idea in any world, but particularly now, when I was pressed for time and looking for answers.

Certainty is a luxury, whether you're dealing with the multiverse or a human being. We're never 100 percent sure what creates a pivot unless we see it form. We never fully understand another person, even those we're closest to. Best guesses and backtracking were imperfect, incomplete pictures, whether you're dealing with branches or boys.

I tried to be logical: In this world, Simon hadn't touched me. We hadn't had that strange, deliciously tense moment. Powell hadn't interrupted us. But what was the result?

"Tell me again when we're meeting?" I rubbed at the back of my neck, trying to quell the gathering tension.

"You forgot?" The movie cast shadows across his face. "Sunday. At the library."

Same as the Key World. He looked identical, but the pitch was definitely different. I gritted my teeth. I should be able to *see* such a significant change.

Unless I was looking at the wrong person. "So . . . you and Bree?"

He sat up, annoyance tightening his features. "Where'd you hear that?"

"Around," I said vaguely. "You two are back together, huh?"

"Taking her to a party doesn't mean we're together. I haven't even told her yes."

She'd asked him out. I could trace the chain of events like dominoes falling. In our world, Bree had seen our interaction and decided to hold off. In this one, he hadn't touched me, and she'd had no reason to wait. His answer would trigger a second pivot, and her response would create a third. Eliot's map should have shown an entire galaxy of Echoes; instead I'd seen a supernova. It didn't add up.

"Anything else exciting happen after class? Anything weird?"

He tapped his pencil on one lean, denim-clad leg. "A girl I just met started asking me a bunch of questions. Does that count?"

"Ah. Weird girl." I was glad it was dark. The sub looked up, and Simon pretended to watch the video until she'd gone back to her game.

"The *questions* were weird."

"Not the girl?"

"Early days." His gaze swept over me, but I couldn't stay to investigate any longer. Class was nearly over, and the last thing I needed was another detention.

"Gotta go." I stood, feeling unsteady.

"You're going to walk out?"

"Trust me," I said. "Nobody's going to notice."

• • •

I made it back moments before the lights came on. The sub blinked at the sight of me, and I waved cheerfully.

Before I could escape, a hand clamped on my arm.

"And where did you sneak off to?" Simon said as we filed out, bending down to murmur the words. "Meet up with your boyfriend?"

"I don't have a boyfriend."

He brushed my hair away from my neck. "Where'd you get the hickey?"

"The . . . oh." I covered my throat with my hand, conscious of how the red welt must look. "It's from my violin."

"Mmn-hmn," he said. "You're telling me you and the skinny guy aren't together? Friends with benefits?"

"Eliot's my best friend." The edge in my voice was audible despite the noisy hallway. "That's it. Why do you care, anyway?"

"I'm trying to get a feel for you."

Someone slammed into me. Simon placed a steadying hand on my hip, leaving it there a beat longer than necessary.

"A feel for me?" I said, trying to sound skeptical instead of scattered.

"We're partners now. And when my partner cuts class, I get curious. I'll figure it out eventually, Del."

"Don't bet on it."

CHAPTER SIXTEEN

Once a cleaving is completed, the First Chair must submit a formal report to the Consort Archive. It is traditional for Walkers to maintain a journal of their personal Walks as well, as a reference for future generations.
—Chapter Three, "Echo Properties and Protocols,"
Principles and Practices of Cleaving, Year Five

U P," SAID ADDIE THE NEXT MORNING.

"Bite me." I pulled the covers over my head. She yanked them back, and I shrieked at the rush of cold air. "What is your *problem?*"

"It's practically noon," she said.

I squinted at my clock. "It's ten thirty. On a Saturday."

"Suspended does not mean vacation. If you were going to training, you would have left hours ago."

"But I'm *not,* thanks to you. Get out."

"Mom said you can either clean the bathrooms or work with me. Your choice."

"You are such a bitch." I sat up and shoved tangles of hair out of my eyes.

"I'll be in the kitchen," she said over her shoulder. "Fifteen minutes, or you're scrubbing toilets."

I stumbled out of bed, shuffled downstairs for a shower, and made it into the kitchen thirty seconds ahead of Addie's deadline. "Where are Mom and Dad?"

"Some meeting downtown with the new teams. They'll be back by dinner." She waved a hand at my wet hair. "Don't drip on the table."

I ignored her, heading straight for the coffeemaker. The caffeine didn't improve my mood any, and neither did the piles of textbooks on the kitchen island, which I deliberately dripped on.

"You haven't been keeping up with your reading," she said with a frown.

"I read journals. That's plenty." I'd studied Monty's journals since I was a kid, deciphering the cramped, messy writing, thrilling at the near escapes and crazy stories. Textbooks were dry and lifeless in comparison.

"You need to understand the theories before putting them into practice," she replied, pushing the pile of books across the table.

I pushed them back. "Or I could, you know, *practice*. Theories didn't help the other day."

"If you'd had a better grip on the basics, you wouldn't have cleaved that Echo to begin with," she said.

"I got us out," I snapped, my temper breaking free. "Not your stupid books. That's what burns you, isn't it? People won't shut up about how perfect you are, how you follow every rule. But it's not because you're smart. It's because you don't have the chops, and I do, and now everyone knows it."

"Screw you," she hissed. "You think you're so special? You're going to fail your licensing exam. When you do, the Consort—and the rest of the world—will finally see you're more trouble than you're worth. And I. Can't. Wait."

I was halfway across the room, arm cocked for a punch, when Monty shuffled in.

"Man can't play a tune with you two shouting. Bet they can hear you five worlds away."

"She started it," I said, as Addie complained about how disrespectful I was.

"Girls!" he boomed. We fell silent. "Are there cookies left?"

I could see Addie counting to ten in her head. "We ran out," she said. "But it's Saturday. Mom'll bake tonight."

"Bake on Saturday. Your mother used to do that." His face brightened. "She'll come home and make apple cake and we'll play a hand of rummy. She cheats at rummy, Rose does. I don't mind, really, but it's better not to tell her."

He'd slipped again, mistaking Addie for my mom.

"Grandpa, it's Addison. Remember me?" She touched his arm, trying to jog his memory.

He blinked at her, owl-like. "I'm old, Addie-girl, not stupid."

Faster than I'd thought possible, he crossed the room to the coatrack and grabbed his battered porkpie hat. "Walk with me, girls. It's a beautiful day, and I haven't lost all my moves."

Addie lifted up a textbook. "Del's supposed to be studying."

"She knows enough to get where she's going." When Addie didn't budge, he added, "Let's show her how it's done."

Addie sighed and scooped up a pile of papers while I slung my bag over my shoulder. Monty winked at me and did a soft-shoe routine out the door.

Twenty minutes later we were surveying the football field. The sky was a pure, clear blue, wisps of clouds drifting across. The air was crisp enough to make me glad I'd worn my coat. Addie consulted her paper map, checking it against the deserted parking lot. "I was planning this for next weekend, but I suppose we could try it today."

I couldn't imagine thinking so far ahead, but knowing Addie, she'd already worked up lesson plans for my entire suspension. Still holding the map, she drew a slim black rectangle out of her purse. Not a cell phone, but it could pass for one if you didn't look too closely. Her fingers flew over the keys as she punched in a string of numbers.

A generator: Input the specific resonance of an Echo and it would play the frequency for you. More reliable than memory, they were for licensed Walkers only. I wouldn't get one of my own until—or unless—I became an apprentice.

"Don't go without us," she warned, and pressed a final button. The generator wheezed like an accordion.

I found the matching pivot almost immediately. "Concession stand," I said, and at Monty's nod, led the way.

The world looked similar to ours, but I barely had time to note the differences, because Addie played another pitch. "Go."

"This is kindergarten stuff," I complained. If this was supposed to be next week's work, she'd planned for a glacial pace. I'd die of boredom—and be months behind for the exam. That was probably her intention. Monty nonchalantly dropped a button while her back was turned.

"Then it shouldn't be a problem," she said sweetly. "Go."

I checked my phone, now running Eliot's map software. The light of the pivot was bright but steady. Safe to go. I found the new frequency and Walked through again, feeling the air flex and settle around me.

"Told you," I said. "Kindergarten."

"Again," said Addie, and picked a new frequency.

By the fifth crossing I'd lost patience. We'd reached the center of town. In each world, the dissonance increased, and so did my frustration. "This is stupid. Can we do something else?"

Monty nudged her. "Wouldn't hurt to push her a bit. You can tell her if she's doing it wrong."

"Oh, fine." She waved an arm at the surrounding buildings, the pedestrians enjoying a Saturday-morning stroll. "Map it."

I blinked. "The entire Echo?"

"Too much?" she replied. "You're such an expert, prove it. We've got two hours left. Mark as many pivots and breaks as you can. We'll compare it to the most recent map when we get home, and you can write up an analysis of the changes."

If her plan was death by dullness, it was working. I opened my mouth to complain, but Monty interrupted.

"Start there," he said, and pointed to a coffee shop across the street. "I need a snack."

• • •

A few minutes later Monty was plowing through a blondie the size of a deck of cards while Addie sipped a cup of tea. I slouched in an overstuffed chair on the other side of the room, a notebook in my lap, the café's floor plan sketched out. I'd tried to use Eliot's software, but Addie was watching me too closely. I'd have to do this the old-fashioned way.

I ignored the indie-folk blaring on the radio and listened. Snatches of conversation floated around me: plans for the rest of the afternoon, gossip, quarrels, friends doling out advice to one another. My pencil flew over the paper, drawing an X for each pivot that formed. I couldn't get a clear read on their strength. If Addie wanted that kind of detail, she'd have to let me Walk more.

The highest concentration of pivots was near the counter, not only at the register, where people placed their orders, but along the open space where people lined up to study the chalkboard menu. Some of the rifts formed and dissolved again with a drone like a mosquito. Transpositions, probably, and I marked them with a small wavy line.

Eliot had been stumped by yesterday's transposition. By returning the girl's note cards, we'd altered the frequency of an entire Echo. But Walkers didn't change Echoes; we cleaved them. Neither my parents nor my teachers had ever suggested another possibility. I wondered why not.

A group of chattering girls, identical in their suede boots and fleece jackets, shopping bags weighing down their arms, approached the register. I didn't recognize any of them, but something about them—their airy confidence, maybe, or the way they expected everyone else to make way for them—reminded me of Bree.

One of the girls, a dishwater blonde with heavily glossed lips, asked, "Is Soren working today?"

The woman behind the counter, who sported an impressive number of piercings and perfectly applied kohl liner, rolled her eyes. "Not for another hour."

"Oh," the girl said, crestfallen. The air around her stirred faintly, the beginning of a break. "We could wait, right? Surprise him?"

"Go for it," the barista said in a tone suggesting Soren would not, in fact, be surprised by the sight of four girls giggling into their skinny caramel lattes.

The café was nearly full—all that was left was a low table in front, with a couch on one side and two chairs on the other. It was the perfect place to see and be seen, and the only spot where the four girls would fit.

As they waited for their drinks, Monty ambled over, handing me a cappuccino. "Having fun?"

"Not particularly."

He gave me a conspirator's wink. "Would you like to?"

"Most definitely."

He tipped his head toward the girls hovering at the counter. "Hard to concentrate with their gabbing, isn't it? Bet you could convince them to leave."

"They're too stable," I said. "The break around Lip Gloss Girl is tiny. Addie would kill me if I interfered."

Addie and Monty had made direct contact so the cashier would notice them and take their order, but I'd been sitting undetected in my chair for thirty minutes. I wondered if I could sneak a nap.

"Influence, not interference," he chided. "Oldest trick in the book."

Before I could stop him, he scooped up my backpack and dumped it on one of the empty chairs.

The ringleader, a tall brunette, had been eyeing the table. She blinked and turned to the others. "Why don't they have more seats?" she complained. "We're going to have to squish in."

Monty's plan became clear. Swiftly, I tossed my coat on the other chair and stretched out on the couch, feet on the cushions, moments before the girls collected their drinks. They stopped a few feet away, confused. In the Key World, I would have been on the receiving end of haughty looks and barbed comments, maybe even a veiled threat.

The Echo clique wouldn't remember any details about me. They knew their plans to sit by the window had been thwarted, but if you asked them to explain why, the best they'd be able to come up with was, "Someone took our seats." I was insubstantial and utterly forgettable, but I could change their path.

"Let's check out the bookstore instead. Maybe that hot guy is working the customer service desk." The brunette tossed her hair and headed for the door, a pivot forming in her wake. The others trailed silently after her, and the break around Lip Gloss Girl steadied.

Monty thumped down on the couch next to me with a grunt and perused my map. I dumped a bunch of sugar into my drink and folded a star from the empty packets, just to pass the time.

"I give up," I said eventually. "What was that? Her break fixed itself?"

"It's called tuning," Monty said as Addie joined us. "Addie's seen it before, haven't you?"

"I have," she said, dropping my backpack on the floor and sitting down. "It's a weird side effect of Walking—when we interfere with a break, their pitch will sometimes stabilize."

"You can bring them back in tune," Monty said cheerfully. "Neat trick, isn't it?"

"Sure, if it doesn't make things worse," Addie replied. "You shouldn't have encouraged her, Grandpa."

I thought back to the note cards. "Can you fix entire Echoes?"

"Theoretically, yes. But there's no point. It's more efficient to cleave Echoes than fix them. Safer, too." Addie waved her hand. "Have you finished?"

"Almost. There's one behind the door, I think."

In the back of the café was a door with an EMPLOYEES ONLY sign.

"Go check it out," she said. "And don't try to fix it. Get the reading, and we'll leave."

I crossed the room, trying to connect Addie's explanation of tuning and the transposition from yesterday. Was it possible I'd tuned the Echo so well it had transposed? Was that illegal? Considering I'd violated my suspension the instant I crossed over, asking Addie was not an option.

The door was locked. I pressed my ear against the wood, trying to hear the break on the other side. The frequency was fluctuating wildly, and I couldn't get a good sense of its strength.

"Can't get in," I said, returning to the couch. I drew a question mark on the map and Addie scowled. She'd never been a fan of unanswered questions.

"Get the key from the cashier," she replied.

"How am I going to do that without touching her?" I shot back. "You wanted me to map the break, and I did. End of story."

"Not end of story," she replied. "Pretend for a minute that hell freezes over, and you actually get your license. Cleavers initiate their cuts as close to the breaks as possible, to keep them under control. You'd need a way into that room."

"I've got a trick for that, too," said Monty. He slapped his knees and hefted himself off the couch. "Time for more fun."

"This isn't supposed to be fun," Addie replied.

"Trust me, it isn't," I said under my breath.

"No need to squabble," said Monty. "Del's supposed to be learning, so we'll visit the school."

"Basketball game tonight?" Addie asked. The statue of George Washington outside the front door was dressed in a fire-engine red uniform. In the Key World, our colors were blue and white, but the tradition was the same, apparently.

"Like I would know?"

Monty headed for a side door, and I chased after him. "They lock it up on weekends. Only the custodians and teachers have keys."

"Haven't bothered with a key since I met Rose," he huffed, and pulled out his wallet. "Watch and learn."

"Lock picks?" Addie said. Her ponytail whipped back and forth frantically. "Grandpa, you can't break into the school."

"Good point." He sat back on his haunches. "You'll never learn if you don't try it yourselves. Del?"

I took the slender metal hook he handed me.

Addie snatched it out of my hand. "No. This is against the law."

Monty tsked. "Whose law? Whose jurisdiction are we under, Addison?"

She struggled to answer, but finally said, "The Consort's."

"Indeed. Any crime committed in service to the Key World is no crime at all. That is what they teach you, isn't it? How they justify what they do?" His voice shook, but his hands were steady as he maneuvered the picks.

A minute later the door swung open.

"In we go," said Monty. I helped him up, his arm knobbly and fragile underneath my grip. Despite his mischief and stubbornness, he was old. I forgot that, sometimes. Forgot the toll his Walks had taken. "We haven't got the whole day. And I need another snack."

The main building was shaped like a rectangle, and we'd entered at one of the corners, the two hallways on either side of us forming an L. Monty's words reverberated down the corridor, past darkened classrooms and banks of lockers.

And every single door had a lock.

My fingertips tingled, the same as before every Walk—so much possibility. So many things to see, even if it was the same school I went to every day.

I'd had freshman geography in the first room I came to. Here it was a German classroom—a flag draped in front of the windows, maps lining the walls, homework assignments and verb conjugations written on the board. Nothing interesting, except that the knob wouldn't turn under my hand. I was about to ask Monty for his picks when Addie recovered her wits.

"That's it," she said, taking his arm. "We are going home. Right now. Someone has to be the adult here."

He tugged away from her, surprisingly forceful. "That's me," he snapped. "We're not leaving until the two of you learn some real skills. You can't rely on the Consort to teach you what you need. They'll only teach you what they need. It's not the same thing."

I shot Addie a triumphant look, and Monty rounded on me. "Instinct isn't enough either. You want to outwit everyone else, you need to practice."

He slapped his hands together and surveyed the hallway. "Let's get started."

Monty's lesson took longer than we thought—but even though we arrived home after dark, dazed and headachy from so much exposure to bad frequencies, my parents were nowhere to be found. Addie checked her voice mail while I texted Eliot to see if he was home from training.

"They'll be home late," Addie announced. "There's a casse-role in the fridge."

"No apple cake?" Monty said mournfully.

"Mom will bake tomorrow," Addie said, and dished up a giant bowl of rocky road to hold him over until we ate. Grumbling, he took it up to his room. When he'd gone, Addie blew out a long, slow breath. "Cocoa?"

"With extra Fluff," I said, pulling a squat white jar out of the pantry.

Addie poured milk in a saucepan, eyes troubled. "We should tell Mom."

"That we spent today breaking and entering? She'd freak out."

"She should."

"You're the one who says Echoes aren't real, so what's the harm? If they think we can't handle Monty, they'll put him in a home."

She was quiet as the milk heated, then stirred in cocoa and sugar. When the mixture was steaming, she finally spoke. "This isn't the first time he's taught you something shady, is it?"

I got down mugs and spooned in big globs of Marshmallow Fluff. "Not shady. Just . . . extra techniques. Like when I stole Simon's wallet."

"Do you really think they're helpful?"

Mostly, Monty's tricks were fun. A way to show off, even if no one noticed. But I'd used them enough to know they could have a big impact, made bigger by the fact that people didn't expect them.

"It's another thing to add to the toolbox," I said, thinking of the leather case full of picks sitting in my bag. Monty had given them to me while Addie was distracted, insisting I would get more use out of them. "You don't have to use it, but it's nice to have the option."

She filled the mugs, and the Marshmallow Fluff bobbed to the surface like a buoy. "It feels . . . wrong."

"It's no different from a screwdriver. Right or wrong depends on how you use it." Learning to pick locks seemed minor compared to Monty's lesson in tuning. No one had ever told me we could repair Echoes. What if I could have prevented Park World's cleaving? Saved Simon and Iggy and the rest? I pushed the mug of cocoa away, feeling ill.

"Maybe." She stared into her cup, glancing up when someone knocked on the front door. "Is that Eliot?"

Eliot used the back door—and he never bothered to knock. For a fleeting second I hoped it was Simon, but that seemed impossible. The knock sounded again. I opened the door and stepped back quickly, as if I'd found a rattlesnake on my doorstep.

"Hello, Delancey," said Councilman Lattimer. "I'd like to come in."

CHAPTER SEVENTEEN

I WOULD NEVER GET USED TO THE WAY THE Consort didn't ask questions. They made statements, a weird formality designed to reduce the pivots around them. Pointless, considering that Walker-created pivots couldn't sustain themselves, but they clung to the tradition.

"My parents are out," I said as Councilman Lattimer crossed the threshold. "Working."

"I'm aware. I'm here for an update on your progress, per your sentence."

"Shouldn't that be Shaw's job?"

He peered into the living room, with its jumble of instruments. "I assure you I'm qualified."

Addie sloshed cocoa everywhere at the sight of a Consort member strolling into our kitchen.

"Not Eliot," I said.

"Councilman!" She shot out of her seat. "We're—I'm—how can we help you?"

"I'm here for Delancey's progress report. Since your parents have placed you in charge, I thought it simpler to get the information directly."

He gave her an expectant look, as if his patience was already wearing thin.

"I haven't written a formal report yet," Addie hedged, "but she did well. We spent today reviewing navigation and cartography, and discussed strategies for directly analyzing breaks."

Impressive. It was a much better spin than, "We hung out at a coffee shop and burglarized a school."

"I trust you've limited her Walks only to supervised training?"

"Yes, sir. We've monitored her very closely."

"We. You and your grandfather, I presume." He looked up at the ceiling, where Monty's shuffling gait was audible. "Are you certain neither of them slipped away unnoticed?"

A direct question from a Consort member was virtually unheard of. He must have been genuinely curious, and his curiosity fueled my own. Was he here to check up on me, or Monty?

Addie was too caught up in the implication she'd been lax in watching me to notice his slip. "The Consort's expectations were very clear. I had eyes on Del the whole time."

I did my best to look obedient and remorseful.

"It's important that you supervise your grandfather as closely as you do your sister, lest he wander off. Also, you should be aware his methodology often conflicts with standard practice."

"He's got years of experience," I blurted. "Why not learn from that?"

He turned on me, predatory as a hawk. "The lessons you can take from him are cautionary at best. You'd do better to learn from your sister. We need more Walkers like her."

Addie straightened, her posture more impeccable than usual as he turned to her.

"We appreciate your willingness to help, Addison. Once your apprenticeship is concluded—and assuming your work with Delancey is successful—the Consort will make sure you're given a position worthy of your abilities."

On the surface the words sounded complimentary. But the underlying message had an ominous note: If I failed, I wouldn't be the only one punished.

"Yes, sir," she said, eyes wide. She'd heard it too. "Thank you."

"Excellent. Send me your written reports, as well as your plans for the upcoming week. I'll continue to check in personally."

"That's not necessary, sir. Del's caused you enough trouble."

"No trouble at all." His smile fell several degrees short of warm. "It's the least I can do for the granddaughters of my old friend. Especially considering that he's in no condition to do it himself."

Before Addie could manage another timid "Yes, sir," he was gone.

"Well, that wasn't creepy." I threw the dead bolt and headed to the kitchen. "Why does the Consort care so much about me? I figured they'd hand me off to Shaw again, especially since they're busy with Mom and Dad's special project."

Addie stared into her mug, lost in thought. "Grandpa was a big deal when he was a Cleaver. A lot of people thought he would be selected for the Consort, before Grandma disappeared. Maybe they think they're doing him a favor."

"Some favor," I said. "Monty and Lattimer can't stand each other."

"No, they can't. But he was important. Mom and Dad are important. They can't publicly show favoritism, but behind the scenes . . ." She shrugged. "Regardless, Lattimer's right about Monty being a bad influence. He keeps losing time, Del. He's slipping."

The cocoa coated my tongue, making it thick and clumsy. "Only a little. When it's important, he focuses."

"It's what he deems important that worries me," she replied.

My whole life, Monty had encouraged me to stretch myself. To find out what I was capable of, instead of blindly following instructions. "Teaching us. Making sure we can find our way home."

"Those are secondary," Addie said. "He wants to find Grandma, and if he can't do it himself, he'll use us. He'll use anyone. He's training us to keep going once he can't."

"You think he knows they're talking about sending him to a home?"

"I think he's not as lost as he seems." She shook her head, rinsed out her cup. "I'm going to write that report."

After she left, I texted Eliot: *U back? Movie night?*

The reply was immediate: *B there asap.*

The textbooks Addie and I had fought over this morning lay scattered across the table. I stacked them neatly, but my mom's office, a narrow windowless room off the main hall, was locked as usual. The only books I could reshelve were the journals, leather-bound diaries kept by my grandparents and other long-dead relatives, stretching back generations. These days most Walkers kept their journals on a computer, but there was something reassuring about seeing row after row, each stamped with the author's initials.

The Monty I glimpsed in the journals was nimble and canny, even if he didn't follow protocol. He relied more on instinct and the deft manipulation of strings rather than the bloodless, data-driven style we were taught in school. His later entries degenerated into ramblings about the Consort and his attempts to find Rose. I didn't read those volumes as much.

My grandmother's journals were more like scrapbooks: a few maps, lots of notes about medical cases she'd treated, home remedies and recipes for the desserts Monty loved, brief melodies she'd composed.

When I was a kid, I'd read my grandparents' journals again and again, looking for clues about where Rose had gone and how Monty had searched for her. I'd thought if I could find her, he'd be restored—not just my beloved, dotty grandfather, but the brilliant Walker contained in those books. He'd be happy, and I'd finally meet my grandmother instead of only hearing stories.

I knew better now. Too much time and too many worlds had passed to find my grandmother. The best we could hope for was to keep Monty from losing himself, too.

I headed into the living room, picking up my mom's viola and running through a few arpeggios, fingers dancing over the strings. The lively, complicated scales usually did the trick when I wanted to fend off melancholy.

Eliot let himself in the back door, calling, "Miss me?"

"Like you wouldn't believe." I met him in the kitchen and gave him a quick hug. "Have you been out this whole time?"

"Yeah. Tricky stuff today." He grabbed a can of pop from the fridge and swallowed noisily. "Boring without you."

"Naturally. Did anyone ask about me?"

"Callie said you should call her. Everyone's bummed you're gone."

I wanted to believe him, but my phone had been awfully quiet since the sentencing. "What about Shaw? Did he say anything?"

Eliot settled into the blue brocade armchair, lacing his fingers behind his head. "'Be nice to Addie.'"

"Pfft. He knows what she's like." I played another arpeggio, pleased. Shaw was on my side. If we could prove the cleaving wasn't my fault, he would back me up with the Consort.

"I went to the Archives after class," he added. "Pulled a bunch of files and read them on the way home."

My pulse kicked up. "What did you find?"

"Nothing yet. A lot of the data was lost in the cleaving. I'll keep looking."

I tried to sound upbeat. "Did Shaw like the map program?"

"I'm not ready to show him."

Eliot would be eighty before he was ready—he was a total perfectionist. Usually it made me nuts, but this time he was right.

"Yeah, the software's glitchy. I meant to tell you yesterday."

His eyebrows shot up. "What did you do to my map?"

"I was testing it during history, and the display kind of . . . exploded." I waved my bow around for emphasis.

"Why didn't you mention it?"

"I rebooted and it looked fine. Besides, it wasn't like we had a lot of time to chat yesterday." Between my detention and his training, I'd barely seen him.

"It's working now," he said, sweeping his fingers over the screen. "What were you doing when it crashed?"

"Nothing! I was sitting in class, testing the range, and it froze. I took it back to the music room so I could check things out in person, and it started working again."

He scowled. "I wish you wouldn't Walk by yourself."

"Shhhhh." Before he could scold me—or ask who I'd seen—I added, "There should have been a million pivots coming from the music room, but there was only one. What's up with that?"

"Only one?" He paced around the room as he worked. "You're sure?"

"Yes, I'm sure. Saw it, heard it, felt it." Rather than watch him wear a path in the carpet, I started playing again, trying to recreate the melody I'd heard at Grundy's. "I bet my mom can figure it out."

"Quit goofing around," Addie called, coming downstairs. "And don't bother Mom. She doesn't have the time to fix your latest gadget, Eliot. No offense."

"None taken," he muttered.

"It's not a gadget," I said, tucking away both the viola and the memory of Echo Simon. Addie's easy dismissal of Eliot rankled. "It's a map. A real-time map. And it's amazing."

"Real-time? Let me see." She plucked the phone out of his hands.

"There are a few bugs I need to work out," he said.

"Let's bring it with tonight," I said. "Test it again."

"You've been Walking with it?" she asked sharply.

"I'm not allowed to, am I?" Which was not exactly a denial, and Addie knew it. She also knew she couldn't prove I'd done anything wrong. I let her stew and turned to Eliot. "We should take off."

"Your wish is my command," he said, easing the phone out of her grip.

"You two aren't going out tonight." She raised her eyebrows, a perfect imitation of my mom. "We're not done training."

"Don't you have friends? Or a date? Something to do that doesn't involve sucking the joy out of my life?"

"For your information, I did have plans tonight. But since I'm not interested in rehashing the adventures of my delinquent baby sister, I decided to pass." She didn't look too upset about it.

"That's the stupidest excuse I've ever heard," I said. "As if you'd even mention me to your friends. What's the real reason?"

"I don't need to justify myself to you. Get your coat, Del. We're going to a basketball game, and you're going to map it."

"Are you joking?"

Her mouth was a tight line. "Do I look like I'm joking?"

"You look like you need to get—" Eliot jabbed me in the ribs, and I glared at him. "What? She does."

"Not helping," he muttered. He gave Addie an apologetic half smile. "We kind of have plans. It's Saturday. Movie night."

"She knows it's movie night," I said. "Saturday is *always* movie night. She's just being a bitch."

Addie sniffed. "Nice, Del. Very classy."

"You can't stop us," I said.

"Can't I?" She brandished her own phone like a sheriff's badge. "I talked to Mom, and she agreed with me. Ask her yourself—they'll be home any minute."

"I'm going to kill her," I told Eliot through gritted teeth, following Addie to the kitchen. "Smother her with a pillow. Garrote her with a violin string. Maybe a poisonous snake in her bed. Aren't you glad you're an only child?"

"It has its advantages," he admitted.

I was tempted to start in on my mom as soon as my parents walked in the door, but she looked so exhausted—bags under her eyes, hair falling out of its usual neat bun, skin pale with fatigue—I bit my tongue.

"Eliot," she said warmly. "I feel like I haven't seen you in ages. How are you?"

"Good. Dad says you're keeping him busy." Eliot's father led another one of the teams Mom worked with.

"Never enough hours in the day," she said with a weak laugh, and then turned to me. "Out with it, Del. What's wrong?"

"Addie says I have to go to a basketball game, but it's movie night!" When she looked unimpressed, I added, "I've spent the whole day training and now she wants to hijack our plans."

"Quit whining," Addie said. "You two can try out his map gizmo another time."

"Map gizmo?" Mom asked, sitting down at the table. Monty wandered in and took his usual seat.

Eliot handed over the phone, bashful and proud mingled together. For few minutes, my mom was lost in it, asking him questions and half-listening to the answers. I tried not to feel hurt that a computer program got more attention than me.

"Impressive. Can I get a copy of the software?" asked my dad. "Could be handy out in the field."

"The code needs a few tweaks," Eliot hedged.

"No time like the present," my mom said, shooting my dad a look. "Send us a copy, Eliot. Tonight."

My mom usually encouraged Eliot's inventions and gadgets, but never with this kind of gravity. If my parents wanted the map, it wasn't for entertainment purposes.

"Mom, Addie's not allowed to take over my whole life, is she?"

"Your sister knows better than to abuse her position." She gave Eliot a sympathetic smile. "It's a shame you two won't have as much time together, with Del's . . . new situation."

She was right. With Eliot on his regular training schedule and me at the mercy of a power-crazed Addie, we wouldn't be hanging out the way we normally did. Eliot was one of those parts of my life that was so familiar I barely noticed it, much like the Key World. He was my constant. The prospect of him moving on to apprenticeship without me pinched my heart.

"The three of you can go together," Mom said. "Addie's right—sporting events are a great way to practice mapping. And, Eliot, you can test the software in a high-stress situation. Everybody wins."

Addie smirked at me. "Told you so."

Monty pushed back from the table, his chair squeaking on the hardwood. He'd been so silent, I'd forgotten he was there. "Sounds like a plan, girls. I'll get my coat."

Addie's jaw dropped, and it was my turn to smirk.

CHAPTER EIGHTEEN

HALF AN HOUR LATER THE SCENT OF POP-corn and nachos filled the air—but instead of the maroon carpet and plush chairs of the movie theater, it was hardwood floors, ancient bleachers, and the staccato squeak of sneakers against the thud of dribbling basketballs. The field house was packed for the first home game, and the four of us were stuck in the nosebleed section.

"Sporting events tend to create really dense concentrations of pivots," Addie said. "Emotions are running high, which leads to more emphatic decisions and more significant repercussions, and the game itself is a compressed cycle of choices and reactions."

"Lots of choices," Monty translated around a mouthful of hot dog. "Lots of branches. Plenty to see, and a familiar face, to boot."

He nodded toward Simon, bushy eyebrows waggling. I pretended not to know what he meant.

The number of pivots opening and closing around us was dizzying. The sound was like the sweep of wind through tall grass, or a thousand birds taking flight—all flutter and rush and thrill. So many worlds, dangling in front of me like brand-new songs waiting to be played.

Rather than explore, I was stuck with my notebook, marking every pivot that sprang up: people choosing where to sit, the players' actions, the referees' calls, and the coaches' directions. It was a tedious, mind-numbing job, and I fought the urge to shove Addie down the bleachers in retaliation.

While I worked longhand, Eliot analyzed the scene with his phone, the lights scattering and twisting like a kaleidoscope. He barely lifted his head to watch the game. No matter where I looked, my gaze kept wandering back to the court.

Back to Simon. I wouldn't have argued quite so much if I'd remembered he would be here. The thought made me feel shallow, so I pushed it away and focused on the sight of him pounding down the court, shouting instructions to his teammates. I'd watched him for years, but tonight was my first basketball game. He moved with an urgency that surprised me. The lazy grace that marked his everyday movements was gone, replaced by a sharpness that verged on anger.

It was easy to sense the pivots Simon created. I didn't need to look at Eliot's display to see the strength of those branches—I could hear them, the tangle of realities tantalizingly complex.

Next to me, Eliot jerked in surprise.

"What's wrong?" I had to shout to make myself heard over the crowd.

"Your partner," he said, tapping the screen. "Watch."

Bright dots were scattered across the display, smaller pixels clustering around them. "That's him," Eliot said, pointing to a pulsing light. "He's drawing the other branches in."

I hadn't heard it, because I'd been so focused on Simon himself. But now, seeing the entire court in miniature, the interplay was obvious. Simon's pivots fed off the smaller lights around him, increasing with every passing moment.

Monty peered over Eliot's shoulder, then down at the floor. "You don't see that every day."

"What is it?" Eliot asked.

"A Baroque event." Addie tilted the phone toward her. "One branch in a group of similar frequencies causes the smaller ones to shift. Once enough of them start to shift, they combine, like they've been transposed. The resulting branch is much stronger. They're not super common, but you see them at sporting events sometimes." She launched into a more detailed explanation, filled with technicalities and citations. It was like listening to someone read their term paper out loud.

"So it's a transposition?" I asked. Eliot slanted me a look, no doubt remembering how we'd transposed Doc Reese's science test.

"Not exactly," she said. "Transposition occurs in newly formed Echoes, before the frequency locks in. Baroque events happen in established Echoes—they're a lot more complex."

"What causes them?" Eliot asked.

"Nobody knows," she replied. "So long as the end result is stable, it's not a problem. These are the right conditions for it, though."

Below us the Baroque event was finally audible. It was like listening to an orchestra tuning up—myriad pitches colliding with one another, making minute adjustments. Not even the regular, everyday game noises—the crowd's stomps and yells, the refs' whistles, the cheerleaders' chanting—could mask the sound spreading through the field house.

"It's kind of cool," I admitted, watching the pivots forming in Simon's wake.

The halftime buzzer blared, putting a stop to the Baroque event. We were ahead, 52–37, and the bleachers shook with the crowd's enthusiasm. The team headed for the locker room, fists pumping, but their absence caused the pivots to fall quiet.

Eliot stood. "Nacho run?"

Addie looked repulsed. "That cheese is nothing but artificial dyes and hydrogenated fats."

"I'm living on the edge," he said cheerily. "Come on, Del. You said you wanted popcorn."

"Popcorn?" Monty said, but Addie caught his sleeve.

"We'll stay here," she said. "Be back before halftime's over."

Taking me by the hand, Eliot led me down the bleachers and into the crowded lobby. Children darted through the crowd while parents chitchatted, and our classmates clustered together, tight-knit little groupings that didn't admit newcomers.

"You hate nachos," I said.

"I didn't want to talk in front of the others. Tell me exactly what the map looked like before it crashed yesterday."

"One big light. Took up the whole screen."

"What did it sound like when you crossed through?"

"Strong," I said, thinking back. "I couldn't have stayed longer than an hour, tops."

"I think you saw the remnants of a Baroque event. Same as now, lots of pivots combining into one. You came in at the end, after the branches were absorbed." His hands traced paths in the air as he spoke. "I bet another one forms during the second half. Do you think Addie would let us take a look?"

"Not unless we spike her pop." But the lure of exploring trumped my concern about Addie. "We could go without her. Wait until she's distracted and check it out."

"She's turned you in once already," he warned. "Don't give her the chance to do it again. Let's ask."

Halftime was ending. Through the doors we could hear the pep band playing a fight song, heavy on the trombone and the bass drum.

"Guarantee you she'll say no." I shrugged. Even though doing the sensible thing fit me like a pair of someone else's shoes, I could see the logic in it. We headed inside and made our way up the stairs. "But you can try."

Addie spent the second half lecturing us on branch theory and Walker protocol. Monty napped, despite the deafening noise of the crowd. Eliot's eyebrows shot higher and higher, his posture ramrod straight as he compared the action on the court to his display. I kept my eyes on Simon and the Baroque event.

Even without looking, I knew the minute Eliot's map crashed—it was the same moment the pivots cramming the floor coalesced into a single, deeply resonant one, tolling like a bell. I clapped my hands over my ears. Even Monty jolted awake.

"And that is how a Baroque event works," Addie said, like

we were kindergarteners and she was the put-upon teacher. The game ended moments later, the crowd on its feet, roaring triumphantly.

Simon led the team through a complicated handshake ritual with the opposing squad, then huddled with his own on the sidelines. He'd played nearly the entire game, turning his uniform dark with sweat and his face ruddy. The triumph in his expression verged on cockiness, as if their victory had never been in question. Fists pumping, the team swarmed into the locker room.

As the crowd dispersed, I turned to Addie. "Did they lose, in the Baroque Echo?"

"Impossible to say without crossing through." Before I could suggest we do exactly that, she held up a hand. "I'm not taking you into a world we haven't planned for, Del. It's not safe."

I shot Eliot an "I told you so" look.

"We'll stay on this side," Eliot promised, towing me down the bleachers.

We hovered on the sidelines until the gym was nearly empty. Pivots covered the court, their edges brushing against me like moths' wings. Ghosts of previous games, they were unaffected by the Baroque event.

I tucked my hands in my coat pockets and zeroed in on the Baroque pivot. It was centered on a curving red line on the far side of the gym, the edges so pronounced that if I hit them at the wrong angle, it would be like walking into a doorframe. Across the room Addie was explaining the finer points of Baroque events to Eliot, who looked like he was longing for escape.

A basketball rolled into my ankle. I picked it up, surprised by the weight of it. Tentatively I dribbled it, listening to the rhythmic whump as I memorized the new frequency. Maybe I could explore it during school, when Addie wasn't around to catch me.

Out of nowhere Simon swiped the basketball away midbounce.

"Gotta keep your guard up," he said, evading my attempt to steal the ball back. "I didn't peg you for a basketball fan."

"I'm not." I swallowed, my throat suddenly dry. His hair was damp and disheveled from the shower, his expression curious. "This is my first time. Congratulations, by the way."

He glanced over at the scoreboard. "It was okay."

"You won. By twenty points." I was pretty ignorant about sports, but even I knew that was a good thing.

"True." He made a show of looking around. "Want to know a secret?"

"Always."

He leaned in, his fingers skimming my shoulder, his breath warm against my ear. "It's more fun when it's close."

I ordered myself not to blush. "Is that so?"

"Winning's always better if you have to work for it." He handed me the ball. "Shoot a free throw."

"I can't make a basket."

"Have you ever tried?"

"In PE. Not pretty."

"Don't be so sure. Watch." He took the ball back and stepped to the line. I watched the shift in him, the way his awareness narrowed to the strip of hardwood, the ball, the net. I'd been on the receiving end of that kind of focus the other night, and the memory stole my breath.

He dribbled twice, raised the ball with his fingers spread wide, and shot, wrist snapping down and hands hovering in the air. I heard the rustle of the net and the bounce of the ball, but my attention was riveted on Simon, who dropped his hands and smiled.

"Very nice," I said.

"That shot won the state championship last year," he said. "In overtime."

"I think I remember hearing about it," I said dryly. No one had talked about anything else for a week.

"Best day of my life, winning that game. They even let me cut down the net." He scooped up the ball and pressed it into my hands, his fingers covering mine, his frequency strong and true. "Now you."

"This is your thing, not mine."

The smile spread, his eyes crinkling in amusement. "Scared?"

I lifted my chin. "Hardly."

"Then let's go. Feet on the line, Sullivan." He spun me toward the free throw lane, poked a finger into the small of my back, and prodded until I was standing where he had been. "Show me what you've got."

The ball barely made it to the backboard. "See? Hopeless."

"Take off your coat," he ordered. "Your range of movement is restricted."

I struggled to pull my arms out of the sleeves, and he helped me, pulling it off with practiced ease and a wolfish grin.

"Okay, you're right-handed, so put your right foot here"—he nudged my boot with the tip of his shoe—"and point your toes toward the basket."

My limbs felt stiff, like a puppet's, like I'd forgotten how to move.

"Bend your knees a little," he said, setting his palms against my shoulders. "Arms up. You're shooting with your right hand—the left is only there for balance." With every command, he touched me, the gentle pressure of his fingers making me light-headed. "Give it a try."

The ball sailed into the backboard and careened away. "Told you."

"Nobody likes a quitter." He retrieved the ball, spinning it like a top. "So, you came to cheer me on in our home opener? I'm touched, partner."

"My sister wanted to come." I tilted my head toward Addie and Eliot, who were half watching the map, half watching me, and wholly unhappy. There was no sign of Monty—but I'd let Addie deal with him this time. "I'm grounded, unless I'm with her."

"And here I thought you cared." He tossed me the ball and stood directly behind me, his arms coming around to position my hands. "Fingers spread out. You need backspin. And keep your eyes on the back of the rim."

I fought the urge to turn and face him. He was the wrong Simon for those kinds of thoughts. Instead I concentrated on the solid expanse of his chest against my back, the way our hands looked together—strong hands, both of us, for entirely different reasons.

His voice was rich and teasing. "Did you do something really bad to get grounded? Please say yes."

I stared straight ahead. "Long story. Suffice it to say I have a problem with authority."

"Shocking." He laughed. "Shoot, Del."

His hands guided mine, and the ball arced through the air, sliding through the net with a faint whisper.

"I did it!" I whirled to see the smile break across his face, mirroring my own.

"With my help," he pointed out. He tugged the little braid I'd woven into my hair. "Grounded for scandalous reasons? Cutting class? I'm getting a very clear impression of you."

"Oh?"

"You're trouble." He made it sound like a good thing.

"Funny. That's what people tell me about you."

"You should listen," he said softly. His skin radiated heat, as it had the other night, and the memory made me bold enough to step closer.

"Simon!" Bree ran up, throwing her arms around his neck. "You were amazing! It's like they didn't even show up, you guys were so good! And that three-pointer was incredible—I swear, the scout from Arizona didn't even *look* at anyone else."

Simon eased away, his smile fading. Bree tipped her head to the side and gave him a beseeching look. "Can I get a ride with you to Duncan's party? Cassidy has a ton of people in her car already."

"Yeah, sure." He turned to me, a note of apology creeping into his voice. "Party. At Duncan's."

"I heard." Cold settled over me, and I scooped my coat off the floor, avoiding his eyes.

"You could probably come, if you wanted. It's pretty low-key."

"Duncan won't want a bunch of people he doesn't know showing up," Bree cut in. "We can't go around inviting everyone."

For one crazy moment I thought he might do it anyway. He had enough social currency stockpiled that he could have brought a leper—an actual leper, not just a social one—and people would have been okay with it. He hesitated, and his choice was obvious.

I beat him to the punch. "Grounded, remember? And high school parties aren't my scene."

"Really," Bree said, dripping sarcasm. "Why's that?"

I smiled at Simon, radiating nonchalance as hard as I could. "No challenge. You two have fun."

"Del," Simon began, but I was already heading for the door. Always better to be the one leaving.

CHAPTER NINETEEN

Aside from the need to keep Walkers secret from Originals and Echoes, romantic relationships are frowned upon for another, more pressing reason: The future of our people and the Key World depend on maintaining the genetic line.
—Chapter Four, "Physiology,"
Principles and Practices of Cleaving, Year Five

Y OU LIKE HIM," ELIOT SAID AS WE SAT ON THE front porch after the game.

"Simon? Hardly."

"You've been acting weird ever since Powell paired you up. Walking when you're not supposed to. Flirting with him in class. He was hitting on you tonight, and you let him. Evidence doesn't lie."

It was Eliot's guiding principle, but that didn't stop me from denying it.

"Did you miss the part where Bree told him not to invite me? And he listened?" I dug my toe into the floorboards and pushed off. The wooden swing creaked loudly as we swayed.

"You should stay away from him," Eliot said. "He makes you unhappy."

"This conversation is making me unhappy." Eliot never liked

the Walkers I went out with either, and I wasn't in the mood for this talk. Besides, I wasn't going out with Simon.

"There's something weird about the guy. Two Baroque events in as many days, and he's at the center of both? Let me look into it before you start throwing yourself at him."

I scowled. "I'm not throwing myself at him! He's not even my type."

"*Who* isn't your type?" asked Addie through the screen door. "That basketball player? The grabby one?"

"Forget it." I slouched down.

"You know it can't go anywhere," she warned. "He's not a Walker."

"He's not anything," I said. "Just a guy."

"Good," Eliot and Addie said in unison.

The order against Walker-Original relationships was stupid. Even the Consort turned a blind eye to it until after apprentice-ship, when people started settling down and relationships turned serious. I understood the need to pass along our genes; without future generations of Walkers, the Key World would eventually crumble. But I wasn't looking to marry Simon. I wanted . . . I didn't know what I wanted, but a white picket fence wasn't it.

Addie went back inside. I must have looked like an idiot, flirting with Simon only to have him leave with another girl. Embarrassment curdled in my stomach.

Eliot slung an arm over my shoulder. "Find someone else, Del. Someone who's actually worthwhile."

I stiffened. "Don't tell me what to do."

"I'm not. I'm saying be smart, for once."

"You're the relationship expert now? I don't see you getting anywhere with Bree Carlson—or anyone else." The words came out nastier than I intended.

"Why would I want to?" His brow furrowed. "Simon's the one who bailed. How come you're mad at me?"

"Why would I be mad? I love hearing Simon Lane couldn't *possibly* be interested in me. Keep going. Tell me more."

"That's not what I—" he started to say.

"You're jealous," I said. His face went cold and remote, and I knew I should shut up, but my humiliation had been festering since the game, turning to anger, thick and oily in my veins. I couldn't stop myself. It was leaking out, contaminating everything, poisoning the one good thing I had left. "You're jealous because I actually go after what I want, and I get it."

"You didn't tonight," he said, voice like acid.

"At least I *tried*. You'd rather spend your time analyzing data than take an actual risk. Jesus, Eliot. Find a girl. Make a freaking move. Maybe then you'd get the hell off my case."

"And maybe if you'd pay attention to anything except yourself for five minutes—" He broke off, like he was stuffing down the words he wanted to say. "You want to be mad? Get mad at Simon or Bree. I saw your face when he chose that party over you, and *evidence doesn't lie*. Don't tell me that you're not falling for him."

"And that's your business?"

"You're . . ." He dropped his head, took a deep breath, and

met my eyes. "You're a pain in the ass, and tonight you're kind of being a bitch, but you're my best friend. I don't want you to get hurt."

The anger leached away at the truth in his words. "You think he'll hurt me."

"He already has." He threw up his hands. "Do what you want, Del. You always do."

He jogged down the porch steps without another word, shoulders hunched, hands jammed in his coat pockets. I wasn't the only one who was mad.

In sixteen years we'd fought only a handful of times. Each one left an awful, hollowed-out feeling in my chest. Now the hollowness was tinged with guilt. Eliot had always been unfailingly, unquestioningly on my side. What if I'd broken our friendship? What if it couldn't be mended?

Inside, Addie was drinking a cup of tea and reviewing a map. "You two were going at it pretty good."

"I'll fix it." Some things, you had no choice. And fixing Eliot and me was one of them.

"Good luck with that."

"It's late," I said, surprised by how quiet the house was. "Where is everyone?"

"Monty's asleep. Mom and Dad are holed up in her office. Again. I wish they'd tell me what the problem was."

"Good luck with that," I mimicked, and she glowered at me, her frustration clear.

My entire life I'd watched Addie follow the rules, gathering praise and attention. There'd been no way for me to match her perfection, much less exceed it. Eventually I'd stopped trying. Addie and the rules were interchangeable, and I'd grown to resent them both. I'd never given any thought to why she was so driven. If people love you because you're perfect, what happens when you screw up? Constant perfection was its own kind of pressure, I realized, and felt an unexpected rush of sympathy.

"He's right about that guy," Addie said. "What's his name?"

"Simon," I said after a moment's hesitation.

"You were talking to him at the park, weren't you? Before the cleaving."

"His Echo," I corrected. Hair so long it obscured his eyes, leather cuff, warm hands and a warmer invitation.

"You shouldn't get involved with him, especially if Eliot thinks he's bad news."

"Eliot's wrong."

"Eliot is biased, but he's not wrong. Be careful."

I rolled my eyes. Sisterly bonding time was over.

Upstairs, I flopped onto the bed, the ancient springs squeaking in protest. Above me, my origami garlands swayed in a draft from the window. Hundreds of stars, twins to the ones I'd scattered while Walking.

Including the one I'd left with Simon, back in Doughnut World.

The Simon who wanted me. The one who'd left a show and a room full of people to spend time with me. The one who didn't judge or scold or do anything except make my heart quicken and my blood sing.

Echoes weren't real, but I was falling for one. Or was I falling for the real Simon, and using his Echo because it was the only way to be with him?

I eased out of the bed, holding my breath. My backpack was still stocked from today's training session—duct tape, Swiss Army knife, matches, candy, and now, Monty's lock picks—and its weight was comforting. I might be reckless, but I wasn't stupid.

I'd snuck out plenty of times before, but never with this much at stake. The smart thing to do was to stay here, figure out a way to make Eliot forgive me, and convince my parents I had learned my lesson.

But ask anybody: Addie was the smart one.

CHAPTER TWENTY

Even though pivots created by Walkers didn't last, most houses contained at least a few—previous owners, plumbers, the occasional visitor. We might not choose to spend time with Originals, but some interaction was unavoidable. The pivots riddling our house were old, but they worked— and provided the perfect escape route.

I tiptoed across the room, feeling for a rent in the air next to my music stand. The edges were soft as mist when I eased my way through, listening for Doughnut World's frequency.

I'd been using this passage out of my room for years, ever since Monty had shown me how. Even though our house existed in countless Echoes, we weren't the owners. Sometimes I'd cross through and find it abandoned and in disrepair, but most of the time, someone else had moved in. I'd grown accustomed to seeing rehabbed master suites, dusty storage catchalls, and home offices, though I never got over the sensation of being a burglar in my own house.

This time I crossed into an empty attic, exactly as it looked before I had moved up here in elementary school. I headed downstairs, surprised to see familiar furniture and pictures on the wall. The house was dead silent and covered in a thick layer of dust, but definitely ours.

Weird as it was, I was more interested in finding Doughnut Simon.

By now he'd probably forgotten me. But I could remind him. I could try again. It had to be better than my real life, even if only for a few hours. I let myself outside and crossed the shadowy overgrown lawn.

At the living room window a curtain fluttered, ghostly white, and fell still.

I flattened myself against the trunk of a maple tree, trying to discern any hint of movement. Had my parents come up to check on me and tracked me through the pivot? Was the Consort monitoring me without my knowledge?

Nothing. The curtain hung straight and unmoving as clouds scudded across the sky. The only sounds were the wind in the leaves and Doughnut World's frequency, even stronger than last time.

I exhaled slowly and set out to find Simon.

I tried Grundy's first. There was a half-decent jazz combo playing, but no Simon. I knew where his Original lived, but couldn't quite picture this version hanging out at home on a Saturday night. Why had I thought I'd know him well enough to guess his movements?

In a corner booth I spotted the basketball coaches, boisterous and laughing over a pitcher of beer. Game night. If the coaches were here, the kids were celebrating elsewhere.

Duncan's party. I might have landed in another universe, but a postgame party was a given. And even if Echo Simon wasn't on the basketball team, he moved with the innate confidence of someone who knew he'd be welcomed in.

The wind cut through my coat as I headed toward Duncan's neighborhood. If there was no party, or if Simon wasn't there, I'd end up with hypothermia for nothing. If he was . . . it would be worth it.

My hunch paid off. I spotted the familiar black Jeep at the same time I heard the bass thumping against the windows of a redbrick colonial. I started for the front steps, then stopped. Simon might not be alone. He could have come to the party with Bree, or another girl. He might want to stay with them. It had been so easy to fall into thinking of him as "my" Simon, but that didn't make it true.

I blew on my fingertips, checked my watch. Past midnight. I could wait for a little while. There was time to scope out the situation, if I didn't freeze first.

That's when the rain began. It was thin and nasty and sharp, finding its way down the back of my neck. I eyed the Jeep, looking cozier by the minute, and sent up a silent thanks that Monty's lessons in petty crime weren't limited to pickpocketing.

Pulling out my picks, I set to work, hands aching with cold. A minute later I was inside—half-frozen but out of the wet—and replaying my fight with Eliot.

Two Baroque events in as many days, and he's at the center of both, he'd said. But Original Simon's frequency was fine. I'd heard it, loud and clear, when we'd touched at the game. If Baroque events were common during sports, it made sense that the captain of the basketball team would be involved. And there were a million factors that could have triggered the problem with Eliot's map. He was blaming Simon because he was worried about me.

Tomorrow, after Eliot got back from training, I'd go over to his house. We'd fix his map and then we'd be fixed too.

The sound of the door opening made me bolt upright and shriek—which made Simon jump back and swear, then peer at me in the glow of the dome light.

He could still see me, as if our previous contact had carried over. I held my breath, hoping his memories had too.

"You do know how to make an impression, don't you?" he said, and climbed inside.

"Rain again," he added as it pattered against the windows. "Am I only going to see you when it's raining?"

I frowned. "What do you mean?"

"I looked for you at school."

"You did?" The idea was flattering. I wouldn't have been there, of course. He would have seen an impression of me, like a figure in a dream that you couldn't quite catch. I allowed myself to imagine a version of Washington where Simon sought me out. "My attendance is . . . spotty."

"Is that why you're grounded?"

"Not exactly."

"Is it because you break into people's cars in the middle of the night?" He lifted my hands to his mouth and blew gently, warming them. I scooted closer.

So much easier to be bold with this Simon, and nothing was more bold than honesty. "I wanted to see you."

"You could have come inside," he said.

"I wanted to see *you*. Not the rest of the school."

His gaze settled on me, and I stared back, my heartbeat *prestissimo*, faster than fast. "Did you break out to see me? Or to piss off your parents? I'm not complaining either way."

I thought back to the jumble of emotions I'd been swamped by tonight, propelling me out of one reality into another. "It was a crappy night overall."

"Poor Del," he said, and brushed the back of his hand over my cheek, the touch whisper soft, and then his fingers slid under my hair, warm and deft. "Bet I can cheer you up."

I tilted my head to the side, pretended to consider the idea. "Okay."

"I'm better than okay." He was close enough now that, even in the darkness, I could see the corner of his mouth curve, irresistibly.

"Prove it." I grabbed the edges of his coat, the leather soft under my fingertips, bracing myself.

His mouth came down on mine—no hesitation, no uncertainty—and while I felt the potential crackle around us, a thousand worlds coming to life at the touch of his lips, every one underscored that *this* moment was exactly what he'd wanted.

What I'd wanted too. The recklessness I felt around Simon was different—sharper and hungrier than my usual impulsiveness. I couldn't stay forever, but he trailed kisses along my throat, his hand sliding up my spine, and I knew I couldn't stay away, either.

The idea should have worried me, but instead it thrilled me more, made me drink him in as deeply as I could.

He drew back, rested his forehead against mine. "That enough proof?"

The words were a challenge, but the gesture was sweet. Rather than answer, I angled my head and kissed him again, slow and thorough, learning the way his hair threaded through my fingers, and the way his breathing changed at my touch, and the tempo of the pulse in his throat. I learned Simon, and if a small voice warned me that this wasn't really him, I ignored it. Ignoring things I didn't want to hear had long been one of my specialties.

"Tell me about the crappy day," he said, when we finally came up for air.

His words brought it back—and I shook my head, trying to dislodge those thoughts. There was no room in the Jeep for anything except the two of us. "It's nothing."

"Not if it made you look so sad."

I traced the bow of his mouth with my thumb, and he caught it between his teeth. Startled, I laughed. "I'm not sad now."

"Glad to hear it. We should go somewhere."

"What's wrong with here?"

He peered out the front window. The party was winding down, people passing by on the way to their cars. "It's a little public for what I was thinking. And cold."

I shivered for reasons that had nothing to do with the temperature. "I should get going."

He let go of me to rummage in the cup holder, coins jingling. "That's what you said last time."

He held out his hand. My star rested in the curve of his palm, the points rounded as if they'd been worn away. The Key World frequency coming off it was barely audible. I brushed a finger along one edge, and the signal strengthened, like a flower unfurling in the sun.

"You kept it."

"You disappeared," he said. "It was proof you were real."

Was the star—or rather, the frequency it carried—why he remembered me? Hard to believe that such a small dose of the Key World could have an effect on him, but his reaction said otherwise. "I'm real. I promise."

"Let's go back to my house," he murmured, lacing his fingers with mine. "Iggy would love to see you. We could watch a movie, or hang out. Get to know each other."

"And then . . ."

There was a wicked tilt to his grin. "Then we'll see what happens." He kissed me again, pressing me back against the door, his roaming hands giving me a very clear picture of what would happen. "Say yes."

"Another time." Disappointment flashed in his eyes, so I added, "I have to get back before someone figures out I'm gone."

"What about school? Will you be around?"

"I'll find you," I said, and tugged my shirt back into place.

"Let me drive you home."

I didn't want to explain my abandoned Echo house. "Better not. I need to sneak back in."

"It's raining." When I hesitated, he simply put the car in drive. "Where to?"

In minutes we were parked at the end of my block, the rhythmic whoosh and slide of the wipers filling the car. "Thanks for the ride. And the cheering up."

"Anytime." I reached for the door handle, and he pulled me back in for one last searing, searching kiss. "Don't make me come and find you, Del."

He couldn't, even if he tried.

I waited until he was gone, then hurried across the yard and up the steps, checking for any signs of movement inside. There was nothing; the entire house stood like a tomb, and the door screeched with protest as I opened it again.

My earlier shoe prints were visible in the dust carpeting the hallway, leading back up the stairs to my room. But I saw something else, too: a path through the dust that had been rubbed out. Not footprints, but the marks of someone trying to hide them.

END OF FIRST MOVEMENT

BEGIN
SECOND
MOVEMENT

CHAPTER TWENTY-ONE

Time spent in Echoes cannot be regained in the Key World. Be aware that events will progress in your absence.

—Chapter Two, "Navigation,"
Principles and Practices of Cleaving, Year Five

I WOKE SUNDAY MORNING WITH GRITTY EYES and nerves stretched to breaking. I'd spent half the night convinced my parents had caught me sneaking out, and the other half certain I was imagining things. There'd been no footprints in the hallway other than my own. The smear of dust could have been an animal, or a gust of air from the door opening and closing. Viewed through the lens of a guilty conscience, even the smallest details look damning.

Addie's smile when I slunk into the kitchen, for example. She was never happy to see me, so there had to be another reason for her good mood. A small, panicked part of my brain worried she'd been the one who caught me, but a slow boil wasn't her style. If she discovered I was sneaking out, she wouldn't wait five minutes to bust me, let alone five hours.

"Why are you so happy?" I demanded, fumbling for a mug of coffee.

"Lattimer approved my lesson plans for this week. He said I was very efficient."

"When did you see him?" I didn't trust his sudden interest in my progress. Lattimer was definitely the sort who would spy on me and save the information for a time when it could do the most damage.

Addie looked at me strangely, gathering up a sheaf of papers and tucking them in her bag. "I e-mailed him. His reply came through about fifteen minutes ago."

Not Lattimer, then.

"You two have big plans this morning?" asked my dad, coming in from his workshop. He hugged me with one arm and grabbed a muffin from the counter.

"We're going to the train station," Addie said, and he nodded approval.

"New or old?"

"New," she said. "More for Del to work with."

I groaned. "If I have to draw one more map, Addie, I'll quit. I don't care if the Consort never lets me Walk again."

"This suspension isn't a joke," my dad said sternly.

"Who says I'm joking?" I slouched over the table, checking my phone. Nothing from Eliot, but I did have a text from Simon, confirming our study date at the library that afternoon.

"Chill out," Addie said. "If you fail the exam, you're going to make me look bad."

"Can't have that, can we?" I said, and my father gave me a quelling look.

"Lattimer agrees we should pick up where we left off before your suspension," Addie said. "Try not to cleave anything this time."

"Very funny." My stomach rolled, and I decided to pass on the muffin. "I have plans after lunch, by the way. School stuff."

My dad dropped a hand on my shoulder. "I'm sure your sister can be flexible. It's nice to see you paying attention to your schoolwork."

Addie kept her voice deliberately casual. "What are you and Mom doing today?"

"Your mother's already downtown. She needed the Consort's computers. The team's meeting me here in a few minutes, and then we're heading out for the day."

"They must be complicated cleavings," Addie said, and my dad nodded before catching himself.

"Nothing you need to worry about," he said, ruffling her hair on his way to the garage. "I'll see you later."

After he'd left, Addie turned to me. "Do you have any idea how much processing power the Consort computers use?"

"Lots?"

She sighed. "Yes, lots. They make NASA's computers look like somebody's science fair project."

Clearly she'd never seen one of Eliot's science fair projects. I missed him fiercely at the reminder. Usually we'd be together by now, on our way downtown for training. "I'm more interested in the fact that it's a local Echo."

"Local?"

"Dad's team usually meets at the Consort building and walks from there. If they're meeting here, whatever branch they're dealing with is nearby." I grinned. "Bet we could find it."

She hesitated and shook her head. "Lattimer signed off on today's lesson. We stick to the plan."

"There's a plan?" asked Monty, appearing in the doorway. "You look tired, Del. Late night?"

I jerked, sending a flood of coffee across the counter. Addie scooped up papers, shrieking, "Del, grab a towel!" while I stared at my grandfather.

I mopped up the coffee as best I could. When Addie's back was turned, I whispered, "That was you?"

He winked, but before I could grill him further, Addie was hustling us out the door.

"Let's review: You're going to locate the vibrato fractums, test them, record the results, and move on," Addie said after we crossed through one of the zillion pivots surrounding the train station.

"Got it," I said. "Find the breaks, get a reading. Lather, rinse, repeat."

Transportation hubs were typically crammed with pivots, and public transit was particularly prone. Flying took planning; by the time a person arrived at the airport, most of their decisions had been made. Trains, subways, and buses were more flexible and more populated, allowing for more interactions.

The Echo we'd stopped in was busier than home. People milled about on the platform, waiting for the next train, and a farmers' market was set up in the parking lot, drawing a crowd. The pivots sounded like popcorn, irregular bursts of sound, and the pitch was a flat monotone that receded into the background. The breaks, on the other hand, stood out in sharp relief. I shook my head, trying to get my bearings.

"No cleaving," Addie continued. "No touching the strings. No flirting with boys or interfering with stable Echoes or picking pockets."

"No fun," I grumbled. "Can I get started?"

"Yes. I'll be right over—Grandpa, come back!" She chased after Monty, who had crossed the street and was peering in the window of a candy store.

I didn't need Eliot's map to help me. The tremors were perfectly audible. But I checked the screen anyway, noting a smattering of emerging breaks and several established spots. One on the platform of the station, one in the farmers' market, and one centered at the ticket window of a dollar movie theater across the street.

If Eliot and I had gone to movie night as planned, we never would have fought.

On the other hand, if we'd gone to movie night, Simon wouldn't have taught me how to make a free throw. He wouldn't have left me standing on the floor while he went off to do God knows what with Bree. I wouldn't have ended up in his Echo's car, breathless and molten.

Every choice we make is both a sacrifice and an opportunity. I wondered if mine had been worth it.

I didn't want to think about Eliot and movie night, so I headed into the farmers' market, listening closely. The crowd worked to my advantage; I could take my readings and jot down a note before anyone noticed I was there. A stand selling honey, a bluegrass trio playing for spare change, a couple holding hands as they looked at bunches of kale: all vibrato fractums, none severe enough to justify a cleaving. The more I wandered the aisles, the more breaks I found, my head swimming. I turned, searching for Addie, but she was obscured by the crush of people.

I bought a steaming cup of apple cider from one of the booths, hoping it would settle me, and heard a familiar laugh.

Simon stood on the corner in a red anorak, hair cut military short, holding hands with a black-haired girl. He pulled her in for a kiss, their bodies fusing together.

Jealousy flared, then died away. Taken separately, the breaks here were insignificant. But cumulatively they might be enough to pose a threat. When I turned in my report, would this world be cleaved? Would I have caused another Simon to unravel? Dizzy and sick at heart, I sank onto the curb.

"It's not lost yet," said Monty from somewhere above me.

"Yet," I said morosely. "How soon will they come to cleave it?"

"Depends." He helped me up. "There's always another way, Del."

Through the crowd, I caught a flash of red. "He's not real. None of this is."

"If that's true, what's got you so upset?"

I didn't have an answer, and he patted my arm. "We can tune the breaks, you know. Tune enough, and they'll ignore this world. I can teach you."

"Grandpa," I said, shaking my head. "We have to cleave. It's what we do."

"What *they* do," he said. "You're better."

Laughter scraped against my throat. "I'm not better. I'm suspended. Tuning breaks instead of reporting them would get me expelled. Addie would turn me over to Lattimer in a heartbeat."

At the mention of Lattimer's name, the fight went out of Monty. He seemed to curl in on himself. "Don't tell," he said, his reedy voice turning small. "Don't tell."

"I won't." I took his hand in mine. "You followed me last night, didn't you?"

"I never left the house," he said primly. "Wanted to know where you were, to make sure you came home safe. I won't tell either."

"Thanks," I said, and gave him the rest of my cider. "Let's find Addie and get out of here."

He nodded, waiting as I nestled a star at the base of the tree.

Addie was sitting on a bench by the train station, watching the kale-loving couple I'd spotted earlier climb into a battered red pickup truck. "Did you get your readings?"

I handed her my notebook and she scanned the entries. "Nice. I'll turn these in when we get home. Good work, Del."

It didn't feel good, but I managed a smile.

• • •

We hit three more Echoes. None had as many breaks as the first, which was a relief, and none contained an Echo Simon. Monty was quiet for the rest of the trip, singing to himself and methodically working his way through a bag of jelly beans. My dizziness faded, but a headache crept across my skull, clamping down with iron fingers.

"One more stop," Addie said.

"Do they serve lunch?" Monty grumbled. "The least you could do is feed an old man."

"Lunch?" My stomach dropped. "What time is it?"

Addie checked her watch. "Oh, wow. Nearly two."

"I'm late!" I took off for the nearest pivot, Addie and Monty following behind.

"Late for what?" Addie called. "Del, wait up!"

Fixing the Key World frequency in my mind, I burst through the pivot back home and headed for the library, a few blocks away. My headache eased, but not my panic.

"I'm supposed to meet someone," I said when Addie and Monty caught up to me at an intersection. I jammed my thumb against the walk button, but the light didn't change any faster. "I was, anyway. An hour ago."

"Your school project? Since when do you worry about school on the weekends?"

"I promised my partner."

"Since when do you care about promises?"

I hit the library at a dead run, heading for the group study rooms. The woman at the reference desk shot me a dirty look.

The glass-windowed rooms stood empty. There was no sign of Simon. I cursed under my breath, earning a second glare.

"Is there another study area?" I asked the librarian.

"Just the desks," she said stiffly, and pointed to a group of tables.

"Was there anyone here earlier? In the study rooms?"

"I saw a young man, closer to lunchtime," she said. "He left."

I checked my phone and groaned. We didn't get cell service in Echoes, but judging from the string of texts Simon had sent, he'd assumed I was ignoring him.

Here.

Where u at?

Booooorrrrred.

U OK?

WTF?

Time is finite. Minutes spent in Echoes are lost in the Key World. It's the cost of Walking, we're taught, and it was a price I'd been happy to pay.

Until today.

On the way home I sent Simon a string of apologies, but my screen stayed dark. No messages from Eliot, either.

U mad? I texted Eliot, while curled up on the threadbare chaise in my room. There was no reply. Maybe he was out with our class. Maybe he was so focused on debugging his map software that he didn't hear the chime. Maybe he was ignoring me.

Sorry. Really. Miss u. I picked up the violin, trying out a few melodies for the composition project. None of them were right—too mournful, too insipid, too clichéd—and I couldn't keep my eyes off my phone.

Patience was never one of my strong suits. I took a deep breath and dialed.

"Hey," I said when Eliot picked up. "Did you get my texts?"

"Yeah." Definitely mad.

"I'm sorry. I was out of line."

"I know."

I began to pace. "I was pissy about Simon blowing me off, and I took it out on you."

"I know."

"And I was sick of Addie acting superior, and I have to put up with it until this stupid suspension is over, and I took that out on you too."

"I *know*," he said, not hiding his exasperation.

"You're very smart. And probably right about Simon." Before he could tell me he knew that, too, I rushed on. "How was class today?"

There was a pause. "Fine. Quiet."

"I'll bet. Did you show your map to Shaw?"

"Not yet. I want it to be perfect."

"Nothing's perfect," I reminded him. "Not even me."

"Definitely not you." Warmth trickled back into his voice, the first signs of a thaw.

"But you love me anyway," I said, giddy with relief.

Another pause. "It's late. I'll see you tomorrow, okay?"

"I'll be here," I said.

I couldn't sleep, imagining the look on Simon's face when he'd finally given up on me. I worked on our composition, but my fingering was clumsy, my pacing off, the melody hovering just out of reach. Maybe a trip to see Doughnut Simon would help. Without thinking, I moved toward the pivot—and then stopped. Another make-out session would be a distraction, not a solution. Eliot might be on the path to forgiving me, but Simon was another question entirely.

Tomorrow, I'd have my answer.

CHAPTER TWENTY-TWO

Judging from the stiff line of Simon's back when I slunk into music the next day, forgiveness was a long way off.

"I'm sorry," I whispered as Powell started the day's lecture. Simon stayed immobile, the chill coming off him practically visible. "I had a family thing."

He leaned over to Bree and murmured inaudibly. She dipped her head toward him, giggling, and Powell frowned at us over her cat-eye glasses.

"Change of plans," she said. "Take fifteen minutes to check in with your partner, make sure everyone's on the same page."

The class split up, but Simon continued to face front.

"Hey." I tapped him on the shoulder. "I said I was sorry."

"Everything okay, you two?" Powell asked, arms folded.

"Great," I said through clenched teeth.

"Simon?"

He sank down farther in his chair. "Awesome."

"Sounds like it," she replied dryly, and circled the room.

"You can't ignore me for the whole project," I said.

"You blew me off!" he growled, spinning around. He looked

more shocked than angry. For Simon, being stood up was probably as incomprehensible as gravity failing.

"Not intentionally. I was out with my family and I lost track of time. And I apologized."

"So what? You're as bad as everyone says," he shot back.

Guilt shifted to temper. "Everyone? Or Bree? How was the party, by the way? Did you two have a nice ride?"

A muscle in his jaw twitched. "You blew me off because you were pissed about the party?"

"Please. Like I care."

"Then why'd you bail?"

"I didn't bail! I had to do something with my sister and it went longer than expected." When his expression didn't soften, I added, "Here. I worked on this last night."

"It's supposed to be a team project," he said, taking the staff paper from me.

"Fine. You do the next part and I'll take a nap," I said. "It's a peace offering, you jerk."

He stared down at the notes. "I don't know what any of this means. Does it sound decent?"

"Of course it does." I moved to Powell's piano. Grudgingly he joined me on the bench, and I played the opening measures.

"It's nice," he admitted. "It sounds like . . . I don't know. Rainy nights."

"A little bit, maybe." I'd taken the music from the band at Grundy's and improvised, adding and subtracting until the song was both familiar and new. Kind of like Simon.

"The party sucked," he said.

"Bummer." Impossible to keep the satisfaction from my voice.

"Would have been better if you'd come." There was no gleam or charm to his words this time, only a quiet honesty that brushed away the remnants of my hurt.

I kept my eyes on the music and my voice light. "Wasn't invited."

He pressed a low C. "I'm sorry. I should have . . ."

I shrugged. "We're even."

"Guess so." The dark blue of his eyes turned thoughtful. "Play it again."

He traced the notes as I played, and I couldn't help remembering the feel of his fingers against my cheek as we'd stood in the rain.

"How do you keep the notes straight?" he asked. "The minute the parts start going in different directions, I'm lost."

"Perfect pitch, remember? I can hold the notes in my head more clearly. Plus, I've been playing violin since I was four."

"Definitely a prodigy," he said, shaking his head. "Your whole family is musical? Even your sister?"

"Addie's good at everything." I rolled my eyes. "Wait. Addie's *perfect* at everything. Good isn't good enough."

I was accustomed to thinking of our abilities as genetic, but Simon's question spurred one of my own. If Walking was my birthright, why did I feel like such an outsider in my own family?

"Could perfect write this? I don't think so." The words were teasing, but there was an undercurrent of sympathy to them. "Perfect is boring. No challenge to it. And you know how I love a challenge."

Flustered, I turned the conversation back on him. "What about you? Brothers or sisters?"

"Neither. I was all the kid my mom could handle," he said, a note of wistfulness creeping in. "It would be nice, though. Especially now."

"Why now?" I asked.

He bumped his shoulder into mine, mouth curving. "I could make them do my homework."

I glanced down at the half-filled score. "I can finish it at home. It's no problem."

"I told you, it's a team project." He scooped up the pages and held them out of reach. This Simon, it seemed, had a stubborn streak. "You don't play well with others, do you?"

Eliot, sitting a few feet away, made a choking sound. I twisted in my seat and glared at him. He put his hands up and made a show of turning his attention to Bree.

"I play fine," I said through gritted teeth.

"Glad to hear it. We're never going to finish this here, you know. Let's get together and"—he tapped the score and leered comically—"make beautiful music."

I threw one of the crumpled papers at him. "Very funny."

"Couldn't resist," he said, batting it back at me. "Look, Del. I need this grade."

I scoffed. "You're not failing the class. Everyone says you're a lock for a basketball scholarship. Who's going to care about your music grade?"

"My mom." He looked genuinely worried. "How about Thursday? I've got three games this week, and my other nights are kind of shot."

Spending time with him outside of school wasn't a hardship. "My sister has taken over my weeknights. What about Saturday?"

"Away game," he said apologetically. "Sunday?"

A full week before I could see him alone, away from school. I fought back disappointment. "Sure, as long as it's in the afternoon. Library again?"

"We need a piano, don't we? What about your house?"

The last thing I needed was Simon running into my family. "What about your place?"

"I don't have a piano." He tapped his pencil, a quick 7/8 rhythm. He might be tone-deaf, but he wasn't totally hopeless when it came to music. "You don't want me to come to your house. What are you hiding, Delancey Sullivan?"

"Nothing." Everything. I wasn't used to people seeing me—really seeing me. At home everything I did was eclipsed by Addie's performance or my parents' work. At school I kept to the fringes, the girl with the wild hair and the thrift-store clothes and the bad attitude, and I cultivated my isolation like a shield.

People see what they expect. Their minds are conditioned to smooth away the impossible until it's transformed to the probable. Seeing the truth requires patience and attention, and seeing the truth of a person is even harder.

But Simon saw me. In the Key World, in Echoes, he saw me in a way that no one else did, and he didn't look away. It was terrifying, and magnetic, and addictive. I couldn't help worrying that one of these days he'd see too much. "You're not exactly rolling out the welcome mat either. What are *you* hiding?"

His pencil skidded over the paper, a slash of black. "Nothing."

Never try to con a con, Monty said. But I smiled as if I believed Simon. "Okay, then. Sunday afternoon at my place."

"Sunday," he agreed. Relief washed over his entire body, the tension ebbing from his shoulders and jaw, his lazy smile coming back. "It's a date."

CHAPTER TWENTY-THREE

Isolating break threads is part of cleaving protocol. By determining which strings are responsible for an Echo's instability, the cleaving can be rendered more efficiently. Be advised, however: Direct contact with a vibrato fractum increases sensitivity to frequency poisoning.

—Chapter Five, "Physics,"
Principles and Practices of Cleaving, Year Five

Y OU SAID YOU WANTED SOMETHING DIFFERent," Addie said, when we went out for a quick lesson later that afternoon.

"I spend eight hours a day here," I said. "This isn't different; it's cruel."

At the Original Washington, only the sports teams were still around, practicing. Here, the halls were crowded with kids in tan pants and maroon sweaters.

"Blame Grandpa," she said. "It was his turn to pick."

When I looked over at Monty, he was mumbling to himself, tugging at the buttons on his sweater. "Why this one, Grandpa?"

"Sounded right."

It did, actually. Strident but stable, with no nearby breaks. It was as safe as an Echo could get.

Addie gestured to the students filing quietly past us. "This *is* different," she said. "You wouldn't last ten minutes in those uniforms."

I looked down at my ripped jeans and "runs with scissors" T-shirt. She had a point. Around us the corridor was rapidly emptying.

"I want something new. Something exciting."

"Exciting is another word for trouble. Which you have more than enough of." Addie headed toward the cafeteria, calling over her shoulder, "We can go home and catch up on your reading, if you'd rather."

Monty shot me a look of apology and followed her.

I trailed after them, twirling the dials of each locker I passed. They spun too freely under my hand, and on instinct I yanked on one. The door sprang open, revealing a tan canvas coat and neatly stacked books. I tried the next one and found the same thing. Four in a row, completely identical.

What kind of high school had no locks on its lockers?

One where theft wasn't a problem.

And privacy wasn't a concern, as evidenced by the surveillance cameras mounted at both ends of the hall. They shouldn't pick me up, unless I touched an Echo—but their presence made me uneasy.

"Cafeteria," Addie called back, and I hurried to catch up. The tables stood in perfectly straight rows. I ran a hand over one, the laminate pristine. At home the lunchroom tables were pitted and carved from years of student graffiti. Monty circled the room, poking at each brick as if he was reading their individual frequencies. Addie watched him for a moment and then turned back to me.

"We're isolating break threads," she said. "So tell me why I picked the cafeteria."

"Not for the smell." The universal scent of disinfectant and boiled vegetables permeated the air. I breathed through my mouth, adding, "Lots of repetitive choices. People choose the same meals and the same seats every day. The pivots sound monotonous, so the breaks stand out more clearly."

She nodded in satisfaction. "Once the Consort authorizes a cleaving, the next step is to isolate the unstable strings. They're the first ones you'll cut, but you have to fix them beforehand."

"Why?"

"If you start cutting while the threads are unstable, the cleaving won't heal properly, and the damage will spread." She gestured to a whiteboard with the day's menu. "Try this one."

I laid my palm flat against it, bracing myself for the tremor of the break. "Doesn't sound too bad."

"Nope. We aren't dealing with anything that would require cleaving. We're finding the thread and letting go. I'll help you through the first few. Curl your fingers and catch the break, like when you choose a frequency midpivot."

I did, the movement natural and familiar. The break intensified, traveling over my skin. I twitched reflexively, and Addie smiled. "You get used to it. Now, keep your hand in contact with the break, and . . ." She broke off as I crooked my index finger, gathering up a group of threads. On instinct I slid my other hand along them and began sorting through them by touch, humming lightly. *Nimble fingers, open mind . . .*

Most of the strings felt smooth and taut, resonating in unison. But one vibrated out of sync with the rest, its surface kinked and rough, and I transferred it to my other hand, shuddering at the contact. *Hum a tune both deft and kind . . .*

"What next?"

Wordlessly Addie reached into the break, her hands covering mine and feeling for the threads. When her hand closed around the one I'd separated, she drew back as if burned. "Let go. Right now."

I did, withdrawing my hands and dragging them down the sides of my jeans, trying to scrub off the feeling of the faulty string. "Did I screw up?"

"No. You did great." She peered at me. "When did you learn that?"

"Um . . . three minutes ago."

"That wasn't your first time isolating a thread." She turned her hands over. "It takes tons of practice. Have you been messing around on your own?"

I didn't think my solo Walks were what she meant, but I picked my words carefully. "I've never tried that before. Ever. I swear."

"How did you know what to do?"

"I don't know! It was instinct, I guess. My hands kind of took over my brain." *Nimble fingers, open mind.*

"You must have picked it up somewhere. From someone."

She straightened and looked around. "Where's Monty?"

The cafeteria was empty.

"Perfect," she muttered. "We'd better track him down."

We headed out the double doors, into an eerie silence. Class was in session, but unlike home, there were no stragglers. No sign of Monty either. I asked, "Which way?"

"I'll go left; you go right. Bring him back to the cafeteria."

"What if he's crossed a pivot?" I called.

"Then he can find his own way back," she snapped. "No. Find me and we'll track him down together."

I headed toward what was the music wing back home. Here it looked like tech classes—industrial equipment and car parts were visible through the windows. I'd wring Monty's neck when I found him. The first time Addie taught me something good, and he'd spoiled it. He was probably off looking for dessert.

Intent on listening for pivots, I hadn't realized someone was rounding the corner until he slammed into me. I fell backward, swearing.

"Watch where you're going!" Simon snapped.

"You?" I was losing track of how many Simons I'd found. Sometimes the strings making up an Echo would cross with the Key World, causing duplication, but I'd never heard of it happening this often. I rubbed my stinging elbow. "I'm fine, thanks. Don't bother to help me up."

He paused and held out his hand. I took it, nearly gasping as the break in his frequency crashed into me. He looked me over, annoyance changing to amusement. "Nice uniform."

"I'm not really a uniform kind of girl."

"Excellent. Maybe they'll leave me alone and go after you."

Now I studied him more closely—he wore the same tan pants and sweater as the students I'd seen earlier, but the chinos were threadbare, hanging low on his hips, and his hair stood in unruly, gelled spikes, porcupine-style. His frequency wasn't the only volatile thing about him.

"They?"

His smile flashed. A tattoo circled around his wrist—a vine, intricate tendrils spiraling across his skin. My mouth went dry.

"They won't care if you're new, either," he said. "'Ignorance of the rules is no excuse for breaking them.' They never mention the part where they keep us ignorant about the real world."

Okay. Clearly this was Angry Dystopian Simon. Monty's choice made more sense now. A world with fewer choices made for a more stable environment, and the breaks would be easier to identify. In his own way, he'd been trying to help. "I'm just visiting."

"Lucky girl."

"You'd think so, wouldn't you? Are you supposed to be somewhere? Everyone else . . ."

"Do I look like everyone else?" He braced an arm against the wall, leaning so close his breath feathered across my cheek.

"No," I squeaked, and he laughed.

"I got called down to the office. You're making me late." He didn't sound bothered. "Might as well cut. Want to come with?"

"Cut?" This was new—Simon as the rule breaker, me as the

voice of reason. "What happens if they catch us?"

"I'm already in trouble," he said, and took my hand, tugging me toward the nearest door. He was in more trouble than he knew. His break was stronger than any of the ones in the cafeteria. If I'd listened to Monty the other day, I could have tuned him. "What's a little more?"

"Del! Where are you going?"

Addie clipped down the hallway, boots clicking on the linoleum, Monty in tow. I couldn't let her hear Simon's signal. She'd know immediately that he was a break, and she'd report it. "I can't really handle any more trouble today. But you should go."

"You're sure?" he asked.

"Another time," I said, not meaning it, but desperate to get him away from Addie's scrutiny. "Someone's coming."

He turned on his heel and strolled away, moving fast without seeming to rush.

"You were supposed to stay with us," I scolded Monty when Simon was out of earshot.

"He was in the office. We're lucky nobody saw him." She squinted at Simon's retreating form. "Is that the basketball player?"

"Kind of." Before she could say anything else, I asked, "Back to the cafeteria?"

"As long as Grandpa stays put," she said.

"Bah. I'm here now, aren't I?" he replied, unabashed. "Let's see how she handles those breaks."

I handled them pretty easily, to Addie's continued surprise. How I'd handled Simon's break was more worrisome.

. . .

Seeing Simon at the reform school, as I'd privately christened it, had put Addie on high alert. For the rest of the week, everywhere we Walked, she looked for him. More often than not, we found him.

There was Simon the drummer, who wore black T-shirts that clung to his biceps and had a line of eyebrow piercings. Shy Simon, who helped me reach a library book I had no intention of checking out and vanished into the stacks. Simon the science geek, who spent the better part of an hour discussing relativity with me until Addie shot down his theory with basic Walker physics. Simon the horndog, who managed to ask Addie *and* me out in the space of fifteen minutes. ("Not my type," she'd responded, witheringly. I'd laughed all the way home.)

"I'm telling you," Addie said. "There's something strange about him."

"It's nothing," I said, checking my phone. Eliot hadn't made much progress researching the problems in Park World, but his map was running smoothly. "Every Walk we take is either at school or in town. He's not the only Echo we keep seeing."

Bree Carlson, for example, though she never noticed me. She shifted as dramatically as Simon did, from Goth to cheer-leader to teacher's pet. In some Echoes she and Simon were obviously a couple, but in others they barely crossed paths. I liked to think the lack of continuity between their Echoes was a sign they weren't supposed to be together in the Key World, where Bree was pursuing Simon like a lioness about to take down a really tall, hot zebra.

"Yeah, but Simon's the one you keep running into. It's not an accident, Del. You're looking for him."

"He's easy to look at." In truth, his frequent appearances unnerved me, too. But aside from Dystopian Simon, his recent Echoes had sounded stable, so I chalked it up to coincidence.

This time we'd found Simon the student council president. Clean-scrubbed, smart and sensible, and not a member of the basketball team. Instead, he was running the concession stand with Bree.

"Who knew filling the popcorn machine was so tough?" I muttered the third time Bree needed Simon's help to make a fresh batch.

"Who cares? The break's somewhere in the concession stand. Isolate it, we'll grab Grandpa and Eliot, and go home."

Monty had wandered off too many times recently, so we'd pressed poor Eliot into service—they were inside watching the game and tracking pivots while we worked in the nearly deserted lobby. Bree's laughter trailed across the room, and Simon's answering chuckle followed.

"Gladly," I said. Simon's back was to me, and Bree was too focused on him to notice anything else—least of all a Walker.

"Cassidy's having people over after the game," Bree was saying. "We should check it out."

"For a few minutes," he said.

"A few?" She pretended to pout, lowered her voice to a purr. "We'd have fun. I guarantee it."

"I bet," he said, a smile in his tone. Jealousy squeezed my lungs.

"Excuse me," I said, leaning over the counter. My fingertips barely touched his elbow, but his frequency—like the feedback from a microphone—ricocheted through me.

Simon turned, his smile broadening. "What can I get you?"

Damn it. *He* was the break, same as at the reform school. This time I couldn't hide him from Addie. My mind raced, and he frowned. "You know what you want?"

For you to stabilize. "A Coke, please."

Bree's gaze shifted to me, and I could feel her annoyance from ten feet away, as clear as Simon's break.

He plucked the can from a cooler and handed it over, melting ice dripping over our hands. "Buck fifty."

"Thanks." I threw the money on the counter and fled back to Addie.

"You didn't do anything," she said.

"He's the break. It's not the counter or the cash box. It's him."

She barely looked up from her map. "So? Go back there and isolate the threads."

My heartbeat quieted. If Addie thought it was no big deal, maybe I'd overreacted. "How? I can't go up and start manhandling him."

"Like that would bother you? You don't have to touch him directly—we do that with beginners, because it's easier. You've got a radius of about three feet to work in. Go on." She shooed me away.

"Working up a thirst?" Simon asked as I returned.

"Something like that." I slid the money toward him. When

he reached for the cooler again, he moved out of range. I'd need to keep him talking.

"So, you're going to Cassidy's party?" I asked.

He handed over the can, looking at me with fresh interest. "Not sure yet. You?"

"Possibly." Below the counter, I caught a fistful of threads and started sorting through them. Hard to explain my twitching fingers without sounding crazy. I pitched my voice low and flirtatious. "It's not my usual scene."

Bree was pouring oil into the popcorn machine, but she glanced over at us, her nose wrinkling. Simon leaned toward me, elbows on the counter. "What is?"

"I heard there's a band at Grundy's tonight that's pretty good." I was too intent on checking the strings to be original. The thread leaped under my fingertips, rough as twine, and I exhaled in relief.

"Did you need anything else?" Bree asked, sliding her arm around his waist. "Honey, I need you to help me with the popcorn machine again."

Honey. I'd found the string but misread Simon completely. My grip tightened without thinking.

Around me the world jerked and stuttered. Alarmed, I let go of the strings and cast a panicked look at Addie, who was already speeding toward us.

"We're set," she said, and hustled me away. When we reached the opposite corner, she glared at me. "I told you to find it, not play it like a banjo."

"My hand slipped. The string's okay, right? I didn't . . ."

"You didn't cleave it," she said, but the break screeched, piercing my eardrum. Addie clapped her hands over her ears and stared at Simon. A moment later Monty and Eliot joined us.

"That was you, wasn't it?" Eliot asked. "I saw the break on the map. It looked like a firecracker went off."

"Of course it was her," Addie snapped.

"How do I fix it?" I turned to Monty, battling back fear. "Can we tune it?"

"Walkers cleave," he reminded me, pious as a saint. "We don't tune."

The words felt like a punishment. "Addie, please. If the Consort thinks I ruined another world . . ."

"I'll take care of it," said Addie, voice tight. She shoved her leather bag at me. "The three of you stay put. And for God's sake, Del, stay away from Simon."

She crossed the room swiftly, standing to the side of the concession stand. Her chest rose as she dragged in a breath, eyes shut. Her hand drifted up until her arm was parallel to the ground, her fingers making tiny, fluid, graceful movements. She was playing the strings, adjusting their pitch to match the rest of this world.

Beads of sweat popped up along her hairline, and stress lines bracketed the corners of her mouth, but she never faltered. Gradually the shrieking ebbed away, the break disappearing. When I looked at Simon, he and Bree were talking as if everything was normal. We'd been the only ones to notice the difference.

Addie kept working, her breathing shallow, her cheeks pale, her fingers patiently curling and smoothing threads the rest of us couldn't see. Finally she exhaled, long and slow. She staggered, and I dashed across the room to catch her.

"You okay, Addie-girl?" Monty asked.

She opened her eyes. "Yeah. Don't let me see you try that, Del. You aren't ready."

"Got it," I said, too relieved to take offense.

Later I ducked my head into Addie's room, marveling at the ruthless tidiness. Not a piece of clothing on the floor, not a single book lying facedown on the green wool rug. She looked up from her laptop. "What's wrong now?"

"Nothing. I wanted to say thanks for tonight. You saved my ass."

She shrugged. "I'm here to help. You've never wanted it before."

"I thought you didn't believe in tuning."

"I don't. You saw how hard it was. We can't tune every break, Del. We can't save every world."

I stepped inside and sat on the edge of her bed. "Why did you do it?"

She set the laptop aside and drew her knees to her chest. "Despite what you think, I'm not completely heartless."

"I don't—"

"You do. Everyone does." She pressed her lips together, but not before I saw the slight wobble. "They think I put the Walkers above everything else because I don't care. That's not true. But caring too much makes you lose sight of the bigger picture. Without the Walkers we'd lose everything, including the people we love. Caring is a luxury, Del, and not everyone can afford it."

Addie had never spoken about Walking with such bitterness and resignation. She'd always said it was a calling, the thing she loved best. But now, as she rubbed a hand over her eyes, I started to wonder if it was all she'd ever loved.

"You're not heartless," I said firmly. "A heartless person would not have helped me tonight."

She waved away the words. "I should have stepped in earlier. I forgot you hadn't isolated a person before. They're harder to manage."

"Because they're moving?" I'd been so distracted by Simon and Bree, I'd lost my focus.

"People are unpredictable," she said. "It makes them dangerous."

"Your grandfather's already in bed," my mom said from the doorway. "Did everything go okay tonight?"

"Nothing I couldn't handle," Addie said. "How about you guys? Are you making any progress?"

My mom frowned. "That's classified information, Addison."

Addie drew back at the sharpness in her tone. "I only asked how it was going."

"It's going. You don't need to know more than that." She raised her eyebrows, probably surprised we weren't ripping each other's hair out. "You're sure tonight went well?"

I held my breath. It would be easy enough for Addie to tell her what I'd done. Mom would freak out and insist we shift back to more remedial work.

But Addie closed her laptop with a decisive click. "I think Del learned a lot this evening."

I thought about the rush of jealousy that had overtaken me, how my instincts had nearly ruined everything, and decided Addie was right.

CHAPTER TWENTY-FOUR

Upon an Original's death, each of their Echoes begins to unravel. Depending on the strength and complexity of their branch, these terminal Echoes unravel at different rates—in some cases up to twenty years after the Original's death. To onlookers it appears as a natural death. Terminal Echoes are easily identified by their complete absence of pitch.

—Chapter Five, "Physics,"
Principles and Practices of Cleaving, Year Five

MORNING, KIDDO," SAID MY DAD. MY MATtress tilted under his weight, and I opened my eyes slowly, blinking away the remnants of a dream where our house unraveled, shimmering away to a gray void. "Brought you some coffee."

Fragrant steam rose from the mug he held out to me, and I struggled upright, scooting back against my iron headboard.

"Daddy?" I'd barely seen him over the past few days. "What's up?"

"I'm heading out on a big Walk. Thought I'd check in before I left."

"You're working? What about the concert?" Another one of my parents' constants—one Saturday a month they took us to the symphony. It was my father's attempt to teach us how to enjoy music for its own sake. I grumbled about being forced to spend an afternoon with my family, but canceling was unthinkable. Whatever they were dealing with must be really bad.

"Maybe next week," he said, but he stared at the floor when he said it, and I knew "maybe" actually meant "not a chance."

"Could I come with today?" When I was little, my dad used to take me on Walks as a special treat. Never to cleavings—my mom had forbidden it—but on the preliminary trips, to monitor breaks. As long as I promised to stick close and hold his hand through every crossing, he'd let me tag along. "I won't get in the way, but maybe I could help?"

"No can do," he said. "It's a big job. Lots to keep track of, and I can't have the team distracted."

I took a tiny sip of coffee, syrupy with sugar, and said nothing.

He ruffled my hair, which only made me feel more like a kid, and I twisted away. "Love you, Del."

I didn't answer.

"You hurt your father's feelings," Mom said when I finally came downstairs.

I dug in the fridge for a piece of last night's pizza—another dinner on our own—and didn't respond.

"This is hard on all of us. We're not thrilled about having to work these kinds of hours, but it's got to be done."

I turned around, slice in hand. "Why? What's the big emergency?"

Addie and Monty were sitting at the kitchen table, poring over an old map. He plucked the pen from her hand and circled something. Addie sighed with exaggerated patience and spun around to face us. "Mom, you're working like crazy. I could help."

"This is beyond your skills," Mom replied, missing the hurt that flashed across Addie's face. She pinched the bridge of her nose and tried again. "I appreciate the offer, but Daddy and I don't want you involved. "

"But—"

"But nothing. If you want to help, be extra careful on your Walks. That's one less thing to be worried about. Del, eat a real breakfast."

I held up the pizza. "Grains, dairy, vegetables—"

"Rose says tomatoes are a fruit," Monty said.

"Sorry. Fruit," I said. "It's a well-balanced meal. And you could at least tell us why it's so hush-hush. We have a right to know why we've been orphaned."

I'd meant it as a joke, but my mom's lips flattened into a thin, bloodless line.

"Your father and I have a duty," she said, biting off the words. "Not only to you, but to the Walkers and the Key World. I realize responsibility is a foreign concept for you, but we take it seriously."

The words felt like a slap, a numbness that quickly turned to a vicious sting. For the last two weeks I'd done everything Addie asked—passed every test, read every textbook, even when they were so boring I would have rather watched paint dry. I'd baby-sat Monty and given up time with Eliot.

And for what? My dad thought I was a distraction; my mom thought I was selfish. What was the point in trying to change when my own parents thought so little of me? If they couldn't see I was trying, how would the Consort?

Even Monty was silent, and Addie bent over her map so far that her nose nearly brushed the paper.

"I'm late for my train," Mom said.

I threw the pizza into the trash, appetite gone.

"She's tired," Addie said softly after Mom had left. "She didn't mean it."

"Whatever." Sympathy was harder to bear than bossiness. "Are we going out today?"

She looked at the paper in front of her, her graceful cursive and Monty's scrawls mingled together, then studied me as if I were another map. "You up for more isolations? People, not objects. We'll even make it back in time for you and Eliot to have movie night."

Eliot and I were supposed to go over data he'd found about Park World, but suddenly I couldn't see the point in trying. Movie night sounded infinitely better: a few hours with my best friend and a chance to forget about Walking and cleaving and Echoes that didn't act the way they should.

"Del?" Addie asked again. "You ready to head out?"

Anything was better than sitting at home, where I would never measure up. "Absolutely. Are you coming, Grandpa?"

"Nowhere I'd rather be," he said.

• • •

"I'm hungry," said Monty, hours later. We'd traveled to countless Echoes, locating people with breaks and isolating their threads. Happily, none of them had been Simon. "Time to head home, girls."

Addie checked her watch. "Ugh. No wonder I have a migraine. Last one, Del. What do you hear?"

A frequency that was eerily similar to Park World, only more stable. My ears were ringing from the sheer amount of time we'd spent among Echoes.

"Eliot's map would be faster," I said for the millionth time, and wished I were with him.

Before Addie could reply, Monty spoke, searching his pockets for a snack. "Too many gadgets these days. The only tools a Walker needs are two good ears and what's between them."

"Says the man who gave me enough lock picks to break into Fort Knox." I cocked my head, listening. "Three pivots, and one break by the bus shelter. I'm hungry too."

Monty pulled out a packet of animal crackers as Addie listened, checking my work.

"Oh," she said softly, and put her hand on Monty's arm. "Hear it?"

"Hear what?" I asked, as his shoulders slumped.

"She has to learn eventually," he said. "Now's as good a time as any."

"What's wrong?" I asked.

"Listen," Addie said to me, but her tone was gentler than usual.

The pitch was sharp and regular—not pleasant, but not

dangerous. Even the minor breaks I'd noted earlier weren't a problem. But there was something else. Something new.

Silence.

It was as if a music box was winding down, the individual notes of the frequency losing strength, punctuated by drawn-out, aching silence. I followed the hush to a shoe store and spotted a middle-aged couple holding hands.

Addie waved a hand toward the door. "You can check it out. It's safe."

I ducked inside. The clerk was crouched on the ground, helping a pigtailed kid slide on a pair of glittery pink ballet flats. I stopped next to the clearance rack and stared.

"Balloon girl?" It was the kid I'd helped in Park World, the one who'd given us a way out during the cleaving. The frequencies must be so similar that people and places were repeating. She'd been so miserable the last time I saw her, but now, as she peered down at her shoes and up at her dad, she sparkled with delight.

If I felt a surge of envy at the way her father looked at her, as delighted with her as she was with the world, it was tiny compared to the relief I felt at seeing her uncleaved and vibrant. From this distance she sounded fine, but the irregular patches of quiet were spreading through the room.

"Plenty of room to grow," the salesman said, pressing a thumb against the toe of the shoe. "Can you walk in them, sweetie? Let us see how they fit?"

She skipped toward me, the glitter winking as she moved, a five-year-old's dream.

"I love them, Daddy!" she trilled, but the sound of her voice warped and wavered. The color began leaching from the room. "They're princess shoes!"

"And you're my—" The sound dropped away completely, his words breaking off.

Someone had cleaved this world.

I started to back away, my only thought to escape. But when I signaled Addie through the window, she held up both hands, mouthing, "Stay put."

The man lay crumpled on the ground, clutching his arm. The woman was crouched over him—I could see her shouting to the clerk, but there was no sound, even as he ran to the phone and dialed, his lips moving frantically.

I whirled toward the little girl. Her mouth was wide open, her chest heaving, her pink shoes now gray. It was as if we were stuck in a vacuum as endless and silent as space. I took a step forward, hoping to comfort her, and froze.

What if I'd caused this? What if my interference in Park World had carried over to this Echo, with its similar signature? What if I'd inflicted some sort of damage on that little girl that showed up in branches across the multiverse? What if, in stopping to fix her balloon, I'd ruined *all* her lives?

Without warning, the frequency of the world began to filter back in, the same as it ever was, growing stronger and surer with every second—except for the man on the ground, who remained stubbornly silent. He'd been the source all along.

"Daddy," the girl wailed, and then Addie was next to me,

her arm around my shoulder, urging me out the door as the girl's sobs increased.

People peered in the window of the shoe store as sirens approached.

"Come on, now." Monty took my hand. "Nothing you can do but let it unfold."

"You knew," I said, my lips numb. "You knew he was going to die. We shouldn't know that. But you both did."

"He was dead before we ever Walked here." Addie's words were careful and kind. "He was a terminal Echo."

She looked at me expectantly. A vague memory of the phrase filtered through the shock encasing me. Something I should have studied years ago, no doubt. "His Original died."

"Yes. He's been unraveling ever since."

"Why did the world go silent?"

"Terminal Echoes suppress the pitch of everything around them as they finish unraveling."

Behind us paramedics rushed inside, equipment at the ready. They'd never revive him. In the Key World, the little girl's father was already dead. This Echo—and his family—had been living on borrowed time.

The numbness was burning away, leaving behind a sorrow I couldn't understand. It wasn't my fault. I hadn't caused this. I couldn't even change it. "It's not fair."

"Who ever told you what we do is fair?" Monty asked. "There's plenty of fun to be had, Del, and I've done my best to show it to you. But Walking isn't about fairness. It's the biggest cheat around, but no one outpaces death."

"He wasn't real," Addie said, as if that made it easier.

"And who are you to say what's real and what isn't?" Monty said, rounding on her.

"Everyone knows . . ."

"Because the Consort tells them? Bah. You can't reduce life to strings and science, Addie-girl."

The weight of the day dragged at me. I couldn't change my parents' lousy opinion of me. I couldn't make Simon choose me. I couldn't save that little girl from heartbreak, and my own heart felt ragged and bruised.

We'd been taught Walking was a noble pursuit. The sacrifices we made and the rules we lived under were for a higher purpose, and this Echo's death was the same: a necessary cost of maintaining order. Somehow that only made it worse. There was no cause other than physics, no choice that had led to this moment. It was, literally, the way the world worked.

And it sucked.

I peered through the crowd, trying to spot the little girl. I didn't know her name. I acted like she mattered, but I'd never even bothered to ask her name.

Addie blocked my path. "You can't change this. There's no way to pivot away from what happened. That's why it's terminal."

The paramedics were heading back to the ambulance, in no particular rush. He was an Echo, but he was also a person. When had Addie become so cold that she could watch someone die—or unravel—and not be horrified? What if the nobility we claimed was simply another word for indifference?

Addie sighed. "Let's talk about this at home."

"I'm sick of talking," I said, and took off.

I moved blindly, turning down streets at random. When I finally looked up, I was across the street from a small cemetery, twin to one in the Key World. Cemeteries were quiet, even by Walker standards. The dead were beyond choosing. The pivots resulted from the living left behind, blunted by sorrow.

Quiet—not silence, but quiet—sounded perfect.

The gate was unlocked. I pushed it open, the rusted metal screeching in protest, and wandered inside. The angels overlooking the headstones had soft, blurry faces. The majority of the markers were worn, their engravings illegible or chipped. I knelt and touched one. An infant's grave, judging from the dates. I wondered if there was a matching one in the cemetery back home. If this, too, had been unchangeable.

I'd thought being a Walker meant freedom, but lately, it was beginning to feel like a cage. Elaborate, beautiful, and so large, the boundaries were barely visible. But still a cage.

I stood, brushing at the dampness on my knees, and realized I wasn't alone. Sitting on the stone wall along the back of the cemetery was Simon.

He'd appeared in tons of the Echoes I'd visited lately, and each time the sight jolted me. Despite what Addie said, I wasn't looking for him—not actively, anyway. Most of the time there was a logical explanation for his presence. But the sheer number of encounters made me wonder if something in his frequency drew me to him, as if he was true north on the map of my life. It was a stupid, secret, self-indulgent thought, but it didn't stop me from wishing.

He was dressed in black—black jeans, black coat, the collar of a black T-shirt visible underneath. The skin of his throat was pale in contrast, and his hair hung down into his eyes under a black knit cap. His fingers curled around an oversize green sketchpad. "Hey."

"Sorry," I said, when I'd gotten over my shock. "I didn't think anyone else was here."

I also didn't think he would see me. I must have inadvertently touched one of the Echoes outside the shoe store.

Simon shrugged. "This place doesn't get a lot of traffic."

He looked thinner. His cheekbones stood out prominently; his lips were a straight, unsmiling line. The midnight of his eyes seemed flatter, giving nothing away. I'd seen so many versions of him that it was easy to pick up the differences, to extrapolate who he was from how he looked. But I looked the same, no matter what world we were in. Did his perception of me change because he did, or was his impression of me constant?

"You look sad."

I touched my cheek, surprised to find it wet. "Ugh. I'm fine."

He nodded, silent and watchful.

"I'll let you get back to . . . whatever you're doing."

He lifted a shoulder and returned to his notebook, pencil flying over the page. Without looking up, he said, "It's not private property. You can stay."

Behind him stood a row of trees, bare branches interlaced like spindly fingers, their trunks so thick around that my arms couldn't have spanned them.

I slid my hand in my pocket and touched the paper I'd brought with me. Addie had been watching me so closely, I hadn't had time to fold a star. I could stay a few minutes longer.

I wove between headstones and sat, leaving a decent-size gap between us. He kept working—drawing, I assumed, based on his frequent glances at the tree behind me and the way he squinted at the page. He didn't offer to show me his sketch, and I didn't ask. I closed my eyes and listened to the faint scratch of pencil on paper, the sound of his breathing, the frequency of this world. You could last longer in an Echo if you let the pitch roll through you, like thunder.

"You come here a lot?" I asked eventually, pulling my knees to my chest. As much as I wanted to simply enjoy this interlude, I couldn't help wondering how we'd both ended up here.

"When I need a break," he said. "It's a good place to think."

"Too much thinking isn't always a good idea." Thinking diminished what I'd seen, transforming a man's death from tragedy to collateral damage.

"You want to talk instead?"

I shrugged. "Won't change anything."

"It might change you." He flipped to a fresh page, too quickly for me to see what he'd drawn. "Show you a different perspective."

My head felt crowded, as if the images and emotions of the day were about to spill over. I looked at the assortment of headstones and marble angels, and thought about the little girl who'd lost her father for no reason other than the laws of a universe she didn't know existed. Thought about how quickly my future had slipped away. I was tired. Tired of walking and getting nowhere, tired of choosing and never seeing a change. Tired enough to confide in a boy who wasn't real and wouldn't remember me.

"My family . . . ," I began. "They're big into making good choices. Big decisions, small ones . . . They believe life is made up of every choice you've ever made, one leading into the next, like the notes in a song."

Simon nodded, his pencil flying over the page, and the misery inside me ebbed.

"But that's crap. You can lead a perfectly good life. You can make great choices, and in the end, completely random events will undo everything." I pointed to the tiny headstone. "That's a *baby's* grave. No one chooses that. No one wants that. People die not because of what they did or didn't do. It's not their choice. It just…happens. Why bother choosing if the world's going to do what it wants regardless? What's the point in trying to make a difference?"

He set the sketchpad down. "Because it matters."

"It doesn't. I watched someone die today." His pencil stilled. "There was no reason for it. He didn't do anything wrong. He couldn't have chosen differently. It was 'his time,' and now he's dead, and nothing he did mattered."

"You're crying again," Simon said. He leaned over to brush at my cheek, the canvas of his coat sleeve rasping against my skin.

"I couldn't stop it," I said softly. "There was nothing I could do."

He smoothed a lock of my hair. "That's the worst."

I nodded and swiped at my nose.

"Del . . ." I looked up, surprised he knew my name. "I come here and sketch almost every day. These trees. These graves. Every day.

"It doesn't bring them back. But it matters that I come here. That they're remembered. Even when the outcome is the same, it matters. And it changes me."

He spoke with such conviction, but I shook my head. Outcomes, not intentions. That's what the Consort taught. "It's easier to be philosophical when they've been dead for fifty years. The man I saw had a family. A little girl. And now she's alone."

His expression hardened. "Would it be better if he'd never existed?"

I thought back to the silent unraveling I'd witnessed. "I don't know. Maybe? To spare people that kind of pain."

"You're wrong." His fingers tightened on the pencil.

"Del!" Addie's voice, distant but coming closer. I slid off the wall.

"I should go." I gave him as much of a smile as I could

226

manage—which wasn't much, and swiveled away, stubbing my toe against a small headstone. Unlike the other graves, its surface was shiny, the engraving crisp. I looked closer.

AMELIA LANE

BELOVED MOTHER

Below that, her dates. She'd died last winter, a few months shy of forty.

"Amelia Lane," I breathed, and turned to Simon, who quickly shifted his attention to his sketchbook. "Your . . . ?"

"My mom." His words felt like a punch to the chest.

"I don't understand." Except I did. Echoes needed their Originals to survive, but not the reverse. I stared at the marble slab. Sixth grade. The cancer diagnosis. She'd beaten it then in the Key World, and lost to it here.

"She was sick," he said, grief etched across his features as sharply as her name in the stone. "For a long time. And then she was gone."

"I'm sorry." Such small words for such a huge loss.

"She mattered," he said. "I couldn't change it, but I was there. I still am."

I nodded, feeling frantic. Feeling like an idiot for mourning a stranger when Simon was grieving for his mom.

Some things were constants. His mother's illness must be one of Simon's. Cancer wasn't a choice. From the minute the first cell turned malignant, every Echo that had sprung up carried the disease within her. The only difference between worlds would be how she treated it.

He stared at the headstone. "That family you saw today . . . Do you really think they would have rather never had him? They made him happy, and he did the same for them. That time mattered more than anything." He met my eyes. "Trust me."

"I do." Whatever I'd learned from the Consort crumbled away under the force of his certainty.

I couldn't help wondering about the real Simon, the one I was supposed to see tomorrow. The one with shadows under his eyes for no reason, and sadness in his voice at odd moments. What if this was his truth, too?

If his mom was sick again, people would know. The whole community had pulled together to help them before; they would do it again. Simon might not confide in me—he'd barely known I existed three weeks ago—but surely he would have told *some-one*. Word would have gotten out.

It struck me that I'd never heard anyone talk about Simon's father, even during the year his mom had been so sick. "Who do you live with now?" I asked. "Your dad?"

His eyebrows snapped together, face darkening. "I wouldn't even know where to find him."

"He doesn't know?"

"He doesn't deserve to know. I can take care of myself."

"I believe you," I said, noting the hardness in his eyes, the lines of sadness around his mouth. He'd tried to take care of me, too. "Thanks for not trying to cheer me up with a bunch of stupid sayings. Most people would have."

There. A hint of the same cocky grin I'd seen so many times. "I am not most people."

"No," I agreed solemnly. "You're better."

It never ceased to amaze me that his Echoes could be so different, and yet the same in essentials: self-assured, perceptive, challenging. And if I was being honest with myself, hot.

My cheeks heated. He'd told me something tragic and private, trying to make me feel less alone, and I responded by wondering what it would be like to kiss him. If there was a hell, I thought, looking out at the tilted, time-worn graves, I was definitely going there.

Addie's voice rang out again, even closer. She must have been tracking my signature. "I really should go."

He frowned. "You keep saying that."

I paused. "Do I?"

"Don't you?" He shook his head like he was trying to clear it, and tore a page out of the sketchbook. "Here. For perspective."

It was a rough sketch of me, my back pressed against the bark of the tree, leaves drifting around me. The lines were too strong and sparse for prettiness, but the girl he'd drawn was striking, the kind of girl people noticed.

"I don't look like that. It's great—it's beyond great—but it isn't me."

"Perspective," he said again, with another grin.

I searched for the words to thank him, not only for the sketch, but for seeing me this way. Words seemed inadequate.

"I don't have anything to—" I broke off, pulled out the origami paper, and swiftly folded a pale yellow star. If I was going to leave a trail, I wanted it to lead here.

I held it out to him, and he took it between thumb and fore-finger, inspecting it carefully. "People used to navigate by the stars," he said.

"That's because they're true." There were worlds where you couldn't see the stars, where light pollution or smog obscured them from view—but they were constant, no matter where we Walked.

Maybe Simon was the same.

CHAPTER TWENTY-FIVE

MONTY PATTED MY ARM AS I REJOINED THEM.
"Feeling better?"

I lifted a shoulder. Whatever Addie saw in my face must
have convinced her to hold off on the lecture, because she was
silent the rest of the trip home.

Monty lagged behind us, and I dropped back, keeping him
company.

"Do you think Echoes are real?" I asked after a block and a
half.

His shoes scuffed through leaves. "Do you?"

"They can't survive on their own. They aren't born—they're
generated when the Echo forms. They don't even notice a cleaving."

"Sounds like you've got it figured out," he said.

"They feel real," I said, thinking of Doughnut Simon. "Their
choices make pivots. They have feelings, and memories."

"What's bothering you, Delancey?"

A million things, but I picked the most baffling. "I keep seeing Simon. Not every time we Walk, but often. I saw him today,
after the terminal Echo."

"You've said it yourself. We Walk in the same areas. It's natural to run into similarities between Echoes."

I lowered my voice. "Is it natural for his Echo to see me without direct contact? Or to know my name?" I'd been too caught up in our graveyard conversation to give it more thought, but he'd seen me before we touched; known my name before I'd given it.

Monty slowed his pace, putting even more distance between Addie and us. "The multiverse is infinite," he said. "But it's not all chaos. There are patterns and connections running through the very heart of it, crossing the Key World and spreading out into the Echoes, and those connections are like music. They give meaning to what we do."

"You think Simon and I are connected?"

"Could be. A person's life is made up of many strands. Who's to say yours and his aren't interwoven?"

The idea thrilled me more than I wanted to admit. It wasn't sensible, but neither was the way we kept meeting. Monty's words explained so much.

Monty continued, wheezing as we turned up the front walk. "I'm not a physicist, Del. I'm an old man with too much time to think. But maybe the universe has an affinity for you and Simon. Maybe it's written in the stars, same as Rose and me." He hummed a song, so faintly I couldn't make out the tune. "That's how I know I'll find her again."

Once inside, Addie gave Monty a muffin, and he wandered to the front room. I could hear him noodling around on the piano, a loose improvisation, but it somehow managed to capture the frequency of the world we'd been to.

"It's an awful lesson," Addie said, taking a seat. "Shaw usually waits until right before graduation to cover it."

"Good to know I'm ahead of the game." The words came out thin and bitter as boiled coffee.

"That wasn't the reason I took you there. I'm really sorry, Del."

"It wasn't your fault. It wasn't anyone's fault."

"I could have prepared you better."

I remembered the pain in Simon's voice when he'd told me about his mom. Knowing he would lose her hadn't made her death easier, just difficult in a different way.

There was a knock at the front door, and she jumped up. "Lattimer."

"You get the door," I said. "I'll handle Monty."

She nodded and dashed down the hallway. I followed behind.

Monty was sitting at the piano, the empty muffin wrapper lying on the bench.

"Do we have a visitor?" he asked.

"Promise you'll be good," I said. Behind me, Addie opened the door.

"Statements like that raise my blood pressure. Who—" He broke off as Lattimer entered. "What's he doing here?"

"Checking up on your granddaughter. I'm a man of my word, Montrose. You remember."

Monty shrank back, as if the words were a threat. I said,

"Why don't we get a snack while Addie and the councilman talk?"

"Something to keep up your strength," agreed Lattimer. "It's Addison I want to speak with."

I herded Monty into the kitchen, set him up with a bottle of root beer and a bowl of chocolate-covered pretzels. "I know you hate him, but please don't make things worse. I need the Consort to let me back in."

"Nonsense. Best thing in the world would be for you to get away from him."

"Not if I want to Walk," I said. "Stay put, okay? I want to hear what they're saying."

He craned his neck, trying to look down the hallway, and then slumped down in his version of a sulk. "Watch yourself. He's a slippery one."

"But that's not covered until apprenticeship," Addie was saying in the living room. "It won't be on the final exam. Besides, Del only started isolating break threads this week."

Talking back to a member of the Consort? It was as if an Echo Addie had overtaken her.

Lattimer's voice was steely. "You said she mastered isolations quickly. If that's true, it makes sense to accelerate her training."

"I thought Del's was a punishment," Addie said.

"She appears to have a native talent that could prove useful, in light of the current situation. We'd be foolish not to take advantage of it."

"The current situation?" I asked, abandoning my attempt at eavesdropping.

Councilman Lattimer's lips stretched over his teeth, his version of a smile. "The anomaly your parents are working on? It's classified, but I presumed Addison, at least, would have pieced it together by now."

Addie flushed and stammered, and I cut in. "She's been kind of busy. Maybe you should unsuspend me, and she can help you out instead."

"The Consort could also revisit your sentencing," he said. "I'm sure you're aware of the usual punishment for unsanctioned cleavings."

I was: a life term in an oubliette. I ducked my head and stayed silent.

Lattimer focused on Addie again. "Your work so far has been exemplary. I hope you'll continue in that vein, now that I've made my expectations clear."

"Yes, sir."

"Excellent. Someone with your talent and drive could go quite far with the proper backing." His pale eyes lingered on the arch above the kitchen door. "Your grandfather seems to be improving."

"The Walks are good for him," Addie said. "They give him something to look forward to."

"That's wonderful to hear," Lattimer said. "He's taken a hand in planning the lessons? Any particular favorites he's shown you?"

"Not really," I said. "Addie runs the show. Monty goes wherever she says."

Addie tensed at the obvious lie, but Lattimer didn't seem to notice.

"Perhaps you should let him do more, not less. I'd be curious to know how he gets on. Be sure to tell him I said good-bye."

When Addie had shut—and locked—the door, I said, "I don't like him."

"Shhhhh!"

"He's halfway down the block by now," I pointed out. "What does he want you to do?"

"You were listening in," she said. "I'm more interested in the anomaly Mom and Dad are working on. How am I supposed to know what it is when they won't talk?"

"They've told us plenty," I said. "They're tracking something, because Mom wanted Eliot's map software, and it's local, because Dad's teams are meeting here. They're using the Consort computers, which means they're either dealing with one really big problem, or a bunch of small ones."

"Or both," she said, motioning me into the living room and lowering her voice. "I'll tell you what else: They're not having any luck. They've got teams from all over the world running around headquarters. It's been weeks now, and nobody's acting like they're heading home soon. Security is crazy strict. Closed-door meetings, reassignments. Every door's got a key reader now, even the areas that used to be open access. I don't know why it's classified. Everyone knows something's up."

"But they don't know how bad," I said. "The Consort's keeping it classified so people don't freak out."

"Well, that's comforting."

"Ironic, isn't it?" In the kitchen, Monty's chair scraped and the freezer door whooshed. He was hunting for ice cream again. "You know what the weirdest thing is?"

Addie straightened the sheet music scattered across the piano. "You and I are getting along?"

"Aside from that. If the Consort's dealing with a huge, complicated, potentially disastrous problem, why the hell is Lattimer personally monitoring my suspension? Why is he accelerating my training?"

"And why does he care what Monty's doing?" she asked. "Lattimer shouldn't be interested in either one of you."

"Maybe he thinks Monty can help them?"

"I don't see how. Besides, Monty would never agree to help the Consort." She paused. "Lattimer must think he'll confide in you."

"And you'll report back." She looked pensive, and I added, "Which you won't, because it would be totally crappy to spy on our grandfather."

She didn't say anything.

"Addie?"

She wrapped a lock of reddish-gold hair around her finger, unwound it again. "Whatever they're working on, it's serious. If Monty knows something, we have an obligation to help find it."

"You'd sell him out to Lattimer?"

"I would do what I'm sworn to do: protect the Key World. And if you really want to be a Walker, you will too." She shook her head, pale and determined. "I'm going to get ready for tomorrow's Walk." The one Lattimer had assigned.

"I have plans tomorrow. For school." No way was I blowing off Simon a second time.

"We'll be back by lunch. You can study then." She went upstairs, and I headed back to the kitchen. Monty was sitting at the table, working his way through a bowl of ice cream the size of a softball, doused with chocolate syrup and caramel sauce.

"Well? What did he want?"

"He's checking in on my training. And buttering up Addie." *He's spying on you,* I wanted to say, but Addie's warning was fresh in my mind.

He poked the spoon at me. "He's after something. Thinks you're the key to it."

"Then he's an idiot," I said hotly. "I can handle Lattimer."

"Smart girl." He patted my hand, his fingers sticky. "But even fools are dangerous if they want something."

CHAPTER TWENTY-SIX

Inversions occur when a vibrato fractum replaces the corresponding area of a nearby branch. They must be stabilized before a cleaving occurs, or else the exchange between branches becomes permanent, allowing the damage to spread.

—Chapter Five, "Physics,"
Principles and Practices of Cleaving, Year Five

WE HEADED OUT EARLY THE NEXT MORNING. Mom had fixed a real breakfast—French toast, eggs, and bacon—given me a hug, and retreated to her office, as if a dose of proper nutrition erased yesterday's fight. My dad had already left.

The sky was the pale blue of a glacier, the sun giving the illusion of warmth. We crossed through a pivot near the football stadium and wove our way through the residential neighborhood. Between houses I caught a glimpse of the graveyard, and wondered if Simon's mom was alive in this Echo.

"The terminal Echo from yesterday," I said. "Does he exist in other worlds?"

"Some, but they'll unravel eventually. They're not real."

The Simon I'd met yesterday seemed real enough. So did

his suffering and his sympathy. "Echoes can die before their Originals, right?"

"Sure. It happens all the time."

Maybe Original Simon's mom was healthy, and I'd worried for nothing.

Monty trailed us by a half block, and I lowered my voice. "What about Grandma? Would the branches she'd Walked through react if she died?"

"No. She doesn't have Echoes, so her impressions would fade away."

I shuddered. If I died, the Simons I'd met wouldn't care. Or would they? Doughnut World Simon remembered me. If I died, he'd wonder why I never came back.

Monty caught up to us. "What are you two looking so serious about?"

"Going over notations," Addie said smoothly. I was impressed—usually she was a terrible liar. Now she eyed him. "Do you know what Mom and Dad are working on, Grandpa?"

"Consort business," he said with a nonchalant wave. "Hush-hush."

"You don't have any idea?" she pressed.

"Plenty of ideas. Mostly about lunch." He stuck out his chin. "Not my fight anymore."

Addie sighed, then turned to me. "Fine. We're here, Del. Are you ready?"

"For what?" I expected to catch the hum of a pivot, but heard nothing unusual. We'd stopped in front of a tiny white cottage with black shutters and a red door, window boxes filled with gourds. Clusters of hydrangeas and mums pressed against the picket fence, a stone frog guarding the gate.

"Watch," she said, and tilted her head at the polished brass mailbox hanging from the fence.

"Very quaint. What's wrong with it?"

"You tell me."

The frequency pulsed in a strange cycle, and I peeked inside, spotting a few slim letters and a magazine. As I reached in, they disappeared. I craned my head for a closer look and they came back. I went for them again, and they vanished.

"What the hell?"

Addie was trying not to snicker. "It's an inversion."

"You're kidding." Another reality, swapping places with this one. Exactly the sort of thing Walkers were supposed to prevent. "Why isn't there a team here to take care of it?"

"There is. Us."

The mailbox shifted from polished brass to rusting white metal and back again. "I can't hear a pivot."

"Pivots come from choices. An inversion is a really bad break. But we can use it like a pivot. If a frequency can make it through, so can we. Right, Grandpa? You're an expert at inversions."

"I've dealt with my fair share." He ambled over and poked at the mailbox. "This is apprentice-level work."

She forced a smile. "The Consort felt Del was ready."

His expression darkened. "You mean Lattimer. I won't be a part of whatever scheme he's cooked up." He picked up a newspaper lying on the driveway and settled himself on the curb. "I'll be here when you get back."

"Grandpa, we can't leave you behind. Mom would kill us."

He rattled the paper. "Then you've got a choice. Disobey your mother or disobey Lattimer. But I'm not crossing that inversion."

We were silent for a moment, Addie struggling to keep her temper, Monty scowling at the op-ed page. "We'll be back soon. Don't move from this spot."

"Wouldn't dream of it," he said airily.

Walking through faint pivots was like threading the world's smallest needle. You needed steady hands, sharp senses, and total concentration.

Crossing an inversion was like trying to thread the needle while treading water. I kept reaching through space, feeling for the vibration that corresponded with the mailbox. A few times I could have sworn it brushed against my fingertips, only to drift away. Even Addie was getting frustrated, her movements jerky as she tried to guide me.

"We're never going to get through if you keep swinging your arms around like a windmill," I said when she'd bumped my hand one too many times. "Let me try alone."

On the curb Monty coughed noisily. Addie turned her back on him. "It's more dangerous than a pivot, Del. I need to stay with you."

"Once I've got it started, you hold on to me, and we'll cross together. Eliot and I do it all the time."

"Please spare me the details of what you and Eliot do together."

I smacked her arm. "Ew. We're not like that."

"Much to poor Eliot's chagrin."

"Stop," I said. "Can we please get to work? I think it's getting worse."

Addie folded her arms across her chest. "If you leave me here I will tell Mom. And the Consort."

"Relax," I said, but it was more for my sake than hers. I shook out the tension in my arms, blew out the breath I'd been holding, and closed my eyes, listening to the wind rustling through the leaves, children playing in a nearby yard, my own heartbeat, and the pitch of this world. A quick burst of dissonance flashed and fell silent.

There was a meter to it, I realized after a few flashes. Irregular, but present, and I started to count, readying myself.

My hand shot out and the sound retreated, but not before I bent my fingers, barely snagging the thread I needed. Carefully, my movements as fluid as possible, I reached for Addie and brought us through.

"Whoa," I said, opening my eyes and staggering. The slightly off frequency I'd heard was amplified, and my arms broke into goose bumps. "I was not expecting this."

Addie wasn't either, judging from the lines creasing her forehead. "I don't understand. Inversions always sound worse, but it wasn't supposed to be this bad."

243

"It's like Park World." I could have kicked myself for not checking Eliot's map before we crossed. This was exactly what he'd worried about. "Remember? The pitch was worse than Mom told us."

"No." Addie's voice shook on the word, but quickly strengthened. "We're not going to cleave this world. I'm going to stabilize the inversion, you're going to watch, and we'll leave."

"What if we can't?" I fought the urge to clap my hands over my ears.

The cottage, like the world itself, was in bad shape—instead of window boxes filled with bright mums and miniature pumpkins, the windows were framed with peeling shutters and rotting wood. The lawn was full of crabgrass and patchy spots, and the fence was more gaps than boards.

"We will," said Addie. She pushed on the gate, and a cat shot out from underneath a bedraggled shrub. "Stabilizing inversions is the last step before a cleaving. The threads of this mailbox are swapping places with the other one. We need to fix them in place again."

"They're going to cleave this world." The knowledge unsettled me more than the pitch.

"Probably. The inversion's only affecting Echoes, not the Key World. And the rest of this place seems stable, so they might not get around to it for a while. But it's definitely a candidate."

The cat hurtled past us a second time, orange fur flashing, its yowls adding to the clamor. Addie said, "What is wrong with that—dog!"

"Cat," I corrected, and then heard it. A deep, joyful barking. "Oh, hell. Run, kitty!"

The cat didn't need our advice—it streaked up a tree, hissing and spitting. Another, larger form hurtled past and took up residence at the base of the trunk.

"Iggy?" I ran a hand over his silky brown fur. "You're messing with me, aren't you, pup?"

He barked twice and returned his attention to the tree.

"Iggy, you psycho," called Simon, exasperation ringing through his words. "Leave Mr. Biscuits alone."

"Mr. Biscuits?" I snorted.

Simon turned to me, recognition lighting his eyes. His hair was practically a buzz cut, and he wore a down vest over his sweatshirt instead of a coat, but otherwise he seemed pretty similar to Original Simon. "I didn't name him. He's not my cat."

Addie made a strangled sound, and I elbowed her.

Above our heads Mr. Biscuits gave an outraged, warbling cry, and Iggy quivered with excitement.

"He's not going to eat the cat, is he?" I asked.

"Not unless the cat's stupid enough to come back down. He likes to taunt Iggy and run home, but the gate's usually locked." He looked at the gate, then us. "Were you looking for Mrs. Higgins?"

Addie whispered, "Get rid of him."

Before I could respond, Simon called, "C'mon, boy. Lunchtime!"

Iggy romped at the base of the tree, pointedly ignoring him.

"Iggy," I singsonged. "Go see Simon."

The dog whuffed and padded toward him, head drooping.

Simon grabbed the red nylon collar. "Good to see he listens to someone. See you around."

I waved weakly.

"Why did he know you?" Addie demanded.

"He doesn't," I lied, searching for an answer that would convince both of us. "I touched his dog. Same as touching another person, and it made me visible."

She narrowed her eyes. "You'd better hope that's it."

It wasn't. From Doughnut Simon's memories to the way Cemetery Simon had known my name, something was off. Even if Monty was right, and the threads of our lives were somehow interwoven, Simon's Echoes weren't following the rules of our world, and I knew firsthand how the Consort felt about rule breakers. Confiding in Addie was not an option—she'd left Monty sitting on a sidewalk rather than cross Lattimer. She'd turn Simon over to the Consort without batting an eyelash.

Around us the dissonance increased, the mailbox flickering more rapidly. I reached past her to tap it, asking, "Should I be worried?"

She shifted into lecture mode, exactly as I'd hoped. "Inversions are strong, and the longer they exist, the stronger they get. We have to stabilize the threads directly."

"A tuning? Isn't that what you did at the game?"

"It's similar, I suppose. Tunings aren't usually worth the effort, because you're only dealing with a few threads. Inversions are a lot more work, and they're riskier." She smiled. "Watch and learn."

She closed her eyes and slipped her fingers through the air, wiggling them slightly. "The first step is to isolate the threads, same as with a regular break."

But she wasn't acting like this was a regular break. Her skin was chalky white, her shoulders hunched. After what seemed like ages, she flinched. "There. Put your hand over mine."

I did, cautiously, pushing aside my memories of Duck Pond World. These threads—a solid handful of them instead of the one or two I was used to feeling—felt knotted and kinked, their instability giving me vertigo. No wonder the effect was visible. "What next?"

"Mimic the frequency you're looking for, and sort of . . . coax the thread." She ran her hand over the bad strings, gently but firmly, humming under her breath the whole time. Gradually they smoothed out, taking on the same frequency as the rest of the world.

"Done," she said, and I eased my hand away, feeling dizzy.

Carefully she withdrew her hand, and took a deep, shuddering breath. Her eyes were shining, and bright spots of color stood high on her cheeks. "Awesome, right?"

"Sure. Lattimer will send in Cleavers now?" I asked, trying to match her enthusiasm. The whole world sounded better; the Simon we'd seen had been stable. Cleaving him seemed unfair. Cruel. And I'd played a part in it.

"Don't worry," she said, mistaking the source of my unhappiness. "You'll be cleaving soon enough."

CHAPTER TWENTY-SEVEN

Choices requiring significant effort on the part of the subject create stronger Echoes than those maintaining the status quo.
—Chapter One, "Structure and Formation,"
Principles and Practices of Cleaving, Year Five

IT MUST BE A UNIVERSAL LAW THAT NO MATTER how absentee your parents have been, the one time you would like them to stay away is the exact time they'll decide to take an interest in your life.

"Del?" my mom said, coming out of her office, coffee cup clutched in one hand, a stack of maps in the other. She folded them in half, hiding their contents. "Who's this?"

"Mom, Simon Lane. Simon, this is my mom."

He stood and shook hands. "Nice to meet you."

"And you as well. I wish I'd known we were having company." She gave me a look implying I had fallen down on the job.

Simon covered his heart with his hand, miming hurt. "Trying to keep me under wraps?"

He had no idea how many secrets I was keeping about him. I waved toward the staff paper on the piano bench. "We're working on a project for music. Counterpoint."

"Del's specialty," my mom said. "Are you two hungry? I made zucchini bread."

"I love zucchini bread," Simon said, but I put my hands up.

"We're fine, Mom. And we've got a lot to do, so . . ."

Her eyebrows arched. "I'll let you get back to work. Dad should be home soon, by the way. I'm sure he'll love meeting your . . . friend."

If there'd been a pivot handy, I would have Walked through and stayed until I was fifty, because it would take that long for me to get over my embarrassment. Simon seemed fascinated by the pattern of the rug, and neither of us moved until we heard the door of her office shut.

"So that's your mom," he said finally. "Where's the rest of the family?"

"My dad's working. My grandfather's upstairs, which is kind of weird. He's usually pretty social." I wasn't complaining. My mom's ability to mortify me paled in comparison to Monty's skill set. "My sister's working in her room." Writing up the report on our Walk. I wondered what she would say about Monty refusing to join us.

"Nice," he said softly. "Having so much family."

"Your dad . . ."

"Took off right after I was born." He swiveled away so I couldn't read his face.

"Ah." Unsure of how much to push, I said, "That sucks."

He picked up my violin, plinked one of the strings. "Don't worry about it. I don't."

"No?"

"Nope. More important things on the radar," he said, and turned back to me.

The most powerful choices are the ones that disrupt the status quo—that break free of momentum and push into the unknown.

They're also the most terrifying.

I could let Simon's remark slide and continue on with our project. Or I could ask the question, knowing it would change us regardless of his answer.

"Things like your mom?"

He set the violin down. I waited, hoping he'd fill the silence between us with the truth.

"Who told you?"

"Nobody. I had a feeling."

He sat next to me and struck a single note on the piano, an E flat, over and over. "The cancer came back. We found out a couple of months ago. "

I'd never wanted to be wrong so badly. "I'm sorry. Is it . . ."

His expression turned haggard. "Yeah. They don't know how much longer she has. A year. Eighteen months, if we're lucky."

Strange to call it luck. In less than two years he'd be an orphan.

"What are you going to do?" I picked out a minor melody, pianissimo.

"Take care of her," he said, jaw set. "Right now she's tired more than anything. Later . . . there are people who can come in and help. That's what the doctors said, anyway."

The circles under his eyes made sense to me now; his insistence on getting good grades for his mom's sake. His wish for siblings. The charm he displayed every day had vanished, replaced by brittle composure. The transformation made my heart ache.

I tried to imagine what it would be like to have no one left in my family—not even Addie. How quiet the house would be. I envisioned myself in those empty, echoing rooms, and my eyelids prickled.

"Why haven't you told anyone?"

"I told Coach. A couple of guys on the team. A few teachers."

"That's it? What about the rest of your friends?"

"Not yet." I must have looked startled, because he said, "It changes how people look at you. How they treat you."

"Maybe not."

"It happened before," he replied, and I remembered the year of casseroles and phone trees and bake sales. Of course he knew how everyone would react. "Once they find out, I'm not *me* anymore—I'm the kid with the mom who's dying."

I'd watched Simon for years, charming and flirting and joking, winning people over at every turn. I'd never stopped to consider what hard work it must have been, convincing everyone to love him instead of pity him. That veneer had never slipped until now, never cracked. The Simon sitting next to me, simultaneously vulnerable and guarded, was as foreign as an Echo, but more real than he'd ever been.

"You told me," I pointed out.

His brow furrowed. "You asked."

"Didn't mean you had to answer."

He looked straight at me, the intensity of his gaze making me forget which world we were in, which Simon I was dealing with.

"I had a feeling too," he said, the words so low they resonated in my chest, and his hand slid to cover mine on the keys.

"I'm glad," I whispered.

"Simon?" called my mom, and he drew away. My pulse beat in a wild, unsteady rhythm. Mom poked her head around the corner. "Would you like to stay for dinner? It's chicken parmesan tonight. You're welcome to join us."

I rolled my eyes. We'd had pizza or sandwiches every night this week. Simon's presence was the only explanation for a return to real food.

"It sounds great, but I can't," Simon said, standing up and grabbing his notebook. "I have a . . ." His eyes slid away. "I have plans."

"Plans" could mean only one thing. A specific plan, with a specific individual.

"Some other time," Mom said. "It was lovely to meet you."

"You too," he said. "And thanks for the offer."

"Of course." She disappeared back into the kitchen, but the damage was done, the sense of connection shattered.

"Hot date?" I asked. I was going for nonchalance: *See how much I don't care you'll be kissing someone else tonight?* But inside, my heartbeat slowed to the tempo of a dirge. He'd confided in me, trusted me with the most awful truth imaginable, but I wasn't the one he wanted. "Bet I can guess who."

He released the arm on the old-fashioned metronome we kept next to the piano, and the steady ticking filled the silence. "Bree's nice," he said eventually. "And it's not serious."

"It never is." Why was he telling me his secrets one minute, and leaving to see her the next? Maybe I'd imagined the connection between us. Maybe he told everyone, making them feel as special as I had. The idea made me feel hot, then cold, and then very, very stupid.

"What's that supposed to mean?"

"Everyone knows you don't stick. When was the last time you had a serious girlfriend?" I kept my voice light.

"They know what they're getting into."

"And they all talk about what a great guy you are." They talked about other things, too, but I wasn't about to feed his ego. "I'm not judging. But I'd have to be blind not to see you've got someone new on your arm every six weeks. And *you're* blind if you think Bree's not after something more serious this time around."

"You want to talk about blind? What about the guy in music class? Lee?"

"Eliot? I told you, we're friends."

Simon scoffed. "If you say so. I've got to run."

"Be careful," I called as he left, surprised at how hurt I felt. "Bree's looking to be more than the flavor of the month."

The door slammed.

I wandered back into the music room, studying the score we'd worked on. I picked up my violin, tightened the bow, and ran through my part. Without Simon's half it sounded thin and lonely.

"Not your usual work," said Monty.

"Hey, Grandpa. It's a project for school. I have to compose with someone else."

"Simon," he said with a knowing smile. "Where'd he go?"

"Date," I mumbled, and shifted to Bach.

"Hmph," he said. "You let him slip away."

I stopped playing with a screech. "What was I supposed to do, sit on him? Steal his keys?"

Actually, I could have lifted his keys. But I wanted him to choose to stay.

I wanted Simon to choose *me*.

Monty shook his head mournfully. "Do you think Rose fell into my lap like an apple from a tree? Make an effort."

"He's not a Walker."

"So?"

"So, isn't that kind of . . . frowned on?"

Monty sucked in air through his dentures. "Since when has that ever stopped you? You've got a connection with this boy, haven't you? When the multiverse tries to tell you something, it's best to listen."

The multiverse was giving me mixed signals. Much like Simon himself. "He's on a date with another girl."

"Find a way around. You can, if you want to badly enough." He played a quick ditty on the piano and pushed up from the bench. "Dinner?"

"In a minute." I stared at the score Simon and I had written together. He couldn't draw a treble clef to save his life. He was dating Bree again. He wasn't a Walker. Bad enough I'd hooked up with his Echo. Falling for his Original would be an even bigger mess.

And it was too late.

CHAPTER TWENTY-EIGHT

Whats on tap for this week?" I asked
Addie as I set the table that night. "More inversions?"

"That's the only one Lattimer told me about," she said. "But
I've got fun stuff planned."

I was afraid to ask what constituted Addie's idea of fun.
Then again, Lattimer had told her to ramp up my training, and
she wouldn't ignore a directive from the Consort.

"What's fun?" asked my mom, dropping into her chair. "I
could use some fun."

My dad rubbed her shoulders. "Sorry I missed your friend
today, Del. Will we be seeing him again?"

"No idea," I replied, and turned to my mom. "What's
wrong?"

"It's nothing," Mom replied. My dad opened his mouth and
closed it again.

"We're not little kids anymore," Addie said. "You don't need
to protect us."

"What are you guys looking for?" I asked. Dad gaped at me,
and I shrugged. "Why else would you need Eliot's map?"

"It's classified," he said.

"And completely manageable," added my mother.

A completely manageable problem wouldn't have turned my mom's skin waxy with fatigue, or threaded strands of silver in my father's sandy hair. It wouldn't have meant whispered conversations and locked doors, late nights and short tempers. Whatever they were dealing with was the opposite of completely manageable.

"Let us help," Addie said. "I'm nearly done with my training, and Del doesn't completely suck."

"Hey!"

My dad shook his head. "Too dangerous. What we need from you two is to be careful. To keep an eye out for anything strange, especially on the Key World side."

"You know you can talk to us," Mom said. "About anything."

At that, I rolled my eyes. Parents *said* you could always talk to them, but whenever you took them up on their offer, it was less of a talk and more of a lecture. I got enough of those as it was.

A thick, uncomfortable silence blanketed the room. Finally my mom pushed up from the table, her dinner untouched. "You two keep on doing what you're doing, and things will be back to normal soon enough."

My dad ruffled my hair and followed her upstairs. Addie surveyed the table, the food lying uneaten at each place. "They're lying."

"Duh."

"Inversions," Addie said, green eyes thoughtful. "He wants to know if we're seeing inversions in the Key World. That's definitely serious enough for the Consort to freak out."

"They're going about it backward, as usual," said Monty. He crammed a piece of garlic bread in his mouth. "Inversions are a symptom."

Addie watched him closely. "What would you do?"

"I've been out of the game too long to do much of anything," he said, and Addie sat back, disappointed. He lifted his eyebrows. "But if I were a younger man, I'd be more curious about the disease, wouldn't you?"

She nodded slowly. "Del, you're on dishes tonight."

"You have plans for this evening?" Monty asked when she'd left. He slanted a look at my backpack, sitting next to the back door.

I poked at my now-cold dinner. "I was thinking about it."

"Be a doer, Del, not a thinker." He winked. "Is it too late for a cruller?"

There was no way the doughnut shop was open at this hour, but I understood him perfectly. "I'll find out."

There was probably a lesson to be learned about the foolishness of Walking without a plan. Walking to Doughnut World was becoming second nature. Even the frequency, stronger than my last visit, was less irritating. But it wasn't until I was standing outside Simon's house that it hit me: He could be out with Bree in this Echo too. Or at a party. Or at Grundy's, or anywhere. A few make-out sessions didn't make this Simon mine, and it wasn't like we'd spent a lot of our time talking, either.

The Jeep was gone, and the shades were already pulled. It

was the same cozy ranch as in the Key World, but it was missing the Washington High pennant hanging in the front window, and the shutters were a glossy green, not red. Neat rows of solar lights lined the front walk, and the hedge along the driveway was carefully trimmed.

I made myself as comfortable as possible on the cement steps. It could be a long wait, and I contented myself with folding star after star, stringing them along a piece of kitchen twine. The temperature was dropping steadily, and I pulled on my fingerless gloves.

This had been a stupid idea. My parents were going to be furious. Addie would know something was up. I'd risked everything, again, and all because I'd been hurt Simon had chosen Bree over me. *Again.*

I reached for my backpack as headlights came around the corner. An instant later Simon pulled into the driveway and climbed out of the Jeep, white plastic grocery bags in hand.

"Hey," he said, catching sight of me.

"I'm not stalking you."

"Glad to hear it. Aren't you freezing?"

"I'll live," I said, hauling myself upright, legs stiff with cold.

"Give me five minutes."

"You want help?"

He shook his head. "Five minutes. Don't leave."

I nodded, and he let himself inside. A low woof caught my attention: Iggy, sitting on the driver's seat, nose pressed against the glass. "Hey, puppy. Did you go for a ride?"

The grocery store, I told myself. Not a date, not a party.

Whatever his Original was doing, this Simon had gone to the grocery store, and the knowledge made me absurdly happy.

Iggy whined and bumped his nose against the window. "You want out? I know the feeling."

I opened the door and held his collar while I snapped the leash on. A moment later Iggy was frolicking on the lawn, running in circles until the leash was wrapped snugly around my legs.

"This was not the plan," I scolded.

"He wants to make sure you stick around," Simon said, jogging down the steps. "Can't say I blame him."

He rested his hands on my shoulders. I held my breath, anticipating a kiss, but the next thing I knew, he was spinning me away from him, untangling the leash from my legs. The world blurred around me, and when he finally stopped, I stood dizzily in front of him, watching the sky dip and sway. The only steady things were his fingers, curving around my arms. "Iggy needs a walk. Keep us company?"

"Gladly," I said, and we set off, hands bumping against each other so often I knew it wasn't an accident.

We passed the cemetery, and I shivered. When Mrs. Lane died in the Key World, this version of her would begin to unravel. This Simon—and every other Simon in the universe—would lose her. There was no stopping it.

It didn't seem possible that the multiverse could contain so much grief, no matter how infinite the branches were. Endless worlds and endless sadness, and I wondered if there could ever be enough joy to balance it out.

There was a small park a few blocks away. Two swings, a sorry-looking slide, and a few benches. Simon unsnapped the leash and took a glow-in-the-dark ball out of his pocket.

"You want the first throw?"

"Sure." I tossed it gingerly. Iggy chased it down and ran back, reproof clear in his eyes.

I threw it again, much farther, and Simon tugged me onto the bench. "I've been missing you."

Part of me thrilled to hear the words, but part of me twinged a warning. He shouldn't miss me. He shouldn't remember me. Every time I came here, I reinforced the connection between his threads and mine. And yet the frequency was stable. I couldn't sense any breaks. It was harmless fun.

Iggy raced over, and Simon's throw sailed to the other side of the park. He touched his lips to mine, slow and lingering and insistent. "Why'd you come by?"

"I wanted to." I tipped my head back to look at the stars, the Pleiades clustered together, the familiar lines of Orion's belt and shield. Fixed points. As close to unchangeable as things got, for a Walker.

The truth was a fixed point too. And the truth was the real Simon was out with Bree right now. Rather than accept it, I'd come here. Guilt snuck under my coat with fingers more icy than the wind. "That's all. I wanted to be with you."

"Then be with me," he said, and kissed me again, pulling me in to him, his hands chasing away the chill. His words were soft and urgent, like the heat building inside me. "My mom's asleep by now. Nobody will bother us. Come back and be with me, Del."

I'd crossed a million lines every time I'd come here. But sleeping with Simon was a line I'd kept well away from. Even so, protests, denials, common sense . . . They trailed away to nothing, and what remained was the feeling of Simon's mouth on my skin, the syncopation of our breathing, and recklessness, coursing through my veins like a drug.

"Come home with me. We can take it slow." He stood and held out his hand.

For once, slow sounded good. I twined my fingers with his.

"Iggy," he called. There was a distant woof, but no dog in sight. "C'mere, boy!"

Yet another constant: Iggy's need for obedience school. Simon whistled, a short, simple melody. Instantly familiar.

"What is that song?"

"Iggy's whistle?" He brushed his lips over my knuckles. "I made it up when he was a puppy."

It was the same tune Simon had suggested for our composition today. "Do it again."

He raised his eyebrows but obliged, the scattering of notes merry and alarming.

"Where did you hear it?" My voice sounded too sharp. Iggy raced over, goofy and delighted. I rubbed his silky ears, taking comfort in the steadiness of his frequency.

"I told you, I made it up."

"Not the last two measures." I'd written them myself this

afternoon. There's no way he would have known them before today. "That's new."

He whistled again, softly, strands of my hair stirring with his breath. "I guess so. You're not the only one who's good at music. Wait. You *are* good at music, right?"

"I'm freaking brilliant," I muttered. Had I told him that? "Tell me your whole schedule."

He rattled off the list, clearly humoring me. He had zero music electives. Dimly a part of my mind noted I knew even less about this Simon than my own.

"Did you ever take music theory?"

"Nah. Art history. What's wrong?"

"Touch me," I ordered.

He grinned and cupped my cheek in his hand, rubbing his thumb over my lips. I pushed aside the want rushing over me and listened as hard as I could.

His frequency was stronger every time we touched, but stable. Simon tilted my face to his. "You're worrying me."

"I can't do this," I said. "Not tonight."

"Did I miss something?" His eyes were intent on mine, like he was hoping to see the answers I wouldn't give him. "Five minutes ago you were ready to come home with me, and now you're bailing for no reason."

"I want to. I just . . . can't. Please believe me."

"I believe you're awesome at leaving." He dropped my hand and stood. "You want me; you don't want me. You show up out of the blue and you disappear for days. Now you're freaking out about how I call my dog? You don't want to sleep with me, fine. All you have to do is say so. Instead, you take off."

He started walking, shoulders stiff, Iggy at his side. "See you around, Del."

"Simon, wait!"

He didn't break stride, and I hurried to keep up with him. "It's not the song. It reminded me of something I need to check on at home. If I don't take care of this now, they'll figure out what I've been doing. It'll be the end of us."

The end of him, I meant.

If Monty was right, Simon and I were connected, our threads twining together across the Echoes. But what if my visits here had strengthened the connection too much? What if I'd some-how triggered an inversion? My father would cleave this Echo himself. This Simon would unravel.

Real or not, I wouldn't do that to him again.

CHAPTER TWENTY-NINE

We have a problem," said Eliot at lunch the next day. He dropped into the chair next to me with a scowl.

"Another one?" I smeared peanut butter onto my apple slice and crunched down ferociously. After I'd left Simon, I'd retraced my steps through Doughnut World, Eliot's map in hand. There'd been no hint of inversions or new breaks. Doughnut Simon was safe, but instead of relief, I felt like disaster was gathering in the shadows.

"More than one, technically. I've been analyzing the other Echoes in the branch system Park World belonged to. I compared readings taken prior to the date you cleaved to ones taken after. A lot of them—not all, but most—are destabilizing at an accelerated rate."

"They're going bad? Isn't that good? Good for me, I mean." If the whole branch was unstable, it proved my case—at the cost of the people in those Echoes.

He picked at the soggy french fries on his tray. "The acceleration didn't kick in until after your cleaving."

I choked on a bit of apple, and he pounded me on the back. "I caused it?"

He left his hand on my shoulder. "It's possible the problems were there all along, and Park World was the first time we noticed it. But the timing doesn't help your case any. I'm sorry, Del."

He looked miserable, like he blamed himself, when all he'd done was try to help.

"Don't apologize. I'm the one who screwed up."

Across the cafeteria Original Simon was eating lunch with the rest of the basketball team, goofing around, laughing and shoving at his friends while he attacked a piece of pizza. Bree was nowhere to be seen. His eyes met mine, and he went still, no doubt regretting he'd ever confided in me. Park World wasn't the only thing I'd ruined.

I'd Walked to a ton of worlds with Addie and Monty since my sentencing. If they all showed the same increase in breaks and inversions, I'd know the problem was me—or Simon.

"Could you run another analysis?" I asked. "Not around Park World. But the branches I've visited since then?"

"Sure, if you can get me a copy of Addie's reports. We'll figure it out," Eliot promised.

I leaned my head on his shoulder. "Thanks, by the way. I feel like I never get to see you anymore. It sucks."

"It does. Addie's pushing you pretty hard, huh?"

"Addie and Lattimer both." The bell rang, sending people scurrying off to class. Except for Simon. To my astonishment, he began making his way across the cafeteria toward us.

"Hold on," Eliot said, oblivious to Simon's approach. "Why is the Consort—"

"Can I talk to you?" Simon asked. "Alone?"

"We have class," I said as Eliot's arm tightened around me.

"I'll walk you."

Eliot's expression darkened, but he didn't say anything as I stood.

Hand on my elbow, Simon guided me out of the cafeteria.

"How was your date?" I asked, pulling away.

He rubbed the back of his neck. "Fine, I guess."

"You two make an adorable couple." I masked my anger with a saccharine smile. How was it his Echoes felt a connection with me, and this Simon—the real one—barely knew I existed? Could be on a date with Bree at the same time he was kissing me in another world?

"It was one date. Probably the only one."

I glanced up. "Why's that?"

"I don't know. It felt . . . off." He dragged a hand through his hair, a gesture of sheer frustration. "Happy?"

I was, but I shouldn't be. "Why should I care? And why are you pissed at me about it?"

He hesitated. "I'm not. It was a weird night, that's all. But I wanted to apologize about bailing."

I started toward the music wing, careful not to look at him. "No big deal."

He caught up to me in seconds. "You really have that down pat, don't you? The indifferent act."

"It's not an act."

"Sure it is. You're pissed, but you don't want me to know it. I can see right through you."

267

My voice shook. "This is why you wanted to talk?"

"I wanted to apologize. And say thanks." I stopped short as he continued more quietly. "For listening. I don't talk about my family much."

"You're welcome."

He flicked one of my dangling earrings. "Apology accepted?"

Behind him, a poster announcing callbacks for the winter play, green block print on yellow posterboard, flickered. The flash of white and blue could only be an inversion.

"Sure," I said distractedly. Echo-to-Echo inversions were a problem. Echo-to–Key World inversions were a disaster. I should report it, but if I did, the school would be swarming with Walkers. They'd scrutinize everyone in the building. Until I knew for sure that the connection between this Simon and his Echoes was nothing to worry about, I needed to hold them off.

I needed to fix the inversion.

I hefted my backpack. "See you later."

"Where are you going?" He blocked me, curling one arm around my waist. Even through the worn flannel of my shirt, the touch warmed my skin.

"Locker," I said, forcing myself to focus. "Tell Powell I'll be late?"

"As usual." He moved closer, and the urge to change course, to let him pull me in, was nearly overpowering. "Are we good, Del?"

I breathed in the scent of soap and clean, soft cotton and smiled, despite everything. "Very."

. . .

I waited until the last bell had rung and the halls had emptied, then headed back to the inversion. The poster was cycling more rapidly, the flashing colors making me queasy as I reached inside. Finally, I located the odd frequency and pushed my way through.

The entire building looked worn around the edges—dingy paint, chipped tiles—and the air smelled like boiled-over chicken soup. There was no sign of Simon, which was a relief. But the longer I listened to the frequency, a ragged blast of noise, the more familiar it sounded.

I searched my memory, calling up the pitches of every world we'd visited in the last few weeks. Finally one clicked. Student Council Simon. The one Addie had tuned.

I looked more closely at the flickering poster—fancy white script announced the winter ball, the blue paper dotted with paper snowflakes. Underneath, the words "For tickets, see Simon Lane or Bree Carlson" blinked erratically.

The tuning hadn't held. I'd done too much damage to that Echo, and now the problem was coming back, affecting anything associated with Simon and his break. How long before the Consort noticed?

I thought back to Addie's lesson, mimicking the way her fingers had curled and plucked at the air until she could find the bad strings. They were easier to find this time, a whole cluster of erratic, unpleasant threads. My movements were small and cautious, tempered by fear. What if I made it worse? What if I cleaved this place? What if someone found out?

But there was nothing to do now except try. *Nimble fingers, open mind, hum a tune both deft and kind.* As I worked, my movements grew more sure, my voice stronger. Finally, I felt the correct frequency take hold, the world stabilizing around me. I let go of the threads by degrees, my fingers stiff.

The poster hung on the wall, and the only thing wobbly about it was the handwriting. I'd done it. I'd stabilized an inversion, completely on my own.

An inversion connected to Simon.

I stopped by the office, dropping off a star while I swiped a hall pass, and took a deep breath before returning to the Key World. The poster had reverted to normal, but it had taken more time than I expected. I slid into my seat nearly twenty minutes late. Ms. Powell shook her head and gave me the Disappointed Look. Happily, I'd developed an immunity to the Disappointed Look sometime around the third grade.

"Pass, Del?"

I handed over the one I'd swiped in the Echo. It was identical to ours, right down to the official time stamp. Powell ran her fingers over the surface and inspected it—and then me—closely. I lifted my chin. The pass was foolproof. The only thing wrong was its pitch.

"Glad you could join us," she said at last, and went back to her lecture on fugues.

"Where did you go?" murmured Eliot.

"Inversion in the commons," I whispered. "It's fixed now."

He dropped his pencil midspin, whispering, "Do you

270

know how dangerous that is? You should have brought me with you!"

"No way. If I get caught, I'm not taking you down with me."

We listened to the rest of the lecture in silence. "Your composition projects are due the week after Thanksgiving, so be sure you're making good progress," Powell concluded.

Simon turned to me. "Want to meet tomorrow?"

"Don't you have practice? And games?"

He considered this. "No game on Thursday. I'll come by after practice."

Bree shifted, clearly listening in.

"Can't wait," I said, as the bell rang.

I thought we'd continue the conversation, but Bree managed to intercept him—and he didn't try to avoid her. Meanwhile, Eliot was strangely quiet as he walked me to lit.

"What's wrong?" When he didn't answer, I hip-checked him. "Spill. More problems?"

"Why did you fix that inversion? You should have notified the Consort instead of going it alone."

"This was faster."

"Bullshit. Key World inversions are a huge deal. Even you know that. You want to be responsible for another Roanoke? You aren't in enough trouble?"

The disappearance of the Roanoke settlement had mystified historians for more than four hundred years. An entire town had vanished into thin air, leaving behind an inexplicably empty settlement. Nobody knew what happened.

Except for the Walkers. The lost colony of Roanoke hadn't vanished. It had inverted, but the Consort of the 1800s—spread thin in a vast country with no efficient means of communication—hadn't noticed until it was too late. What had begun as a small inversion had grown to take over the entire island, swapping places with an Echo where Europeans had never found North America, and the area was populated by the Croatan tribe. When the inversion had finally taken root, the Originals had been swept away, leaving behind a few pieces of their settlement—fence posts, a ring, the fort—that had slipped through the strings.

Not our proudest moment. Even today, Walkers patrolled the area, shoring up the weakness left behind, trying to prevent another inversion of that magnitude.

"You're overreacting," I said. "It was tiny. I fixed it. Addie showed me how the other day."

"Well, gee. If Addie showed you one time, I'm sure you're totally qualified. Nothing to worry about."

I swallowed. This was Eliot. I could trust him. "Remember how I tried to isolate a break at that basketball game, and Addie had to tune it?"

"Hard to forget," he said.

"The inversion came from that Echo."

His face went blank, and I knew he was calculating odds in his head. "That's not a coincidence."

"I think it was my fault. I couldn't let the Consort find out, or they'd blame me." And cleave the world, with Simon in it.

He blew out a breath. "You can't do that again. No more

Walking on your own, Del. Between inversions and the increased breaks . . . it's too dangerous."

"That's why I have your map, boy genius. I'll be fine."

"No. From here on out, I'm going with," he said, gripping the straps of his backpack.

I thought about the things that Eliot did not like: Breaking rules. Walking to unmapped branches. Simon Lane. All of which he'd see in abundance if he came with me. "You don't have to. If they catch us . . ."

"I'd be in the same situation as you," he finished with a half smile. "I can think of worse fates."

I sighed. "This is very unlike you."

"Or maybe it isn't, and you never noticed."

The thought settled uncomfortably in the pit of my stomach. For the first time in ages I studied him. He wasn't bad-looking, actually. He had the narrow, lean build of a swimmer, but you could hardly tell under the baggy cargo pants and too-big oxford he wore unbuttoned over a T-shirt. The tight curls of his hair were starting to poke out in odd directions, in need of a trim. Behind the thick black-framed glasses, his eyes were warm, and his smile was wide and sweet, a dimple peeking out on one side. If he put the slightest effort into it, he could have girls falling all over him.

It was a strange notion: Eliot as heartthrob. He didn't realize it. He probably wouldn't do anything about it even if he did.

"You're impossible," I said, untwisting his collar. "Do you even look in the mirror before you leave the house?"

He covered my hand with his. "Del. No more Walking without me. Promise."

I smoothed his shirt and drew my hand away. Then I nodded, and he smiled. "I'm not giving up on Park World, either. You'll get reinstated, and we'll live happily ever after."

"Sounds like a plan," I said. When I looked away, Simon was watching us across the hallway, eyebrows raised.

CHAPTER THIRTY

By the time Simon arrived at my house to work on our project Thursday night, I was worn-out and cranky from the week's sessions with Addie. I'd avoided his Echoes, afraid of triggering a break or an inversion or Addie's suspicions. But the sight of his tall frame hunched over the piano made me forget about the anxiety that had driven me over the last few days.

"You really are terrible." I laughed, resting the violin on my knee.

"Told you. We should have done something with drums."

"And I told you, you can't do counterpoint with percussion. Unless you've decided to take up the marimba."

"Um, no. Strictly a drum-set kind of guy."

"Why did you stop playing?"

"One of the high school coaches saw me play basketball in seventh grade. Told me if I got serious, I could probably win a scholarship. It wasn't like we had a lot of money lying around, so I got serious, and the other stuff fell away. Between practice and conditioning and camps and tournaments . . . I had to make a choice."

The range of his Echoes made more sense. Each one had

followed a path he'd turned away from. Each one had taken up a life he'd left behind. He'd followed his path with the same single-mindedness I had. "Do you miss it?"

He lifted a shoulder. "Sometimes. I wasn't terrible."

He would have been a good drummer. He had an innate understanding of rhythm. It was melody that tripped him up. Hands that were agile and precise on the basketball court fumbled constantly on the keys, mangling signatures and chords. He didn't need the metronome—his timing was perfect—but his playing was a disaster.

"Congratulations," I said. "You are officially the worst piano player I've ever heard."

"I could whistle." He pursed his lips, making a noise like a deeply angry seagull.

"What *was* that?"

"Our song." He looked hurt. "You couldn't tell?"

"We'll figure something out," I said. His Echo had whistled well enough to call Iggy the other night, but he'd had years of practice.

"I don't understand why we have to play it. It's music *theory*, right? That's the opposite of performance. This is not what I signed on for, you know. Before Powell took over, this class was an easy A. It's like a bait and switch."

"You're mad because you're used to getting what you want. Everything comes easy to you, doesn't it?"

"Not everything," he grumbled. "You know what else isn't fair?"

Idly I played a few notes. "That you're partnered with a virtuoso? I admit, it's very yin-yang of Powell."

"I was thinking more along the lines of how you keep cutting class. Nobody ever busts you."

My fingering slipped. "What do you mean?"

"I know you're at school. I see you in music, which makes sense, because it's the only class you pay attention in. But you've managed to sneak out of history how many times in the last week?"

"Keep your voice down," I hissed. Addie and my father were both out, and Monty was napping, but my mom was only down the hallway, locked in her office. Despite the soundproof door, I was afraid her motherly instincts would kick in, and she'd overhear us.

He whispered, "Yesterday, I saw you take off before second period. You and Lee didn't get back until the end of lunch."

"Eliot," I said. "You know his name. Use it."

"Sorry. You and *Eliot* have been ditching all week. What's your secret?"

"No secret," I said, but his skeptical look told me he wasn't buying it. We'd decided to check the other branches I'd worked on, taking readings for Eliot to analyze. "It's different for you. You're king of the mountain. People are always watching. But they don't look twice when I walk in. Easy to slip out again when no one notices you."

"I notice you," he protested.

Wanting to believe something doesn't make it true, the same way wanting someone doesn't make them yours.

"Really? Did you know my name before this project? I've known you since grade school. We've had classes together for three years in a row, but you had no idea who I was until Powell paired us up."

"Were you waiting for a formal introduction?" he said irritably. "It's not like you make it easy. You walk in every day with a scowl on your face, you only talk to Eliot, and half the time, you're cutting class. You're busting your ass to convince everyone you don't give a damn. Want to know what I think?"

I flushed. "No."

"I think you do care, and it scares you. So you try to scare them off instead."

"This is a music assignment, not a psych class. We're done." Had I wanted him to notice me? I was an idiot. I laid my violin in its case and snapped the latches shut. The skin between my thumb and index finger caught in the brass fitting, and I swore.

"You're scared," he repeated. "I get it."

"You really don't," I said, stung by the accusation and unsettled by the truth behind it. I rubbed at the welt on my thumb, blinking rapidly.

Walkers were encouraged to stay as separate from Originals as possible. We dedicated our lives to something they couldn't comprehend. And if I couldn't be a part of the Originals' world, if I was meant for something else, it was easier to tell myself I never wanted it in the first place.

I'd believed it too, until Simon came along.

"Let me see your hand," he said, crossing the room. The air

felt charged, vibrating with possibility. It happened sometimes, right before a pivot formed, as if the fabric of the world recognized what was coming.

Must be nice.

"You're as bad as I am," I said.

He turned my hand palm up, examining where the latch had caught my skin. "People *like* me, if you haven't noticed. No offense."

"People adore you. Talk about busting your ass—you're on a mission to charm every person who comes within a five-foot radius. You keep back anything that might make them pity you. That might scare them away." I shook my head. "Isn't it exhausting?"

"Not as exhausting as being relentlessly cranky." He was edging toward cranky now, judging from his grip on my hand.

"It's more than wanting to be popular, isn't it? You need everybody to think you're great, because if they didn't . . .what? What might happen?"

He stared at me, as unhappy as his Doughnut-World Echo the other night. *I believe you're awesome at leaving.* The answer slipped out before I could stop it. "You think they'll leave."

"People leave," he said, a sudden bleakness in his expression. "They leave all the time."

"And you're knocking yourself out so they'll stay."

A muscle in his jaw jumped. "You don't know that."

"I've watched you for three years," I said. "I'm pretty confident."

"Three years?" He raised his eyebrows. "Long time to watch someone."

"I wasn't . . ."

"Watching me?"

Damn it. My cheeks went hot as he lifted my hand to his mouth. My voice was so soft I could barely hear myself say, "Let go."

"I don't think so." The light in his eyes, intent and amused, made me edgy.

"Let me *go*."

"Or what? You don't scare me, Delancey Sullivan." He pressed a kiss squarely in the center of my palm. A shock ran through me, every single nerve in my body crackling to life. "Better?"

Words fled. Reason fled. I nodded, and he bent his head down, his mouth inches from mine.

The back door slammed.

"Del! Check it out!" Eliot called, his words carrying down the hall. He stopped short when he spotted Simon. "What's he doing here?"

"Wondering why Del doesn't have better locks," Simon muttered, dropping my hand. Then, more loudly, "Powell's project."

"Great," Eliot said, making it very clear he considered this anything but. "I have something you should see."

I knew better than to ask if it could wait. Already Simon was pulling on his coat.

"No problem," he said. "I've got to get home anyway."

I followed him out to the hallway. "Simon . . ."

"Tomorrow," he said. But there was promise in it, and enough heat to make my knees wobble, and I held on to the doorframe as he jogged down the front steps to a red Jeep across the street.

He was going to kiss me. I'd felt the pivot form in the instant before his lips brushed my palm, and it was still there, tantalizingly close. I could cross over and kiss him back.

I wasn't even remotely tempted. Walking to that Echo and kissing Simon would be no different from any of the other times I'd interacted with his Echoes. And suddenly it didn't feel like enough. I wanted this one. The *real* one.

The knowledge made my knees buckle again. I'd told myself making out with his Echo and befriending his Original was enough. Now I had the chance for more. I had a chance at *everything*.

Until Eliot scared him off.

"Knocking," I said, stomping back in. "Have you heard of it?"

"Self-control," he shot back. "Have you?"

He looked angry. Really angry—the cords in his neck standing out, his hand clutching a sheaf of papers so tightly they crumpled. It wasn't like him. Eliot was the good-natured, even-tempered one, and I'd managed to royally piss him off twice in one month. I thought back to our previous fight, the strange, icy tension between us, and my stomach clenched. I didn't want that again, so I dragged in a breath, let it out, and carefully closed the piano lid.

"I'm using it right now," I said, keeping my voice even instead of snarky. "What's wrong?"

"We need to talk."

I couldn't stay in the music room and talk with Eliot—not with the pivot of Simon's almost-kiss hovering like a ghost. "Can we talk and eat? I'm hungry."

Eliot followed behind, papers in his hand. I grabbed a pear from a green ceramic bowl and bit in.

"Talk," I said through a mouthful of fruit. There was no reason for me to feel guilty. The most Eliot would have seen was the two of us standing together. Close together. Simon's hand cradling mine, our mouths inches apart.

Eliot had seen plenty.

"You promised you wouldn't go out on your own," he said, his words like knives. "You've been cleaving worlds."

It was the last thing I expected him to accuse me of. "You're insane. I'll be happy if I never cleave another world again."

"I don't believe you. Here's the branch we took readings from Tuesday." He slapped a paper map on the counter. The primary Echo was a thick black line, with offshoots crowding around it like suckers on a vine. The sight made me claustrophobic.

"So? We'd seen it was throwing off a lot of Echoes. What's the problem?"

"I ran another analysis today." He slid a second paper in front of me. The thick black line remained, but more than half the offshoots were missing. The ones left were nearly twice as wide as before, but they were bare, no other worlds springing from them like unfurling leaves. "The Echoes are gone. They must have been cleaved."

"Not by me," I said, a tremor in my voice at the idea of someone unraveling so many worlds.

"Then who? Those branches were stable," he said. "The Consort wouldn't waste time cleaving them. But they're gone, and none of them showed traces of other Walkers having visited. The Consort's going to find this, sooner or later, and they're going to blame us. We're both going to get kicked out."

"I didn't do anything!"

He threw the papers at me. "Evidence doesn't lie, Del. But you do."

My throat closed, the words a ragged whisper. "Not this time."

He turned away.

"Look at it," I said, grabbing the paper. "Really look. If I'd cleaved those branches, the ones left behind would look the same. But these are stronger." I raced around the table and held the paper out to him, my hands shaking. "I'm not brilliant like you, but I know cleavings. I've lived through one. That world was gone seconds after we escaped. There was nothing left. You said Park World destabilized the branches around it, but these Echoes are stronger."

"As if they absorbed the weaker ones," he said, taking the paper from me.

And then I understood. "They're Baroque events. Like the basketball game and the music room. The maps are showing a bunch of Baroque events."

"Maybe," he admitted. "But there are too many for them to occur naturally. Something's triggering them."

I voiced the worry that had been gnawing at me for days. "Me?"

"You've been Walking for years, Del. There's got to be another variable. Something new." He nudged his glasses up and studied me. "Or someone. Simon Lane was at the center of both those Baroque events. I told you there was something off about him. You know who has that kind of impact on the Key World? Abraham Lincoln. Hitler. Bill Gates. Not some dumb jock kid from the suburbs."

"He's not dumb," I protested, and Eliot threw up his hands in frustration.

"We have to tell Addie."

"Not yet." The Consort was looking for a problem. I didn't want them to decide it was Simon. "Can't you check if there's something wrong with his frequency? I don't want to tell anyone until we have proof."

"Why does it matter if we have proof? Why does *he* matter, Del?"

Before I could answer, the back door banged open and two Walkers carried my unconscious father inside.

CHAPTER THIRTY-ONE

Overexposure to off-key pitches may result in frequency poisoning. While mild cases cause headaches or disorientation, prolonged or repeated exposure will result in hearing loss, cognitive impairment, and reduced stamina. The most extreme cases can be fatal if not treated immediately.

—Chapter Four, "Physiology,"
Principles and Practices of Cleaving, Year Five

THE PAPERS FELL FROM MY HANDS LIKE wounded birds. "Daddy?"

"Get him to the couch," grunted the man to his left. "And find your mother."

They half dragged, half carried him into the family room. A stream of gibberish poured from his mouth.

"What's wrong with him?"

"Frequency poisoning," said one of the men. Clark, I remembered dimly. My dad's Second Chair. They eased him down on the couch, the other guy checking my dad's pulse. Clark staggered, bracing a hand on the bookshelf for balance. "We got separated, and the frequency destabilized too fast. We were lucky to get him out."

"Magnet maple twisting fence. Lilac glissando, turning box," my dad cried out, thrashing wildly. I rushed to help him. Eliot ran to the office and pounded on the door.

"Never staircase rumpling the blue dog." Dad's eyes darted around the room, showing too much white around the irises, and he struggled to sit up.

"Daddy, can you hear me? It's Del. Lie down." I'd seen mild cases before, when my dad came home disoriented and absent-minded. This was the kind of massive dose Monty had endured, over and over, before the Consort called us home.

"Foster?" My mom shoved Clark and the Third Chair aside. "Foster, I'm here."

She bent over my father, making soothing noises, brushing his hair back with trembling hands.

"What's the commotion?" Monty asked, peering around the corner. He spotted my dad, and his face turned grim. "Del, get the tuning fork from the office. And brew a pot of strong tea, plenty sweet."

"Petals and thorns," Dad said. "Mockingbird falling through stars."

"Did you see Rose?" Monty brushed past me. "Where?"

"Dad, it's nothing!" my mom snapped. "They're random words."

"You don't know what he saw!"

"Neither do you," she said fiercely. "Del, tuning fork. Now!"

Eliot gave me a gentle push. "I'll make the tea."

I stumbled into the office. Neat rows of tracking instruments and mapmaking tools lined the shelves. The main desk was a broad expanse of maple, littered with papers and printouts. Her monitor showed a map like an air traffic controller's, all circles and movement and blinking lights. Above it was a shelf, empty except for a leather box the size of a pencil case. I grabbed it and ran back to the living room.

I held the case out to Monty. "Will it cure him?"

"It will help. Why haven't they taught you how to treat frequency poisoning?"

"They have. Just not for cases this bad."

Mom held out her hand. "I'll do it."

"She needs to learn, Winnie. You were younger than she was, the first time."

She bit her lip and nodded. "Go ahead, Del. Strike hard, and hold it near his head. Keep doing it until I tell you to stop."

I set the box down on the end table and opened it. Nestled into the navy velvet were a rubber block the size of a hockey puck and a steel tuning fork, the tines shaped like a U, the ends squared off. I gripped the handle so hard it cut into my palm, and smacked the block. A sweet, familiar sound pealed through the room.

We fell silent. It was the exact frequency of the Key World, instantly recognizable. My dad sighed.

"Again," my mom ordered as the note faded away, and I repeated the motion. With each strike, my dad struggled less. When he finally whispered her name, Mom motioned for me to stop.

"Tea's ready," said Eliot.

Nobody knew why you gave sugar to someone with frequency poisoning, but tea was the standard treatment. Strong, sweet black tea. I'd never thought about it before, but Monty's insatiable sweet tooth suddenly made sense: He'd gotten hooked, after so many years of Walking.

My mom held the mug steady as my dad took a tiny sip. In the kitchen Clark and the other Walker spoke in low tones, faces drawn. Neither of them looked particularly good, and I poured them each a cup of tea, then set more water on to boil.

"Here," I said. "You were out a long time too."

They drank deeply, nodding their thanks.

"Foster?" Mom said, when my dad had finished the cup. "How are you feeling?"

He blinked, and his voice was thick and muzzy. "Candlewax linen, burning away." He paused, breathed deeply, and spoke again, the words slow and rusty as an old hinge. "I'll live."

"Did you see Rose?" Monty demanded, but my mom hushed him.

Dad closed his eyes, his head falling back on the pillow. "More tea," my mom said, and I hurried to bring it over.

"Del, take over. Give him a little at a time," Mom said, eyeing the pair of Walkers at our kitchen table. She touched her lips to his forehead and whispered something, then crossed the room to speak with Clark.

I sat on the very edge of the couch. "Daddy, drink more."

He mumbled something incomprehensible, and I looked over at Eliot. "How long will he be like this?"

"It depends on how long he was exposed," he said. "Most cases take a few days to recover, at least."

In the kitchen, my mom said sharply, ". . . gone that long! I was very clear!"

"It was worse than we expected. If we'd known—" Clark said.

"Are you saying this is my fault?" Her voice took on a dangerous note, and Monty, Eliot, and I turned our heads in unison.

"Let's finish this in my office," she said. "Del, get me if his condition changes."

There was no way to hear the rest of the conversation, and none of us had much to say. I gave my father more tea, and he gradually came back to himself.

"Winnie?" he asked.

Did he think I was her, the way Monty sometimes mistook my mom for my grandmother? "She's in her office. She's debriefing Clark and the other guy."

"Franklin."

I nodded. His knowing their names was a good sign. "Do you want me to get Mom?"

He grimaced. "Cool down."

"It'll be quite a while before she cools down," said Monty, handing my dad a square of chocolate.

"What went wrong?" I asked.

"Everything," he said.

"But—"

Eliot closed his hand over my shoulder. "Later. Let him rest."

"Did you see Rose?" Monty asked again.

Dad's eyes drifted shut as he mumbled, "Too far gone."

I didn't know if he was referring to my grandmother or himself.

"You're back now," I whispered as he fell asleep.

"This is why you can't Walk alone," Eliot said as we sat on the porch swing that night. "Now do you believe me?"

I curled up, head against his chest. "I've never seen my dad so sick."

"The doctor said he'd recover. It'll take time, that's all."

After Clark and Franklin had left, my mom had summoned a Walker doctor, who'd said what we both expected and feared. My dad could Walk, once he'd recovered. But his resistance was lower. He'd have to be more careful, limit his exposure.

Frequency poisoning built up slowly. Usually, the damage didn't present itself until Walkers were Monty's age, the effects cumulative. But a massive dose, like the one my dad had received today, was harder to come back from. He'd lost years of future Walks in one afternoon.

"He knows the risks. So do you."

"I know. I just thought…"

"That you were immune?" He wasn't mocking me. If anything, his voice was careful and kind, our fight forgotten.

It sounded ridiculous, when he put it like that. No Walker was immune to bad frequencies, but my tolerance had always been higher than anyone in our class, higher than even Addie.

More like my dad, or Monty, both of whom were known for their ability to withstand dissonance.

Except their abilities had failed them. Monty had lost my grandmother and his mind. My dad was upstairs in bed, barely coherent, lucky to be alive. What if mine failed too? What if my time with Echo Simon was actually destroying me—and my future?

I didn't want to ask Eliot. The topic of Simon was too raw between us. Instead I said, "He's my dad. I thought he could do anything. It's weird to see that he can't."

"The Echo acted like Park World," Eliot said after a brief hesitation. "Worse than predicted, accelerated destabilization. The only difference is that they were already planning on cleaving it."

"You think Park World is part of the anomaly they're looking for?"

"Could be. I'll do some more digging. If we can prove the anomaly affected Park World, the Consort would have to overturn your suspension."

Which was great, but it didn't help my dad. Addie rapped on the kitchen window and beckoned me inside.

"Do you want me to stay?" he asked.

"It's pretty late. I'll see you tomorrow." I hugged him tightly, felt his lips brush my crown. "I'm glad you were here."

"Me too."

I stayed outside after he left, listening to the creak of the swing and the wind rustling in the trees. The air had that late-fall, damp-leaf smell, spicy and earthy and faintly musty, like something locked away for a long time.

My mom never would have sent my father into danger without preparing him. Even if an Echo destabilized unexpectedly, my dad and his team should have known to get out.

The easiest explanation was that my mom had made a mistake in her calculations. But that didn't fit. My mother, like Addie, didn't make mistakes. And it didn't explain how my dad had misjudged the frequency. Eliot was right: The anomaly was the only explanation.

The minute I'd stepped into Park World, I'd known the frequency was worse than she'd told us. The fabric had cleaved so easily, so quickly—like frayed rope. Eliot had insisted that there'd been something wrong, and I'd been equally certain my mom was right.

Maybe they'd both been right. Maybe the branches were shifting faster than anyone realized. Inversions, Baroque events, Echoes that cleaved too fast—something was pulling worlds off balance, creating Echoes too strong and flawed to sustain themselves.

And Simon was caught in it.

Addie pushed open the screen door. "Are you coming in? I made cocoa."

I stretched, trying to ease the tension in my muscles. "How's Dad?"

"He's resting. Mom's with him. It's the longest she's been out of her office in weeks."

I sat down at the island, poked at the glob of Marshmallow Fluff bobbing on the cocoa's surface. "It's worse than they told us."

"I know." Her mouth was a flat line, her eyes fever bright. "Monty's not doing great, by the way. He's convinced Dad saw Grandma out there. I had to lock his door from the outside."

That didn't mean he'd stay; it was Monty who'd taught me how to use pivots to sneak out in the first place. But Addie had enough to worry about.

"I'm tired of them cutting us out," she said in a low voice. "I don't care if it is classified. Dad could have died today."

He hadn't known me. For an instant my father had looked at me without recognition, and I knew we'd come closer to losing him than the doctor admitted. "You're the one with the plans," I said. "Tell me what to do."

"We can't go back to that Echo," she said. "But we could find a similar frequency. It might give us an idea of what he was dealing with. Where was he today?"

"No idea. Mom and I aren't exactly on the best of terms lately. But she'd have a record in her office."

We both looked at the heavy oak door.

"It's locked," Addie pointed out. "If you ask her for the key, she'll know we're up to something."

"I don't need to ask." I smiled, relief breaking over me. Finally, something concrete to do, instead of sitting around worrying, making tea and plans. "And I don't need a key."

CHAPTER THIRTY-TWO

Hurry up," Addie hissed.

"Stop crowding me. And quit whispering. She'll think we're up to something."

"We *are* up to something." Addie wrung her hands like a little old lady while I worked the lock picks.

"No wonder you never do anything wrong," I said. "You suck at it."

"And you have way too much practice," she said, as the last pin clicked into place.

I turned the knob and the door swung open silently. "Ready?"

"She's going to kill us if she catches us."

"Then let's not get caught." I stepped inside the darkened room, Addie tripping over my heels.

Unlike Addie, I didn't spend a lot of time in my mom's office. I'd never noticed the snapshots propped on shelves and taped to the wall. Pictures of us on vacations, on Walks. Shots of Addie and me in matching outfits—which we'd stopped wearing, thankfully, by the time I turned four. My dad carrying me on his shoulders while we hiked the Grand Canyon. Monty's birthday party, when I was a newborn in a pink terry-cloth sleeper. Our family's history, and she kept it close at hand. The resentment that had been fueling me over the last few weeks ebbed slightly.

Addie put her finger to her lips and tiptoed across the room, sitting down at the desk with exaggerated care.

"It's soundproof," I said. "She's not going to hear us."

Addie ignored me, scrolling through windows on the computer. "It's got to be here."

I stooped to examine the haphazard pile of books on the floor. "Some of these records go back twenty years. They're totally outdated."

"Archivists keep baseline readings of an Echo forever. Helps with deep analysis." She peered at the display, her fingers flying over the keyboard. "They're total pack rats."

Her tone was surprisingly affectionate, considering how much Addie hated clutter. "Know a lot of archivists? Anyone special?"

She shot me a dirty look.

I plopped down and paged through the nearest record book. "Two decades of Echoes," I said. "Can you imagine how many pivots have formed since then? That's a crazy amount of data to analyze, even for one branch. It would take years."

"Not if you had a Consort computer," Addie said. "Like the one Mom's been using downtown. They must think the problem is in one of the older branches."

I scanned several reports. "Monty was First Chair on a lot of these Walks. Maybe that's why Lattimer is interested in him. He thinks Monty knows something about these branches that didn't get recorded."

"Monty can't remember what day it is," she said. "He's not going to remember details from a bunch of Walks he took twenty years ago."

"It's new stuff he can't keep track of. His long-term memory is fine—look at how upset he gets when Lattimer comes around."

"He blames the Consort for Grandma disappearing," she said dismissively. "He thinks they didn't look hard enough, and seeing Lattimer again has brought it all back. He's using our Walks to look for Grandma, you know. He insists on picking which Echoes we visit."

I'd figured as much. "Do you remember her?"

Addie shook her head, strawberry blond waves rippling. "I was only four when we moved back. She smelled like lilacs, I think."

"Do you think she meant to leave, or was it an accident?"

"I think she's gone," she said. "The why doesn't matter. Monty's damaged either way."

It made me think of Simon, trying desperately to charm people into staying, because everyone who was supposed to love him had either left him or was going to.

She made a noise of surprise. "That's weird. When the new teams came in, they were averaging six or seven cleavings a day. Now they're down to one or two. Sometimes even less."

"They're making progress."

"Not according to these maps." She sifted through the papers next to the computer, comparing them to the display. "Okay, this makes more sense. The teams started out cleaving the most unstable Echoes, but they were fairly recent branches. Two or three years old at most. They're moving backward now, cleaving bigger, older branches. Cleaving Echoes that complex takes more time."

"Which increases your chance of frequency poisoning?"

"Exactly. I'm looking at the record of Dad's Walk, and the Echo was twelve years old. According to Mom's analysis, the cleaving should have taken four or five hours."

"Dad's team stayed a lot longer than they'd planned to." I paused. "The instability is a sign of an infection, and it's spreading—newer Echoes to older ones, smaller to bigger. That's why they've brought in so many teams. They're trying to stop the infection."

"Monty was right," Addie said darkly. "They're going at it backward. They're treating the symptoms. We need to find the source."

We left the office as we'd found it, locking the door and creeping upstairs. Addie was taut as a bowstring and as likely to snap. I should have felt relieved. The Consort had discovered the anomaly before I'd cleaved Park World, before I'd started seeing Simon's Echoes, before he'd triggered Baroque events. Whatever was wrong in the Echoes, it wasn't my fault or Simon's. Even so, I was worried. We were symptoms, and that's what the Consort was hunting.

CHAPTER THIRTY-THREE

Rarely, an individual will choose not to participate in the calling of the Walkers. In deciding to leave our community, they forfeit the right to Walk, and in doing so, their freedom.

—Chapter Ten, "Ethics and Governance,"
Principles and Practices of Cleaving, Year Five

HOW ARE YOU FEELING?" I ASKED MY DAD the next afternoon. He was resting on the couch on orders from my mom, who'd put me in charge while she finished up work. I handed him another cup of tea.

He pushed it aside. "Ready to get off this couch."

"Good luck with that. Mom's on a rampage."

Something between a grin and a grimace crossed his face.

"Are you better?" I asked.

He was quiet for a long time, and the fear opened up like a chasm at my feet. He had to be all right, because that's what dads are supposed to do: Be all right. Make everything all right. Anything less was unacceptable.

"I'm better," he said eventually. "It was . . . not a picnic."

When I was a kid, we'd gone on plenty of picnics. Short jaunts to get Addie and me used to the sensation of Walking. As my parents had risen in the ranks, family outings had fallen by the wayside. Monty had been the one to step in and teach me the basics.

But I'd Walked with my dad enough to know he should never have contracted frequency poisoning. The anomaly wasn't only damaging the multiverse, it was hurting people I cared about.

"You're going back out, aren't you?"

Again, a silence. I'd heard my parents fighting earlier that morning. Mom wanted him to retire, but Dad refused. "The Consort needs me. They need as many people as they can get."

Monty spoke from inside the pantry. "They're asking too much. As usual."

Funny how Monty was too deaf to hear when I asked for help setting the table, but he could eavesdrop with no problem. He added, "We're cannon fodder to them, nothing more."

"Nobody's forcing anyone to Walk," said my dad. "It's a choice, like everything else."

"Until it isn't," Monty growled.

"I want to be a Walker." I squeezed my dad's hand, a gesture of solidarity.

"Bah. You want to Walk," Monty replied.

I shrugged. "Same thing."

He wandered over, bag of chips in hand. "It's not the same. Walkers leave. Doesn't mean they stop Walking."

"Montrose," my dad said, rumbling like a kettledrum.

"Leave?" I asked.

My dad patted my hand. "It's incredibly rare for someone to renounce their place within the Walkers, Del. But . . . if someone chooses that path, they're not permitted to Walk again. They're monitored."

"Is that what they call it these days, Foster?" Monty's gnarled fingers gripped my arm, stronger than they looked. "What did you think Free Walkers were? An army of bogeymen? They're the ones who escape."

"Escape?" I was intrigued, despite myself. Free Walkers were like urban legends, or something out of a comic book, a group of anarchists and religious fanatics working to unseat the Consort. But they were a myth. Without the Consort, the Key World would fall, and the multiverse would unravel. Even anarchists weren't that crazy. Nobody over the age of six believed Free Walkers existed.

Six-year-olds and Monty.

"Enough!" my dad barked. Then, more quietly, "The Free Walkers are a story, Del, like a fairy tale. People tell it to remind us why our work is so important. The Consort exists to guide the Walkers. The Walkers exist to protect the Key World. This is our calling, and even if it's difficult—if there are costs—"

Monty snorted.

"If there are costs," Dad repeated, "they're necessary. For our own survival, for the Originals . . . for the multiverse. You've paid more than most, I know, Monty. But Winnie and I have raised our daughters to be aware of their responsibility. We'd appreciate if you didn't try to undermine that. This is who we are."

"But is it who Del wants to be?" He looked at me, eyes sharp despite the rheumy film. "Is it?"

I nodded. "Of course."

But there was a piece of me that wondered if Monty was right. Was it possible to Walk, even without the Consort's approval? After all their threats and punishments, was there another way?

A better way?

CHAPTER THIRTY-FOUR

ELIOT SHOWED UP SATURDAY NIGHT WITH A movie and a jumbo box of Lemonheads. "I figured you might not be up for going out to the movies."

"Definitely." I filled him in on the fight between Dad and Monty while I made popcorn.

He blinked. "Do you believe him?"

"About the Free Walkers? No. Who would want to destroy the Key World? It's suicidal. I do wonder about Walkers who don't work for the Consort. Would they really never Walk, just because the Consort said not to? I do it all the time."

"Don't remind me," he said, and sampled the popcorn. "Needs more butter. I suppose there are things the Consort could do. Anklets, like the courts put on people who are under house arrest. If you set it to go off when the surrounding frequency changed, that might work. Or a device to alter your frequency, so you couldn't get through a rift. Or—"

"You're having too much fun with this," I said, shoving the bowl at him. "Movie time."

When we were settled on the couch, I picked up the DVD case. "Again? We've seen this one a million times."

"You know I love a good space western." He hit play. "I like it when the good guys win."

"That's because you're such a good guy," I said as the previews rolled. "Hey, how's the project with Bree going?"

"Great," he said, a smile in his voice.

"Seriously?" I twisted to face him. "Bree Carlson. It's going great?"

"Sure, as long as I let her do whatever she wants. Not unlike working with you."

I punched him in the arm and he laughed. "Kidding!"

"You'd better be." I hesitated. "Have you had a chance to run Simon's frequency?"

His laughter evaporated. "No. Strangely enough, I can be around the guy for five minutes without touching him, so I haven't recorded a sample yet."

"Somebody's in a mood," I said, and slumped down. "Forget I asked."

"I'd love to."

Halfway through the movie, someone knocked at the front door.

"Let Addie get it," I said, curled up under a chenille throw. "I'm too comfy."

"Too lazy," Eliot said affectionately, but he didn't move either.

I heard Addie at the door, the conversation obscured by the explosions on screen. A minute later the lights came on.

"Hey!"

"We have a visitor," she said, and Councilman Lattimer strolled in.

"You're late," I blurted. Eliot and I both scrambled up.

"I don't recall setting a specific time for our visits. Apologies if this is inconvenient." His tone made it clear he didn't care.

"It's perfect," Addie assured him.

"Excellent. I came to check on your father's progress, as well. We're quite eager to have him back."

"He's better, thank you," Addie said, her voice tight. "Are you seeing an uptick in frequency poisoning lately?"

My breath caught. She was telling him she knew about the anomaly. Addie had never been any good at cards. She couldn't bluff, she bet too low, and she always showed her hand too early.

"We are. It's quite troubling." Lattimer assessed her coolly. Then his face broke into a smile. "You've put it together, then. Well done."

"Thank you, sir. I'd be happy to help, if the Consort needed me."

That was her game. Impress Lattimer, get in on the anomaly, move up in the Consort. Not a bad plan, but one lucky hand didn't make you a good gambler.

"I don't doubt you'd be a great asset to us," he said, and Addie glowed, then dimmed.

"My parents don't think so."

"Your parents are not in a position to dictate how we deal with the current crisis. I, however, am." His eyes flickered to me. "It's important to ally yourself with those people who have the greatest value."

My father had nearly died trying to fix "the current crisis." Hearing Lattimer dismiss him so easily reminded me of Monty's tirade. "What about the Free Walkers? Are they valuable?"

It was a shot in the dark, but it struck true.

He swung around, the motion as smooth and dangerous as his tone. "Free Walkers don't exist. But if they did, they—and anyone who associated with them—would be tried for treason. I cannot imagine who would tell you such dangerous tales."

Beside me, Eliot tensed, silently willing me to shut up.

Lattimer waited for an extra beat, as if daring me to answer. When I said nothing, he shifted back to Addie. "Your grandfather must be improving."

"He's better," Addie said cautiously.

Lattimer nodded. "I look forward to this week's report. I'm always curious to find out exactly what the three of you have been up to."

What Monty had been up to, he meant. Addie fell all over herself agreeing and saw him out. When she came back, she snapped, "Do you want to get expelled? Free Walkers? Have you lost your mind?"

"He's a jerk."

"Who cares? He is your way back into the Walkers, Del. You should be trying to impress him, not acting like a lunatic conspiracy theorist." She turned to Eliot. "Can't you talk sense into her?"

He backed away, looking slightly panicked. "I'm just here for the movie."

She rolled her eyes. "Del's the only one stupid enough to believe that."

"I'm not stupid!"

"What you did tonight was the textbook definition of stupid. All risk, no reward. You want to be crazy and reckless, fine. But at least do it for a good reason." She turned on her heel and stomped upstairs. Wordlessly Eliot turned the movie back on.

Addie's words stung, but she wasn't completely right. I knew a bluff when I saw one. Lattimer was lying about the Free Walkers, and that was all the reward I needed.

CHAPTER THIRTY-FIVE

Y OU COMING TO CLASS TODAY?" SIMON ASKED
me on the way to history Monday afternoon.

"I'm walking with you, aren't I?" Walking with Simon—
even a short, ordinary walk down the corridor—was an exercise in syncopation. He slowed his pace, long legs eating up the
ground, and I lengthened my stride to keep up.

"Doesn't mean you're going to stay," he said. "Are you even
passing the class?"

I was. Barely.

I tipped my head back, the charge of those dark blue eyes
zinging down my spine. "This from the guy who keeps falling
asleep?"

According to Eliot's research, the pattern we'd seen in the
Echoes—a spike in branches, then a series of Baroque events—
was another symptom of the anomaly. We didn't need to keep
checking on it, and he insisted I start showing up to class.

I didn't complain too much. It gave me time to study Simon.

His frequency was fine. The tremor I'd felt when he kissed
my hand had nothing to do with dissonance. Simon sounded
clear and true as the Key World itself. He sounded like home.

But there was no denying he was a victim of the anomaly. He'd spotted me in Echoes, he'd been at the center of at least two Baroque events, he remembered me when he shouldn't. If the Consort found out, Simon *and* his Echoes would be in danger.

I needed to figure it out first.

He ushered me through the open door. "So, if you're not off hooking up with Eliot, who's the lucky guy?"

"You always assume there's a guy," I said.

"Isn't there? If not, I know one. Tall. Athletic. Astonishingly good-looking. Loves dogs and zucchini bread."

The corner of my mouth twitched. "Sounds perfect. Does he have any flaws?"

"Tone-deaf," he said sorrowfully. "And charming. I know how you hate that."

"It's a deal breaker," I said, sliding into my seat. I looked at him under my lashes. "And we could have had so much fun."

He leaned across the aisle, and I did the same, close enough to see the hint of stubble along his jaw. "Still could."

An inch more—maybe two—and my lips would graze his skin. I could meet him halfway, fit my mouth to his. Every muscle in my body tightened, fear and anticipation so closely intertwined I couldn't separate them. An inch, and everything would change.

Mrs. Jordan cleared her throat. "If we can get started, Ms. Sullivan? Mr. Lane?"

"Another time," I murmured, leaning back.

"Mr. Lane?" she repeated.

"Bet on it," he said, voice low. Then he flashed Mrs. Jordan a trademark grin and made a joke about last night's reading. She laughed despite herself, and I marveled at how well Simon read people.

Including me.

I slid down in my seat as she outlined our newest assignment, declaring today was a research day. Everyone gathered up their books and trudged, en masse, to the library. I found an empty table by the periodicals and set my bag down, as everyone around me chose seats and research topics. Pivots filled the air with a fizzing sound.

"Secluded," Simon said, taking the other chair. "I approve. What's your topic?"

"No idea," I said. "You?"

He pursed his lips and considered. His hair was disheveled, like he'd run his hand through it. I fought the urge to repeat the movement. The air shifted and I held my breath, wondering what decision he was about to make.

"Chancellorsville," he said, and reached for a notebook. The pivot formed with a crack like a gunshot.

"That's it?" Twenty-odd kids had picked a research topic and not a single one had sounded so loud.

"You have a problem with Chancellorsville? If Jackson hadn't been shot there—by his own men—he would have been at Gettysburg. The South would have won."

I was familiar with the battle. We spent the first few years of Walker training studying the way history had shaped the multiverse. But it didn't explain the size of the pivot he'd created. I took a moment to memorize its pitch and stood up. "I'll be back in a few."

Simon glanced over at Mrs. Jordan, who was catching up on her grading and giving kids dubious looks when they grew too loud. "She's going to catch you one of these days."

"Probably," I said. "Enjoy your nap in the stacks."

"I will. Maybe I'll dream of you."

I checked Eliot's map before I crossed over. Lights covered the library in tiny pinpricks, except for the place Simon and I had been sitting, which shone like a beacon. I slipped through a pivot in the girls' bathroom and navigated to the newly formed branch. Through the library window, I could see Simon's Echo heading into the stacks. This world was so young he looked exactly like the Simon I'd left minutes ago. Even the frequency was similar to the Key World's—but louder than I expected for such a small decision.

He would have gone into the stacks for research either way, so his behavior hadn't altered. This Echo should be quiet. Instead, it was as blazingly insistent as a trumpet and growing louder every second. And then it hit me.

A Baroque event.

The class had made a lot of decisions in a short period of time. Simon's decision, stronger for reasons I couldn't explain, would draw the smaller Echoes in.

I wasn't sure I should stick around for the entire Baroque event, but it would be stupid not to do some research of my own. I found Echo Simon in the nonfiction section, head tilted to read the call numbers. Ducking into the next row, I peered at him through the space between shelves.

"Find what you're looking for?" I whispered.

To his credit, he barely jumped. "Can't quite put my hands on it. What about you?"

I'd been careful not to touch him, but he'd noticed me. Was it the amplification, or the similarity between frequencies, or the newness of the Echo? Any of them seemed plausible, and for once I wished I'd paid more attention to Addie's and Shaw's physics lectures. "I'm figuring it out."

He craned his neck. "Are we really going to have this conversation through a bookshelf? I can barely see you."

"I thought some distance might be good," I said.

He raised an eyebrow. "Scared?"

"Cautious." I wasn't scared of Simon. Intrigued. Concerned. Attracted. But nothing about Simon—in any universe—scared me.

"And yet you're hiding behind . . . What's over there, anyway?"

I checked the titles. "The Roman Empire."

"Thousands of years of history between us. Looks like scared to me."

I tossed my braid over my shoulder and strolled around the corner, stopping a foot away.

"See?" he said. "Not so hard."

"Never said it was."

The silence between us quivered with unspoken words. I poked my finger through a hole in my sweater.

"So . . . ," he said, and trailed off.

"So."

"Funny meeting you here."

"Funny, that."

He edged closer, and I backed up until my knees hit the Great Depression. "You meet a lot of girls in the stacks?" My voice sounded unsteady, even to my ears.

"Not really. I'll have to keep it in mind for next time."

"Next time?"

"Turns out we're going to spend the rest of the week on research. So we've got four more days here, minimum."

"That's a lot of research." Casually I tucked a bright orange star between two books, curious to know how a Baroque event would affect it.

"Lot of time back here, anyway." He rested one hand on the shelf above my head. "Not the worst way to spend an hour."

There was a discreet cough, and Simon drew back as someone tapped him on the shoulder. "Another project for Mrs. Jordan?" Ms. Powell asked.

"Um . . . yeah." Simon stuffed his hands in his pockets. "We were . . ."

"Making good use of your time?" Ms. Powell was very carefully not looking at me. Her eyes moved from Simon to the shelves to the floor to the light fixtures—anywhere but me. I'd never actually repelled an Echo before. Then again, Simon hadn't touched me. All she could have seen was my impression.

The frequency swelled dramatically, reminding me how easily Eliot and I had mistaken Baroque events for cleavings on the map. Time to go.

"I forgot my notebook," I said. "See you in a minute."

I crossed the pivot as the Baroque event began to toll.

Back in the Key World library everything seemed normal. Low conversations hummed around the room, the occasional muffled squeal of laughter from a table or the stacks. Simon had triggered the Baroque event, I was certain. There had to be a connection—and I headed for the stacks, determined to find it.

He stood, one hand on the spine of a book, the other dangling at his side. "Miss me?" I asked.

No response.

"Simon?"

He ignored me.

"You're mad I left? I was gone for five minutes." My own temper bubbled up. I stepped closer, ready to tell him off, but the words died in my throat.

When Addie was little, she used to sleepwalk. Not the world-hopping kind, but the garden-variety, standing-in-the-middle-of-the-pantry-at-three-a.m. kind. We'd find her playing Rachmaninoff, or organizing everyone's shoes, or reading a book upside down. In the morning she'd have no memory of her ramblings. She hadn't done it in years, but there was something about the stillness of Simon's face that reminded me of it.

I touched his hand. "Are you okay?"

He jerked once, a full-body shudder so violent it knocked the book he'd been touching off the shelf.

"Find your notebook?" he asked, warm and familiar. "I thought—why are you looking at me like that?"

"Did you fall asleep standing up?" The shadows under his eyes were even more pronounced than usual.

"I wasn't asleep. I was talking to . . ." He looked up and down the row. "Guess I did."

"Late night?"

"Not really." He observed me like a painter with a subject, noting every detail, and my skin warmed.

Flustered, I scooped up the fallen book. "Here."

"Thanks." The cellophane cover crinkled in the silence between us. "Did I, um, say anything? When I was out?"

Out. Not sleeping. I wondered if his choice of words was deliberate. If this wasn't the first time it had happened.

"Nope," I said, watching his reaction. "You didn't say a word. It was like you were somewhere else completely."

He looked more relieved than surprised. "And you brought me back. Woke me up." He grinned now, mischievous. "Kind of like a fairy tale. You should wake me with a kiss, don't you think?"

Something in me fluttered wildly at his words, too chaotic to have a rhythm, too impulsive to resist. "A kiss?"

"Del." His voice inexplicably urgent. "You promised me another time."

The bell rang, and I winced, like always.

"Yeah," I said unsteadily. "But this isn't it."

"Then when?" He ran a hand through his hair, frustrated. "I want to see you. A date. You and me. No running off to cut class or get something out of your locker, nobody interrupting at the worst possible time. No stupid bells. Tonight, Del."

"We're supposed to work on our composition," I said, and wanted to smack myself.

"Screw the composition. Come out with me. An actual date."

"Why?" My mouth was so dry I could barely force the word out.

"Because I cannot figure you out, and I want to." His hands flexed at his sides, like he was trying to keep from reaching for me. "Isn't that enough?"

I couldn't figure him out either. Maybe this was my chance. Maybe a few hours alone with him would explain the Baroque events. Maybe it would give us a clue about how to fix the worlds.

Maybe I just wanted to be with him.

"More than enough," I said.

CHAPTER THIRTY-SIX

Synaptic Resonance Transfer occurs when strings of two separate branches overlap and resonate in unison. While uncommon, it is not typically a cause for alarm (see: *Case Studies in Quantum Psychology*).

—Chapter Four, "Physiology," *Principles and Practices of Cleaving, Year Five*

YOU'RE WEARING LIPSTICK," ADDIE SAID AS I came downstairs that night.

I covered my mouth with my hand. "I wear lipstick."

"Yeah, but this looks pretty. And you changed your sweater."

"Leave her alone," my mom said. "You look very nice, sweetheart. Are you and Eliot doing something special?"

"Eliot's got a school project," I said. He'd complained about meeting up with Bree, and I'd commiserated without telling him the change in my own plans.

"Big night?" Monty asked.

"I thought you and Simon were working on your composition?" Addie asked.

"We might go out instead," I said, trying to sound nonchalant.

"You and Simon?" Mom pinched the bridge of her nose. "Del? Really? He's an Original. There are rules."

"I'm not breaking any of them. It's not serious," I said. "He doesn't *do* serious."

"How reassuring," she replied.

The doorbell rang, and Addie slipped down the hallway before me.

"Let her go, Winnie," said Monty from his place in front of the TV. "What's the harm?"

She sighed deeply. "Fine. Be home by curfew. Not a minute later."

"Thanks, Mom." I grabbed my bag.

"What about me?" protested Monty. "I'm the one who told her you should go."

"Thanks to you, too," I said, and gave him a quick kiss.

Simon stood in the entryway, looking nervous. Addie was grilling him about his family and his hobbies, no doubt gearing up to ask about his intentions. I took him by the arm. "Time to go."

The Jeep was parked across the street. A memory of the one in Doughnut World—black, not red—rose up, startling me.

"I'm supposed to get that," he said as I reached for the handle.

"I can open my own door."

"Not on a date. Let me at least start off like a gentleman."

"This is weird," I said, but let him open the door and help me inside.

"I'm the same me," he said.

But he wasn't. I felt vaguely guilty. Was it cheating if you were dating the same guy in two different worlds? And since Doughnut Simon and I weren't a couple—just two people who ended up making out every time we saw each other—did going out with *anyone* count as cheating?

I nudged a tooth-marked Frisbee with my foot. "Where's Iggy?"

"When did you meet Iggy?" He looked genuinely confused.

A million times in Echoes. Never here. "Everyone's heard about that dog," I said, laughing weakly.

He joined in. "He's so spoiled. He's home with my mom, probably sneaking treats."

"How's she doing?"

"Pretty much the same." He squared his shoulders, resolutely cheerful. "Does the Depot sound okay?"

"Sounds great." Familiar ground and not too crowded. "Definitely better than one of the mall restaurants."

"I figured you weren't a huge fan of the mall," he said with a grin.

"What gave it away?" I smoothed the thrift-store sweater I'd changed into—dark green with a wide neck and a slim fit—dressier than I usually wore, but comfortable.

"If I said you're not like other girls, you'd think it was a line."

"It *is* a line."

"Doesn't make it untrue. Besides, you like it that way."

"For someone who never spoke to me before this semester, you've certainly turned into the expert."

He raised a shoulder. "Tell me I'm wrong."

"Basketball," I said, desperate for a neutral topic. "The season's going well?"

"Yeah."

"Did you end up talking with the scout?"

He stared at me, slowing down enough that the person behind us laid on the horn. "What scout?"

"The one from Arizona. Bree said . . ."

He swallowed. "It's not in the cards for me right now."

Of course not. He couldn't go halfway across the country when his mom was so sick. I touched his sleeve. "I'm sorry."

"Don't be. It's my choice, right?"

I bit my lip. Somewhere there was an Echo where he'd chosen to go. "Definitely."

We pulled up in front of the restaurant. The clean, art deco lines seemed both vintage and timeless, and the bold colors emphasized the structure instead of competing with it. The disparate elements blended together in a quirky, compelling harmony.

"You come here a lot?" he asked when he came around to open my door. He took my hand as I climbed out, kept it as we crossed the parking lot.

"Sure," I said, pausing at the small bronze plaque next to the doors. The air was filled with pivots, their edges like tattered silk.

The train crash on this site had left thousands of worlds in its wake. Twenty years later, the Echoes formed from those pivots were some of the strongest around. We'd taken field trips to this site every year since I started training. If I crooked my fingers, I could have caught a pivot and Walked to countless realities, but I was perfectly happy in this one.

The Depot smelled like warm bread, candle wax, and coffee. Simon guided me to a table in the back.

"This seat good?"

"It's my favorite," I said, and pointed to another bronze plaque on the wall next to my seat. "I like the marker."

"You *are* here a lot. With Eliot?"

Happiness evaporated. "Would you lay off the Eliot thing? I've known him since I was in diapers. That's it."

"According to your sister, you two make a great couple."

"Don't listen to Addie," I said. "I never do."

"So you and he aren't . . ." He fumbled with his napkin. "Promised, or something?"

I nearly spewed water across the table. "I'm going to kill her."

"I'll take it that's a no."

"How about this? You stop giving me shit about Eliot, and I won't mention Bree again."

"Bree? I told you—"

"I know. And I know how she looks at you."

He scowled. "You've got a deal. No more questions about Eliot."

"Excellent."

"Your sister is . . . intense," he said cautiously.

"She's a control freak," I said. "But that's a much nicer way to put it."

"You two don't get along?"

I made a face and scanned the menu. "We've been better lately."

"Must be. You're not grounded anymore, right?"

Had I told him I was grounded? I must have, but the fact

that I couldn't remember served as a warning. Too many worlds. Too many Simons. I needed to get a grip. "Kind of. My folks are easing up."

"I'm glad."

"Me too," I said, as the waitress approached. After we'd ordered, I leaned forward. "Want to know a secret?"

His slow, dangerous smile muddled my thoughts. "Definitely."

"I would have come out anyway."

"Snuck out? For me? I'm flattered."

"You should be."

His hand covered mine, his thumb sweeping over my knuckles. "Does this mean I'm your secret now? Like when you disappear at school?"

"Hard to keep you secret when you show up on the front porch. Are you telling people about us?"

He leaned back. "There's not really an 'us,' is there?"

The heat that had been washing over me receded. Stupid, to assume that flirting in the library and one date meant we were together. This was Simon. Charming, casual, loved-by-many, in-love-with-none Simon. I'd been fooling myself.

It was so easy to fall back into old defenses. They fit better than any outfit I might have worn tonight.

"Flavor of the month?" I said, lifting my chin and plucking a roll from the bread basket. Calm. Indifferent. He hadn't gotten close enough to hurt. "Figured you'd mix it up? Go slumming before you try again with Bree?"

"Dial it down, will you?" His eyes flashed. "It's our first date.

I haven't even kissed you yet. Can we save the relationship talk until after dessert?"

I paused in the middle of tearing my roll to bits, hearing exasperation, not anger, in his voice. Foolish as it was, I let myself hope.

"Yet?"

He looked at me blankly.

"You said you haven't kissed me *yet*. Were you going to?"

His mouth curved. "To start."

"Oh," I said, my voice fainter than I intended.

"Yeah." His eyes met mine again, and now it wasn't anger sparking in them. "So eat up."

Both of us made a deliberate attempt to keep the conversation light and inconsequential during the meal. Finally he asked, "Did you want dessert?"

What I wanted was to go somewhere without a table separating us and a crowd of people watching. "Not here."

"My mom was at the crash, you know," he said offhandedly, signaling for the check.

I gaped. "Was she hurt?"

"She was running late that day. She spilled tea on her outfit and had to change clothes. She was in her car when the train derailed, but the people she usually sat with? Dead. Every one. Switching outfits saved her life. Hard to believe."

"Not really," I croaked, and took a long drink of water.

"That's where she met my dad. He worked for the NTSB, investigating the accident. She says by the time the interview was over, she knew he was the one."

I thought about Simon's dad. I'd never met a version of Simon where his dad was in the picture, but surely, somewhere, he'd made the decision to stay with his wife and infant son. There had to be a world where Simon didn't have to carry the burden of his mother's illness on his own. "And you're really not going to tell him about your mom?"

"He doesn't deserve—I never told you that."

"Sure you did." My stomach dropped.

"No. I don't talk about him." Uncertainty crept into his voice.

"You did," I said, hoping my insistence would overcome his doubt. "You don't talk about your mom, either. But you told me."

He ran a hand through his hair. "Maybe I did. . . . Do you ever get déjà vu?"

"Never," I said, forcing a laugh. "Is that even a real thing?"

It definitely was. Synaptic Resonance Transfer—SRT—was the technical term for when the memory of an event transferred from an Echo to an Original, or vice versa.

But he'd used Doughnut Simon's song for our composition. Doughnut Simon remembered me each time I visited. Cemetery Simon had known my name. Usually SRT was a familiar feeling, not a concrete memory, but this was too similar to be anything else. I had my answer, and it was harmless.

I folded my napkin, the cloth forming a droopy star. Simon watched it without speaking. "Ready to go?"

Outside, the moon glowed orange and heavy. "Where to next?" I asked as he helped me into the Jeep.

"Anywhere I get to be with you," he said, his hand lingering on my arm.

"Book Park," I said. It wasn't really a park but a bunch of sports fields behind the library. At this time of night it would be deserted.

Perfect.

We sat on the football field's bleachers, near the end zone. A single halogen light gave everything the look of a vintage photograph.

The field was crammed with pivots, but they were old and faint, easily ignored. I focused on Simon, who was watching me with dark eyes and a shadowed face. "You're cold," he said, noticing my shiver.

"I'm okay."

"Liar." He shook out the blanket he'd pulled from the back of the Jeep and draped it over my shoulders. "Better?"

"Almost." The shape of his mouth was soft and inviting even in the half-light. It shouldn't have felt new, but it did, my nerves tingling, my palms damp. I was as nervous now as I'd been outside Grundy's, a world away and a lifetime ago.

Something rose up within me—a yearning so fierce it resonated through every cell I had, burning away fear and doubt, stealing my breath and blotting out everything but Simon in the moonlight.

I leaned forward, close enough that we were breathing each other's air, and he went perfectly still, eyes locked on mine, familiar and foreign. His hand skimmed over my shoulder, along my pulse, around the back of my neck.

"Del," he said, the word more shape than sound, more question than anything else.

I waited. It seemed vitally important, this time, that it was Simon's choice. I'd made mine, over and over again. In the Key World, though . . . it needed to be his decision. Here, it mattered. Here, it was real.

His lips brushed over mine—once, twice, three times, more certain with each kiss, hungrier with each touch—and the pale cold moonlight disappeared as I shut my eyes and gave myself over to the heat of him.

He wasn't the same Simon. His skin felt softer under my fingertips, and he tasted like autumn sunlight, like almonds and honey. The relief I felt—*not the same, different,* better—was dizzying. The uncertainty dropped away, and in its place was the knowledge that, for once in my life, I was exactly where I belonged. His lips traveled across my cheek, and I nipped at his earlobe, laughing when his arm tightened around me, opening my mouth to his when he came back for another kiss.

The blanket fell away, and I never even noticed, too intent on the feel of Simon's hands, pulling me closer, the sound of his breathing, unsteady as it skated over my skin. "I dream about you," he murmured. "About this. Us."

I smiled against his neck, feeling hazy and languorous. "How's it stack up?"

"Better," he said. "It's always raining when I kiss you."

END OF SECOND MOVEMENT

BEGIN
THIRD
MOVEMENT

CHAPTER THIRTY-SEVEN

I DREW BACK. "RAINING? IN YOUR DREAM. IN your kissing dream."

"Too creepy?"

Not creepy. Potentially disastrous, but not creepy. I forced myself to breathe, kissed him again like his words hadn't upended everything between us. "Tell me about these dreams."

"We're going there already? You seemed like such a nice girl."

"Appearances can be deceiving."

"They're not X-rated, if that's what you're asking. I'm not a perv."

"Dreams. Raining. Talk."

"It's jumpy. Like bad reception on TV," he said. He leaned against the bleachers, gathering me in the circle of his arms, running his fingers through my hair and coaxing out the knots. "But it's you, and it's raining, and you're just . . . there. Like I've been waiting for you, even if I didn't know it. And suddenly you're there, and we're kissing, and when I wake up, I swear I can still taste you. But they were only dreams. This is better."

"Because of the rain?"

"Because it's real."

He tipped my face up to his and kissed me again, gentle and persuasive, and for a moment longer, I savored him. But when we came up for air, I pulled back, needing to see the truth.

"And it's always raining?"

"Not always," he admitted. "The other day, in the library? I was daydreaming. And you were there, but Powell interrupted us. That's when I decided I was done with dreaming."

The rain, at least, was a coincidence. Nothing else was. His dreams—and his weird fugue state—weren't dreams. He was tuning in to his Echoes. His SRT was stronger and more severe than anything I'd heard of.

I drew out an old English assignment from my coat pocket, trying to calm myself.

"What's the deal with those things?" he asked as I began folding.

"It's origami."

"I know that," he said. "Why do you do it?"

I looked at the paper, seeing the beginnings of a star through his eyes. "Habit. Some people crack their knuckles or twirl their hair. You like to tap your pencil when you're thinking," I pointed out.

"And you fold origami?"

"My grandfather taught me. He used to say that each fold was a choice. That I could make whatever I wanted, if I chose carefully." *Make a choice and make a world.*

"Can I see it?"

I finished quickly, my fingers unsteady, and dropped it into his outstretched hand. It sat there, white with pale blue lines and smudged pencil marks, an entire reality's worth of choices in his palm.

"Why do you leave them behind?"

"I didn't think anyone noticed." I only did that when I Walked.

"I don't know when I started noticing them." He held the star between his thumb and forefinger, spinning it slowly. The gesture was so familiar I wanted to cry.

"Probably the same time you started noticing me," I choked out as the pieces came together.

All the times his Echoes spotted me. The way he'd zoned out in the library. He started paying attention to me in the Key World *after* we'd hooked up in an Echo. The threads of his worlds weren't merely similar. They were interwoven. Like a duet, where the melody and harmony trade places, or the two lines merge.

Like counterpoint.

He touched his lips to my forehead, my eyelids, the tip of my nose. "It took me too long," he said. "But I'm glad I did."

He kissed me, sweetly, the sort of kiss that gave more than it took. Something prickled behind my eyelids, and I suddenly understood the biggest difference between this Simon and the others. He knew me. I knew him. Now I was falling for him—not his looks or his hands or the way he felt, but *him*.

I'd wanted to believe this moment was inevitable. That his

feelings for me were so right, so undeniable, he'd fallen for me in two worlds, because the universe wanted us together.

I'd been wrong. Whatever feelings he had for me weren't because of me, of us, the conversations we'd had and the time we'd spent together. They were residual. A memory of us hooking up in the Echo world. The fabric of the universe mimicking itself and mocking me.

This Simon had never wanted me at all.

CHAPTER THIRTY-EIGHT

CRYING IS USELESS. CRYING GETS YOU nowhere, and nothing, and in the end, all you've done is waste time and energy when you should have been fixing whatever situation made you want to blubber in the first place.

So I didn't cry when Simon dropped me off at my house, kissing me without realizing his feelings belonged to someone else. I didn't cry when my dad came out of his bedroom to check on me. I didn't cry up in my room, alone with the knowledge that my Walking—my reckless, selfish, stubborn Walking—had turned out far worse than even Addie had predicted.

Instead I gritted my teeth so hard that by morning, my jaw was stiff, my head ached, and I still didn't have a solution. Talking hurt, thinking hurt, and I wasn't in the mood to do either anymore.

I'd stayed up past dawn, replaying every moment of my interactions with Simon. No matter how I looked at it, the evidence was clear: The Original Simon was being influenced—guided—by his Echoes. He wasn't the same person as they were. He hadn't made the same choices. Left to his own devices, he never would have noticed me. His feelings were grounded in someone else's memories. He'd never be able to trust them 100 percent, and neither could I.

But Simon understood me in a way that no one else did, saw things in me that everyone else overlooked. I wasn't sure I was ready to give that up, even knowing the truth. Maybe eventually the self-doubt would ruin us, but for now . . . I couldn't leave.

If there was a way to separate Simon and his Echoes so he wasn't influenced by them, his true feelings would surface— and maybe they'd be strong enough that we could make it work.

I was willing to tell myself that, if it meant I could keep him.

But at the root of my fears was one undeniable fact. Simon was more tightly tied to the problems in the Key World than I'd ever guessed. If I was going to free him, I couldn't do it alone.

Eliot always woke up before me. But I'd never gone to sleep, so for once I had the jump on him. I showed up at his house, coffee in hand, a few minutes after seven in the morning.

"Del!" said Mrs. Mitchell, giving me a hug. "Is my clock wrong?"

"I'm early," I said. "Is Eliot ready?"

She glanced uncertainly over her shoulder. "I'm not sure he's awake yet."

"I'll get him." I headed upstairs, throwing open his door. "Wake up, genius boy. We have a problem."

The lump on the bed stirred briefly.

"Eliot." I crossed the room and poked at the covers. "Get up."

"Five more minutes," he mumbled, and pulled the blanket more tightly over his head.

"I'm not your mom," I said, setting my coffee down. "And I hope you're wearing pajamas."

"Wha—"

Grabbing the covers in both hands, I yanked them straight off the bed and dropped them in a heap on the floor.

"Gah! Cold!"

"Glad to see you're not naked. I pictured you as a boxers type of guy."

"Del!" He shot out of bed, no shirt, navy boxer briefs snug enough that I looked the other direction. "What are you doing?"

"Wishing you'd put on some pants." I kept my eyes closed and listened to the squeak of his dresser drawer. "Can I turn around?"

"It's ten after seven. Why are you even awake?" He'd put on a pair of sweatpants, but he still wasn't wearing a shirt.

"We have a problem."

He took the coffee from me and drank half. "What did you do this time? Hold on. Don't speak." He shut the door and sat down at his desk. "Okay. Go."

"How much do you know about SRT?"

"Synaptic Resonance Transfer?" He tipped his head back, studied the ceiling, and recited as if he had the page in front of him. "Common. Harmless. Confined to Originals and Echoes."

"What about really extreme cases? Could an Original ever share consciousness with their Echo? Experience what their Echo is doing in real time?"

"SRT that strong would present as some kind of mental illness. Schizophrenia, maybe, or some sort of psychotic break. Trying to process the experiences of so many Echoes would burn out their synapses."

Simon wasn't experiencing all of his Echoes' lives—only the ones who ran into me.

"Theoretically, it's an interesting problem, but I've never heard of it happening," he said.

Eliot would hear about that kind of thing.

"You think you found someone with advanced SRT?" He scrambled out of the chair, thrilled at the prospect. "That's beyond awesome, Del. The Consort will love it!"

Somehow I doubted the Consort would look favorably on my actions. I picked up the battered old recorder Eliot kept on his desk, played the first few notes of "Greensleeves."

"You're not acting like it's awesome." He folded his arms across his bare chest. "What did you do?"

"Why do you assume it was me?"

"Because you're up at the crack of dawn, you look like death, and you're about to turn my recorder into kindling." Gently he pried my fingers off the instrument. "Tell me."

I sat on the edge of the bed, and he joined me, slinging an arm over my shoulders.

"Remember how I told you something was off with Simon?"

Eliot tensed. "I checked his frequency. There's nothing special about him."

"He's sharing memories with his Echoes," I said. "Not

just feelings. Memories. Entire events. Special enough?"

Eliot whistled, long and low. "He told you this?"

I shifted. "Kind of."

"Kind of? Did he say, 'Funny thing, I keep having crazy super-detailed déjà vu'?"

"It came up in conversation."

"Hell of a conversation," he said tightly. "Fine. He has SRT. Why is this a problem for us?"

"When I interact with one of Simon's Echoes, his Original zones out. He thinks he's dreaming, but he's actually seeing through his Echo's eyes."

Eliot's face went cool and remote, analyzing my words. "And he's seeing you."

I picked at a loose thread on my sweater. "His Echoes notice me. They remember me. When I go back, they ask where I've been."

"Why would you go back?" There was a long, excruciating silence, and then he jerked away from me. "You're hooking up with his Echo."

I cringed. "I know, I know. I'm a horrible person. Can we focus on what's important here, please?"

"This *is* important. You promised me you wouldn't Walk by yourself. You gave me your word."

I covered my face with my hands.

"I don't understand. They're not even real." He sprang up, disgust lacing his words. "Why would you do it?"

How could I explain that the rush I got from being with

Simon was nearly as strong as the thrill of Walking? Better, even. When I Walked, I felt free, but the Consort could snatch it away at any moment. With Simon, I was myself, and it was enough, and that was a kind of freedom I'd never had before.

"He makes me happy."

"Happy?" Eliot's mouth twisted like he'd tasted something foul. "You risked your entire future for him. Our future."

"Our future?" I looked at him, misery and betrayal written across his face, feet braced wide and arms folded like he was trying to ward off a blow or hold one back.

"Oh, Eliot." I pressed a fist against my heart. "I didn't—" *I didn't know,* I'd been about to say, but that was a lie. I hadn't *wanted* to know.

"You've thought about it. You must have thought about it. We're good together. We're an amazing team, Del. Everyone says so. Even you."

"We're the best," I said, cutting him off, afraid to hear any more. We couldn't undo this conversation. We couldn't forget it. And I knew, with a sickening certainty, it would change us in ways I never wanted. "It doesn't mean . . ."

"I'm the best when you need help. When you need someone to cover for you, or fix a problem. I'm good enough to use, but not enough to love," he spat.

"I do love you," I said, searching for the balance of honesty and kindness. "Just . . . not that way."

"No, you save that for Simon. What else are you saving for him? Or did you already give it up?"

"Stop it!" I shoved him, hard.

His mouth snapped shut, and he drew a long, shaky breath. We stared at each other in silence, my chest hollow and aching as if my heart had been knocked out.

Finally he spoke, voice harsh. "Those girls are a game to him. They're conquests, and now you're one of them. I hope it was good."

"He's not like that." My own temper reared up then, much more satisfying to hang on to than the guilt and hurt bleeding through me. "And so what if I did sleep with him? It doesn't make me less. It doesn't mean I'm *damaged*."

"I have been in love with you since first grade," he said, breath coming fast and shallow. "When you threw up on Tommy Bradshaw's shoes after he stole my lunch money. More than half my life. I thought if I waited . . . but you won't even give us a shot, because Simon Lane has some crazy hold over you."

"I didn't mean for it to happen. Any of it."

"You never do." I flinched, but he kept talking. "He's going to make you miserable. He's going to treat you like one of those girls. I won't fix it. I won't fix you. Not this time."

"I never asked you to." It was like running toward a cliff full tilt and skidding to a stop at the edge, fighting momentum to keep from plunging over into nothingness. I needed to slow us down. To make Eliot see reason. I grabbed for his hand, but he evaded me. I tried again. "I'm sorry. I should have told you about Simon, but I was afraid."

"You were afraid I'd stop you. Like I could. You don't listen to anyone else. You don't *think* about anyone else. You don't think about the consequences. You care about yourself, and that's it."

I was used to disappointing my family. I didn't care what my teachers thought. But this was Eliot, hurting and hurtful, and my already-battered heart was breaking into pieces at the sight. I'd done this to him. Useless to cry, I reminded myself, and swiped a hand over my eyes. "Fine. I'm a bitch. But I'm right, too. The anomaly my parents have been looking for is related to Simon. We have to do something."

He looked at me like I was a stranger. "The only thing you need to do is leave."

"Don't make this about us. Please."

"It's about you, Del. Same as always. But I'm not interested." He made a sound like a laugh, only strangled and horrible. "Now you know how it feels."

CHAPTER THIRTY-NINE

ELIOT AVOIDED ME AT SCHOOL ALL MORNING, so I wasn't surprised when he was a no-show at lunch. I sat at our usual table anyway, endlessly twisting the metal tab on my Coke. I was as selfish and self-centered as he'd said. For years, he'd dropped hints but I'd ignored them or laughed them off because they'd made me uncomfortable. Because he was my dearest friend, but only a friend, and telling him so might have ruined us.

Now we were beyond ruined. I didn't know how to make it up to him. The one thing he wanted was impossible for me to give.

People milled around the cafeteria, and I watched as they made choice after choice, world after world, ignorant of the weight their decisions carried. I didn't know whether to envy them or feel sorry for them. Could I have chosen differently? Eliot and I made a great team, but I'd never thought of him that way. He'd never made my heart skip and my head swim the way Simon did.

But I could have been honest.

I pressed the heels of my hands against my eyes, trying to relieve the aching behind them, and took a shuddering breath.

"Missed you this morning." Simon's voice came from overhead. "I thought maybe you'd disappeared."

I opened my eyes, my pulse kicking up at the sight of him. "Right here," I said, smiling despite myself.

He dragged a chair over and straddled it, folding his arms over the back, all easy confidence and long limbs. "Are we good?"

When I nodded, he surveyed the table, empty except for my can of pop. "This is not a proper lunch."

"I'm not hungry."

"Guess not. Where's Eliot?"

I couldn't get the words out, but he must have understood, because he stood up and tugged at my hand. "Come on."

"You wanted to sit with the jocks?" I eyed the table brimming with letter jackets and school spirit.

"Another time. Today you need a break."

We'd gone only a few feet when Bree stopped us.

"Hey, stranger." She gave Simon a friendly push, but her smile was strained. "Duncan wants to talk to you about some sports boosters fund-raiser. Got a minute?"

Simon's hand tightened on mine. "Not right now. Sorry."

"But I saved you a seat," she said, a plaintive note to her voice.

"Give it to someone else," he said gently, and led me away without waiting for her response.

I blinked. "You didn't need to—"

"Yeah, I did."

I felt the stares as he led me through the maze of tables and out the side doors, but Simon didn't seem to care. What must it be like to be so sure of yourself and your place in the world? I'd thought I had that, once, but my certainty had unraveled weeks ago.

"Where are we going?"

"Equipment room," he said. "Nobody's in there this time of day."

I stopped short and gave him a dubious look.

"It's the only place in the building where we don't need a hall pass. I'm in there all the time for team stuff, and since I'm captain . . ." He reached into his pocket. "I've got a key."

He looked so pleased with himself I decided not to mention I didn't need a key.

"How'd you end up as captain when you're only a junior?" I asked. "Isn't it usually for seniors?"

"My cocaptain's a senior," he said, and pointed at the trophy case nearby. "But I was on varsity last year, and we won State, so . . ."

He kept talking, but something in the display caught my attention. I eased closer, nodding as if I were listening.

One of the net-draped trophies winked out of existence, replaced by a smaller, far less showy one. In an instant they swapped again, and everything looked exactly the way it should.

Another inversion in the Key World. Another one connected to Simon.

"I just remembered," I said, smacking my forehead. "I have to turn in a library book."

"Now?"

"It's way late. Fines in the double digits, and the librarian's threatening me with another detention." I shooed him off. "You go ahead and I'll catch up."

The frown cleared. "Del, chill out. I wasn't going to put the moves on you. At least, not a lot."

"I'm looking forward to your moves. I'll meet you in a few minutes."

Easy enough to say I got caught without a hall pass, or that the librarian had made me shelve books as a way to pay off my fine. I'd come up with a story, but for now, I needed to get rid of him.

Reluctantly he let go of my hand. "Go on," I said, shoving at him. I made a show of heading in the opposite direction, toward my locker, glancing back to check his progress.

Once he was safely out of sight, I raced back, shielding the trophy with my body. My pulse drummed in my ears as I pulled out the lock picks and got to work. With any luck, the few passersby would think I'd suddenly become a basketball fan.

As soon as the lobby was empty, I shoved the panel of glass aside and reached for the blinking net, listening for its shifting pitch.

Nimble fingers, open mind. I caught the frequency on the second try, drawing it closer, out of the display case. With light, careful movements I enlarged the pivot enough to squeeze through.

One last check around the deserted lobby, and I stepped into the rift, holding my breath at the tight fit.

When I emerged on the other side of the pivot, the trophies were smaller and the room was dotted with people who took no notice of me. One look at the team picture explained the difference. Simon had never moved up to the varsity squad, and the team had never made it to State.

If the inversion took root in the Key World, would my Simon lose his place as captain? Would people treat him the same way? Would he forget me again? I wasn't sure how he'd be affected, but it wouldn't be good.

I touched the trophy, trying to find the strings that contained the inversion. Over and over, my fingers slipped. My hands ached from searching so meticulously through the threads, testing each one without altering it, and my head pounded. No wonder my dad had contracted frequency poisoning.

My shaking fingers snagged on a thread, and I froze. If even one line snapped, it could cause another cleaving. I had to empty my mind of everything—Simon, my dad's illness, the anomaly threatening the Key World. The only thing I could think about was finding the bad strings.

Nimble fingers, open mind.

And there they were. Once I found the first, the rest were easy to locate. I coaxed them back into tune, painfully aware that the filaments beneath my fingers were connected to this Echo's Simon. I wondered how my actions would alter him, if it would cause him to choose differently, or nullify the decisions he'd already made. It was too much power for one person to have over another, Echo or Original.

The frequency shifted, a grinding, grating, reluctant drop, and I checked my watch. Not bad for fifteen minutes' work.

The empty lobby was both a surprise and a relief. Both the net and trophy were back in place, resonating at the Key World frequency, exactly as they should be. I slid the glass door shut and reached in my bag for the pick that would relock it.

"If you wanted to see it up close," Simon said, stepping out from behind the vending machine, "all you had to do was ask."

CHAPTER FORTY

THERE ARE THREE REASONS WALKERS ARE almost never caught:

> They're good.
> They're careful.
> People don't pay attention.

As long as you had two out of three, you could usually escape detection. I was good, but not careful. And Simon was definitely paying attention.

Basically, I was screwed.

"Don't we have a date in the equipment room?" I said, scrambling for a distraction, hoping he hadn't seen the truth.

One look at his face dashed those hopes. "Nobody who cuts class as often as you worries about library fines. Did you really think I was going to buy that story?"

I lifted a shoulder. "Saying yes doesn't make either of us look good."

"None of this makes you look good, Del. Start talking."

"It's complicated." The idea of telling him made my stomach roil.

"So talk slow. Use small words. But start talking, because what I saw was impossible."

"Nothing's impossible," I murmured, but he folded his arms and stared until I caved. "Can we do this somewhere else?"

"Equipment room," he said grimly. "The truth this time. All of it."

You don't think about anyone else, Eliot had said. *You don't think about the consequences.* He was right. It had been the Walking that mattered most, not the worlds I found. But now I'd found Simon. Irresistible, inexplicable, problematic Simon.

Walkers valued the Key World above all else, but secrecy ran a close second. We'd had it bred into us, generation after generation passing down the gene for Walking and the warning to keep it hidden. Could I really betray that trust for a *boy*? I ran through a million stories as we headed to the equipment room. Surely one of them would be more believable than telling him the truth. Safer, too. If the Consort discovered I'd told, they would come after us both.

Most lies aren't meant to ruin; they're meant to protect what we hold most dear, whether it's a person or an idea or a way of life. But even the noblest lie eats away at the truth, until you're left with the facade and what you were protecting crumbles to dust.

I could lie, and save Simon, and myself, and the Walkers' secret.

And in doing so, I would lose him.

When we reached the equipment room, just inside the field

house doors, he gestured to the dead bolt. "Did you want to take this one, or should I?"

"Be my guest." My hands were shaking too hard to turn a door handle, let alone pick a lock.

The equipment room was actually a big closet—high ceil-inged and windowless, smelling of rubber and dust. There were carts of basketballs and volleyballs, towers of plastic cones, and hockey sticks corralled in a trash can, ends sticking up like the bristles of a brush. A single fluorescent light fixture buzzed over-head, too dim to reach the corners.

He closed the door and leaned against it, the implication clear: We weren't leaving until he got answers.

"Nice place," I said, boosting myself onto a waist-high stack of gymnastic mats. "You bring a lot of girls here?"

Once again he looked at me with too much perception. "Wouldn't be much of an escape if I did."

"Makes sense."

"More than I can say for you," he said.

"Tell me what you saw."

His expression hardened. "So you can make up a story to match?"

"Simon, please. I'll tell you the truth. I'll answer your ques-tions. But it'll be easier if I know what you saw."

"I am not interested in making this *easy* for you." He rubbed the back of his neck wearily. "You were lying about the library book. I thought it was because you were nervous about coming in here, so I started to follow you, to tell you we could go somewhere more public. When you turned around, I hid behind the vending machines and waited to see what you were up to. You're pretty handy with a lock pick," he added. "Are you some sort of teen superspy?"

"Really not," I assured him. "What next?"

"You know how in the desert, the heat makes the air shimmer? You reached into the case, and the whole thing kind of . . . rippled, and you walked toward it. But instead of running into the wall, you disappeared, a little at a time. Like you were a mirage."

He must have thought he was losing his mind. He was astonishingly calm for a person who had to be questioning his sanity, though. "What did you do?"

"I poked around, but everything looked normal. The only reason I didn't think I'd dreamed it was because the trophy case was open."

"What kinds of trophies were inside?"

"The ones I was telling you about. When we won State."

"You're sure? Did you actually see them? Or are you remembering?"

"I'm positive. I straightened the net on top." The inversion hadn't caused any permanent damage. At least one part of my day had gone right. He continued. "When the air started to move again, I hid. Thirty seconds later, you were back."

"You didn't tell anyone else?"

"Who would believe it?"

He had a point. The question was, would Simon believe me? I was surprised by how much I wanted him to. I should have felt only fear, but somehow it was tempered by a sense of relief that I could finally come clean.

"Everything I tell you has to stay secret," I said. "You cannot even begin to imagine the trouble we'll be in if they find out I told you."

I could imagine it perfectly. Permanent expulsion. Thrown in an oubliette. I'd never see him again. But the risk of losing him, of going back to a time when he looked past me as if I were an impression, was equally awful.

"They?" he asked.

I swallowed. "My family. My . . . people, I guess you could call them. Do you promise?"

"Not to tell anyone that I'm hallucinating during second lunch? Done."

I wiped my sweaty hands on my jeans and dove in. "When you play basketball, do you ever wonder if the game could have gone a different way? Like, what if the lineup changed? Or if you'd called a time-out instead of playing through? Taken a shot instead of passed the ball? Do you ever wonder what would have happened if you'd made different choices?"

"Sure. Everyone does."

"Not me. I don't have to, because I can see it."

My words started out halting and low, wilting in the face of his skepticism. But my need for him to believe me was greater than my fear, and I used that need to lend my voice strength.

"Every time you make a decision, from what you had for breakfast to who you fall in love with, the universe splits in two.

One half is the part you remember. It's real. That's the decision you made. The other half is the what-if."

"Like parallel worlds," he said with a frown.

"Yes. Except, this is the only one that counts. We call it the Key World."

He opened his mouth and closed it again.

"The other worlds are called Echoes. They're filled with copies of people, and those people make more choices, and their choices make more worlds, and it goes on and on. For infinity. Sometimes the Echoes cause problems, and the Walkers—my people—have to protect the Key World."

"You're crazy."

I was a lot of things, most of them bad. But crazy wasn't one of them. I hopped down from the mats and stalked toward him. "Then what did you see?"

"You cut class to visit parallel worlds. You're actually telling me that."

"I'm telling you there are entire worlds out there, ones you can't imagine. Worlds where we're still British subjects. Worlds where penicillin was never invented. Worlds where women never got the vote, or the Beatles never broke up. It's not even big choices, sometimes. In sixth grade I took a field trip to a world where Texas seceded because someone forgot to send a telegram."

He shook his head. "This is a joke. You're taping me, and you're going to upload the video."

"Do you see any cameras?"

His face softened, turned sympathetic. He took my hands in his. "You're upset."

"Of course I'm upset. I'm not supposed to tell people like you. Hell, there's now a world out there where I *didn't* tell you." There were worlds where Simon hadn't caught me. But those Echoes wouldn't last, because I couldn't sustain them—and there was something painfully ironic about that fact. Now that I'd told him the truth, it felt inevitable, like we'd been guided to this moment by the same universe that had twined us together in the first place.

"Is there a world where you and Eliot didn't fight?"

There were worlds where Simon hadn't chosen me. There were worlds I hadn't gone after him. But Eliot and I lived in *this* world. No Echoes, no second chances, no way around the fact I'd broken his heart. I felt sick at the thought. "It's more complicated than that."

"It's really stressing you out, isn't it? Have you tried talking to him?"

I yanked my hands away. "You think I'm making this up because of *Eliot*? You think I'm delusional because we fought? That's the stupidest thing I've ever heard. You asked me for the truth, and I'm telling you. I'm a Walker. What you saw was me Walking to another world, fixing it, and coming back."

His sympathy vanished. "Prove it. Take me with you."

I recoiled. "That's impossible."

"Nothing's impossible," he mimicked. "Isn't that what you said before? Teach me how to Walk to one of these other worlds."

I couldn't teach Simon how to Walk any more than I could

teach him to fly. "It's a genetic condition. You can't do it if you aren't born into it. And you weren't, trust me."

"How do you know?"

"Remember how you keep saying I'm a music prodigy? It's a Walker thing."

"I suck at music, so I'm not allowed to go with? That's crap."

"That's life," I said, Monty's words coming back to me. "I didn't say it was fair. Trust me, that's one of the first things we learn. Life isn't fair. The good guys don't always win. There are plenty of worlds where the human race is better off, but we don't get to pick and choose. Our job is to protect the Key World. Anything else is gravy."

"Fine. Do it again, and I'll watch."

I started to protest, but he cut me off. "Either you're crazy, or you're lying, or you're for real. But only one of those ends up with us leaving this room together, Del. Your choice."

My shoulders dropped. "Am I going to come back and find the school psychologist?"

"I promised you I wouldn't say anything. I keep my word."

"I'm crossing over and coming straight back. If you're not here . . ." I couldn't think of a dire enough threat. Anything I could imagine was child's play compared to what the Consort would do.

"I'll be here," he said.

I closed my eyes and listened for a pivot. A freshly formed one hovered less than a foot away. It must have sprung up when he'd decided to hear me out.

"Ready?" I asked, opening my eyes to find him watching me. It was a physical sensation, sweeping over me from my forehead to my toes and back again, turning my entire body to pins and needles. I felt oddly exposed as I reached for the pivot, its edges sharp as a paper cut. Even after everything I'd revealed, it was terrifying to let him see this part of me.

The weight of Simon's gaze propelled me through the rift.

The equipment room stood deserted, the door swinging wide. I heard a slam and peered out at the empty field house. His Echo had left, true to his word. Even without the dissonance, this was not a world I wanted to stay in.

I ducked back through and crashed into the broad planes of Simon's chest. His arms wrapped around me, and I soaked up the sound of the Key World streaming from him like sunlight.

"I thought I could find it." He looked down at me, pupils huge and astonished. "I figured I'd follow you through. But you . . . vanished. You left."

There was something in his voice beyond surprise. Bewilderment, maybe, and hurt.

"I came back."

"You came back." He kissed me softly, and then less softly, and then he was backing me toward the mats I'd been sitting on, his hands woven through my hair, my hands sliding along his back. "It's real. It's amazing, Del. You're amazing."

"Glad you finally noticed," I said between kisses.

If this was what happened when you were honest with people, I'd have to try it more often.

Then again, I wasn't being entirely honest. I didn't tell him that he was sharing memories with his Echoes, that I'd kissed him in other worlds. Too much at one time, I thought, feeling liquid and golden from his touch. Better to tell him when I understood what had happened.

The muffled sound of the bell stopped me from saying anything else. "Class," he said against my neck.

I touched my swollen lips, envisioning Eliot's reaction when he spotted us. This room was a refuge, a world of its own, and I didn't want to leave. "Let's skip."

He stepped back, but left his palm curved around my side. "Coach benches us if we cut. Can I see you later? After practice?"

His mouth came down on mine, silencing the whisper of doubt inside me. Later, I'd tell him about his Echoes. We'd figure out how to free him from the anomaly. We'd start fresh. We'd be happy. Simon's kiss made it all seem possible, the choices before us as limitless as the multiverse itself.

"Sounds good," I said, and let myself believe.

CHAPTER FORTY-ONE

I T WAS EASY TO THINK I'D DONE THE RIGHT thing with Simon whispering those exact words in my ear. But as the day wore on, doubt crept back in. I'd told an Original about the Walkers. I'd let him see me Walk. I was still keeping secrets from Simon, and Eliot was still avoiding me.

It was probably for the best. I could only imagine what Eliot would say if he knew I'd told Simon about us. He'd probably turn me in to the Consort himself. Maybe he already had.

When I arrived home, Mom was waiting by the kitchen island with her coat on, a giant leather tote at her feet. Her shoulders sagged with relief.

"Del! Where have you been?"

"School. Like every other weekday. Am I in trouble?" Guilt surged, and I turned away, fumbling with my coat and scarf.

"I'm in a hurry. The Consort needs me to come in right away, Addie's at her apprenticeship, and I didn't want to leave your grandfather alone."

"I can hang out with him." In the family room, Monty was watching a documentary on the History Channel, arguing with the narrator about the outcome of the Korean War. "How long will you be gone?"

"We should be back by dinner. Addie said she'd be late too, so you're off the hook for training tonight."

At least Simon and I would have some measure of privacy.

"I've got to run, sweetie. Bye, Dad. Love you both."

Monty joined me as I made a cup of tea. "How was your day?"

"Strange." I wrapped my chilled hands around the mug. "Simon's coming over later to practice our composition."

"Was it him who put those roses in your cheeks?" he asked with a grin.

I touched the side of my face, and the loneliness of my trip home faded. "Maybe."

"It'll be good to see this young man up close, considering how much time you've spent with him." He winked. "And his Echoes."

I stared into my mug. "I should have known better."

"Bah. People will do all sorts of things for love. You can't blame them for it."

"I'm not in love with Simon." I wasn't quite ready to confess the extent of my feelings—or my actions. Not even to Monty, who'd been paying closer attention than I realized. "There's something different about him."

"I don't doubt it," he said, and patted my hand. "Not to worry. I'll keep your secrets and you'll keep mine."

I hoped so. I leaned back against the island and checked

him over. Neatly dressed, hair combed, lucid despite his ongoing argument with the television. One of his better days, and I hoped it held. "You're not going to hover, are you?"

He shot a mournful glance toward the empty cookie jar. "Your mother hasn't made cookies in ages. Did you notice? Oatmeal chocolate chip would hit the spot."

I was not in the mood to bake. "Why don't I fix you a bowl of ice cream?"

"Too cold for ice cream. Rose made sure to keep oatmeal chocolate chip in the house. We never went without. Your mother uses her recipes. Did you know that?" His eyes went distant, his voice wavery. "I wonder if she has some right now. If she's making them wherever she is."

Hard to tell if he was genuinely confused, or putting on an act to get what he wanted. But real or feigned, the last thing I needed was Monty slipping in front of Simon. If an hour of baking would buy me a peaceful afternoon . . . "Cookies it is."

By the time Simon rang the bell, the island was covered with racks of cookies and Monty was at the table with a plate full of crumbs and a glass of milk, seemingly content.

"I'll get it," I said, brushing at a lock of hair that wouldn't stay tucked into its braid.

Monty made a noise of agreement and helped himself to another cookie. I'd lost track of how many he'd eaten. My mom was going to kill me.

The minute I opened the front door I forgot about my mom

and sugar comas. Simon, rangy and lean and breathtaking, crowded out everything else.

"Hey." I didn't know what to do with my hands. Was I supposed to hug him? Kiss him? I wanted to melt into him, but with Monty down the hallway, it seemed like a recipe for disaster. "How was practice?"

"I was distracted." He set his backpack on the floor, midnight eyes crinkling at the corners. "You have stuff on your face."

"Flour." I swiped at my forehead. "I was baking."

He sniffed the air appreciatively, and rubbed his thumb slowly over my cheek.

"Did I not get it?" My voice sounded too breathy.

"You did." His fingers curved around my neck and he touched his lips to mine.

I figured out what to do with my hands: slide them over his shoulders, pull him closer. His hair was damp from the shower, his skin smelling soap-and-water clean. He tasted like toothpaste and mischief. With one hand he unwound my braid, while the other slid along the strip of bare skin above my jeans.

Whatever trouble we were in was worth it.

"You must be Del's friend," Monty said from the kitchen doorway.

Simon froze. "I thought you were home alone," he said against my mouth, and straightened.

"Simon Lane, sir." He took a full step away from me and extended his hand.

"Montrose Armstrong. I've been wanting to meet you for

quite a while." He held the handshake for a beat too long, reading Simon's frequency. I tried to interpret his expression. If there was a problem, Monty would feel it.

Finally he let go, nodding in approval. My lungs resumed working. "Del's my favorite, you know."

Simon's hand rested on the small of my back. "Mine too."

"She made cookies," Monty said. "You should have one."

I glared at him, but we went into the kitchen, where Simon made enthusiastic noises about the cookies and I plotted our escape.

"You two are working on a song for music class?" Monty asked.

Simon finished the cookie before responding. "I lucked out, getting paired with her. She's a genius."

"You're not musical?" Monty sounded surprised.

"No, sir. But Del says it runs in your family. Being good at music, I mean."

"Told you that, did she?" Monty said vaguely, but his gaze sharpened.

"We'd better get to work," I said, and dragged Simon to the living room.

"Is he one too?" Simon whispered. "A Walker?"

"Everyone in my family is. Eliot, too. But Monty . . . he's done it for too long. He's not quite right now."

He sat at the piano. "Seemed fine to me."

"He has good moments and bad ones," I said. "And he made a special effort for you."

"Am I special?" He hooked a finger through my belt loop.

"Very," I said, giving him a slow smile.

"I thought about you all day. About this. It doesn't seem possible."

"Anything's possible."

His hands closed tightly over mine. "Is there's a world where they've cured cancer?"

My smile fell away. "I don't know. Probably. But . . ."

"Could we take my mom there?"

I couldn't look at him, at the hope shining in his face, knowing I would be the one to snuff it. "She couldn't get through," I said. "Like when you tried following me. If you're not a Walker, you can't cross."

The shadows under his eyes deepened, but he rubbed a hand across his face and tried again. "What about bringing the medicine here?"

Breaking news gently is a misnomer. News doesn't break. People do, no matter how you try to cushion the blow.

I tried anyway, more careful with my words than ever before. "Bringing objects over from Echoes is forbidden. It's too dangerous."

He scoffed. "It's medicine. How dangerous could it be?"

I thought about the drawing his cemetery Echo had given me, how blithely I'd tucked it into my backpack. Even now, hidden in a dresser drawer, the faintest trace of dissonance drifted from it. But the sketch was a reminder, not a catalyst.

"It's not the size of the object; it's the change it creates, and there's no greater change than someone's existence. An alteration that big is against the rules."

He dropped my hands, shocked and furious. "You won't save my mom because you don't want to get in trouble?"

My anger rose to meet his. "I *can't*. If I gave her medicine from an Echo, the difference in frequencies might end up hurting her." I thought about the anomaly, the plague of inversions, the way Simon seemed to be caught in it. "It could rip her apart. And the damage could spread. To you, to anything or anyone she comes in contact with. You could fade right out of existence, and I'm not doing that to you again."

He went very still. "Again?"

I ran my fingers over the cool ivory keys and said nothing.

"Del?"

For a place that wasn't real, Park World managed to ruin every part of my life. "I'm not grounded. I'm suspended from the Walkers. Addie and I went out a few weeks ago, to an Echo that was really unstable. You were there with Iggy. I messed around with the threads, and . . . they broke. I cleaved the entire branch."

"Cleaved?

"Like pruning, only the branch . . . disintegrates." I sank onto the bench next to him.

"I disintegrated?" His laugh sounded nervous, the kind that preceded a complete freakout.

"Your Echo did. You're an Original. You belong to the Key World, so it didn't affect you. But if we start bringing stuff over from other branches, and it damages the fabric of this one, especially around your mom, you could unravel too. Both of you."

I touched my forehead to his shoulder. The muscles beneath his T-shirt were clenched and unyielding. "I'm so sorry. I wish . . ."

"Don't," he said. I flinched at the harshness in his voice. "What good is it, then?"

A chill crept over me. He'd thought Walking was amazing, in the equipment room. He'd thought *I* was amazing.

I can't figure you out, and I want to. Now he had, and I wasn't a puzzle, or the girl he'd kissed in the rain and in dreams. I was a means to an end.

But hadn't I done the same? I'd used Walking to get what I wanted but couldn't have.

"What's the point if you can't save people? Make the world better?"

"Walkers believe that the integrity of the Key World matters more than anything," I said. "It's the only world strong enough to sustain the weight of all the choices that spring from it. It's like the trunk of a really big, really ancient tree, and all the other worlds are branches."

"The world is a tree. Great. Very green."

"If the branches are damaged, and it spreads, the tree gets weaker. If it happens too many times, the tree won't survive. So we try to contain the damage, as much as we can, but sometimes that means letting bad things happen."

"That's crap. She's *my mom*." He took my hands again, and I wanted to weep at the desperation in his words. "You said it might hurt her. That means it might not. Anything is better than her odds right now. Please, Del."

"I can't."

"You *can*. You break rules all the time. You broke one today, telling me about the Walkers. Why not now, when it might actually do good?"

I felt myself weakening, the wave of his sorrow battering my resolve. My gaze fell on our composition, the notes he'd borrowed from his Echo, the song we'd made together a reminder of all I'd done wrong. I shook my head, finally understanding what my parents had been trying to teach me. "I'm so sorry, Simon. Just because something's possible doesn't mean we should do it."

Turns out, telling your almost-boyfriend you won't save his mother's life puts a damper on the relationship. He left a few minutes later, distant and wounded and avoiding my eyes.

I didn't blame him, exactly. But I doubted him. I doubted myself, for confiding in him, for believing in us.

"Delancey!" called Monty from the kitchen, moments after Simon left, pulling the door shut with a solid thunk.

"Please don't tell me you're hungry again," I said.

Monty sat at the island playing a phantom tune, his fingers gnarled but certain on an imaginary keyboard. "You told him about us."

Too wrung out to bother with denial, I said, "He saw me Walk. I didn't have a choice."

His eyebrows lifted, two furry white caterpillars arching in unison. "He left in an awful hurry. You two have a falling out?"

"His mom is sick. He wanted me to bring back a cure from the Echoes."

"From the look on your face, I'd guess you told him no."

I picked up one of the cookies, but my stomach rebelled. "What was I supposed to tell him? We don't know what could happen, especially with the anomaly causing so many problems. He doesn't understand what's at stake."

"Does anyone? You toss around the word 'infinity' like you know what it means, but you've not the faintest idea. None of us do. Whatever you imagine, whatever you think you know, infinity stretches farther. It's a bit like people. They're capable of so much more than they realize."

I broke the cookie in half, and in half again, until crumbs showered the countertop. "He's never going to speak to me again."

"Bah. Do you trust him?"

Underneath the hurt and the doubt, the answer was as clear as the Key World. "I do. There's something about him . . . I don't know what it is, but he matters."

"I don't doubt it. And if there was a way to save his mother without risking the Key World, would you?"

"Of course."

"Tell him so. And then find a way to do it." He twinkled at me. "Infinity, Del. Anything is possible."

CHAPTER FORTY-TWO

DESPITE MONTY'S PEP TALK, I WASN'T READY to tell Simon anything. I was a collection of hurt feelings and unanswered questions. Better to go to him when I had something worthwhile to offer. Something more than myself.

Over dinner, everyone was subdued, lost in their own thoughts. "Things didn't go well with the Consort today?" Addie finally asked.

"We're not making the progress we'd like," my mom said.

"I did some research today," Addie said. "I have a theory about the anomaly."

My mom set her fork down. "I thought we made it clear that you were to stay away from the situation."

"You did. But Councilman Lattimer thinks I could be helpful."

Monty made a face like a petulant child.

"Delightful," Mom said. "Did a member of the Consort give you express permission to involve yourself with a classified situation?"

"Not exactly," Addie said. "But I thought . . ."

My dad said, more kindly, "It's nice that you want to help, honey. But this isn't a school project. We need you to focus on your apprenticeship and keeping your sister out of trouble. Leave this to the adults."

"The adults?" Addie said faintly.

Mom shook her head. "I expect this kind of behavior from Del, Addison. Not you."

Addie's face went white, then red, then white again. "May I be excused?"

She left without waiting for an answer. Monty tsked. "She's not a child."

"She's my child," Mom replied. "I'm not putting her in harm's way if I can avoid it."

"Can you?" he asked softly. "Desperate times, Winnie."

"Not that desperate. Not yet." She swallowed, reached for my dad's hand. "The girls are to stay away from anything having to do with the anomaly. That's our decision, and it is final. Are we clear?"

Monty nodded slowly, looking smaller, and I felt a twin rush of emotion: sympathy for him, irritation with my parents. Without speaking, I cleared my place at the table.

"The same goes for you, Del," my father said. I stared at the floor. "The last thing you need is to be caught defying the Consort."

"Got it," I said.

I had no intention of getting caught.

Upstairs, Addie was lying on the bed, eyes closed, headphones on. I sat down next to her and plucked them off. Rachmaninoff came through the earbuds, tinny and strident.

"They're worried," I said. "They're so worried they can't hear anything else."

"Whatever," said Addie. "You get away with crap constantly. Why not me? Not even once?"

"You got caught because you told on yourself," I said impatiently. "When we broke into Mom's office, I locked it up again and kept my mouth shut. I didn't sit down at dinner and say, 'Hey, Mom, you need to invest in a better lock, because I picked yours in under ninety seconds.' You don't want to get caught, learn how to be sneaky."

She opened her eyes. "Oh, good. I'm taking advice from a delinquent. This is what my life has come to."

"A very successful delinquent, who's willing to teach you her ways," I added, and hit her with a pillow. "Tell me your theory."

"We're supposed to leave it alone."

"You're supposed to be teaching me," I said. "Consider this a teachable moment."

She snorted, but sat up. "Fine. I think they're approaching the whole problem backward. The Consort's looking for the anomaly in the Echoes—moving from newer to older, smaller to bigger. But the biggest, oldest world is this one."

"You think the source is here? The Consort would have found anything that disrupted the Key World."

"You know the Queen Anne's lace in the backyard? It's a weed, technically. An invasive species."

As a kid, I'd picked enormous bouquets of Queen Anne's lace—broad white crowns and spindly stems that left my fingers smelling like carrots. "It's a flower. Not a very pretty one though."

"It's a weed. We're used to it, so we don't think about pulling it when Mom tells us to clear the flower beds. But she's got enough other plants back there that it doesn't take over. The Key World is the same way: Even if the anomaly is here, our world is stable enough to keep it in check. But the Echoes aren't as stable. There's room for it to take root, and each Echo generated from one of the infected branches is even *more* infected. It's cumulative."

"But what about here? Would it affect Originals?"

"You mean Simon?" She rolled her eyes. "It's more likely to affect his Echoes. He's popular at school, right?"

"He's popular *everywhere*. You've seen him."

"Some people are natural pivot points. The Consort physicists haven't studied it super closely, but they've found that a small segment of the population has a tendency to form significantly more branches than others."

I thought back to the maps Eliot had shown me, thickets of lines crowding around the Key World. "Why would that happen?"

"We don't know. It's like their decisions have more resonance. Historically, those people end up in positions that underscore those tendencies—they become politicians, or prominent in a given field, or celebrities. If that's the case with Simon, he's popular *because* he's a pivot. He literally can't help it."

"That's crazy. Does it make them less stable? Do they have SRT?"

"It doesn't affect their stability. They're like any other Original." She paused. "They do display a higher rate of SRT, but that's simple math—more Echoes means more chance of an overlap."

More Baroque events, too. Situations with lots of choices meant lots of Simons, operating on similar frequencies. If they overlapped, it would account for his extreme SRT. And more Simons meant he was more likely to be affected by the anomaly.

But unless I wanted him to end up as the Consort's guinea pig, it was smarter not to mention that to my sister.

"So, what's next? If we're going to figure this out, we need a plan." Nothing distracted Addie like a plan.

She reached for a nearby map, then tossed it aside. "First thing is to find the branches that are being affected. Eliot can help us narrow it down, can't he?"

My voice sounded small. "I don't think Eliot's interested in helping me right now."

"Why not?"

I traced the floral pattern on the duvet.

"I see," she said. "Give him some time. He'll come around."

Time wasn't the answer. But all I said was, "I've got a copy of the software we can use."

Addie looked relieved. "Excellent. Between the anomaly and the cleavings, none of my maps are working. Fork it over."

I had an instant of panic Simon would text me about Walking while she was using it. Then I shoved my paranoia aside. He wasn't going to be texting, or calling, or acknowledging me anytime soon.

"This software is awesome, Del. I don't know why you won't give Eliot a chance."

"On the strength of his programming abilities? He's my friend. I don't think about him that way."

"You might if you tried."

"Could you make yourself fall for someone you didn't want, just because it would make life easier? Find some nice Walker guy instead of a nice Walker girl?"

"Point taken." She cocked her head to the side. "There's a pivot in your room."

My hands went cold. "There are pivots all over the house. No big deal."

"This one's strong." She headed for the stairs. "Someone must have used it recently."

"I bet it's a glitch." I scrambled after her. "Eliot hasn't finished debugging the code."

She ignored me, and I had a horrible, slow-motion sense of watching disaster unfold. She threw open the door, wrinkling her nose at the mess of papers and clothing scattered everywhere. Map in hand, she turned in a circle until she found the pivot. It pulsed loudly, a drumbeat announcing my guilt.

"Tell me you didn't." She stalked toward the rift.

"I didn't!"

She stopped in her tracks and faced me dead-on. "Tell me the truth."

I looked away.

"Oh, my God. You've been Walking behind my back? Using

this to sneak out and . . . what? Mess around in the Echoes? Were you trying to make me look bad?"

"No! Why would I do that?"

"I don't know, Del. I don't know why you would violate your probation, and risk your entire future, and lie to the Consort, and . . . You're crazy. That's why. You're insane. They don't let crazy people Walk, you know. It won't matter if you score one hundred on the exam. They're never going to give you a license."

I knotted my fingers together. "They will if you don't tell."

"Lie for you." She scoffed. "You've definitely lost it."

"You don't understand," I said, desperation flooding me. "Addie, please."

"I understand you're a lying little weasel. I've been wasting my time babysitting when I could have been helping Mom and Dad. I put my own reputation on the line. I told Lattimer he should consider ending your suspension early, that you were a lock to pass the test. I told him you'd learned your lesson." She laughed. "We're both idiots, I guess."

Addie had backed me up with Lattimer?

"You never told me."

"I didn't want to get your hopes up. Unlike you, I don't lead people on. Make them believe something that was never true. Like me, thinking you'd changed." She waved the phone at me. "Or Eliot, thinking you cared about him."

I snatched the phone back. "Leave him out of this."

"What did you do to him? Eliot would walk through fire for

you, so it must have been something big. Was it because you were Walking without him? Or did he get sick of your weird obsession with Simon Lane?"

I forced myself to look away from the pivot.

"It's both," she said softly. "Simon and Walking. You were chasing after his Echoes. That is . . . pathetic."

"You can't prove any of it," I said, fear turning ugly and vicious inside me. "Nobody's ever interested in your theories, Addie."

"I'll find proof," she said, heading toward the stairs. The smile she leveled at me was as brilliant and hard as a diamond. "And once I do, I will bury you."

CHAPTER FORTY-THREE

I STOOD IN MY EMPTY ROOM, THE PIVOT THROB-bing in time with my head. How long before Addie tracked down the proof she needed? My first instinct was to call Eliot, but he wasn't an option anymore. My second was to ask Monty for help, but when I found him, he was sitting in the living room while my parents washed dishes ten feet away.

I was running out of choices—and time.

"I'm going out," I called.

Mom turned. "It's nine o'clock at night. Where are you going?"

"Eliot's." The lie rolled easily off my tongue.

From the living room, Monty broke into a coughing fit. "Aren't you going to say good-bye?"

I gave him a quick hug. Before I pulled away, he pressed something into my hand, curling my fingers around it. "Just in case."

It was a small silver pendant, a tuning fork like Addie and my mom had. I wasn't supposed to have one until I got my license. "Thanks, Grandpa."

"Use it well." He settled back into the recliner, eyes shut.

"It's a school night," my dad reminded me. "Be back by curfew."

Making curfew was the least of my worries.

I'd left origami stars behind in every Echo I visited, and they were still resonating at the Key World frequency. But instead of guiding me home, my breadcrumbs would lead Addie straight to the proof she needed. I couldn't even collect them without my signal laying a fresh trail.

Even without proof, an accusation would be enough for the Consort to look more closely at what I'd been up to. When they did, they'd find Simon, with his SRT and his Baroque events.

Simon, who needed me to save his mom's life.

What's the point if you can't save people? Make the world better?

My future with the Walkers was unraveling faster than any cleaving. If the Consort was going to cast me out, I might as well use my last few Walks for good.

When I looked up and found myself standing across the street from Simon's house, the choice was easy.

Iggy heard me coming before I could knock on the door, his big bass woofs rattling the windows. Simon's shadow appeared, and then he was standing in front of me, one hand gripping Iggy's collar, one hand braced on the doorframe. The clever things I'd imagined saying—the defenses I'd counted on for so long—flew out of my head.

He was backlit, the lamp glow keeping his face in darkness. I couldn't tell if he was pleased or angry to see me shivering on the steps.

"I can't promise," I said, huddled in my coat. "And if it puts you in danger, I won't do it. But I'll try."

There was a long, awful pause, a pivot swelling as he studied me.

He held out his hand.

I took it, and he pulled me into the warmth and the light, into him. The awful tightness in my chest loosened, finally, and I could breathe him in, soap and sunshine even at night.

"Come and meet my mom," he said.

The front room was clearly for show, with furniture that looked too small for Simon's height and sprawl. He led me through the narrow kitchen, with white cabinets and cheery, apple-green walls and a round table with three chairs. It opened up into a bright, cozy family room. The woman sitting on the couch, feet tucked under her, a red chenille throw on her lap, looked up expectantly. A book lay facedown on the table in front of her, a teacup at her elbow.

"You brought a friend home! Why didn't you tell me?" Mrs. Lane said, and started to get up. Simon went to her side immediately, but she waved him off.

She was taller than me, but not by much. He must have gotten his height from his dad. A scarf covered her head, a few wisps of honey-blond hair poking out at the edges, but her eyes were the same dark, sparkling blue as her son's—intelligent, lively, and right now, full of speculation.

"Mom, this is Del Sullivan."

"It's lovely to meet you, Del. I'm Amelia."

"You too. I didn't mean to interrupt."

"You're not. I was reading, and Simon is entertaining that monstrous dog." Iggy nosed his way over to her, and she gave him an affectionate scratch around the ears. "Take her coat, Simon. Please, sit down."

Iggy plopped down in front of her. "I was talking to our guest, you beast. Del, would you like tea?"

"No, thank you." Simon slipped my coat off my shoulders, his fingertips grazing the nape of my neck. I wrinkled my nose at him—getting grabby in front of his mom was not the impression I wanted to make—but his face was a picture of innocence. He nudged me toward an overstuffed armchair in a red-and-white stripe, and I perched on the edge, ready to bolt.

"Simon says you're working on a music project together?" she asked. "I hope he's not making it too hard on you."

"Hey," he said, sprawling on the floor at my feet. "I'm not that bad."

I saw Simon in her grin. "You absolutely are, and you know it."

He hung his head in mock defeat. "I'm going to make it up to her. I'm going to teach her the finer points of a pick and roll."

"I'm sure Del will find that tremendously useful," she said. She shifted her attention to me. "In your career as a professional basketball player, of course."

"It's always been my dream," I said, drawn in despite myself. The affection between them was so obvious, and they included me as if it was perfectly natural. A pang of envy ran through me.

He ran a hand along my calf. "Don't tease, Delancey. I have other talents."

I kicked him as discreetly as I could.

"He makes an excellent toasted cheese sandwich," Amelia said, as if she was giving the matter great thought. "And his chicken soup has come a long way."

Simon nodded gravely. "I'm amazing with a can opener."

"Delancey," Amelia mused over her teacup. "That's a pretty name. Unusual."

Traditional, for Walkers. "I was born in New York," I said. "But my parents knew we were coming back here, so they named me after the subway stop near our apartment. I'm lucky we didn't live near Flushing."

"They named you after a train stop?" Simon said. "Wait. Addison? Montrose?"

"My family has a strange sense of humor," I said weakly.

Simon raised his eyebrows. "Your family is strange, period."

"All families are," Amelia said, a hint of strain showing around her eyes. The teacup clinked as she set it down. "Chamomile makes me sleepy. I think I'll turn in early, give you two some privacy."

Simon clambered up. "You okay?"

"I'm fine," she said. "It was wonderful to finally meet you, Del. Promise you'll come back again."

Iggy padded along beside her as she left. Simon watched, worry etched around his mouth and eyes.

Finally, she'd said. As if he'd mentioned me before today. Before he knew the truth.

"Is she okay?"

"Yeah. She gets tired pretty fast."

"I shouldn't have come," I said, and he dropped onto the ottoman, one leg on either side of mine.

"I'm glad you did. So is she. Besides," he said, sliding his hand around my neck and drawing me in for a brief kiss, "she's heard a lot about you."

"You didn't tell her about . . ."

"How could I explain it? And after you said it was impossible, there wasn't any point." He fit our hands together, his fingers twining with mine. "You said bringing back a treatment could do more harm than good. What changed?"

"Me," I said. "If we do this, I have ground rules."

He leaned back. "Never thought I'd hear you say that."

Neither had I. "One, if it puts the Key World in danger, we stop. Two, if it puts either of you in danger, we stop."

His jaw tightened, but he nodded.

"Three, your mom has to be sure."

"I'm sure," he said quickly.

"Not you. *Her.* I can't guarantee that I'll find a treatment, but if I do, you have to tell her the risks, and she has to sign off on it. I won't use my Walking to take away her choices."

He bent his head, his words muffled. "Fine. Once we find a cure—if we do—how do we get it back here?"

"I don't know yet. It's fine to bring things from the Key

World to Echoes. When I Walk, I leave stars behind. They're so small, hardly anyone notices them—we call them breadcrumbs, because we can use them to find our way home if we get lost."

"Does that happen?"

"My grandmother," I said after a minute. "A few months before I was born, she went out for a Walk, and she never came back. That's when Monty started to lose it. It's why we left New York—to take care of him."

He brushed his lips over the back of my hand. "I didn't know it was dangerous."

"We navigate by listening to the differences in frequencies. That's why we've got such good hearing, but the sound wears us down after a while. It's not bad in limited amounts, but if you stay too long, it starts to scramble your brain. The longer you stay, the worse it gets. That's why we usually go with a partner."

"Like Eliot."

Not anymore. "My grandmother went out alone. People do it, especially on short Walks. But she disappeared."

"You don't think she left on purpose?" He sounded skeptical.

"No. We think she got disoriented, and the farther she Walked, the more lost she got. The Consort—our leaders—sent people to look for her. My grandfather is still looking. But she's gone. There's no tracking someone through the multiverse after so much time."

He squeezed my leg, the contact scorching even through my jeans. "At least she didn't bail on you guys."

Unlike his dad. "How long ago did he leave?"

He grimaced. "I was three days old. I have it on good authority that I was a delightful infant, so I guess he wasn't cut out for fatherhood."

"I'm sure you were adorable," I said.

"I really was."

Something buzzed at the back of my mind, a warning prickle, and I tried to focus on it. But Simon kissed me again, and it slipped away like water through cupped hands.

"You said medicine from an Echo might hurt her. How are we going to get around that?" he asked.

"I think the trick is not to bring the drugs themselves. That way we're not introducing a new frequency to the Key World. I could track down the formula, and then we could. . . ." I trailed off. We could what? Open an illegal pharmaceutical lab? Find a chem major at the university who was willing to experiment? And what if it wasn't medicine, but a surgery? What if I'd given Simon a second round of false hope? "I'll find a way."

"*We'll* find a way," he said.

"You can't go with me," I reminded him. "And if there's a problem with the frequencies overlapping, I'm calling it off. I can't put you or the Key World in danger, even if it means you hate me for the rest of my life."

"You're risking your own life to help her," he said. "How could I possibly hate you?"

I shrugged. Easy for him to say that when he didn't know what I'd done. "Just so we're clear."

"Crystal," he said, and kissed me again, pulling me onto

his lap, one hand sliding along my back, his lips tracing my ear. "Take me with you."

"You tried, remember?" I sat up, braced my hands against the wall of his chest. "You couldn't follow me through."

"You could help me," he said. "Like a guide. Come on, Del. Pretend I'm a breadcrumb."

"I'm not a guide," I said, tugging the hem of my shirt back into place. "And you're not a breadcrumb."

Simon wasn't the way home. He *was* home.

"What's the worst that could happen? I get left in the equipment closet again?"

"I don't know what the worst is. I don't know how the frequency would affect you. The equipment closet was a terrible location, by the way."

"It lacked ambiance, but I enjoyed it." His hand inched along my thigh.

I smacked him. "For *Walking*. It's easier when the pivots are established."

"So we'll find one that's established."

"You passed a bunch of them the other night at the Depot, and you never noticed. It won't work." But part of me wondered. I'd learned to Walk by holding on to Monty's hand and letting him lead me through Echoes. My dad's team had carried him back unconscious.

"One try. If I can't cross, I won't bug you again. If I can, and there's a problem, we'll come back right away." His touch made me light-headed. "Let's go break some rules."

. . .

Twenty minutes later we were sitting in the Depot's half-full parking lot, staring at the train crash's memorial.

"How does it work?" he asked in a low voice.

"Why are you whispering?"

"I don't know. Felt like a whispering kind of moment. Clandestine."

"Everything with you is clandestine," I said.

"It doesn't need to be. You want to announce to the school we're together, I'm more than fine with it."

"One thing at a time, okay?" Bree's reaction didn't worry me nearly as much as the Consort's.

I climbed out, Eliot's map in hand. The edges of pivot points caught on my coat, stronger than before. We needed a large, stable rift, one I could cross without much concentration. No sense making this more difficult than necessary.

"You have to hold on to me." I checked the screen and headed for the far end of the parking lot. "Don't let go, even for a second."

"Got it." He gave me a smile that tilted toward nervous, and took my hand in his.

"I can do this alone," I told him, trying to give him an out. "You don't need to come with."

"Yeah, I do. It's dangerous, right? Even for you?"

"It can be. But I am very, very good."

His smile quirked up. "I'm sure you are."

"Do you see the rift?"

The air around the pivot looked more dense, a sliver of night that the amber glow of the streetlamps couldn't penetrate. I gestured, and his eyes locked on my hand.

"Nope. But I feel weird, like an electrical storm is coming." He took my hand. "Go ahead, Del. I trust you."

Not many people did—not even me. But belief is a powerful thing. In that moment I was trustworthy because he believed in me. Simon's faith transformed me into the person he thought I was.

With Simon's hand gripping mine, I felt my way through, the air oppressive and unyielding. I breathed out, slow and steady, my entire body attuning to the frequency, fixing the sound in my mind, pushing away thoughts of Simon, of the Consort, of anything except the world I was trying to reach.

My foot slid forward a few inches, the air resisting the entire way.

It had to be Simon. His frequency was locked into the Key World, holding us back.

When I looked over, his jaw was set in concentration. He'd never agree to quit.

I pressed on, inch by inch, and gradually my hand pushed into the other world, the resonance unpleasant but not painful. Foot, knee, elbow, shoulder, head, each a struggle.

Finally I was clear, except for my hand holding his. I willed the pivot to part, planted my feet, and tugged.

There was an awful, excruciating tension as the pivot ground along my wrist. It wouldn't work. I'd lose him. Maybe I'd lost him already, and he'd disintegrated in the subatomic spaces between worlds. I swore under my breath, hauled as hard as I could, channeling my panic into action.

Like a cork from a bottle, Simon burst free. We went down in a tangle of arms and legs on the pavement.

"You're here," I said. "Oh, God, you're really here. I thought—"

"It worked?" Wide-eyed, he took in the nearly deserted parking lot. We'd landed at the end of a row, at the base of a parking meter. "We did it? Holy crap, Del."

I fought back tears of relief. We'd made it. Simon could Walk, and everything I'd ever been taught was wrong. I flopped back onto the ground, heedless of the gravel biting into me, and stared up at the sky, surprised the stars were lodged in their familiar constellations. My whole world tilted on a new axis. The stars should be different. Everything was different.

I listened carefully, gauging the pitch and stability, searching for any breaks that might hint at a problem, but the Echo sounded safe. How had the Consort been so wrong?

It wasn't the first time. I thought back to the girl with the note cards, how I'd caused an Echo to transpose. How Monty had promised tuning could stabilize entire worlds. Maybe they weren't wrong. Maybe the Consort wasn't telling us everything.

Simon pulled me to my feet. "Are you okay? You said it can make you sick."

"We've got a few hours before frequency poisoning kicks in. Hear the difference?"

He shook his head. "Still staticky, though. Where are we?"

The Depot was gone. In its place stood a boxy redbrick building, and the platform was lined with benches and warning signs. "New station. I bet the crash happened, but they didn't move the location. But we can't know for sure."

Simon took it in, his eyes catching every detail. "It's so real."

"For the people in this world, it is." I wondered if Simon would be visible, or go unnoticed, the way Walkers did.

"And my house is here? Can we check it out?"

"That's not a good idea." Echo objects weren't supposed to come in contact with their Originals, and I assumed the principle applied regardless of where the meeting took place. The strain on the threads could be dangerous. "Maybe we should—"

"Do you think my mom is there?" He started off, not waiting for my response.

I chased after him. "Wait! You don't know what you'll find. It's not a good idea to rush off."

God, I sounded like Addie. All caution and common sense, while Simon viewed the world like he'd gone through the looking glass. My usual recklessness waned when he was at risk.

"Listen to me, okay? We can check out the house. But she's not your mom. She's your Echo's mom. She might not even be home."

"I have to see," he told me. "You said we have to find a world where she's cured. Maybe this one is it."

"On the first try?" Unlikely. But he looked so hopeful, I matched my stride to his, and we went in search of his family.

"The town moved," he said after a few blocks.

At home it was the north side of town that was busy, even at night. Restaurants and shops and lots of pedestrians, even when the weather was lousy. But here the business district had shifted south, toward the train station. We passed by Grundy's, and he paused.

"Some things are the same," I said, nodding at the familiar sign. "It's hard to predict what changes from world to world."

"But it's only the Key World that matters?" He sounded troubled.

"Echoes matter," I said softly. "But not in the same way. And not to all Walkers."

Our words made smoky puffs in the cold air. "Is that why you don't get attached? Because you can always find something similar. Or better."

"Real is better," I said quietly. My time with the Walkers was running out, but maybe I could forge a future with Simon in it. "It matters more."

"Does it? This place *feels* real."

Was Doughnut World Simon real? To me, yes. Was he enough?

I'd thought so, for a while. If I'd spent time with him over music and coffee and free-throw lessons, I might have gotten to know him beyond making out in a car. But the Simon standing in front of me was the one who'd told me about his family and asked about mine, who'd taught me how to shoot free throws and learned how to play the piano, however poorly. This was the Simon I wanted, not because of which world he belonged to, but because of who he was.

I pointed to his house. "There. Your mom's Echo might be inside. She might be healthy. Would you rather have her, or the one back home?"

He eyed the door with a new wariness. "We have to see if she's sick."

"I'll go in," I said. Better not to risk an encounter between Simons. "Echoes don't notice me unless I make an effort. What should I look for?"

"Check the cabinet to the right of the sink for medication. Or the calendar by the phone—look for doctor's appointments."

"Give me ten minutes," I said.

"Can I—can I watch? Through the window?"

I wondered how he felt, witnessing a life that looked like his but would never be. Until now, all the people I cared about were Walkers, so I'd never had to watch their Echoes. Lonely, I thought. A different kind of loneliness than the one I'd known, but it still pinched at me.

"Of course."

Worlds can form or fall apart in an instant.

We turned into the driveway, the door at the side of the house opened, and Simon's Echo came out, the porch light glinting off his shaggy hair as he hefted a paper bag and took it to the recycling bin.

Behind me, my Simon froze. "That's me."

I shoved him into the hedge separating the cottage from its neighbor and dove after him. The branches rustled around us, and I prayed Echo Simon would blame the wind, that his tendency to notice me worked only when I was in plain sight.

There was a pause, then the sound of footsteps on gravel, diminishing as he walked back to the house. I sagged in relief.

And then I heard a sharp whistle, a metallic jingle, and the delighted bark that could only be Iggy.

"Bad dog," I muttered.

An instant later Iggy nosed through the shrubbery, and my hand was covered in enthusiastic slobber.

"You can come out now," Echo Simon called.

Simon grabbed for my wrist, but I shook him off.

"Stay here. Do not come out, no matter what happens," I whispered, and stepped into view, my hair snagging in the branches. "Call off your dog."

"Tell me why you're trespassing," Echo Simon replied. He shoved inky-black hair out of his eyes and peered at me. "You're that girl. From school."

"I'm that girl," I said, forcing myself not to look at the shrubbery, where Iggy was still barking.

"Iggy, come," he said, but the dog ignored him. "Who else is back there?"

"Nobody." I widened my eyes and gave him my best smile. "I swear."

He smirked. "You're cute, I'll give you that. But I'll take the dog's word over yours."

I studied him, trying to figure out who this Simon was. Rail thin, lip ring, alt-metal-band T-shirt, and a look in his eyes that suggested he had at least a few of the real Simon's memories.

He grabbed my arm and I yelped. Iggy's barks turned frantic.

"Let go of me!" I tried to yank away, but he held fast.

"Last chance," Echo Simon called as I struggled against him. "The dog might look goofy, but he'll attack if I tell him to."

"I doubt it," the real Simon said, stepping onto the driveway, rubbing the top of Iggy's head. "Sit, boy."

Echo Simon dropped my arm. The dog looked between the two of them and whined in confusion.

"Oh, *hell*," I said, as the world cracked open.

"What the fuck is this?" said Echo Simon, staring at the Key World version of himself. "Some kind of joke?"

"It's bad," I said, grabbing Original Simon's hand. "Very, very bad."

Around the three of us a tear was forming—not the usual pivot but a gaping slash. Iggy turned in fretful circles, but neither boy seemed to notice it.

The dissonance pouring out of the rift was so strong I nearly dropped to my knees. "Time to go," I said through clenched teeth.

"What about my mom?" asked Original Simon.

"Mom?" said the Echo, looking poleaxed. "What about her?"

"We have to leave," I said, as the rip grew. Around us the world started to flicker and dim, the first stirrings of a cleaving. "Now."

"Is she sick?" Simon asked. "Did the chemo work? Or the surgery?"

Echo Simon shook his head, eyes somber. The rusting Toyota changed to a Volkswagen and back in a blink.

They looked at each other, two versions of the boy I'd fallen for, carrying a grief so big it crossed worlds. "Simon," I said, and they turned in unison. "My Simon. You can't be here."

I stumbled into him, the world wavering as the breach widened.

"What's wrong with her?" asked Echo Simon.

"Frequency," I gasped, as Original Simon slid an arm around my waist, keeping me upright. "Go back."

"To the Depot?"

I nodded. We needed distance. The crack hadn't formed until the Simons had been in close proximity. If we could get away, it might slow down; if we left, it might reverse. Most importantly, I had to keep Simon safe.

"Take my car," said Echo Simon.

"No!" The Toyota was cycling through different vehicles. If we were in it, we might get sent to another frequency and never find our way back. "Walk."

Original Simon shook his head. "Run," he said, and we took off as the world around his Echo continued to crumble.

I was right about the proximity. The farther away we got from Echo Simon, the more stable I felt. Behind us the erratic pulse of the tear slowed and steadied, a heartbeat returning to normal. The world took on substance and color. But Simon urged me along, not bothering to waste air or concentration on speech. When we reached the train station, I skidded to a stop, trying to hear the Key World. Simon barely looked winded. Leaning against a light post, I wheezed, "Thanks."

"For starting . . . whatever that was?" He waved angrily in the direction of his house. "I couldn't hide. Not when he was—I was—hurting you."

"You'd never hurt me, here or anywhere else. You got me out."

I couldn't concentrate. My mind was whirling, trying to understand what had happened, trying to grab hold of the frequency I needed. Panic left me too scattered. I couldn't get us back on my own.

I dug in my bag for the necklace Monty had pressed into my hand. How had he known I'd need it tonight?

The pendant was a miniature tuning fork—three inches long, perfectly balanced, with the worn patina of something much loved. The chain puddled in my palm as I tilted it under the light and saw the name etched into the tines.

Rosemont Armstrong.

Monty had given me my grandmother's pendant. Which meant she hadn't taken it with her when she disappeared. I couldn't think about it now, but I would. Soon.

"What's that?" Simon asked.

"The way back," I said, and struck it on the light post. The sound rang out, soft but true, and the Key World pivot fluttered in response. I grabbed Simon's hand and brought us home.

CHAPTER FORTY-FOUR

Damage to the fabric of a world results in a weaker frequency, rendering the affected threads more prone to future vibrato fractums and other problems.
—Chapter Five, "Physics,"
Principles and Practices of Cleaving, Year Five

EITHER PRACTICE REALLY DID MAKE PERFECT, or desperation counted for more than I realized, but the return trip was easier on both of us.

Not that it was easy. My legs trembled, my lungs burned, and my head ached like a New Year's Day hangover. Simon looked better—the benefit of being a jock, I guess.

We sat in the Jeep with the heater on full blast. It was filled with fast-food wrappers and dog toys. I never wanted to leave.

"Hell of an introduction," he said. "Is it usually this crazy?"

I curled up against his side, listening for any hint of damage. "Usually it's pretty calm." Except for cleavings.

His hand moved gently over my hair, removing twigs and leaves. "Iggy recognized me."

"My grandfather says animals are better at that kind of thing."

He touched his lips to my forehead. "What happened back there? I couldn't see it, but it felt bad."

I had no idea. This was uncharted territory. Thinking out loud, I said, "It wasn't a pivot. Those come from decisions. It wasn't a cleaving, because you can't stop a cleaving after it starts, and this stabilized once we left. This was like the fabric of the world couldn't handle both of your frequencies at once, so it ripped, then wove back together when we left."

Was it possible for threads to re-form?

I checked the map, but the pivot we'd come through shone like a miniature sun—strong and steady. "It's a freak thing. We might never know."

Eliot would. Addie, too. Neither one of them was going to help me now. Monty, but he wasn't exactly a reliable source. I clutched my grandmother's tuning fork. Why hadn't she taken it with her on that last Walk? She could have found her way home.

I slipped the chain over my head. Monty had answers; I'd simply been asking the wrong questions.

"You can't Walk anymore," I said. "We can't risk running into your Echo again."

"And you can't go alone."

"I do it all the time."

"Not anymore," he said, and kissed me.

"You are not the boss of me," I said a few minutes later. "But I appreciate the concern."

"I nearly lost you," he said, tracing the chain of my necklace. "What if—"

"Everything is a what-if. That's why I love it." I paused.

"We'll find your mom. A healthy version. It'll take time, that's all."

Time I might not have if Addie blabbed to Lattimer.

It was as if Monty had a secret ability—an ability other than Walking—that told him to lie low when he was about to be grilled. I waited as late as I could the next morning, hoping he'd show up in the kitchen and I could ask him about my grandmother's pendant, or the strange dual-Simon tear or anything else. But my mom caught sight of me first and ordered me out the door to school, where Simon greeted me with a slow, knee-buckling kiss.

The entire corridor went silent, then filled with a hurricane of whispers.

"What was that for?" I'd wanted people to see me, but this wasn't quite what I'd had in mind.

"Everything. Nothing. For being you, mostly."

"For helping with your mom." My heart twisted the tiniest bit.

"For offering, sure. But this—" He gestured to the space I'd put between us. "This started before I told you about her. It started way before I knew what you could do."

It had started when I went after his Echo. But my guilt kept me from saying so. "Walk me to orchestra?"

"Gladly." Before I could stop him, he hooked his arm around my waist, casual and obvious.

We passed by the trophy case, and I looked over my repair from yesterday.

And then I stopped cold.

"What's wrong?"

"The trophies," I said, fear gathering in my stomach like a leaden ball. "They're different."

"What do you mean?" He let go of me. "Wait. This is a conference trophy, not State. And where's my net?"

"It must have slid back," I said. "That's what I was fixing yesterday, when you caught me. It was another world merging with this one. You were on the JV squad, I think."

"I'm not in the picture at all," he said. "Is this because of last night?"

"It must be." I thought back to the cottage. The one-car garage. "Your Echo house didn't have a basketball hoop."

He closed his eyes, like he was trying to picture it. "No, I guess not."

The Echo we'd met didn't look like a basketball player; piercings aside, he *moved* differently than Simon, slouching instead of striding.

"The world bled through. When I fixed the trophy inversion yesterday, the strings must have been left vulnerable, so when your frequencies met last night, the damage showed up here." Simon looked utterly perplexed. "Part of last night's Echo has overtaken the Key World. Your doppelgänger didn't play basketball. In that reality, the basketball team had a different season last year. These are *their* trophies."

"I remember winning," he said. "I remember cutting down the net. Won't other people notice too?"

"I don't know. This is advanced stuff. College level." The

pitiful little trophy didn't move, which meant the inversion had taken root. "I need to Walk through and fix it."

"For a trophy? No way."

"It's an inversion," I said. "It will keep spreading until I fix it."

"What if you don't come back?" His fingers hooked in the pockets of my jeans, drew me closer. "Don't go."

"I'll come home," I said, and fished the pendant out from beneath my shirt. "I'm a Walker. This is what we do."

"But . . ."

I skimmed my fingers along the glass, feeling the traces of the bad frequency blending with the Key World. The Consort would find this, I realized. With so many teams scrutinizing the area, nothing would draw their attention faster.

"Quit arguing," I said. "Go to class. I don't want you near the pivot when I go through."

"Del—"

I brushed my lips over his cheek, like it was no big deal. "I'll see you soon."

He went, walking backward, his eyes on me the whole way.

I ducked into the girls' bathroom, hid until first period had started and the commons had emptied out. There was no telling how quickly my mom or one of the other navigators would pick up on the inversion. I needed to move fast.

My hands shook as I found the frequency from last night and felt my way along it.

When I landed on the other side, the dissonance slammed into me like a hammer to the skull. The world swam in front of my eyes, the lights blurring. I planted my free hand on the wall to steady myself.

The fabric of the world was densely woven, nearly impossible to penetrate. I ran my hands lightly over the quivering material. No wonder the inversion was so stubborn—the problem strings were wound so tightly around the others, I couldn't unkink them enough to restore the proper pitch.

I had no idea how much time had passed while I worked. Nausea washed over me in a greasy wave, and I took careful breaths. *Nimble fingers, open mind, help to seek what you would find.* There. I isolated the first strand, vibrating wildly out of tune.

It was the opening I needed. The more threads I fixed, the easier it was to repair others, the damage as pervasive as a choking vine. The vertigo was overtaking me, and I anchored myself with thoughts of Simon.

The last tangle of threads resolved itself, the resonance clear and stable, the inversion fixed.

Fixed too late.

My knees gave out, and I crumpled as the frequency poisoning kicked in. My grandmother's pendant hung heavy around my neck, but my fingers were too cramped and numb to reach it. Is this how she'd felt, when she'd been lost? Would Simon miss me the way Monty missed her? The world tilted around me, going dark at the edges and narrowing rapidly.

Someone grabbed me by the shoulders, and a face appeared above mine, dear and familiar. Eliot.

The tunnel closed.

CHAPTER FORTY-FIVE

SOMETIMES THE MOST WELCOME SIGHTS ARE the most unexpected.

I woke up on the floor of a supply closet, burning with fever and teeth chattering.

"Bathroom," I said, trying to curl up on my side. "I'm going to be sick."

"What's she saying?" I heard Simon ask. "What language is that?"

"It's frequency poisoning," Eliot said. "Her cerebral cortex is scrambled."

"Sick," I said, my tongue thick and clumsy. "I need to throw up."

"Get her a Coke," Eliot ordered, prying the tuning fork from my hand.

The chime of the pendant sank inside me, tamping down on the nausea. "You came for me?"

"Don't try to talk," he said, and tapped it again.

"The inversion. Is it gone?" My whole body shuddered, and someone shoved a sweatshirt under my head.

"She's not making any sense," Simon said, his voice rough.

I felt Eliot prop me up and heard the crack-hiss of a can being opened. The syrupy taste of Coke filled my mouth. "Swallow," he ordered. The sugar hit my system and my muscles eased.

"Someone's going to come by any minute," Simon told him. "Can we move her?"

"Better now," I slurred. A little of the tension went out of Eliot's body.

"You're better," he agreed. "Welcome back."

"The hell she is," Simon growled. "Del? Can you hear me?"

I struggled to sit up, the cement floor cold and uncomfortable. "I have perfect hearing."

"Not anymore," Eliot said grimly, brushing sweaty strands of hair from my face. "And he's right. We need to get you out of here."

"Wait. Did it work? Are the trophies . . . ?"

"Screw the trophies," said Simon. "I'm taking you home."

Eliot touched my cheek. "It worked. Barely."

"I'm bringing the car around," Simon said. "Stay put."

I drifted off. When I came to again, I asked Eliot, "Did you see me on the map?"

He made a face that was almost—but not quite—a smile. "Your boyfriend pulled me out of orchestra. He thought you were acting crazy."

"Ah."

"I told him that you're reckless, not crazy."

"Don't forget selfish," I said.

"That too."

"What did he say?"

Simon rejoined us. "I said he could help you or I could break his legs. I'm more than a pretty face."

I drank deeply, feeling better with every second. "You are pretty, though."

"Ruggedly handsome," he said, and helped me to my feet. "Let's go."

There wasn't a lot of talking on the ride home. I concentrated on not throwing up, and both boys were silent. I didn't know what Simon was thinking, but the computer in Eliot's brain was definitely working overtime.

No one was home—even Monty was gone—so the boys helped me upstairs. After they'd settled me on the bed, Simon turned slowly, taking in the stars scattered everywhere, the maps I'd drawn, the battered furniture, the collection of instruments around my music stand. He looked like I must, every time I Walk into a new world. "Breadcrumbs," he said softly.

"I came home," I pointed out. "Told you I would."

Some emotion I couldn't read crossed his face.

Eliot coughed.

"Can you give us a minute?" I said to Simon. He looked at Eliot, then me, and nodded.

"More pop would be good," Eliot said. "Her blood sugar's dropped off the charts."

"Got it." Simon disappeared down the stairs.

When he'd gone, Eliot paced the room. "You shouldn't have gone in there alone."

"Turns out I didn't," I said softly.

"I would have helped. Even if he hadn't threatened to knee-cap me. You know that, don't you?"

I hadn't. I'd assumed Eliot was as selfish as me, and my eyes filled. "I'm sorry. For everything. For being so stupid and horrible and scared. You are totally right to hate me."

"I don't hate you." He sat down on the bed. "I'm angry. But we're a team. Always have been . . ."

". . . always will be." I dashed a hand over my eyes. "I screwed up."

"Yeah," he said, and I knew from the way his voice caught we were talking about more than frequency poisoning. "He shouldn't be able to Walk."

I winced. "He told you?"

"I can't work with limited information. And I can't believe you told him about us."

"He caught me. I couldn't lie." When he raised an eyebrow, calm and skeptical, I amended, "I didn't *want* to lie. Speaking of which . . . I didn't tell you the whole truth."

"Shocker." He sighed. "What now?"

"There's something wrong with him. Really wrong, Eliot. He was one of the breaks in Park World. His Echoes have been seeing me ever since. I run into him constantly. Every inversion I've found involves him. It's not just the SRT, or the Walking. It's something bigger. I think he's caught in the anomaly."

"We have to tell the Consort," he said. "They'll handle it."

"They'd handle it by making him disappear." I grabbed his

hand. "Addie knows I've been Walking to see him. She's going to tell Lattimer as soon as she finds proof. I need to get him clear of the anomaly before she turns us in."

He drew his hand away. "And you need my help."

I'm good enough to use, but not enough to love. Even woozy and exhausted, I recognized the danger. "No. If you're involved, they'll punish you, too. I'll take care of this."

"Yeah. You've got things totally under control," he deadpanned. He kissed my forehead, eyes troubled. "Rest up. I'll be back later."

"Eliot . . ."

He waved and jogged down the stairs. I heard him say something to Simon, their voices too low to make out, and I sagged back against the headboard.

"I hate sitting here," I said when Simon came back in.

"Bummer for you," he said, and handed me a bottle of root beer. "Drink up."

When I'd finished, he set the bottle on the floor and stretched alongside me. I shifted until my head rested on his chest, directly above his heart.

"You know, this is not how I was planning to get into your bedroom." He trailed his fingers up and down my arm.

"Sorry to disappoint you."

"Not disappointed. Worried. Are you sure you're okay?"

"Frequency poisoning wears off fast." To begin with, at least. The next time would be worse. I nestled in closer to Simon and tried to sound nonchalant. "I'll be fine by tomorrow morning."

"Eliot said you're supposed to stay put for another day or two."

"Eliot worries."

"Eliot is in love with you." There was no censure in his voice, only calm certainty.

"I'm such an idiot." I closed my eyes, let the beating of Simon's pulse resonate through me. "How did you know?"

"Recognized the signs."

"Oh." My eyes flew open. I didn't know what startled me more—what he seemed to be implying, or how much I wanted him to mean it.

The silence between us grew weighty and he laced his fingers with mine. "You can't take off like that again."

I twisted to look at him. "How else will we find a cure for your mom?"

"It won't help us if your brain is fried," he said. "I couldn't understand you when you came back."

"Side effect."

"What about next time? Or the time after that? No more, Del."

"Don't tell me what to do," I said sharply. "You've known about Walking for forty-eight hours. I've done it my whole life. This is my choice, not yours."

"What about rule number three? My mom has to sign off on it? Does she get a say?"

"I meant the treatment itself. You can't tell her about the Walkers. What would you say? 'Hey, Mom, do you mind if my girlfriend goes into an alternate dimension to find a cure for your cancer? It's kind of dangerous, and it might not work, but are you in?' She'll have you committed."

"I was thinking I'd try for a little more subtlety."

"We stick to the plan. I find the cure, we figure out how to make it work here, and then we loop her in."

"She's not going to go for it, Del. Trust me." Tension radiated down his arm; his words were tinged with bitterness. "She wouldn't even want you to look."

"You're angry with her," I said softly. "She's accepted it's terminal, but you haven't."

His body angled away from me, and I squirmed until we were face-to-face.

"It doesn't matter how far down you are in a game," he said. "You play until you hear the buzzer. You give it everything."

"Until you can't," I said. "What if she's tired of fighting?"

"Then I fight for her. But that's my job, not yours."

"I won't stop Walking," I told him. "Not even for you. You might as well let me help."

His eyes met mine and he gave the slightest nod.

"Good. Once I'm back on my feet, we'll get started."

Before we did, though, there was something I needed to stop.

CHAPTER FORTY-SIX

Every action we take is a choice. Some are deliberate, some are automatic, but each represents a decision between paths. Viewed in this light, even inaction is a choice, albeit a weak one.

—Chapter One, "Structure and Formation,"
Principles and Practices of Cleaving, Year Five

THE WORST THING ABOUT FREQUENCY POISON-ing is how long it takes you to recover. If you go out again too soon, your resistance is half what it should be. I wasn't in fighting form, but I also didn't want to put off what I had to do for a moment longer. Eliot told my parents I'd caught a flu bug going around school, which got me out of Addie-time—but it also kept me from seeing Simon. On Friday, stir-crazy and missing him, I headed back to school, despite Eliot's protests.

I trudged through the day in a fog. Only Simon was clear, urging sugar on me at lunch and keeping Bree at bay during music. By ninth hour, I was so worn down that even Mrs. Gregory believed me when I asked for a pass to the nurse's office with only ten minutes left in the period. "She's probably high," Bree whispered.

I ducked into the girls' bathroom, found the pivot, and crossed to Doughnut World.

I'd asked this Simon about his schedule the last time I'd seen him. He was in Spanish now, and I moved through the hall on autopilot. The bell rang and the corridor filled with laughter and chatter and shouts, kids bursting free of the constraints of the day. Already the frequency was wearing on me, familiar and ominous. I wove around clusters of people and couples reunited, my hand wrapped around my pendant. Lingering here was not an option.

Finally I saw him.

And he saw me.

Shock. Relief. Heat. Anger. The expressions washed over Echo Simon's face, warring with each other, and finally settled into something I hadn't anticipated. Wariness.

Hatred would have been easier. Would have protected him better. Hope and fear mingled together this way only meant more damage.

"Hey," I said, and gave a small wave.

"Where the hell have you been?"

"Can we go somewhere else? Talk?"

"So you can give me another lame excuse? Don't bother."

I wished I'd never returned, but he'd trusted me. I owed him the truth—or a version of it. I had seen what happened when people left without explanation, how badly it wounded the ones left behind. It tainted everything that had come before and twisted what came after. Simon's father had done it; so had my grandmother. Their absence was as tangible as their presence. "I told you I'd come back."

He slammed his locker shut and stalked toward the side

door. "For how long? I can never find you, Del. You're a god-damn ghost. It's like you're not even real."

"I am." So was he, despite everything I'd been taught. I rubbed at my arms, trying to ward off the encroaching frequency. "But I can't come back again."

"Won't." He pinned me with a cold, contemptuous look.

"Can't," I replied. "I don't belong here. Every time I see you, I'm hiding. I have to stop."

"Hiding from what?" He thawed slightly. "Are you in trouble?"

"I'm trying to fix it." Emotion wouldn't help me, but I couldn't stop the ache in my chest. "I wanted to say good-bye. You deserve a real good-bye."

Because he *was* real, every bit as much as my Simon. He deserved better than the moments I'd stolen.

"Don't do this." He shook his head, bewildered. "Whatever the problem is, whoever you're hiding from, let me help you. I can protect you."

He touched my cheek gently, like I might shatter. Maybe I would.

"From myself?" I pressed my fingers to my eyelids. "You wouldn't believe how many people have tried."

We always have a choice. It's one of the first things Walkers learn. There is always a choice.

It turns out my teachers were wrong. The more you care, the fewer choices you have. If you care enough, sometimes there's only one. A single, impossible way forward, and you have to take it. Because it's the only way to live with yourself.

CHAPTER FORTY-SEVEN

CAME BACK JITTERY AND NAUSEOUS AND exhausted. I didn't know if it was from Walking too soon or leaving Simon. Not my Simon, I reminded myself as I sat in the commons and downed a can of Coke, hoping to ward off another bout of frequency poisoning.

I'd cleaved one Simon, flirted with countless others, and wounded another moments ago. But the Simon who mattered most was the one who knew me best, and he was *here*. I would fix whatever problem was affecting both him and the Key World, we'd find a way to help his mom, and then we could be happy, here, together.

No more Walking to find other Simons. Never again.

Never didn't last nearly long enough.

The sound of running feet caught my attention. Poking my head around the corner, I spotted the school nurse dashing toward the gymnasium, medical bag in hand.

"—says he's fine," said one of the other basketball players as they ran. "Coach didn't want to take any chances."

I might have been failing trig, but I could do the math.

I followed them to the field house, clammy with fear.

Simon sat on the bench, barely visible behind the wall of teammates looming over him. The nurse shooed them away, brisk and cheerful as she pulled out her blood pressure cuff. "Let's see what we have."

He waved her off, looking haggard. "Put me back in, Coach. It was nothing."

"That was not nothing," the coach growled. "Looked like a damn seizure."

"I pulled an all-nighter," Simon replied. "I'm good."

"The hell you are. We've got a game against Kennedy tomorrow. I can't have you fainting like a thirteen-year-old-girl at a rock concert in the middle of a full-court press."

I could see Simon's flush of embarrassment from across the room.

"Plenty of fluids and a good night's sleep should do the trick," the nurse said. One of the other players brought out a duffel bag and set it near Simon's feet.

"Go home, Lane," barked the coach. "Get some rest."

"I don't need—" Simon started to protest, but he caught sight of me and straightened, the set of his shoulders combative. "Sure, Coach. I'll be back tomorrow."

"Damn straight," the coach said, and blew his whistle. "The rest of you—this isn't a tea party. Get moving!"

Simon's eyes never left mine as he crossed the room—it was like he was freezing me in place, and the closer he got, the colder I felt.

"Car," he said, hefting the duffel bag. We reached the Jeep without another word. When he was behind the wheel, he turned to me. "I saw you Walking."

I didn't bother denying it. "How much?"

He snorted. "Everything. This whole time, I thought they were dreams, and you were . . . what? Hooking up with me in other worlds? It wasn't enough that I fell for you here? *I* wasn't enough, so you had to go and mess around with my Echoes?"

"No! It wasn't like that!"

"And then you dumped me? Were you thinking you'd break up with both of us, make the worlds match?" He sounded insulted. "You were cheating on me *with me*."

"I wasn't! I haven't been back there since before our date. Before things changed with us."

"Things changed with us a long time ago."

My own anger flared up. "Did you ever wonder why? You said it took you too long to notice me, but did you ever ask yourself what changed?"

"The project," he said. "Powell put us on the project. And that night . . ."

"You dreamed about me. In the rain."

"Outside Grundy's. You gave me a star," he said.

"You barely talked to me when Powell paired us up. You didn't have an epiphany in the middle of music class. You noticed me because your Echo had kissed me the night before."

He folded his arms. "You didn't stop him."

"Why would I? Nothing was ever going to happen between

us. You're the star of the basketball team, and I'm the freaky orchestra girl. So, yeah, when the guy I've had a crush on for years wants to kiss me, I go for it, even if he's an Echo."

"You went back," he accused.

"You went out with Bree."

"This is different. Don't you dare tell me otherwise. You've been lying to me the whole time we've been together."

"You didn't know about the Walkers. How could I explain?"

"That's bullshit, Del. You could have told me in the equipment room. That would have been the perfect time."

"I've been a little busy," I shot back. "You know, trying to save your mom's life?"

"She's not a bargaining chip," he said fiercely. "You don't get a pass on being honest with me because you said you'd help her. They're totally separate."

"The hell they are! You found out about the Walkers and asked me to help her on the same afternoon. When I said no, you took off. When I said yes, we were back on. If you want honesty, let's start by admitting that the reason you're with me is because I can help her."

My breathing was ragged, my voice tight, and Simon drew back as if I'd slapped him.

"I was a dick," he said. "When you told me about the Walkers, I didn't think about whether it was dangerous, or how it would cost you. All I could think about was saving her. You risked your life for my mom, and that's huge. I don't even have words for how huge that is."

413

I dug my fingernails into my palms, waiting for him to continue.

"But I'm with you—I *was* with you—because I was crazy about you. Walking had nothing to do with it. At least I thought it didn't. Walking made a lie out of us, and that's your fault."

I bowed my head. "I didn't want to lose you."

"How's that working out? Because from what I can tell, the me in that world isn't exactly your biggest fan right now." He grimaced. "Something else we've got in common."

"Simon . . ." My head jerked up, but his gaze was fixed on the wheel.

"You were kissing *me*. You think my feelings were caused by him, but what triggered his feelings? Maybe I would have noticed you completely on my own. And now we'll never know, because you don't have any faith in me, and I sure as hell don't have any in you."

I grabbed his arm. "Hold on. What triggered him? He noticed me, and he shouldn't have."

"The low-self-esteem act is getting old," he said, reaching across me to open the door, waiting for me to climb out. "You should go."

I braced a hand against the doorframe. "Not self-esteem, you jackass. Physics. Walkers cast impressions in other worlds, but Echoes don't remember them. He shouldn't have noticed me, because we weren't interacting. Here or there."

"Maybe you stalked me in another world," he said. "That seems to be your specialty."

414

"I wasn't stalking you. The only other time I'd run into you was at the park." The truth came together like parts in a score, combining to voice what I'd missed. "You saw me at the park."

"What park?"

"The world I cleaved," I said, thinking of the duck pond, and balloons, and small changes that changed everything. "It was unstable, and you touched me."

"It won't happen again. I can't stop you from coming after me in other worlds, but in this one? We are *done*."

He drove off, leaving me alone in the parking lot.

Grieve later, I told myself. My thoughts felt tentative and light, like when I was picking a particularly sensitive lock, how pushing too hard would cause a tumbler to trip and I'd have to start over at the beginning. *The park.* I closed my eyes, losing myself in the memory of Simon's hand curving around my thigh, how he'd steadied me and thrown me off balance with a single move.

The wrongness of his frequency, how strong the dissonance was every time we'd touched, in every Echo.

He'd noticed me in Park World because something was wrong with its frequency.

He'd noticed—and remembered—me in Doughnut World because there was something wrong with *him*.

He'd noticed me here, and the inversions started.

I'd had it backward. Park World Simon's frequency hadn't been wrong because the world was unstable. The world was unstable because there was something wrong with Simon.

415

Because there was some sort of connection—bigger than SRT, bigger than a single frequency—between his Echoes. The more I interacted with them, the greater the transference. The stronger the frequencies. The more unstable his worlds became.

My parents had been looking for something in the Echo worlds that would cause so much instability, but the problem wasn't an Echo.

The problem was Simon.

CHAPTER FORTY-EIGHT

I WALKED HOME ON AUTOPILOT, MY NEW-found realization—Simon was the anomaly, and I'd amplified the effects—turning the world around me ashen.

Every time I'd crossed realities and found him, whether it was Doughnut World or a lesson with Addie, I'd strengthened the connection between his Original and his Echoes. That's why his SRT was so strong; it's why the sky had torn when they'd met—their combined signal had been too much for one world to handle. It's why the inversions I'd found were connected to him. It's why he'd been caught in the Baroque events—because he'd created them.

He was the disease, not the symptom.

I was the carrier.

And I had to find a cure.

I didn't notice Addie's car until I nearly ran into it.

"Get in," she snapped through the open window. I reached for the handle, stopped when I saw Eliot sitting in the passenger seat, expression somber.

I sighed as I slid into the backseat. "What did I do now?"

"You don't know?" Addie asked, dour and disbelieving.

"It's a really long list. Narrow it down for me."

Eliot made a noise of warning, and I remembered that Addie's search for proof could implicate him, too. If I wanted to help him out of this, the way he'd been helping me all along, I needed to draw her fire.

"For starters," Addie said, "let's talk about the Original you're sleeping with."

"I'm not sleeping with him! Why does everyone assume—I do have *some* self-control, you know."

"You've demonstrated a breathtaking lack thus far," she said. "Fine. You're making out with him instead of going to class. He's a problem, Del, and you have to end it."

"Already done," I said. "But there's a bigger problem with Simon."

"He's the anomaly Mom and Dad have been looking for," Addie said.

"How . . ."

Next to Addie, Eliot coughed.

I shoved his shoulder. "You told her?"

"She knew something was up."

"The flu?" Addie said scornfully. "Hungover, I would have believed. Not the flu."

Eliot twisted to face me. "I recorded a sample of Simon's frequency while we were at your house. It sounds fine on the surface. Even my map didn't pick up on it. But if you listen—really drill down and look at the individual oscillations, not the overall pattern—there's a flaw. A minor correction in every cycle, like it wants to veer off-key but gets pulled back into line."

"I have a D-minus in physics. What the hell does that mean?"

Addie spoke slowly, making each word distinct, like she was talking to a little kid. "He's a pivot. His choices make stronger worlds. They'd be stable, if his frequency was right. But it's not. So every time he creates a world, it's not just off-key. It's magnitudes off-key."

Eliot took over. "It takes a while for the world to destabilize, because the flaw is so small. But when it finally goes bad, it goes bad fast."

"Like Park World," I said.

Eliot nodded. "I told you there was another reason."

"And you told Addie first?" The betrayal stung. "Why?"

"You haven't exactly been a model of restraint and clear thinking lately," Addie said. "Leave him alone, Del. He was worried about you."

I glared at Eliot, who shrugged. Apparently the days when I could boss him around were gone.

"What would do that to someone's frequency? How do we fix it?" I asked.

"We tell Mom and Dad. They'll tell the Consort, and the Consort will take care of it."

They'd cleave him. "No Consort. We'll handle it ourselves."

We pulled up to the house, and Addie hit the brakes so hard that I almost slid off the seat. "This is why Eliot told me first. You've seen the damage he's done. There's no way we can fix it without help."

"Then we ask for help," I said, running through the possibilities in my head. Only one stood out. "But not from the Consort."

CHAPTER FORTY-NINE

IT'S DEFINITELY A SITUATION," MONTY SAID, once we were gathered around the kitchen table. He helped himself to another cookie. "You're positive it's the Lane boy? I met him, and he sounded fine."

"The flaw in his frequency is so small, it's impossible to detect without computer analysis. But it's definitely there, and it's allowing other frequencies to interfere with the Key World," Eliot said. "Because he's a natural pivot, he creates more Echoes than usual, and every one of them carries the flaw—so they're all more likely to destabilize. The longer the Echo has been around, the longer it can withstand the flaw, but the newer branches are more vulnerable."

Addie chimed in. "Every time he interacts with Del in an Echo world, the signal there boosts—and his Original remembers it. It's like he goes into a trance here, and his entire consciousness is wherever he's engaging with her," Addie said.

"Just you, Delancey? No other Walkers?"

"I'm the only one he knows."

He chewed thoughtfully. "You're sure?"

"I'm not sure about anything," I said. "Except that we have

to help him, Grandpa. If the Consort gets hold of him, it's the end of everything. His mom's really sick, and he's all she has."

"And you'd miss him."

I looked down at my coffee. I missed him already, but this was more important than my feelings.

"Look," said Addie. "Not that Del's heart growing three sizes isn't great, but Simon is endangering the Key World. If we can't figure out a way to stop the damage, we have to tell the Consort. That's the rule. No exceptions."

"I still don't understand why his frequency is off," Eliot said. "Or how he was able to Walk with Del."

"The last one, I can explain," Monty said, getting up from the table and reaching for his hat. "Let's go find your boy, Del."

Ten minutes later I was gathering my nerves on Simon's doorstep while Addie, Eliot, and Monty watched from the car.

"I don't want to fight again," he said through the screen door.

"I'm not here to fight. The thing is—"

He spoke over me. "What you did was not okay."

"I know."

"I trusted you. I told you about my mom. I told you about my dad. You made me look like an idiot in front of the team. Every single truth you've told me, I had to drag out of you."

I stared at the sunflower-strewn welcome mat.

"And I can't blame you."

My head snapped up, and he said wryly, "Well, maybe a little. But I didn't give you much reason to trust me. You told me about the Walkers, and all I could think about was my mom. And considering how I acted at school—three years, and I looked right past you—I wouldn't trust me either."

"I do," I whispered.

The faintest smile tugged at his mouth, and he put his hand against the screen. "That's a good start."

I matched my palm to his, the contact warm through the cool mesh.

"There's something else you should know," I said, and his smile faded. "Can we come in?"

"We?"

I pointed at Addie's car, idling at the curb.

He sighed and pushed open the door. I signaled to Addie, then turned back to Simon. "I really am sorry about this."

"Good to see you again, Simon." Monty stuck out his hand as the others filed in.

Simon shook it, giving me a faintly disbelieving look, like he couldn't believe we were going to waste time on social niceties.

"Where's your mom?" I said, keeping my voice low.

"Resting. We'll stay out here."

I got the message. The back of the house, with its cheery kitchen and cozy family room, was off-limits for now. We still had ground to make up.

Addie spoke, brisk and businesslike. "There's a problem with your frequency. A flaw that gets progressively worse with each iteration of your Echoes. We don't know what's causing it, but we do know the result: Some of the Echoes you appear in are destabilizing, and the damage is now spreading to the Key World."

He looked at her blankly.

"Something in your frequency is off," I translated. "And it's causing problems across the multiverse. Big problems."

Addie continued. "The damage is increasing to the point where the Consort will soon be able to track it back to you. If we can't solve the problem before they do . . . Del thinks you and your mother could be in danger."

He looked at me for confirmation. I swallowed hard and nodded, expecting him to get angry again. Instead he regarded Addie coolly. "Delivery like that, you should consider a career in oncology."

She inclined her head. "Someone here has to think straight, and we all know it's not going to be Del."

I ignored her. "The Consort's going to figure it out soon. We don't have a ton of time, and we need your help."

"I'm assuming you have a plan," he said. Everyone was perched on the spindly furniture except for Simon, who stood at the door like he was about to throw us out again. Iggy padded in and made a beeline for me, resting his head on my knees.

"There's always a plan," said Monty. "They don't usually work out like you'd expect."

"You would know," said Simon's mom. We turned in unison as she walked in, clad in yoga pants and one of Simon's old sweat-shirts. "Hello, Montrose. I wondered if I'd see you again."

"Hello, Amelia," said Monty. "Wasn't sure you'd want to."

CHAPTER FIFTY

WHAT THE HELL?" I SAID, AND ELIOT ELBOWED me. "You two know each other?"

Monty dipped his head. "How long has it been?"

Amelia clung to Simon's arm, her eyes red rimmed, the bright smile replaced by one more faded and resigned. And suddenly, I knew.

"Seventeen years," I said. Every head in the room swiveled toward me.

"That's my girl," Monty murmured.

"I don't understand," Simon said.

"Seventeen years. That's how long my grandmother's been gone," I said, edging closer to Simon, the way you would an animal about to bolt. "And so has your dad."

"Del?" Eliot asked, putting it together. "Are you sure?"

"Sure about what?" Simon asked, his patience clearly at an end.

"Your dad's a Walker." My certainty grew as I spoke.

Simon shook his head. "My dad *left*."

"Same as my grandmother. When's your birthday?"

"January third."

I looked at Addie, who shrugged. "Grandma disappeared on the ninth."

"Not quite," Monty corrected. "I needed to muddy the trail a bit. Give her a few days' head start."

"I'm a Walker?" Simon said.

"Half Walker," Addie said. "Half Original. *That's* why your signal's so strong."

"And why you were able to Walk with me," I said. "You can't find the pivots—you didn't get your dad's hearing—but you can move through them."

Simon tensed, and I couldn't tell if it was to attack or run. "You can't ask for help like a normal person? You have to manipulate people? She's lying," he said to his mom. "Isn't she?"

Amelia's mouth trembled, and she ran her hands over his shoulders, smoothing imaginary creases from his T-shirt.

"Mom?"

"We were so careful not to leave a trail," she said. "Rose delivered you here at home. We never put your father's name on any records. We weren't even legally married." She touched the gold band on her ring finger. "He hid us away as best he could, to keep us safe until the Consort was finished. When he didn't come back, it seemed safer to keep hiding."

"The Consort discourages Walker-Original relationships because they weaken the genetic line," Addie said. "They monitor the kids closely."

Monty snorted. "If you believe that poppycock, Addison, I've got a bridge in Brooklyn to sell you. Those children aren't monitored; they're taken—if they're lucky. And the child of a Free Walker—Gil Bradley's son, no less—would have been a special prize."

"The Free Walkers?" Eliot said. "Don't they want to destroy the Key World, or something?"

"Hardly," Monty replied. "They want to save the Echoes. Inversions aren't the only things that can be stabilized. You can tune entire Echoes, rather than cleave. Protect all those lives."

"Echoes aren't alive," Addie said. "There's nothing there to save."

"Who taught you that? The Consort, because it serves their purposes. They'd rather sacrifice the Echoes for their own gain, so they lie and tell you cleaving's the only way."

Eliot spoke. "You're saying the Consort has been systematically deceiving Walkers for . . . how long? Twenty years? That's impossible."

"Nothing's impossible," Monty said morosely. "This has gone on much longer than twenty years. Generation after generation, we've drifted further from the truth, until we've forgotten what we were meant for. The Consort's taken advantage, and the Free Walkers are working to stop them. They're not madmen, or anarchists, or whatever other stories you've been spoon-fed."

"I don't care about Echoes," Simon said in a voice hard as granite. "Whatever war you people are fighting has nothing to do with us."

"But it does," Amelia said, taking his hands in hers. "Your

father was one of the Consort's top navigators, but he'd been secretly organizing a group of Free Walkers to move against them. If they'd found out he had a child, they would have used you—used both of us—as leverage."

"He bailed to protect us? You believe that? Mom, I know these people. They don't care about anything except themselves and their stupid Key World."

"I thought you'd be quicker, son," said Monty. "Your father didn't leave. He was taken by the Consort three days after you were born."

"You're working with them," Eliot said to Monty. "You're a Free Walker."

"I did my part, back in the day." Monty settled himself on the couch. "Once Rose was gone, there wasn't much point to it."

Addie tore her gaze from Simon and Amelia. "You and Grandma? Both of you?"

"She and Gil worked together. When he was caught, we knew he'd be interrogated." Monty grimaced, and Amelia pressed her hand to her mouth. "Chances were good they'd find out about Rose, so she ran."

"I don't believe you," said Addie. "If Grandma was a traitor, we would know. The Consort would have told us."

"She wasn't a traitor," Monty snapped, anger distorting his features. "She fought for the good. You've met Randolph Lattimer. He'd cut out his tongue before he admitted that some of their top people revolted."

Addie's mouth opened and closed soundlessly.

"If you and Rose were both involved, why aren't you in prison?" Eliot's tone was cool and logical.

"Who says I'm not?" Monty said softly.

"That's why Lattimer wanted us to keep an eye on you," Addie said. "And why security's so tight. They think Free Walkers are behind the anomaly. He was hoping you'd lead them to the Free Walkers."

"Lattimer's a fool. If I knew how to find them, I would have by now. Would have found Rose, too."

"Why didn't Grandma get in contact once the coast was clear?" I asked.

Monty sagged. "She got lost. She must have been terrified, and she ran so far and so fast, she couldn't find her way home." He clutched my sleeve. "We can find her now, Del."

I covered his hand with mine. I didn't want to tell him we'd be chasing a ghost. Nobody could survive in Echoes that long.

"Where's my dad?" Simon broke in. "You said the Consort took him. Where?"

After a beat, Monty said, "An oubliette, no doubt. One of our prisons."

Eliot cleared his throat apologetically. "This doesn't change the fact Simon is a threat to the Key World."

"You're looking at it wrong," said Monty. "He's not weakening the Key World; he's strengthening the Echoes. The boy's signal is so strong, he even triggers Baroque events."

"That's exactly the problem," Addie said. "There's a flaw in his frequency making them unstable. If you start with ten bad

Echoes, and you combine them, you end up with one really, really unstable Echo."

"Easier to tune one world than ten," Monty said. "We can use him. Take him into the worst of the Echoes, trigger a Baroque event, and tune the remaining branch. We do enough, and the problems with the Key World will disappear."

"Hold on," I said. "You want to take Simon into the Echoes?"

"Fastest way to do it," he said. "And the Consort's getting closer every day."

"It's a temporary fix," Eliot warned. "The flaw in his frequency will keep causing problems. We need to know what's causing it."

"This buys us time to find out," I replied.

Silence fell as we mulled it over. Amelia lowered herself into a chair, hands clasped in her lap.

Then Simon spoke, his voice razor edged. "Del? Kitchen?"

Amelia's tea, steeping on the counter, had gone cold. A book of crossword puzzles lay next to it. The table was covered in Simon's school papers, and I could picture the two of them joking around as he worked. Our arrival had stolen the moment from them, and I wondered if they would ever reclaim it.

"I had no idea about your dad, honestly," I said, gripping the back of a chair. "It never even occurred to me."

"My dad isn't the problem." He looked drained, face shadowed, and I wanted to put my arms around him. But tension crackled through him, like a downed power line, holding me at bay. "I keep thinking there's something else. Some other bomb you're going to drop."

"I've told you everything I know. If there's more, it'll surprise us both."

"It's too much. My dad, and these problems with the Echoes, and . . . It's too much." He ran his hand over his head. "My dad. Jesus, Del. I can't even think about him right now."

I tucked my hands in my pockets, trying not to reach for him. "You don't have to Walk. We'll figure out a way to keep you out of it."

"But it's my frequency causing the problem. It's my fault." He hunched his shoulders. "The Consort. The people who steal kids and threw my dad in prison. They're the ones in charge? And the Free Walkers fight them?"

"I guess. I thought they were a story, not real. Not organized, or powerful."

"Maybe they wanted it that way," he said. "If we don't fix this, the Consort will find me. They'll take me away from my mom, like they did to my dad. The best chance I have to stay here and have a normal life is to help you."

"Last time you Walked, we almost died. It ripped the fabric of the multiverse. I don't want to risk it."

"More tears?" he asked.

"You. I don't want to risk losing you." *Any more than I have already,* I added silently.

"Because you care about me." I nodded, and the tightness around his mouth eased. "But you don't believe I care about you."

"What you felt for me was rooted in your Echoes," I said. Pictures of Simon hung from the fridge, and I studied them to

430

keep from looking at him. They went back to grade school, a little boy clutching a basketball with undisguised glee and the same clear, direct gaze weighing on me now. "I'm not the choice you would have made on your own."

"So, the Echoes' feelings are real, but they aren't. And I'm real, but my feelings aren't. Works out pretty well for you."

"Excuse me?" I wheeled around.

"If we crash and burn, regardless of which world you're visiting, we weren't real. And if it's not real, it doesn't hurt."

It hurt plenty, so much that my throat tightened and my breath came shorter at the reminder. But I held my hands up in a gesture of surrender. "Can we back-burner the psychoanalysis for today? We've got bigger problems."

"You're scared."

"The multiverse is about to start coming down around our ears. I'd be an idiot if I wasn't scared."

"You told the other me you'd been hiding. This is what you've been hiding from. Reality. There's a million worlds for you to visit, but only one that counts, and you can't control it and it terrifies you."

He stalked toward me, and I edged away until my back hit the counter.

"You gave up on us pretty damn quick, didn't you? Because it was real and you could have gotten hurt."

"I am hurt," I said, but it came out softer than I'd hoped.

"Me too," he said. "It hurt to think of you with anyone else, even if it was me. You and I are real, Delancey Sullivan. I'm not letting you hide from that in this world or any other. So I'm coming with. You said my choices make worlds?"

I nodded, my breath coming too fast.

"Then I choose the world where you and I are together, and we solve this. Got it?"

He slid his hand around the nape of my neck, tipped my head back. "Got it," I whispered, and he swallowed my words as we fell into the kiss.

"I would tell you to get a room," Addie said from the direction of the doorway, "but you're too young, and we don't have the time."

"Go away, Addie," I said, eyes closed.

She clipped across the floor. "We need to get ready. And I'm sure Mrs. Lane would like to talk with her son. Which she cannot do while you're mauling him."

Simon pulled back, hands framing my face. "Tomorrow," he said. "We'll talk tomorrow."

"Tomorrow," Addie said, "we save the world."

He kissed me again, lightly, and we went back to the living room, where Eliot was carefully inspecting the wallpaper. Monty waggled his eyebrows at me and turned to Simon's mom.

"We'll be off, then, Amelia. I'm sure we'll see you again soon."

She stood, fragile but determined. "I wouldn't recommend waiting another seventeen years, Montrose."

"No indeed," he said, sadness in his smile.

"I'm sorry we brought this down on you," I said to her, when everyone else had filed out. Simon stood behind me, hands on my waist.

"It was always a possibility," she said. "Especially once Simon brought you home."

"You knew who I was?"

"Not at first. But when you told me your name, and Simon mentioned Montrose, I knew it was coming." She sounded miserable and resigned, and I wanted desperately to make her feel better. To make them both feel better.

"We'll figure it out," I said. "Monty's really good. He must seem like he's slipped a lot since you knew him, but—"

"I don't think he's slipped at all," she said. "He's exactly as he used to be."

I relaxed slightly, and she pressed my hand between hers. "Please be careful. I know Walkers believe the Key World matters most, but Simon is *my* world. Take care of him."

"I will. I promise."

CHAPTER FIFTY-ONE

In rare instances, the destabilization of one branch can spread to others, creating a cascade effect and requiring swift action.

—Chapter Five, "Physics,"
Principles and Practices of Cleaving, Year Five

SATURDAY MORNING I WOKE EARLY AND found my mom in her office, door thrown wide. "Del," she said, barely looking up as she shoved file folders and rolled-up maps into her bag. "You three are on your own today. I'd prefer it if you stayed out of the Echoes as much as possible."

"Is there a problem?" I said, trying to sound curious instead of alarmed. Inside, my heart was pounding triple-time. "Some development with the anomaly?"

"We're very close," she said. "I'm hoping that the analysis we run today will pinpoint the source, but I need the Consort's computers. And since your father's not fully recovered, he's going to coordinate the teams." She slung her bag over her shoulder and headed for the kitchen. "We're hoping this is the end, honey. Once we can get rid of the source, life will go back to the way it was."

The source was Simon. Getting rid of him was not an option.

Besides, after Monty's bombshell last night, going back to the way things used to be had lost its appeal. The future was equally murky; how could I work for the Consort if Monty's stories were true?

"Mom?" I asked. "What was Grandma like?"

"That's an odd question," she said. "Why do you ask?"

"Monty's been talking about her a lot lately," I said. "But you know how he gets. What was she really like?"

She poured coffee into a travel mug, dosed it with cream and sugar. Finally she said, "She was strong, I suppose. Practical, but not rigid. Not quite as . . . exuberant . . . as Monty. She loved your grandfather, and she loved what she did. She was absolutely devoted to her patients, to the teams under her care. They were like family to her. Sometimes I thought she cared more about them than she did our work. Or us."

She snapped the lid on her mug. "I have to run. Be careful today."

Before the car pulled away, I was texting Eliot and shaking Addie awake. We convened around the kitchen island, reviewing one last time.

"Simon spends the most time at school," Addie said. "He's already created a bunch of branches there, so they're our best shot at triggering Baroque events. Grandpa, you're going to help Simon. Del and I will handle the tunings. Eliot, you're going to navigate. Everybody clear?"

"What about Lattimer?" I asked. "He always checks in on Saturday."

Addie chewed on a fingernail. "He'll be busy with Mom

and Dad's big meeting. As long as we're home in the evening, he won't find out."

"You're assuming we'll finish this in one day," Eliot said. "And that the Consort won't be monitoring the area."

"Maybe we shouldn't bring Simon with," I said. "When we were in music, he triggered a Baroque event without leaving the Key World. Why can't we do it that way?"

"There's no time," Monty said. He pointed to the map in front of us. Addie and Eliot had circled several thickets of black lines, unstable but strong, that we would target today. "Lattimer's coming. Your parents are close to finding Simon. The branches are growing more unstable by the day. The longer we wait, the greater the danger."

"He makes worlds stronger," Addie chimed in. "By bringing him into the Echoes, we can place the Baroque events exactly where we want them."

She handed Monty a six-pack of pop and a package of chocolate bars, our defense against frequency poisoning. "Can you put these in the car, Grandpa?"

He took the bag and shuffled outside.

"It's a Band-Aid, not a cure," Eliot said, gathering up the maps and shoving them in his messenger bag. "There's no way to change Simon's frequency. He's going to keep inverting the Key World. We should tell the Consort."

"How can you say that after the horrible things they've done? They tortured Simon's dad. They steal Walker-Original kids." I folded my arms. "I don't trust them."

Eliot and Addie exchanged glances. "Del, there's no proof any of those things happened. I'm not saying Monty's lying . . ."

That's exactly what he was saying.

". . . but you know how easily he gets confused. A few weeks ago your mom was ready to put him in a home. Now he's got this elaborate conspiracy theory. . . . It doesn't add up."

"I believe him," I said. "And you do too, deep down, or you wouldn't be here."

"I'm here for you," he said. "That's it."

"Even if there's some truth to it," Addie said, scattering the awkward silence with trademark efficiency, "the fact remains that the Key World trumps everything else. If it falls, the entire multiverse unravels."

"I know."

"Okay, then. If this doesn't work, would you let the whole world crash to save your boyfriend?"

"This will work," I said, heading out to the car. It *had* to work.

"I hope so," Addie called after me. "Or I'll turn him in myself."

I threw my bag in the backseat of Addie's car. Monty patted my arm reassuringly. "Don't listen to her," he murmured. "We'll figure something out, you and I."

I leaned my head against his shoulder, breathed in the scent of shaving soap. "Thanks, Grandpa."

"You carry too much with you," he said, his usual complaint. "A good Walker does more with less."

"I like to be prepared."

"You're heading into infinity," he said. "There's no way to prepare for it. Did you bring the necklace, though?"

I fished the pendant out from beneath my shirt. "Why did she leave it behind?"

Monty reached out a gnarled finger and tapped it lightly, the high, clear tone carrying through the air. "You hold tight to it."

Which was not an answer, and I was about to say so when Eliot and Addie appeared, Addie buttoning her coat, Eliot bobbling the rolled-up maps. I tucked the necklace away and tried not to worry about what they'd discussed when I was out of earshot.

We drove to the school in silence. The parking lot was empty except for Simon's Jeep. He met us at the doors to the gym, freshly showered from practice.

"Everyone else is gone?" Addie asked.

"Yep. I hid in the equipment room till they left," he said, and I blushed at the memory.

We moved through the field house in a loose knot, Eliot monitoring frequencies on his phone, Addie consulting the map we'd drawn up last night, Monty as nonchalant if he were out for a stroll. But his eyes were sharp and his hands were steady as he felt for vibrations in the air.

Simon hung back, his arm around my waist. "What are we looking for, exactly?"

"Listening," I corrected. "For the pivot we need to go through."

"I can't hear it," he said.

"You don't need to. I'll bring you across."

"We have a problem," called Eliot, his voice echoing through the room. He pointed to a banner at the top of the bleachers. As we watched, it flickered rapidly, popping in and out of sight.

I swore, and even Addie looked worried. "An inversion?"

"Two birds with one stone," said Monty. "We bring Simon through to the inverted Echo, trigger the Baroque event, and tune the entire branch while you fix the inversion."

Eliot tapped his screen. "You'd have to nail the timing. Tune it too early, and it won't carry over into the final branch. Too late, and the inversion will have taken root permanently."

"Fabulous," Addie muttered. "Let's get moving. The Consort's monitoring for inversions, and this one's big enough to grab their attention."

"Why sports events?" Simon asked as we started up the bleachers. "First the trophy case, now the conference banners. Why is it always sports?"

"Sporting events form strong pivots. You form strong pivots. Put them together, and this is what you get," Addie said.

Monty groaned from exertion. Simon and I helped him up the last few steps, and Eliot trailed behind, muttering about rates of oscillation and dampening effects.

When we reached the top, directly under the banner, I left Simon near Monty and placed my palm against the heavy felt.

"I can do it," Addie said.

"I can do it faster."

She looked like she was going to argue, but I closed my eyes and shut out everything except the frequency before me, isolating the bad string and following it back to its source, moving parallel to the wall. I was dimly aware of people fumbling behind me, but I kept pushing until I was through, gasping like I was coming up for air.

And nearly stepped into empty space. The bleachers were pushed in, and I bobbled on the ledge, fighting to keep my balance—only for Addie to knock me into the metal railing as she crossed. I tipped over empty space, my center of gravity too far off to compensate. My arms windmilled, trying to break my fall.

Addie caught my hand and hauled me upright. "Great start."

"Your timing's good, at least." I clutched the railing so tightly my knuckles turned white.

An instant later Eliot appeared, and we steadied Simon and Monty as they came through, the five of us balancing on the top row.

Simon shuddered. "Am I ever going to get used to that?"

"Let's hope you don't have to," Addie said. The pitch clashed with the buzzing of the giant fluorescent lights in their wire cage. I rubbed at my ears, feeling as if something were crawling inside them. On the floor below, the girls' basketball team was practicing, oblivious to all of us.

"We're invisible," Simon said wonderingly.

"Welcome to my worlds," I muttered. "Eliot, how long will the Baroque event take?"

He held his phone up to Simon, checking the readings. "Less time than I thought. It's like we're picking up momentum. I'm guessing three or four minutes, tops. Go ahead and isolate the inverted threads, Addie, but don't tune them till you hear my signal. Be ready to move."

"As long as there's no pressure," Addie said. I wondered if she was having second thoughts about helping me. But she simply closed her eyes and reached back into the inversion.

"How does it feel?" asked Eliot after a minute. Addie's face was pale and strained, but there was a hint of triumph at the corner of her mouth.

"I've got the threads. Can I start?"

"Not yet. The Baroque event hasn't progressed enough."

Monty nudged Simon. "Move closer. It'll speed things up."

"Get over here," Addie said, not bothering to sound polite. Simon brushed past me, and I went a little weak-kneed at the sensation, despite the seed of doubt unfurling within me. Something was off.

Simon stretched out a hand, inches above Addie's, and the frequency ratcheted up. Monty and I both winced, clapping our hands over our ears.

"Go," Eliot said, his voice wavering. "It's moving fast. Ninety seconds, Addie."

She bit down on her lower lip, brow creasing as her fingers made minute adjustments.

"Sixty seconds," Eliot warned. Around us, the entire gym started to flicker, the Key World version alternating with this one, creating a strobe effect with the lights. Beads of sweat popped on Addie's forehead.

"Thirty seconds."

"Almost there . . . ," Addie breathed. "Got it!"

The room trembled as if the molecules were rearranging themselves. The frequency crescendoed, rippling through us like a sonic boom, and Monty staggered into Simon. An instant later the pitch dropped back to almost normal, and our ears filled with the sounds of basketball practice—squeaking sneakers, basketballs on hardwood, the shouts of the coach. The banner was nowhere in sight, safely locked in the Key World.

"Knew you had it in you, Addie-girl," Monty said.

"Time to go," Eliot said. "Even if it's tuned, we don't want Simon boosting an Echo any more than necessary. The longer we stay, the stronger this place gets."

One by one we edged through the pivot, easier the second time. I clung to Simon's hand, pulling him through. Eliot dropped onto the bleachers, which were fully extended once again.

"We have to do that how many times?" he asked, looking haggard.

"As many as it takes," I said, hauling him to his feet.

Simon touched my cheek. "Are you sure you can keep this up?"

"No problem," I said.

An hour and a half later it was clear we had a very big problem indeed. We'd tuned the Baroque events according to our plan, but we'd also run across several inversions, each one bigger than the previous one.

"I don't understand," I said. We sat on the floor of the

commons, Simon's arm draped around my shoulder. I huddled against him, shaking. "Why isn't it stabilizing?"

"We're losing ground," Addie said, massaging her temples. "The Baroque events are holding steady, but the inversions are increasing."

"We've got to get ahead of it," I said.

"We can't," Eliot said wearily. He took a bite of his chocolate bar. "The inversions are coming through faster than we tune the Baroque events. Look."

He tossed me his phone and I scrolled through the map—the inversions showed up as pixilated blurs where there should be steady lights. Another burst of static took out the lower right corner of the screen as I watched. "How do we stop them?" I asked. "What's causing it?"

"I don't know," he snapped. "I can't think like this, with all these frequencies . . ."

"We need to tell the Consort," Addie said. "They're going to pick up on it anyway."

"Not yet," I pleaded.

"We need to start cleaving," Eliot said. "It's the only way."

"Absolutely not," said Monty, as a high-pitched whine filled the air. The room flickered around us.

"Time to go," said Simon, hauling me up by the arm. "We can argue when we're clear."

We ran for the main office, and Monty dropped onto one of the wooden benches. When his breath evened out, he said, "We could cover more ground if we split up."

"That is a terrible idea," Eliot said. "In the entire history of movies, there's never been a case where splitting up turned out well."

"It's a better idea than cleaving," I said. "This isn't a movie; it's Simon's life. We're running out of time."

"Del, we need to discuss this," Addie said. "Review our options."

"Discuss all you want. In the meantime, I'm going to stop the inversion." I sprinted back down the hallway.

The noise streaming out of the commons hit me like a tidal wave. It was cycling rapidly, electric-blue carpet and white chairs changing to the familiar beige and maroon.

I plunged into the inversion before Simon or anyone else could stop me.

The dissonance was doubly strong on this side, furniture blurring, ground swaying. The damage was so widespread, I didn't need to find a specific object—I closed my eyes and reached into the air, the frequency abrading my skin. Fighting the instinct to pull away, I dug in, and the fabric of the world peeled back. I began sifting through a million different strings, trying to find the ones out of tune.

The threads were as weightlessly strong as spider silk. Resilient, too. When I pushed, they pushed back, weaving together more densely as the world grew stronger. I imagined Simon on the other side of the pivot, trying to find a way through. He'd be furious when I got home.

If I got home.

Reckless, I thought, as the signal increased and threw me off-kilter, interrupting my search. That's what they were always saying: Addie and Simon and Eliot, my parents, my teachers, the Consort. My recklessness had brought me this far, but now I needed to be more. I needed to be as good as I'd claimed, and that meant gathering up all my skills and all my wild jaunts through the multiverse to find the one strand that would calm this world down.

I breathed out, pictured Simon, breathed in, and reached through the threads one more time.

And found a piece of silk that twisted and kinked and sang in a key far different from the rest of them.

I grabbed it, traced the damage back to the snarl I'd been hunting, a cluster so large I needed both hands to span it. Bit by bit, I smoothed the strings, rocking them back and forth, coaxing and nudging until they chimed in harmony with the rest of the threads.

Done.

The instant I let go, the frequency roared around me, and I dropped to my knees, fumbling for the tuning fork at my neck. I tapped it once, twice, and followed the signal home.

Four pairs of hands grabbed at me. The room spun like a top winding down. "I did it?"

"Yeah, you did it. And you nearly gave me a heart attack." Simon gathered me up in his arms. "Are you okay?"

"Never better," I said, teeth clenched.

Wordlessly Eliot passed me a chocolate bar.

Addie's face was bloodless, save for two splotches of red high on her cheeks. "What were you trying to prove?"

"We can split up, like Monty said. Cover more ground."

"It's too dangerous. Besides, without Simon, Eliot and I can't trigger Baroque events. "

"We'll still fix double the number of inversions. Hold off the Consort." I stood, Simon's arm tight around my waist. "Please, Addie. We can't quit yet."

Monty piped up. "If she's willing to try, I'm willing to keep an eye on her."

"It's getting late," said Addie, consulting her watch. "One hour, Del. If we haven't turned this around by then, there's no point in trying more."

"Got it," I said, and next to me, Simon and Monty made noises of agreement.

"Good luck," Addie said, but Eliot scowled at Simon, and then he and Addie took off.

"What next?" Simon asked, looking from me to Monty.

"Next we start looking for another inversion. That way," I said, and gestured toward the music wing.

Simon took my hand and we started moving, only to realize that Monty wasn't following. He'd sat down on one of the couches in the now-stable commons, face slack and hands trembling.

"Grandpa? Are you sick?"

His eyes were a pale, watery blue. "We're never going to get ahead of the inversions."

"But you said . . ."

He tugged me down next to him. "Like calls to like. Every Echo he's ever created carries the flaw. They're being drawn here at the same time his flaw is weakening the Key World. It doesn't matter how many we tune, they won't stop coming. They'll only get faster."

"Then why did you want us to split up?"

"We need to take Simon away. Find another branch. Hide him from the Consort." His voice dropped. "The minute they realize what he is, they'll kill him."

"You want me to run?" Simon sounded insulted. "Won't I bring the inversions with me?"

"If we could find a world where we knew he never existed. A major branch, one without an Echo of him in it, would be more resistant to the inversions. It would buy us time." Monty clutched at my arm. "Time's the only thing we can't choose. It runs like a river no matter how the world branches. But we can slow the damage if we draw him away. Let the Key World restore itself, repair the Echoes."

It sounded crazy, but I couldn't see another option. We needed time to fix the Key World, time to fix the flaw in Simon's frequency. Time we didn't have here, where reality was degrading.

"I don't know any Echoes where he doesn't exist, Grandpa." I'd watched Simon for so long, I couldn't even imagine a world without him.

"A place he'd never even been born," Monty mused. "Your

447

parents met at the train crash, didn't they? Near the Depot."

"If the crash never happened . . . ," Simon said, understanding. He fished in his pocket for his keys. "I'll drive."

"Best we hurry," Monty said, struggling to his feet. "The others will notice soon enough."

I stopped cold. Addie would track us. "Someone has to stay behind and throw them off the trail."

"Nonsense," Monty replied. "We should all go. She won't guess where we've gone."

"If we vanish, she'll turn us over to the Consort. We need you to stay here and talk her down. Stall her."

"And we'll go back for him later?" Monty frowned. "You know the risk, Del. It's better if we stick together."

"You said it yourself. There's no time. Please, Grandpa."

"Do you think you can handle Addie?" Simon asked.

Monty drew himself up, offended. "She's just a girl. I've handled worse."

"Then let's go," Simon said.

CHAPTER FIFTY-TWO

THE DEPOT WAS BUSY WITH THE SATURDAY lunch crowd. Through the window I saw black-clad waitresses toting trays of lattes, oblivious to the disaster bearing down on us.

"Good date," Simon said.

I smiled despite my nerves. "We'll do it again soon."

"I'm holding you to that."

We climbed out of the Jeep. "Is the pivot at the memorial?"

"The Originals' memorial marks where the train hit. The Walkers' is where the engineer chose to maintain his speed instead of slowing down. If he'd applied the brakes a few minutes sooner, there would never have been a crash."

We circled the building, crossed the grassy median between it and the tracks, and followed them a hundred yards, holding hands. I spotted the small cairn of white pebbles at the same time the pivot tugged at me.

"This is the spot," I said, nudging a stray pebble with my toe.

"Your memorial is a pile of rocks?"

"It's symbolic. We build it up each time we cross; the vibrations from the train knock it down. Entropy."

I slid my arms around him, trying to fight off the panic crawling over me. "Ready?"

He nodded, jaw tight, eyes looking past me at a rent in the air he couldn't see and was about to give himself over to.

"You shouldn't get frequency poisoning. You'll be safe."

"How will you find me?" he asked.

"Wait at the school until I come back for you," I said, taking his face in my hands, forcing him to meet my eyes. "I will come back."

"I know." He kissed me until I felt weightless. "The sooner we start, the sooner I see you again."

I laced my fingers through his, memorizing the way we fit together, the feel of his skin against mine, the syncopation of our heartbeats. We'd crossed worlds together, but this time I would have to leave him behind. The thought of the Key World without him in it—for a day, an hour, a minute—felt as wrong as a world missing the color blue.

My phone trilled. "What?"

"Where are you?" Eliot hissed.

"About to cross a pivot," I said, which was technically true. "Why are you whispering?"

"Addie's on the phone with your mom. The Consort picked up on the inversions at the school. They're sending a bunch of teams out to start cleaving. Your mom called to make sure we were staying home today like she asked."

Cold gathered along my spine.

"We need to get out of here before they catch us," Eliot said.

"Grab Monty and go," I said. A train rocketed by, my hair whipping in the rush of air. When I could hear again, I added, "I'll take care of Simon."

Eliot was quiet for a long moment. "Del, for once in your life, think. This isn't going to work. You can't hide him forever."

"I don't need forever," I said, and hung up.

Simon frowned. "Everything okay?"

"It will be," I said, and reached for him.

Simon twitched when we came through, like Iggy shaking himself dry. The frequency here was flat but solid. A good sign.

We headed north, toward the school. The town had shifted toward the train station, storefronts jammed with high-end boutiques and gourmet restaurants. "What do I do while you're gone?"

"Whatever you want," I said. "People won't notice you unless you touch them. You don't have to worry about running into yourself."

"Could I check on my mom? She might be healthy here."

"Amelia Lane exists in this world," I said. "But she's not your mom. She never met your dad at the crash. She might not even live here anymore."

She might not be alive at all.

"The Consort's coming," I said when we reached the front doors of the school. "I need to get home and come up with a cover story."

"Is that why Eliot called? To warn you?"

I nodded, pressed my cheek against his chest. "I'll come

back tonight to give you an update. It's good that your signal's so strong—I'll be able to track you without a problem. In the meantime—" I dug in my bag and found the package of origami papers. "Better start teaching yourself. Now that I know you can Walk, imagine the fun we'll have."

He smiled, but it twisted and disappeared before he could make it work. "You'll take care of Iggy, right? And . . ."

"I won't need to take care of Iggy," I said, my throat aching. "Or anyone else. I won't leave you here."

"Del—just in case—"

I stopped his words with a final kiss, telling him everything I couldn't bring myself to say, listening to everything I couldn't bear to hear him speak.

"Tell me later," I said.

"Tell her now," Addie said, and I jerked away from Simon to see her standing at the edge of the parking lot, cold and white as marble. "You're not coming back, Del. Ever."

CHAPTER FIFTY-THREE

 OW DID YOU FIND US?"

I pushed Simon behind me as if I could shield him.

"You're not hard to track, Del. He's like a freaking siren." She darted forward and wrenched me away. "Are you insane? Do you have any idea what you're doing?"

"He was pulling the inversions into the Key World, so I moved him. How did you find us?"

"Eliot heard the train when he called and put it together. Moving Simon isn't enough."

"It will stabilize the Key World and get the Consort off his trail. That's what matters."

"His signal's too strong," Addie said. "When he was in the Key World, it drew the Echoes there. Now it's drawing them here."

"That's good," I said. "The inversions will stop."

"*All* the frequencies," she said, and took me by the shoulders, spinning me around. "Even the Key World's. Look."

A cast-iron replica of a steam engine stood at the front entrance of the school. As we watched, it shifted to a statue of George Washington. "I don't understand."

"I do," Simon said, coming to stand next to me. "Did you know they changed the school mascot?"

"Did you know I don't care?"

"Twenty years ago," he said. "We used to be the Iron Horses. After the crash, they renamed the school."

The sky tilted, the world going dim. "I don't know what that means."

"This world's mascot is a train, not a president. But the Key World is being pulled here. Toward me."

"We can't win." Addie's eyes filled with pity. "The Consort was at the school when I left. They're already cleaving the inversions. They'll find this world, and they'll cleave it."

My stomach wrenched. All those Echoes, gone. All those Simons. All those lives we'd worked so hard to save, rippling away.

"Breathe," Simon said, rubbing slow circles on my back. "Breathe, Del. In and out. Come on."

"No. *No.* There's got to be a way around this." I dragged Addie to the edge of the sidewalk. "If we bring him back, the Consort will kill him."

"We don't know that for sure. They might fix him."

I laughed. "They don't want to fix things. It's inefficient, remember? Why bother tuning an Echo when you can cleave it? Why bother saving a life when you can end it?"

"They're preserving the Key World. You know this. It's kid stuff. It's what they've always taught us."

"Exactly," I said. "Did it ever cross your mind that they aren't telling us the whole truth?" *As fluid as water, as faceted as diamonds, as flawed as memory.* What were the other facets? What was the Free Walkers' truth? The Echoes'?

What was mine?

"Del, listen to me. You are the best Walker I've ever met. You can go anywhere. You can Walk to any world, have anything you want." She gave me a gentle shake. "But you can't have him."

It was the easiest choice I'd ever made.

"Then I don't want to be a Walker."

"Do I get a say?" Simon asked. He rejoined us, tucking me against his side.

"Only if you can talk sense into her," Addie said.

"You want to hand me over to the Consort," he said, with the same shrewd look he used when sizing up the opposing team.

She met his eyes squarely. "You're a nice guy. You care about Del, which is not easy, and you make her happy. If there was another way, I'd take it. But there's not, and I won't let the multiverse crumble because of one person, no matter who it is. I'm sorry."

"Monty said this world was safe," he pointed out.

"Monty was wrong," I replied. Monty had been wrong about a lot of things lately.

"If they don't get the inversions under control," he said, "if the Key World keeps degrading . . . what happens to my mom?"

I didn't say anything. He looked at Addie, who turned her hands skyward, helplessly.

"And if I don't go back?"

"They'll cleave this world," Addie said. "Once they figure

455

out the source is here, the easiest thing to do is unravel. That would stop your signal from affecting the Key World. Or any Echoes not connected to this one."

"So either I hand myself over to the people who took my dad, or they cleave me." He swallowed hard. "I gotta say, for people who deal in choices, the ones you're giving me suck."

"Choices," I murmured. The plan came bright and fast as a lightning strike, a charge running through my body and stopping my lungs. Simon must have felt it too, because his eyebrows arched as he looked down at me.

I went up on tiptoe to kiss him, saying against his mouth, "Trust me?"

"Always," he said.

I pressed closer to him, drawing out the kiss, savoring the taste of him, gaining strength from his signal and his steadiness.

Addie cleared her throat. "Del. We have to go."

I turned toward her, wiping my eyes. "Five more minutes, Addie. Please. They'll take him the minute we cross back. You know they will. This is my only chance to say good-bye."

She hesitated, but Simon met her eyes and nodded once. Inches away, a pivot swelled into being.

"Privately," I added.

"Fine." Addie checked her watch. "I'm going to wait around that corner of the school. But in five minutes and one second, if you two aren't walking toward that pivot, I will drag you both back there by your freaking hair."

"You won't have to," I assured her.

CHAPTER FIFTY-FOUR

 $\bigwedge$ S SOON AS ADDIE ROUNDED THE CORNER, I
turned back to Simon. "Ready to go?"

"What?"

"We've got five minutes. Less, the longer we stand here
talking." I listened for the pivot he'd just created. "Kiss me again,
in case she's looking."

"We can't run."

"If we keep moving, they might not be able to find you."

"Running won't help. You said so yourself. No matter where
I go, the Key World will follow me. As long as I exist, everyone I
love is in danger. My mom. Iggy. You."

I leaned my forehead against his chest, feeling the tears start
in earnest. "I'm not giving you up."

"These Cleavers that everyone keeps talking about. What do
they do?"

"The Echoes are connected by threads. The Cleavers cut the
ones tying a specific Echo to the rest of the multiverse."

"So they're completely separate? No possibility of a cross-
over?"

"Cleaving unravels the entire fabric. Once the strings are

cut, the Echo—and every Echo that came from it—disintegrates, from oldest to newest."

"So it's not instantaneous. You'd have time to get out."

And then I understood.

"No," I said, my voice cracking. "I'm not leaving you."

He slid his hands through my hair and I closed my eyes, willing the tears back as his mouth came down on mine, more fierce and frantic than ever before. He tasted like salt and sunshine, and he smelled like the rain that was threatening to fall, and I knew I couldn't let him go, not in a million worlds.

"Will it hurt?"

"I'm not doing it!" I tried to twine my arms around his neck, but he gripped my wrists, evading me.

"Will it hurt?"

"I don't know! Echoes don't feel anything, but you're real. You're *mine*."

"You have to help me, Del. I can't find the threads on my own."

"Don't do this," I begged. "You're the only person who has ever seen me, in my whole life. You see me, exactly as I am, and you still . . ."

"Love you," he finished. "And this is how I save you. Save everyone."

Except it wasn't his job to save everyone. It was mine.

There was no getting around the truth this time. Simon was the heart of the anomaly, and my heart, and there was only one way to reconcile the two. To be both a Walker and myself.

"We stay together," I said. "It's a big world. It'll take time to unravel. We keep moving, and we don't give up."

"You'll be okay," he said.

"So will you."

"Show me the strings," he said. "If I'm going to destroy the world, I'd like to at least know what it looks like."

"They're threads. Like a tapestry, but they don't show a picture. They make a symphony. The most amazing symphony you've ever heard."

"Then let me hear it," he said. "Please. Before it goes bad."

"And then we run," I said. "Promise me."

He kissed me, infinitely sweet, infinitely slow.

I traced his face with my fingertips, feeling the hint of stubble, the sharp line of his jaw, the shape of his mouth. I took his hands and kissed his palm, the way he'd once kissed mine.

Then I reached into the pivot beside him, feeling for the threads at the center of the world.

There. Just like I'd told him, a tapestry of strings and sound, strong and sturdy, off-key but not unpleasant, like hearing music from an unknown land.

His eyes met mine, sharp and dark and sorrowful. He slid his hand along my sleeve, over my hand, his fingers overlaying mine.

"It's amazing," he said, his face a mixture of wonderment and fear.

"It's the fabric of the world. You're touching infinity."

"And I'm breaking it," he said. "I'm sorry, Del."

"Don't apologize. We're going to fix it."

"No. We're not." Before I could ask what he meant, he wrenched the strings away, snapping them cleanly. The frequency screeched and skipped.

"I'm so sorry," he repeated, and the world began to cleave.

CHAPTER FIFTY-FIVE

IT'S A BIG DEAL, THE END OF THE WORLD. THERE should be thunder and lightning and the parting of seas. It should look as momentous as it feels. As it is.

Around us, the few leaves clinging stubbornly to the trees turned muddy, the silvery bark going a dull gray. The sandy-orange brick of the school changed to beige, matching the mortar. Addie shot from the side of the building.

"Cleavers!" she shouted. "Time to go."

"It wasn't the Cleavers," I said, feeling sick. "It was us."

She skidded to a halt. "What? Why?"

"Because it was the only way," said Simon. "Leave me here and the inversions stop."

"Leave *us* here," I corrected, unease creeping over me. "We have time to find a solution."

"No! Del, this isn't a solution. This will kill you. We have to go home. Now."

"She's right." Simon brought my hands to his lips. "You promised you'd take care of my mom."

"What?" I stared at him. "You promised we'd run!"

"I never promised."

He hadn't. He'd been so careful not to promise. "You are such a *jerk*." I beat my fists against his chest. I wanted to scream the world down. To hate him for breaking my heart after he'd been the one to make me open it in the first place. "I'm not leaving you."

"You're not leaving. I'm telling you to go." He pushed me toward Addie as the grass around the school turned silvery white. "Take her back."

I shook her off and ran to him. "Don't do this," I pleaded. "Come with us."

"Delancey Sullivan," he murmured. "The girl who Walks between worlds. No wonder I kept falling for you. Can't imagine a world where I wouldn't."

"I love you," I said, crying now, finally. I didn't think I'd ever stop.

"Glad to hear it," he said, and stepped back as Addie caught me, her shouts lost in the ragged sounds of my sobs.

There was a ping, and a streak of silver raced across the ground between us, the inversion at the school splitting the Echo like a chasm. On his side of the flickering line, the world dimmed as if the sun had hidden behind clouds. On my side, the buildings swayed and slumped, the ground softening like tar. If I didn't get back to the train station, I'd be trapped here—with Simon on the other side of that line, forever out of reach.

Simon made worlds stronger, Monty had said. Maybe his side would unravel more slowly. Maybe even slowly enough for me to get back and rescue him. I threw my backpack over the widening gap. If I was right, he'd need those supplies more than I did.

"Don't get caught in the unraveling," I shouted as he slung it over his shoulder. "Keep moving. I'll find you."

"Del!" Addie screamed over the white noise of the cleaving. "We have to get out!"

"Go!" he shouted.

I went, reality toppling around me.

CHAPTER FIFTY-SIX

My FEET POUNDED ALONG THE ASHEN, SAG-
ging pavement, trying to outrun my grief. It followed behind
me like a tangible thing, a weighty shadow blocking out rational
thought. Addie urged me along, shocked into silence.

I reached the pivot, lungs on fire, muscles quivering. The
white cairn on this side had scattered, stones tumbled across the
grass. The power of entropy. I sank to my knees.

Grief caught me in its jaws and snapped me in two.

"Up," Addie said. "You can lose it when we get home. Stay
with me, Del."

I listened for Simon's frequency, trying to hear it one more
time, but it was pointless. I'd never find him, I'd never be able to
save him. The Key World was damaged, and it was all because
of me.

Ignoring Addie's pleas, I picked up a rock and threw it as hard
as I could at the encroaching grayness. It flickered out of existence.
I threw another. And another. And another, as if I could stop the
unraveling somehow, as if my actions could freeze it in place. And
then my fingers reached for another pebble, and brushed against
something else. Smooth plastic instead of rough stone.

I wiped my eyes on my shirt and looked more closely at the inch-wide disk in my hand. Navy blue, the same as Simon's eyes. Four holes in the middle, arranged in a square, just big enough for a needle to fit through.

My mom, handing my grandfather his sweater. "I don't know how you manage to lose so many buttons."

Monty, finger to his lips, winking at me.

"Breadcrumbs, Delancey. To mark the way home."

It sat, humble and innocuous, in the palm of my hand, proof that Monty had been here. I combed through the remaining stones, and more buttons tumbled out. Tortoiseshell, polished wood, tarnished brass filled my hand, each one familiar, each one an indictment, each one bringing the truth closer, along with the cleaving.

Monty, who'd known Simon was half-Walker since the beginning.

Monty, who'd insisted we hide here.

Monty, who would do anything to find my grandmother.

"I don't think he's slipped at all." Simon's mom, eyes troubled. "He's exactly as he used to be."

"Simon needs to go into the Echoes. The plan won't work without him."

The crack of Addie's palm against my cheek brought me back. "Quit throwing rocks," she snapped. "We have to get out. Now."

"Monty," I said, showing her the buttons. "He came here a bunch of times."

"Who cares? He won't be coming back, and neither will we."
She took my hand and reached for the pivot.

But Monty hadn't known we'd cleave it. He'd sent Simon to this specific world, knowing he'd amplify it. Believing we would come back. But for what?

What he always wanted. Rose.

She'd been a practical woman, my mom said. She and Monty would have had a plan. She must have fled here, a world that was sturdy enough to sustain her, dissonant enough to hide her tracks, with plenty of branches to hide in. She'd left behind her pendant because she'd never intended to return.

She wouldn't have left a trail for the Consort to follow. But a sign. Something small that only Monty would have understood. Breadcrumbs.

Rose is my home.

Monty wasn't trying to bring her back. He was trying to join her.

The plan had gone wrong, somehow. Maybe the Consort had been watching too closely; maybe Monty had been captured. The breadcrumbs faded and the trail was lost.

Why aren't you in prison?

Who says I'm not?

For my grandfather, any world without Rose was a prison.

But Simon made worlds stronger. Once he was here, her breadcrumbs would have regained their strength, standing out like flares.

Monty must have thought he'd follow them right to her.

It was impossible. After so much time, it was practically impossible.

Nothing's impossible, Delancey.

Especially if you were willing to risk the whole world.

I thought of Simon, his hair curling over his collar, eyes challenging me, hands drifting over my skin. I imagined him fading to gray, flickering with static. Simon, lost among the worlds.

My mother, shaking her head. "You and Monty are peas in a pod."

She was more right than she'd realized.

CHAPTER FIFTY-SEVEN

I SHOVED A SINGLE BUTTON IN MY BACK POCKET and followed Addie through the pivot, salt drying on my cheeks.

"Del!" Eliot raced toward us, Monty tottering behind him. "Are you okay?"

"Where's Simon?" asked Monty, peering toward the pivot. "What did you do?"

"I cleaved it. Once it unravels, everything will be . . ." I swallowed down bile. "Finished."

Addie wrapped her arms around me, but didn't say anything.

"What do you mean, you cleaved it?" Monty said, face going gray. "The whole branch? With Simon in it?"

"What else could she have done?" Eliot turned to me, his voice kind and tentative. "The Consort has teams at the school, patching things back together."

"Great." My chest felt hollow, my limbs numb.

Monty sank down on a nearby bench, head in his hands.

"I'm calling Mom," Addie said. I didn't move.

"Lattimer's on his way," Eliot said, studying me as if I were an equation he couldn't solve. "Tell me how to fix this, Del."

"You can't."

"Lattimer doesn't know about Simon," Eliot said. "We told him you and Addie came here to tune inversions."

"You lied to the Consort," I said, barely interested. The numbness had spread through my whole body. "Why?"

"Because I have a theory to run by you."

"Hold on." I walked over to Monty. He looked as broken as I felt, a colorless lump in a worn cloth coat. Anger surged, breaking through my numbness, giving me momentum. I called to Eliot, "Can you grab me a Coke? I picked up more frequency poisoning."

He glanced at Monty uneasily. "Back in a minute."

I sat down next to my grandfather and said nothing. Pivots crowded around us, big and small, choice after choice overlapping, the air dense with possibility. All I had to do was pick one.

"I never thought you'd go through with it," he said.

"Who says I did?" I pulled the button from my pocket and held it just out of his reach.

Monty stiffened.

"Eliot will be back soon, and Lattimer's on his way," I said, low and fast, urging him to believe me, not to question my story. "I cleaved the world partway. It's still there. It's not stable. It's shifting, and it's getting stronger, but I cut enough threads to stop the inversions. That's why they think it's gone."

"Partway?" he said, the stirrings of hope clear in his voice. "I didn't think that was possible."

"Nothing's impossible, right?" I pasted on the sly smile he used with me. "It should fool them for a few weeks. Long enough to track him and Grandma. We can do it, but we have to go now."

"Now?" He blinked at me. "But . . ."

"Simon has to keep moving. The longer we wait, the harder he'll be to find. Eliot's coming," I said, tugging at his sleeve.

His hand closed over mine, his eyes bright and sharp.

"Walk with me, Delancey." The same words that had started off every Walk we'd taken since I was a child.

Eliot called out, but I waved him off as Monty and I strolled behind the Depot. He frowned, but instead of following us, he headed for Addie.

"There," I said, gesturing to a tiny pivot hovering nearby. "I used another pivot to get out, like with the balloon."

"That's my girl." Monty chuckled. "Always said you were my favorite."

He stepped through the pivot and disappeared.

"You were mine," I said to the shimmering air.

"It sounds different," Monty said when I'd joined him. This world was nearly identical to ours, down to the cars in the parking lot. It couldn't have been more than a few hours old—Monty should have caught on immediately. But desperation makes people believe in impossibilities. Desperation makes us foolish.

"That's Simon," I said. "He must be close."

Monty hurried around to the front of the train station, more youthful than I'd seen him in years. Midway across the parking lot he stopped and peered around. "Are you sure we're in the right place?"

"Dead sure." I curled my fingers around the spindly threads of this Echo.

"I thought you said you'd cleaved it." He turned. "Del?"

"I didn't cleave anything," I said. "Simon did. He made me show him the threads and he ripped them apart. And now he's gone."

Confusion clouded his features. "You said . . ."

"I *lied*." My rage rose up, choking me. "I'll assume you're familiar with the concept. How long have you been planning this? Since I cleaved Park World? Since you heard Simon's name? How long have you been using us?"

"You don't understand," he said, gaze locked on my shaking hand. "Rose is waiting for me."

"How long?"

"After Gil was taken and Rose disappeared, the Consort came for me. A public trial would raise too many questions, but they had questions of their own. They took me into the Echoes and held me there till I was half-dead from frequency poisoning. Every day, for weeks. Told everyone we were searching for Rose, but they were making an example of me to any Free Walkers that heard the tale. Lattimer supervised it personally."

"My God," I breathed. Sympathy stirred, but my own loss crushed it.

"Finally they figured they'd made their point. But it was too late. I couldn't hear Rose's signal. That was the true torture, you know. They laughed as they watched me lose her."

He dragged a hand over his face. "The Free Walkers had

scattered. Amelia cut me off, thinking she'd protect Simon. There was nothing I could do. And then there was you, Del, bright as a button, bold as brass, my very best girl. You came home, and I knew you'd be my salvation."

"Everything you taught me . . . all those tricks, all our Walks . . . were a scheme?"

"You were too good to waste on the Consort," he said. "Only a few months younger than Gil's son. Who better to watch over him?"

A flash of memory. "You picked Doughnut World. He went there every Thursday, and you threw me into his path. You called him to the office in Angry Dystopia World so I would find you both. You arranged our Walks so I'd run into him."

It wasn't the universe pushing us together; it was Monty.

"I figured if he saw you in Echoes, he'd trust you in this world. Despite the boots and attitude, Delancey, you've a soft heart. Once he asked you to help Amelia, everything fell into place, and then the inversions knocked it down again. I haven't puzzled that one out quite yet."

"You used me. You used both of us."

"You would have done the same," he wheedled. "You wanted to hide him away, even when you knew how dangerous he was. You would have damned the world to keep your love safe."

"A Walker's duty is to the Key World," I said dully. "I couldn't do it."

"Ah, but you would have. It was Simon who cut the threads, wasn't it? Not you." He moved closer, hands up, his eyes never leaving the pivot. "It's not too late. We can save them."

"Stop lying!" I screamed. "Simon is *gone*. So is Rose. *Forever.*"

"Because you abandoned them!" he snarled, and caught himself. The momentary rage, replaced by sympathy and remorse. It was an act, and I wondered if his dementia was an act too.

Even fools are dangerous if they want something.

"I was going to stay. Save the Key World. Save Simon. We were going to run, but he stopped me." My fingers twitched. "It's a shame he's not here now."

"Delancey," Monty said nervously. "Think."

"I am. I'm thinking about when Simon asked me if it would hurt when he unraveled. I didn't know. Would you like to find out?"

I heard the shimmering sound of the pivot, the Key World ringing out on the other side, beckoning me back to a place where Simon wasn't. Where he was never going to be.

A hand came down on my shoulder. "Del, stop."

"Addie?" I twisted to face her, but I wouldn't let go of the threads.

Monty called out, "Addison, she's not well. She overdid it, and the frequency poisoning's back. We need to get her home."

"I agree," she said.

"No. You don't know what he did," I pleaded.

"He tried to use Simon to find Grandma." At my startled look, she shrugged. "I told you Eliot put everything together. He's worried about you. Come on."

A three-man team came through the pivot, but I tightened

my grip. "No," I said. "He's not leaving. It's a tiny world. No one will care if I cleave it."

"You'll care," she said.

"Simon's gone." Something inside me shattered, glass ground to dust.

"I know." Gently she pried my fingers off the strings. Her nails, usually perfectly manicured, were bitten to the quick. "He did it to save you. Don't waste it, Del."

She pulled me back through the pivot, where Eliot and my parents waited. My mom clutched my dad's arm, and they raced over as soon as we were clear. Lattimer followed behind, solemn but pleased.

All I could see was what wasn't there.

I stood unmoving as my parents fussed over us, my mom smoothing my hair, my dad gathering me up in a bear hug. When he released me, Lattimer cleared his throat, and my parents stepped aside.

"You did well, Delancey," Lattimer said. His hand dropped on my shoulder and I steeled myself not to flinch. "I knew you'd realize where your future should be."

Behind me the pivot wavered as the team brought Monty back through. Lattimer's face transformed, the proud smile turning predatory.

"Del! We can get them back! It's not too late!" Monty shouted.

Out of the corner of my eye I saw the team drag Monty toward a black van, engine rumbling. He shouted again, "He's more important than you know!"

He was everything. What could be more important than everything?

"There's another way! People who can help us! Nothing's done, Delancey! Nothing's—"

The sound of the van's door slamming cut off his cries, and then there was only silence.

CHAPTER FIFTY-EIGHT

IT TURNS OUT, THE END OF A WORLD ISN'T THE end of the world. It only feels like it. Life pushes on, a vast unfurling that should be uplifting. Reassuring. An affirmation of the things we hold dearest.

I didn't feel affirmed. I felt insignificant. Life pushed on, dragging me in its wake like a piece of driftwood. The music of the multiverse turned as distant and tuneless and monotonous as my days.

I walked, but not between worlds. Not anymore. I walked Iggy, long rambling trips that left us both shivering and exhausted. Easier to fall asleep that way, easier to ignore the dreams of paper stars in a gray sky and a bright-eyed boy beckoning me closer.

A week later I appeared before the Consort for the second time in as many months. My parents stood on either side of me, Addie near the door. Monty's absence was palpable.

Councilwoman Crane folded her hands and spoke in the grave, formal cadence of the Consort. "Your suspension was to last until the end of the term, Delancey. We had hoped that the time would allow you to develop not only the techniques, but also the restraint required of licensed Walkers." She peered over the top of her glasses, her smile dry as bones. "You can imagine our surprise when we learned of your involvement with the anomaly."

I stared at the ballet flats I'd borrowed from Addie. The fluorescent lights made tiny, star-shaped reflections in the patent-leather toes.

Councilwoman Bolton spoke next, tapping the papers in front of her with one finger. "We have determined the anomaly was a collusion between Montrose Armstrong and the Free Walkers, created to destabilize the Key World. Now that the source has been cleaved, thanks to your actions, the multiverse is no longer in danger."

I slanted a look at Addie, who kept her eyes fixed on Councilwoman Crane. She and Eliot had coordinated our stories before the Consort debriefed us, making sure to leave Amelia and Simon out of it. It had meant throwing Monty under the bus, but neither Addie nor Eliot seemed too guilt-ridden about it. I figured he'd gotten off easy.

I'd expected Lattimer to speak next, but he sat back, watchful and silent, as Crane took over again. "While your behavior was unconventional, it demonstrated your commitment to our highest principles: obedience, diligence, sacrifice. Your decision to keep Montrose Armstrong contained prevented him from taking refuge with other Walkers who are themselves fugitives."

Other Walkers. *There are people who can help us.* Another one of Monty's lies, and I dug my fingernails into my palms.

"Therefore, we are reinstating you, effective immediately.

You shall resume your formal training, with credit given for your recent service."

My mother exhaled, her relief audible. My father squeezed my elbow gently, but I didn't respond. As quickly as they'd taken my future away, they handed it back.

I wasn't sure I wanted it anymore, wasn't sure where it led.

"Furthermore," intoned Lattimer, "we would like to make a request."

That got my attention.

"Your sister accelerated your training at my urging. It was clear that you had considerable talent, however undisciplined you might have been, and I'm pleased you rose to the challenge."

He'd been testing me. Grooming me every bit as much as he'd groomed Addie, and I'd been too blind to see it. What else was I missing?

"As you've discovered, the Free Walkers do indeed pose a threat to our way of life. Our efforts to repair the Key World are ongoing. Considering the abilities you've demonstrated, and your knowledge of the situation, you're . . . uniquely qualified to deal with the aftermath. Naturally, we would take this into account while determining your apprenticeship. Would you be willing to assist us, should we need you?"

A bribe. Help the Consort, and I would have my pick of assignments. I'd have more freedom than ever before.

What would I do with freedom? Walk to worlds where Simon wasn't? I didn't want his Echoes. I definitely didn't want to watch his Echoes fade in front of me, like the man from the shoe store.

What I wanted was the truth. About the Consort and the Free Walkers, about my grandmother and the Echoes. Lattimer didn't need my help; he had some other reason for recruiting me, and I wanted to know that, too. He'd never tell me outright, but he didn't need to. Watch someone's lies closely enough, and they'll give away the truth.

"Happy to help," I told him.

I almost meant it.

Later that night, Addie knocked on my doorframe. "Mom says you're going to school tomorrow."

"I'd like to see her make me," I replied, and pulled the covers over my head.

She yanked them back again. "Stop moping."

"There are a zillion worlds out there, Addie. Please go visit one of them. Or all of them."

"I'm worried about you. Even Mrs. Lane is doing better than you are."

"Mrs. Lane gets as many drugs as she wants," I pointed out. "And she's not doing better; she's a wreck. I see her every day." Simon had made me promise to take care of her, but we were taking care of each other.

"He wouldn't want this for you, Del. He saved your life. The least you could do is get back to living."

"Go to hell, Addie. Do not try to tell me what Simon would want. You barely knew him, and you didn't like him. You sure as hell don't speak for him."

"Fine." She hesitated at the door. "Monty's sentencing was today. He pled insanity."

My body clenched, waiting for her to continue. The Consort couldn't let him go free. Not after what he'd done.

"They sent him to an oubliette. They said he was too dangerous to be allowed out."

My muscles went lax. "I hope he rots there."

"He freaked out. He was screaming for you. Started singing that song he made for you." She nibbled a nail. "I'm sorry."

I shrugged. "It's not music, Addie, just noise. And I never have to hear it again."

It was time to write my own song.

CHAPTER FIFTY-NINE

MY MOTHER WAS RIGHT. I DID GO TO SCHOOL the next day, worn down by nagging that began at sunrise and ended when Eliot escorted me off the porch.

"She's going to text me every period to make sure you don't cut," he warned.

The sky was a faded blue, the sun a pale circle. I shoved my sunglasses farther up my nose and kept walking. "You can lie."

"I could. But I won't. You need to keep busy. You should come back to training, too. Shaw's been asking about you."

"Not ready," I said.

He was silent for the rest of the trip, but there was a kindness to it. I was alone, but he wouldn't let me be lonely.

All day I found myself looking for Simon. *Not here, not here, not here,* I whispered to myself. I couldn't help searching. Couldn't help hearing people who were wondering why Simon Lane had transferred out of state so suddenly, without even a word to his coach, despite the big tournament coming up.

Music was the worst. I stared at Simon's empty chair, ignoring Bree's glares and Ms. Powell's lecture.

When the bell rang, Ms. Powell approached me. "Del? Can I speak with you privately?"

"I'll wait outside," Eliot said.

She gave him a thumbs-up and perched on the edge of my desk. "I'd like you to present your composition tomorrow, if you're ready. The rest of the class completed their assignments while you were sick."

"Yeah, I guess." Simon and I had nearly finished the sixteen measures. I could knock out the rest that night, after I'd walked Iggy. It would give me something to do. I bent down to pick up my new backpack, much lighter than the one I'd left with Simon. I had no intention of Walking, so I didn't bring my tools.

"The funniest thing happened yesterday," Ms. Powell said, almost as an afterthought. "I could swear I saw Simon."

"He moved," I said when my heart started up again. "You probably saw someone who looked like him."

"Maybe," she said. "This guy did seem a little different. He needed a haircut. And had a metal bracelet around his wrist. It looked like a big shiny nail."

A glint of silver in the glow of a streetlight. "A railroad spike."

"I'd never thought of it that way, but . . . sure. Not the sort of thing you wear on the basketball court, is it?"

"Where did you say this was?" I choked out.

"I didn't." She smiled broadly, waved at one of the other students straggling out. "It was right outside this great dough-nut shop downtown. Corner of Main and Evergreen? Do you know it?"

"I think so," I said. There was no doughnut shop at Main and Evergreen. Not in the Key World.

"I like to visit there sometimes. Their Bavarian cream is out of this world." She met my eyes. "He sounded great, Del. You know what I mean?"

Ms. Powell had seen Simon's Echo. Yesterday. "You're a Free Walker."

"I'm a friend. Here. I've been meaning to return these to you."

She held out her hand. Cupped in her palm was a mound of paper stars. My stars, the ones I'd dropped over the last few weeks, from the world I'd fled to after the first cleaving to the one I'd left in the library. I looked closer, but the dark green star I'd made in Doughnut World wasn't among them.

"It's an impressive body of work, Del. You've been through a lot. But it's time to concentrate on where you want to go, instead of where you've been."

Eliot stuck his head in. "We're going to be late for class," he called, as the bell rang and the three of us winced in unison.

"We'll talk soon," Ms. Powell said.

Not soon enough.

"If you're hoping I'll call you in sick for the rest of the day, guess again," Addie said when she answered her cell.

"Why would Simon's Echoes still be around?"

"You're supposed to be in class. Let's talk tonight."

"Just answer the question. Why haven't they unraveled?"

"They might be complex enough that they'll stick around for a while. It's not instantaneous, you know. Some terminal Echoes take years."

"But they wouldn't have a frequency, right? If his Echo was terminal, it would sound weird?"

"Yes. Did you go looking for one?" Her voice took on a sympathetic note. "I'm not sure that's a good idea."

"I didn't. Let's say he wasn't terminal. Why else would his Echo be around?"

If Ms. Powell was a Free Walker, she would have known I couldn't get back to Simon. Why would she tell me about his Echoes? And why had she waited so long to reveal herself to me?

Addie sighed. "Echoes won't fade while the Original exists, but the Consort checked. The world Simon cleaved is no longer broadcasting a frequency. It's completely unraveled."

"Addie, this is important. Please, think really carefully. Is there any other reason why Simon's Echoes wouldn't be unraveling?"

"There is no other reason. He's gone."

But Simon's Echo hadn't faded, which meant his Original wasn't gone.

He'd escaped the cleaving, and now he was lost in the Echoes.

And I was going to find him.

I'd promised, after all.

END THIRD MOVEMENT